F
J15   Jacobs, Israel.
            Ten for Kaddish.

Temple Israel Library
Minneapolis, Minn.

Please sign your full name on the above card.

Return books promptly to the Library or Temple Office.

Fines will be charged for overdue books or for damage or loss of same.

Ten for Kaddish

for Kaddish

Israel Jacobs

W · W · NORTON & COMPANY · INC ·

NEW YORK

F
J15

Copyright © 1972 by W. W. Norton & Company, Inc.

75-43   4-2-12   Geltman   695/560

Dedicated to my father,
Rabbi Samuel Jacobs.
(1907–1942)

"The righteous are to be remembered for blessing."

Acknowledgments

To

Joel Goldblatt for his initial readings of *Ten for Kaddish* and for finding it of sufficient interest to recommend it to W. W. Norton and Company.

Merrill Pollack, Managing Editor at W. W. Norton and Company, for his criticism and suggestions and for the tact and wit with which he persuaded me to use them.

My children for the time I took from them to write this novel.

Selma for the grace, charm, and dignity she infuses into a complex and oftentimes lonely role.

That infinite source of all existence and mind that has vouchsafed me life, granted me intelligence, and inspired me to write this novel.

Boruch Atah Adonoy

Ten for Kaddish

Now there was a king who possessed a beautiful orchard.
He appointed two watchmen to guard therein, one lame the
other blind. One day the lame said to the blind, "I see fat
tasty figs in the orchard. Come take me upon your shoulders,
that I may pluck them, and we shall eat them." So the lame
mounted the blind, plucked the figs, and they ate of their fill.
Some time after, the king came and inquired of them, "Who
has plucked my beautiful figs?" The lame denied his guilt
and argued, "Have I then feet to walk with?" And the blind
argued in a similar manner, "Have I then eyes to see with?"
What did the king do? He mounted the lame upon the blind
and judged them together.

Sanhedrin, 91a–b

One

Rabbi Morris Kleinman pondered the asymmetry of the fowl
offering before him. Amazing! Utterly amazing is God's
handiwork. The King of Kings fashioned every chicken in
the stamp of the first, and yet none of them resembles his fellow. Even a chicken wing dormant on a plate possesses a
uniqueness all its own. No two are alike. They may all taste
the same like warm water, but they're different. The unini-
tiated may not perceive the difference; probably all humans
look alike to a chicken, too. But probe. Search. Investigate

in depth and discover the profound dissimilarities. A chicken wing can be narrow or broad. Thick skinned, spotted, flaky, or smooth as a baby's bottom. Heavy with bone or weighed down with flesh. A thousand variations and combinations in a chicken wing, not to mention a whole chicken. Yes, indeed! Each chicken is a creation unto itself.

And Kleinman had become a chicken connoisseur. Particularly of boiled chicken. Also boiled potatoes. Also anything boiled bland and tasteless.

"Nothing spicy or too salty," the good doctor had ordered. No alcohol, of course. Make *Kiddush* on *challa*, but make sure the *challa* isn't fresh. It'd be better if your wife toasts it."

Toasted *challa*? Fah! Like starching a roast beef.

Rabbi Kleinman was less than enraptured by his doctor's orders; but what was this minor discomfort compared to the martyrdom Israel has suffered. Self discipline! Is this not the foundation of all morality? And dietary restrictions! This is new for a rabbi? The moment an infant breaks away from the warmth of a Jewish womb he is bounded by restrictions, . . . dietary laws being the least of them.

So Kleinman found consolation, even a secret pride in his martyrdom. Except for that Sabbath morning schnaps. That he sorely missed: when the handful of *daveners* circled the lone table set up downstairs in the empty ballroom, with sponge or honey cake for chasers.

The thought of *Kiddush* conjured up Max Mendelson, the synagogue's hard-nosed, self-appointed unpaid sexton, and Kleinman chuckled at the picture. Mendelson standing guard, warning all and sundry: "Nothing; don't touch nothing till the rabbi comes downstairs to make the *broche*." A good man, Kleinman reflected; returned to the synagogue late in life, but making up for every lost day.

For a fleeting moment fond memories of *Kiddush*, of *matjes* herring lying on a slab of Spanish onion, of fried cutlets, of hot *cholent,* sparkled in Kleinman a feeble rebellion at the boiled chicken to which his wife, Beth, had him chained. Then he remembered the furnace in his stomach that could turn his insides into an inferno at the least provocation. No more *Kiddush;* not over *schnaps.* At the bi-weekly Sunday morning bagles and lox breakfasts sponsored by the men's club and served after services in the Chaim Cohen Auditorium as a bonus to the faithful who pried themselves from warm beds to make the morning *minyan* at nine, Bill Morely, synagogue custodian and the *rebbitsen's* diligent deputy, saw to it that Kleinman's menu was limited to toast and warm milk. Cigars, too, which he enjoyed puffiing away at on occasion— particularly at meetings and at the weekly chess games with Canon Robert—he also had to surrender. Deprivation piled on deprivation.

"You're not the first clergyman with an ulcer," Dr. Gross of stony heart had said, refusing to empathize. "Stop ten people on Main Street at random and at least one will be a member of the ulcer society. Why, it's a mark of distinction."

"A rather painful way to make one's mark," Kleinman had wryly retorted.

Actually, when after three series of GI examinations ordered by Dr. Gross, the ulcer in his duodenum finally showed up on X-ray, Kleinman breathed easy. For almost a year he had lived with the dread thought that the volcano spurting hot lava into his entrails was symptomatic of something more final than an ulcer. No! it wasn't the restrictions, food or otherwise, that troubled Kleinman. What frustrated him no end was that the painful spasms, though not as frequent or intense as they had been, refused to decamp. And from the information he had picked up about ulcers, culled from medical books, medical journals, from interrogation of doctors in his congregation, from anyone who had or ever had had an ulcer, Kleinman had determined that after all this time his ulcer should have been cured.

He struggled to be objective about his ulcer. It was merely a question of taking stock, of looking at the problem dispassionately. Of bringing to self-analysis the same cold logic he exercised when attacking a difficult talmudic passage. And logic did not dictate conceding to Dr. Gross that the distress in his stomach originated in his mind. Not that Gross denied he suffered pain. No, the ache was real enough. The pain was not imaginary by any means; the rabbi's stomach was a mess. But the acid eating into his duodenum, the doctor insisted, was due to an agitated mind. And so long as whatever was troubling him up there remained unresolved, the problem below would not go away either . . . and that was even less acceptable to the rabbi.

Yes! He would admit he was human, vulnerable to the same physical disabilities that affected other mortals. In fact, Beth had him pegged as a minor hypochondriac. It was something else again to adjust to the idea that he was susceptible to maladies of the mind. The one thing that had never occurred to him was that he, Morris Kleinman, could become emotionally ill. A physical breakdown? Yes, that could happen. Mental? Not in control of his mind? Absurd. Preposterous. Simply out of the question. . . .

Yet so were those recurring dreams absurd, too. Jolting him from sleep. So vivid. So real. Awakening him to a cold sweat. Over and over again. Projecting inside his skull like an old movie revived for the thousandth showing: *An appointment. He has an appointment. Is on his way . . . going from somewhere to somewhere. Whatever his destination, it's imperative he arrive on time. A matter of life and death. He hurries. Can't find the car. Thousands of cars in the vast parking lot. He drags leaden feet round and round the block, . . . but there are no blocks in shopping centers. Tenements.*

Row on row of tenements. Gray. Threatening. No car. Where did he park? Can't remember. Thieves! The tenements are full of thieves. Blocking his path. Late . . . he'll be late. Frantic. The subway! Must find the entrance. Down. Deep down into the blackness. The pit. Such a long trip to Blueport via subway. So many stops. So many changes. Never make it. His notes. What happened to his notes? Left them in the tenements. Lost. Unprepared. Mind won't function. Head feels stuffed. Ideas won't come. Thoughts slip from his brain. Can't get hold of them. An ocean of eyes staring up at him . . . and nothing to say. Dumb. Three times a year they come. Packed sanctuary. Every pew taken. They sit and stare. Brilliance. They demand brilliance. He must meet their expectations. He must impress them and be dynamic. The notes . . . must find them. No sermon. No idea, an emptiness in his head. . . .

Peculiar nightmares. Taken by themselves the contents of his dreams were innocuous. If his car were lost or stolen, would it be such a tragedy? It's insured. What is his destination in the dream, the appointment that evokes such anxiety? The subway? He had spent half his life riding subways. Why should a subway frighten him so? Notes lost, forgotten. This should worry him, a seasoned speaker? A hundred times if it were once that he spoke extemporaneously. Strange that under Morpheus these minor inconveniences should take on such dreadful dimensions.

Fourteen centuries before Freud, Samuel son of Nahaman taught his disciples: "A man is shown in a dream only what his thoughts suggest." But what do these dreams suggest?

"Aren't you hungry?" Beth worried at the sallowness of her husband's complexion; his face was a pallid contrast to the thick black hair cresting his high forehead.

"Yes," Kleinman said. "I was just thinking."

"What of?"

Kleinman turned flippant. "The boiled chicken."

Beth's mouth, pert and full-lipped, puckered into a line of matriarchal authority. In another month she was to close the door on thirty-nine. Yet her face, sweet and oval with a hint of plumpness and hued in natural pink, retained a schoolgirlish charm.

"You know I can't give you anything heavy or spicy. There isn't much choice on an ulcer diet." The pout above her dimpled chin disappeared. "I wish I could vary the menu a little."

Kleiman chuckled mischievously. "There's nothing wrong with the chicken, honey. It's fine. I really don't mind eating it seven days a week. Twice on Saturdays."

Beth's pout returned. Quickly, Kleinman moved to stem the hot flood his teasing was about to release. "Really, dear, I'm grateful I can eat anything at all. I was just thinking how I worked myself into such a state."

Beth relented again. "You didn't do it all by yourself. The congregation did their part. There's just so much pressure a person can take."

"Nobody forced me to become a rabbi. I knew what I was getting into when I decided to enter the seminary."

"Nobody can possibly know what he's getting into until he's been in the rabbinate at least half a lifetime," Beth said.

"I suppose you're right, honey. Anyway, if I have to eat boiled chicken, I'm thankful it's yours. After all! Who can cook up a fowl like the *rebbitsen* of the Blueport Jewish Center?"

Beth waved her hand in mock impatience. "*Nu!* if it's so good, eat it already."

Kleinman stabbed his fork into the pale chicken wing, but her comment subverted his thoughts: *Nobody can possibly know what he's getting into until he's been in the rabbinate at least half a lifetime.*

Half a lifetime. That's how long it seemed he had been in Blueport. He was forty-two. Sixteen years and one ulcer in the rabbinate. Ten of the years served in Blueport. My God, is it that long already? Kleinman marvelled, bewailing the rapid flight of time. Ten years! Bizarre, how memory contradicted itself. On the one hand it seemed only yesterday that he had been elected to the Blueport synagogue, and yet he felt as if he had been living in this town all his adult life.

"You know, Beth," he said. "Thursday next week will be ten years since I conducted my first service in Blueport."

"Funny you should be thinking that," Beth said. "Ruth Cane and I were just discussing it the other day."

"Ruth? When did you speak to her?"

"Tuesday. She dropped in to ask me about Par-cream. Wanted to know if she could use it at a meat meal."

"Asked you? I'm the rabbi. Why didn't she ask me?"

"I suggested she ask you," Beth said. "You know what she answered?"

Kleinman swallowed the bait. "What did she answer?"

"Oh, maybe I'd better not," Beth demurred.

"Come now, Beth. Don't keep me in suspense . . . doctor's orders. I'm not supposed to get excited."

"If you insist. Ruth said—and these were her words, Morris, not mine—'When I want to know what's permitted in the kitchen, I may as well go directly to the *rebbitsen*. The rabbi's going to ask her anyway',"

"How did Ruth uncover that secret? Did you tell her?"

"Heaven forbid! I wouldn't let the cat out of the bag. I guess it was her woman's intuition."

"My ego has been punctured. I am deflated." Kleinman puffed his cheeks and exhaled like a ruptured balloon. Beth laughed at the mimicry; he grinned. "Ruth is a fine woman," he said. "She's sincere and determined to maintain a good Jewish home."

The smile froze on Beth's face. "Yes! She's determined to have a Jewish home. Too bad she gets no encouragement from that husband of hers."

Deftly, Kleinman sidestepped his wife's hostility toward Ira Cane. "To get back to my original question. How did my tenure come up in your womanly talk?"

"How do women get around to talk about anything?"

"Ask a Jew a question, and you get another question. So how can you expect a straight answer from a *rebbitsen?*"

"Don't be so clever, please," Beth chided. "We happened to be talking about how fast our children are growing up. Her son, Stanley, is in his final year at Blueport High. The Canes are looking into several colleges. Ruth is anxious to get Stanley out of Blueport and into a different environment. She's had her hands full with him this past year. Stanley's been running with a fast crowd, spending two, three nights a week at those awful taverns down at the bay. When I hear such stories I'm grateful our Jonathan is away at the Yeshiva all week; just keeping him from falling under the influence of that crowd makes it worth all the trouble and expense. . . . And Stanley's marks have been nothing to boast about. Ruth is concerned that he might not make any of the first rate colleges. Anyway, I remarked it seems like yesterday our boys were *bar-mitzvah,* and soon they'll be college students. . . . You know how women talk."

"I sure do," Kleinman brashly agreed. "Every Friday night I get a sample. Generally, in the middle of my sermon."

Beth pointed menacingly. "You think you're a regular comedian, Morris Kleinman! Let me tell you a thing or two. If it weren't for the women you'd be sermonizing to yourself. It's the women who drag their husbands to *shul.* Instead of criticizing you should be grateful."

Kleinman threw up his hands. "Okay, you win. . . . I

surrender. Should have known better than to start. Please go
on. So what did Ruth say?"

"Yes, I'll go on. But you'd better think twice before you
criticize us women." Beth continued: "Ruth commented
that we've set a record in Blueport. She said she remembers
when the synagogue was housed in a storefront on Main
Street. That's nearly thirty-five years ago, when she was a
little girl. And no rabbi in all that time has even come close to
staying on that long. She complimented you; said you've
done the congregation proud and the Jews in Blueport a lot
of good, and she hopes we're here to stay permanently. . . .
That's all. Now suppose you return to your dinner."

Kleinman returned dutifully to the chicken wing, sliced off
a piece of white meat and began to chew absent-mindedly.
As he ate his mind worked. It went round in circles. This
was his bane. He couldn't shut his mind off. It was constantly
tuned in, day and night. The channels in his brain switched
of their own volition, like an automatic TV tuner that has
usurped the controls from its owner. This incessant cerebra-
tion had turned him into an insomniac, waking him in the
middle of the night tossing and turning; his mind refused to
yield to the unconsciousness his body craved. Often he
watched the dawn come up after no more than an hour of
sleep. Once or twice he had even resorted to barbiturates;
in his wildest dreams he had never imagined that he could become hooked. Fortunately, he was able to gather the will
power to withdraw from those little colored demons. One
could get a lot of reading done in the wee hours of the morning.

Ten years at Blueport! Kleinman marvelled that he had
lasted so long. In the twelve years before he came to town,
his congregation had worked its way through seven rabbis,
less than two years per rabbi. He was amazed at his survival
power. Being a rabbi in Blueport was like walking a tight-

rope buffeted by gusts blowing from opposing points of the compass.

On one side, threatening to push the rabbi off his precarious perch, were the compulsive traditionalists, the Jewish counterpart to Christian fundamentalism, demanding that the synagogue conform to all the minutiae of time worn ritual. It was not piety that clamped their minds against change; of that Kleinman was sure. It was a syndrome of guilt, fear, superstition. Piety embraced humility and compassion, both of which were conspicuously absent in their opinionated stances, in their cutting assaults on those who differed. In a sense, Max Mendelson's need to stack the prayerbooks in precise piles of ten and arrange chairs in symmetrical sections was kith and kin to the irrational resistance put up by the hard core traditionalists to innovation of any kind. Some of them panicked if Cantor Rosenberg so much as changed the tune to *"Adon Olam"* on the rare occasions when they attended services to hear it.

Meyer Schwartz, doggedly orthodox, refusing to yield an inch for fear that tomorrow someone would demand a yard, it was true, did not fall into this category of mindless traditionalism. He was sincere; his way of life was consistent with what he postured at board meetings. He demanded of himself what he asked of the synagogue. However, the coterie who found in Schwartz an impassioned spokesman were for the most part nonobservant orthodox Jews. Amongst them were to be counted merchants for whom the Sabbath meant business as usual. Their homes were kosher, but on weekends you could find any number of them in Sing Lee's chop house or dining in any good restaurant, kosher or not. Their business ethics, too, left much to be desired. But, they insisted the synagogue had to conform to every jot and tittle of the law. The synagogue had to fill the lacunae in the lives of the guilt ridden traditionalists.

And the liberals! The pseudointellectuals! They put the pressure on from the other side. After a time, Kleinman discerned that the difference between traditionalists and liberals was superficial, a matter of form rather than substance. The liberals were as rigid and self-righteous as were the traditionalists. They clashed over shallow issues, but on the deeper question of the right to hold another opinion, there was little difference. It was beyond the progressive section of the aisle to concede even the possibility of merit in the traditional point of view.

Kleinman expected criticism no matter which way he turned, but he had been pushed off balance by one bumptious matron from Manor Park. She took offense because "Rabbi insists on clinging to obsolete customs." And what was the obsolete custom that had slighted her sensibilities? One Sabbath morning she had overtaken the rabbi on his way to services and honked her Cadillac to offer him a ride. The rabbi declined.

"It's all so ludicrous," she crowed at a sisterhood meeting. "For the life of me I can't understand why the rabbi refuses to drive his car on Saturday. He looks positively ridiculous walking to the synagogue in all kinds of dreadful weather. . . . And he makes me feel guilty."

"No organ in our *shul*," screamed the traditionalists.

"Our services are dry, sterile," the progressives countered. "Organ music will beautify the services and attract more people".

"Rabbi! The only way to keep the synagogue kosher is to be firm. You can't permit anyone to bring food in. No matter who they are."

"Rabbi, we're having a cake sale. The ladies would like to bake at home and sell their cakes at a sisterhood meeting; it's a good fund raiser. Surely you're not going to insult good sisterhood members. Can't you bend a little?"

"Rabbi, you've got to commit yourself. Take a firm stand."
"Rabbi! You're too rigid. You should be more flexible."

Yes! Beth was right. One needs to be in the rabbinate half a lifetime before one can fully understand what the profession is all about. His seminary training, his professors, the uncounted texts he was required to master, hardly prepared him for the real problems ahead.

But more disturbing than the nitpicking he had to contend with was a nagging doubt, a growing confusion as to his purpose. On that radiant day when the seminary pronounced him rabbi, teacher, preacher, he clearly knew to what he stood committed. The ground of his religious convictions was secure. In the beginning there was no hesitating. He was a rock on all moral issues and ritual questions. He was the rabbi, the *morah d'asrah*. Synagogue policy, if not synagogue members, was obliged to conform to his value judgments—particularly, on religious issues. But lately, certainty had fled. He wasn't sure of anything anymore, not of the cogency of his convictions or their relevancy. Black was merging with white and forming large gray areas. His occupation forced him to touch every emotional base in the lives of his congregants: joy and sorrow, happiness and suffering, birth and death; all telescoped into months, weeks. Sometimes he was called on to shift gears on the same day, running from a funeral in the morning to a wedding at night. Whether the synagogue catering facilities were one hundred percent kosher or not, whether the organ was played at services or not, were matters that were losing their compelling urgency before the accelerated human dramas racing past him from which he strained with ever increasing frustration to squeeze some meaning.

And, as if the agony of working through his own conflicts wasn't enough, he now had taken on Raymond Purnell, Blueport's superintendent of schools and gift to public education. It was a drastic way to get his message across. There would be repercussions, probably the most vociferous and indignant from Jews. But there was no way to make them take their blinders off other than to force them off. Not much more than a generation after Hitler, and Jews were lulling themselves into a false sense of security. He had to get his people to pull their heads out of the sand. . . .

"How was the chicken, dear?" Beth brought him back to the prosaic subject of poultry.

"Fine, honey. I enjoyed every morsel," Kleinman said, smacking his lips. He slid the plate aside and began to chant the grace that followed meals. Beth cleared the table, stacked the dishes into the dishwasher, and rejoined her husband. Pensively, she studied the pinched lines zigzagging his brow and waited for him to finish. He raised his voice, signaling the final verse: "May He who established peace in the heavens grant peace unto us and unto all Israel."

Sunk in her own thoughts, Beth waited for him to initiate conversation.

"Did you hear from Jonathan?" Kleinman said.

"Yes. He called. He won't be home this weekend. He'll be staying at the dormitory. The varsity has a game scheduled Saturday night."

"Another game?" Kleinman showed annoyance. "Is this what I send him to *yeshiva* for? So that they should turn my son into a basketball star?"

"Now let's not get on that subject again," Beth shrugged off her husband's petulance. "You know he needs some diversion. His grades are good. You can't expect him to bury his nose in books every minute of the day. Besides, I heard you boasting to Sy Wasser the other day about Jonathan making the team."

"Boast! Who me? That wasn't boasting. I just mentioned it to Sy in passing, so he should know that a boy can go to

Yeshiva and still be an all-around American, even an athlete."

"It seemed to me, Morris, you were overdoing the bragging."

"So I bragged a little. A father's not allowed to be proud of his son?"

Before he could answer himself, the doorbell chimed. Kleinman started for the door.

"Sit, Morris. I'll see who it is."

"That's okay. I'm through; I'll answer it."

Beth waved her husband back into his seat. "No. I'll go. You relax in the study."

She walked to the door and opened it.

Beth was not easily flustered, but standing tall and broad-shouldered in the doorway of the thirty-year-old stucco house provided by the Jewish Center for their rabbi was the last person she had ever expected to see there.

In the few seconds that Beth stared open-mouthed and mute at Dr. Gabriel Gross, her memory went back some ten years. Jonathan had run a high temperature and was complaining of cramps. Beth had called the office and had asked that Dr. Gross come over as soon as possible. She was politely but firmly told by the receptionist to bundle her son up and drive him to the office.

"Let me speak to Dr. Gross," Beth had said.

"The doctor is busy with a patient."

After much insistence on Beth's part, the receptionist had finally yielded and connected her with the good doctor.

"My son is running a temperature of one hundred and four," Beth expostulated. "And your receptionist tells me to bundle him up and ride him to your office in this cold weather."

"Don't be alarmed Mrs. Kleinman," the doctor replied jocularly. "We allow patients with temperatures of over one hundred and two to use the side entrance."

The retort, which Gross evidently thought to be the acme of urbane wit, and with which he no doubt relaxed untold anxious parents, failed dismally to amuse Beth. Having no choice, she drove Jonathan to the office. Gross diagnosed the trouble as a virus, gave Jonathan a shot, and in three days he was as good as new. But Beth could never find it in her heart to forgive Gross for that smart-aleck quip when she was so worried.

And here was the great man himself . . . without even being called.

"I'm sorry for stopping in without notice," Gross said, intruding into Beth's memories. "I'm leaving town for a few days, and I'd like to speak to the rabbi before I go. I'll only be a few minutes."

Beth recovered enough to manage a smile. "Please come in. I'm sure my husband will be delighted to see you." She took his hat and coat and wordlessly led the doctor into Kleinman's study.

The room was square and high ceilinged and panelled in scratched mahogany. Shelves laden with books covered most of three walls. A green carpet that had seen better days did not quite cover all of the stripped wooden floor. Kleinman was studying a large book on his desk when the squeak of the study door demanded his attention. He looked up. With hardly less astonishment than his wife, Kleinman gaped at Gross.

"Dr. Gross! This is a pleasant surprise," Kleinman said, finally remembering his manners. He rose, stepped around his desk and firmly grasped the doctor's hand.

"I'm sorry I didn't call before coming," Gross repeated his apology. "I'll only be a while. I really don't want to intrude on your evening."

"Intrude on my evening? Nonsense! I'm delighted to have you in my home. Somewhat surprised, to be frank, but it's a privilege."

Kleinman beckoned the doctor to a wide comfortable

chair set catercornered at one end of the room. Gross sat down. Kleinman took a seat on a low slung studio couch. Beth started to leave.

Gross checked her exit. "Please stay. I'd like you to hear what I have to say to the rabbi."

Gross pressed forward, leaning heavily on his elbows. He interlaced his fingers and looked broodingly at the floor. The Kleinmans waited circumspectly. For several moments the doctor seemed to drift off. His mouth tensed, quivering ever so slightly. He brushed his eyelid as if to remove a mote.

"My mother has cancer," Gross said, letting loose his burden. "Last month we found it. . . . I have a feeling she knows, although she doesn't let on."

Kleinman was startled at the pronouncement. When Evelyn Gross had telephoned, asking him to call on her mother-in-law, Kleinman surmised that the old lady was suffering from more than a bad cold. And when he paid the sick call he could tell she was ill. But not cancer; that had not crossed his mind. He felt his stomach contract into tight knots.

"I'm sorry to hear such news. There's no question it's cancer?"

"The X-rays confirm it; she hasn't much time left." Gross inhaled deeply, trying to hold on to his composure but not quite succeeding. "I don't know why I didn't think of calling you—should have thought of it myself. But I'm glad Evelyn did. Your visit meant a great deal to Mom. She appreciated it very much. . . . Kept on repeating, 'What a fine rabbi . . . Must be such a busy man, yet he finds time to spend an hour with an old sick woman.' Yesterday she said to me, '*Nu, mein kind*, you see? Sooner or later there comes a time when what you can do for a sick body is not enough. That is when God sends a Rabbi Kleinman.' "

Gross put his finger to his eye, again to remove a mote that Kleinman now knew wasn't there. The doctor hesitated, uncertain how to proceed.

"I'm sure you know my views on God, religion, prayer . . . I've not kept them secret. I support the synagogue and have accepted membership on the Board because I feel the synagogue should be available to those who want it. But, at the moment, my theology is irrelevent and of no help to my mother—which you were. I wanted to call you. Write you. But I felt I had to come and personally thank you."

A moment passed before Kleinman allowed himself to speak. He searched for a statement to give some weight to his emotions; he found it, and the sentences bubbled to the surface as if they had a life of their own.

"You know, my profession can be frustrating, which I'm sure must be true of yours at times. But as a doctor you have an enviable advantage. You diagnose, prescribe treatment, and most of the time—not always, after all you are not God —you help your patient. I envy you the privilege of being God's instrument in restoring a man to health. A rabbi, what can he do? He listens to *tsuris*, tries to reassure the sick, to console the bereaved. But in the face of the pain and anguish, he is called upon to witness, mere words seem so inadequate, and he begins to wonder if he really is of any use to anybody. Then once in a while there is a whisper that what he is doing is not clutching at the wind. You take the time and trouble to come to my house and tell me I have comforted your mother. To be able to go on, even a rabbi must occasionally be told that his work is not futile. . . . Dr. Gross, I thank you for your thanks."

During the latter part of the colloquy Beth sat, twisting and wringing a handkerchief. The scene was proving too much for her: Gross' frightened announcement dooming his mother, the almost childlike helplessness in his voice, and her husband unburdening himself. She dabbed at her nose and stood up.

"Let me serve you a cup of coffee. Maybe a piece of cheese cake?"

Gross held up his hand. "Please don't bother, Mrs. Kleinman. I must leave. I still have to make a stop at the hospital tonight."

Kleinman escorted Gross to the door and handed him his coat. "Tomorrow at the *minyan*, we will make a *mi sheberach* for your mother."

"You do that, Rabbi. You do that. That's all there's left to do."

Kleinman closed the door and walked slowly back to his study. The large book was still open to the page he had marked for further study. He stared at the columns of text with unseeing eyes. Beth came into the room.

"You must have made quite an impression on his mother."

Kleinman raised his eyes from the Talmud. "It went both ways. His parents impressed me as much, if not more . . . and surprised me."

"In what way?"

"Would you believe it? Dr. Gabriel Gross, the agnostic, has parents who are orthodox Jews. I mean really orthodox. When I came into the house, the old man was wearing a tall black *yarmulke* and studying the weekly *sidra*—with Rashi yet. His mother, poor woman, wanted me to read a *kapital tehilim* with her. And as I left, the old man asked that I make a *mi sheberach* for his wife."

"Why should that surprise you?"

"I'd never think to associate Dr. Gross with orthodoxy. He, the suave self-assured agnostic, and his wife, Evelyn, svelte and sophisticated. . . . They just don't go with orthodoxy."

"You talk as if you just discovered a new fact of life. Children are not carbon copies of their parents."

Beth was right. Why was he so surprised? It wasn't the first time he had uncovered such anomalies. Couples devoid of any visible trace of Jewish tradition springing from parents deeply committed to Jewish ideals.

"Anyway, he's a fine man. A very good son. Shows you, Morris. Even an agnostic can be a fine person."

"Yes, it seems so."

Dr. Gabriel Gross, son of orthodox Jewish parents, doubts God's existence and remains a fine human being. But Rabbi Kleinman questioned whether these humane traits Gabriel Gross had inherited from his parents could be transmitted to his children without the support of religious sancta. And Kleinman detected similar doubt in Gross. Despite agnostic predilections, the good doctor was a synagogue trustee. And he put his son through Hebrew school. And he evinced pride. . . . Yes, he had been proud, as any of the faithful, when Melvyn Gross chanted the service on his *bar-mitzvah*.

Kleinman glanced at his wrist watch. "My goodness; it's eight-thirty already. I've got to go to a meeting."

"Tonight?"

"Yes, dear. I almost forgot. Blueport's Ministers Association."

"Can't you skip it? You've been out every night this week. Stay home tonight," Beth implored.

"I better go. They're assigning parts for the Brotherhood Week service. That ecumenical-minded friend of mine from St. John might just take it into his head to assign me a reading from Hebrews."

"So what would be so terrible if the Gentiles heard Hebrew in their church?"

Kleinman chuckled. Playfully, his fingers curled to tweak her nose.

"Hebrews, my dear *Rebbitsen* is a book in the New Testament."
"Oh."

Two

In Blueport, St. John's Episcopal Church was the church and Canon John Robert its sacerdotal sovereign. Father O'Conner's mass drew more of the faithful, but the collections at St. John pulled in larger denominations, and its steeple rose higher as did the stature of its minister.

During the first half decade of Kleinman's incumbency, the rabbi and the Episcopalian minister rarely crossed paths. On the rare occasions when they did, Kleinman received scant notice from Blueport's senior spiritual leader—until that memorable dinner celebrating the thirty-fifth anniversary of Robert's call to St. John.

It was an extraordinary testimonial. Dinner. White tie. No fund raising. A thousand guests paid fifty dollars a plate to honor John Robert. Kleinman was impressed by the splendor and the panoply of personages. Anybody who was somebody was there, and hundreds who were trying to be. Kleinman recognized politicians high in county and state government. Senator Garvitz, tall and stately, his bushy mane fluttering with every nod of his handsome head, was seated on the first dais. Next to him sat Sam Rabinowitz, the lieutenant governor, a Jew in name and deed. The governor had accepted the invitation, but a legislative crisis prevented him from putting in an appearance. Even Hollywood was represented by comedian Sid Bogel and his third wife, Lorreta Pierce, a star in her own right. Bogel, born in Blueport, had made the big time via the *borsht* circuit, but he never gave up his home or old friends.

No doubt about it, St. John could muster the powerful and famous. It was an influential church, and Canon John Robert was genuinely esteemed by the community at large.

Kleinman was herded to the dais together with six other clergymen who headlined Blueport's half dozen churches. Father O'Connor, who in a gesture rare for that pre-Vatican II era had agreed to a temporary truce, was placed to the right of Robert. The chairman recognized Christianity's debt to the Old Testament by centering Kleinman on the crowded second dais, slightly below but in line with the honored guest.

Perhaps it was proximity, perhaps the evenings exhilaration sharpened his awareness, but that night Canon John Robert noticed Blueport's rabbi. Possibly they would have been thrown together by some other event and eventually would have clicked anyway. But on the night of Robert's testimonial the catalyst that made the mixture was tuna fish.

Shrimp cocktail, which traditionally launches non-Jewish testimonials (and many a Jewish one) was served first. Kleinman passed. Vegetable soup spiced with strips of beef followed; this too, Kleinman dispatched without so much as a taste. Then came roast beef, thick and juicy, its red tenderness promising nirvana. A thousand knives and forks dived into a thousand plates, greedily carving and ripping and carting chunks to a thousand chomping mouths.

A thousand minus one.

Through the meat course Kleinman nibbled away at a salad while rotating his second scotch between damp fingers.

Sitting behind Kleinman's elbow, Robert couldn't help noticing the rabbi's abstinence. It made the guest of honor uncomfortable, and with each mouthful his own roast beef became tougher to chew. Finally curiosity pushed Robert into an investigation. He half rose, reached over the width of his table and tapped Kleinman on the shoulder.

"Rabbi Kleinman!"

Kleinman turned in surprise.

"You've been eating nothing but salad all evening. Are you a vegetarian?"

"Oh, by no means," Kleinman said. "I'm waiting for the house specialty."

The *maître d'*, short and stocky, clad in tux, black tie and white gloves moved between the closely spaced chairs with the agility of a ballet dancer and deposited a steak-sized platter in front of Kleinman.

"And here it is my favorite dish, the *pièce de résistance*." Kleinman rubbed his hands over the plate. "Tuna fish salad!"

Robert stared disbelievingly. His nose bunched into a wrinkle; there was definite reproach in his eyes. "You're not a vegetarian, and you prefer tuna fish to roast beef?"

Kleinman made an heroic try at gravity. "It's really not unusual, Canon; it happens to many rabbis. Tuna fish and rabbis—we develop a rare attachment for one another. If it weren't for tuna fish, many a rabbi would leave many a testimonal a hungry man. These sumptuous feasts give us a unique perspective on the versatile tuna, a fish appropriate to any occasion. We are connoisseurs of the delectable tuna. Nothing tickles our taste buds as does the majestic denizen of the deep green sea, the tuna."

Robert's knife clinked to the plate. He looked the picture of confusion. Suddenly, he slapped his forehead. "Am I dense! I should have realized. You're a kosher rabbi. That's it, isn't it?" Robert's palm cleared his forehead, leaving the imprint of his slap. "You're the first rabbi I've come across in the longest while who still practices the dietary laws. I thought Jews didn't observe them anymore."

Kleinman tried to keep a sober face, but the priest's earnestness made it a losing battle; he grinned. "Oh, they're still practiced, Canon; you must have been moving in the wrong circle of rabbis."

Robert scratched his chin, pinched his nose and said nothing. Interpreting Robert's silence as condolence and not wanting to be the object of pity, Kleinman daintily tucked some tuna into a lettuce leaf and munched happily on the mouthful.

"And it's got a lot less calories."

Robert stared suspiciously; through narrowed eyes he watched Kleinman smack his lips, undecided whether the rabbi belonged in the theater or really had a crush on tuna fish. He went back to his roast beef, apparently without coming to any conclusion.

The program called for Senator Garvitz to speak after dessert. He strutted importantly to the rostrum and for twenty minutes sang praises to Robert. Sam Rabinowitz was next. His greetings from the Capital took another fifteen minutes; he sat down to scattered applause. After the lieutenant governor, Kleinman was called. He spoke briefly, wishing Robert the strength and wisdom to continue to serve his church and community with the same distinction and effectiveness he had served the last thirty-five years. He sat down and was followed by three more speakers. After the last of the testimonials, Robert rose to a standing ovation.

"Words, speeches are my stock in trade," Robert began on a serious note. "But tonight I'm at a loss for words. I feel inadequate to the occasion, too deeply moved by your kindness to me and my wife to do justice to my feelings." Robert smiled benignly at his wife, an exquisitely groomed silver-haired woman in her late sixties who looked ten years younger. "I'm particularly privileged tonight to be the drawing card for so many distinguished clergymen."

Robert's serious opening trailed into a lighter banter. "One of them seated on the dais put me on for a while . . . till I figured his bag." Kleinman dared a look up and caught the twinkle in Robert's eye.

"The rabbi's put-on reminded me of how one enterprising entrepreneur converted a liability into a fortune. This fellow had started canning white salmon. Well, in his town no one had ever seen white salmon. Pink salmon was the only kind they would have any truck with. So the man's product went begging, and he would have lost his shirt. Then he hit on a scheme that just about put his competition out of business . . . on every can he pasted a label that read: 'This salmon is guaranteed not to turn pink in the can.' "

An unbroken vista of smiling faces encouraged Robert to continue. And continue he did, with relish.

"The good rabbi turned down the main dish for tuna salad. When our lovely waitress set down the main dish it made my juices flow. Then I watched the joy—no, rapture would be better—with which Rabbi Kleinman dug into his tuna fish. Well! I really thought I was watching a man in paradise. He near convinced me to turn in my roast beef. But before I give up meat for fish I intend to arrange a kosher roast beef dinner at St. John and invite the rabbi. Then I'll see what he really prefers."

The guests roared. Though on the butt end of Robert's humor, Kleinman laughed with the crowd. Robert waited for the laughter to subside, then reverted to the seriousness with which he had opened.

"You have come here to heap praises on me, praise of which I would be happy to deserve a fraction. What does please me no end and which I like to think I have had a hand in creating is the climate of fellowship and harmony in our community. I see it dramatically in evidence tonight, and it gives me much joy. We may vote for different candidates and worship in different churches, but we respect each other.

We are a community that has put into practice our Lord's spirit of love and fellowship. I pray to our Lord Jesus Christ that this spirit of love and fellowship will always prevail. For my part, I shall continue to work toward that end."

Kleinman's smile faded. If Robert's orison to brotherly love was meant to please the rabbi, it seemed to have the opposite effect. An optimist in most things, Kleinman's experience had conditioned him instinctively to read himself and his religion out of the charmed circle whenever any Christian clergyman preached love and fellowship. And Robert's invocation of the Lord Jesus Christ to the assembly which included a sizeable Jewish delegation gave Rabbi Kleinman little reason to question his instincts.

Nevertheless, after that memorable evening, rabbi and priest subsequently met at other community functions: Memorial Day parades, the dedication of the new library, interfaith services. Soon a friendship evolved and they discovered their mutual passion for chess and arranged a weekly game. The location of the game alternated, one week in Robert's study, the next in Kleinman's. They played every Monday morning, starting at nine-thirty and breaking at noon. The game would be cancelled only in the event of an emergency. A funeral might be considered an emergency, and even funerals, whenever possible would be put off to the afternoon so as not to interfere with their chess schedule.

Kleinman was Robert's equal and better across the board, and when he survived Robert's brutal opening moves he played a powerful game. But these occasions were too few and far between to suit Kleinman. Usually, the priest relentlessly pressed his opening advantage and brought Kleinman to his knees.

The rabbi's Ford crunched to a stop in line with the entrance to the First Methodist Church of Blueport. A waist-high picket fence separated Main Street from the church lawn. Two tall narrow windows, their stained glass patterns only faintly discernable in the dark, peered invitingly onto the cold street. From the car, the wooden frame building, topped by a lofty steeple rising to a gracious tapering spire, presented a picture postal card serenity. A bright yellow beam boldly illuminating the church bulletin board announced Reverend William Wright's Sunday service and Bible class. It was snowing gently. Shimmering like polished diamonds, the crystals drifted past Reverend Wright's bulletin board, danced briefly in a sparkling exhibition of infinitely varied configurations, then fell to the whitening ground.

Kleinman raised his coat collar and made directly for the door, his steps biting a trail of dark footprints in the fresh snow. He entered the vestibule and turned right, heading into the new wing. Voices muffled by the textured sound-absorbent ceiling filtered through the halls, urging Kleinman on to the classroom in which the clergymen were conducting their meeting. Kleinman was late again; if he knew his canon, the meeting must have been on for at least a half hour. To John Robert, eight o'clock meant just that. Not seven forty-nine or eight thirty-one. It meant eight sharp. The rabbi made a coward's try at slipping unobtrusively into the room.

Robert caught him in the act.

"How do you do, Rabbi? Glad to see you could make our meeting. Better late than never, I suppose."

Nine pairs of eyes shifted in Kleinman's direction. Bennet Graham, another inveterate latecomer, who had arrived ten minutes before and received similar chastisement, chuckled at Kleinman and waved him to a vacant chair. Kleinman sat down meekly.

"We were just discussing where to locate for our next meeting," Robert said, bringing Kleinman up to date on the deliberations. "We've all had a round. How about the Jewish Center, Morris?"

Kleinman hunted inside his jacket. He drew out a diary-calendar and thumbed the pages. "That'll be the first Tuesday in March, right?"

"Yes."

"That'll be fine, John. Be happy to have the meeting at the synagogue."

"Okay. That's out of the way. Let's see how we did on our aid to Biafra project."

The clergymen announced the pledges made by their respective churches. Frank Simpson, chairman of the drive to aid Biafra, tallied the sum. The figure hugged a thousand dollars. Kleinman's pledge of two hundred on behalf of the Blueport Jewish Center was topped only by St. John's, which pledged two hundred fifty.

John Robert was pleased. "Very good. We'll send the money to the Biafran Relief Fund as soon as the pledges are honored, and I hope to God the food it buys will get to those poor people in time."

The ministers added a prayerful amen. They were united in their concern for the starving wretches in Biafra.

"Now to get to the problems at home," Robert continued, hastening to the next item on the agenda. "We've run into a roadblock in our push for low-cost housing in Blueport. The real estate people, backed by the Civic Association, are opposing us. Not openly; they haven't the guts to come out into the open. But they managed to throw a monkey wrench into the works. The town council has quietly shelved our petition for a rezoning. Any suggestions on where to go from here?"

Miles Porter, the black minister of Blueport's Baptist Church, raised his hand. In angry mood he blasted the unconscionable delaying tactics of certain known parties out to kill low-cost housing in Blueport. Passionately he reminded his colleagues of the acute need to get his people out of the slums and of the Ministers Association's pledge to fight on no matter whose toes were scuffed. There was unanimity regarding this problem, too. Robert appointed a delegation to meet with Mayor Downing, which he agreed to head. He assured Porter that the Ministers Association would continue to apply pressure to the end. John Robert gave every impression of sincere concern for the needs of Blueport's less fortunate citizens, although his parish for the most part consisted of the town's elite and well heeled.

Thinking ahead in the meeting and of what he wanted to say, Kleinman considered the canon. To the rabbi, John Robert remained a question mark, their friendship notwithstanding. And despite the surface camaraderie between himself and the disciples of Christ, he was under no illusions. He hesitated to make the appeal for fear of being rebuffed, but he was duty bound to try. In good conscience he couldn't remain silent; that would appear as if he were disinterested. Worse, it might be interpreted as concurrence on his part with the hypocritical condemnation headlining every newspaper. As a rabbi he was obliged to speak out. He didn't expect much from the others. Robert, however . . . maybe, just maybe, he might understand. And if he did, he had enough influence to swing the entire group.

Even seated, the pastor of St. John's Episcopal Church was an imposing figure. His face was long and high cheeked. Gray brows, thick and scraggly as an untended hedge almost met above the bridge of an aquiline nose that sloped downward above a square shelf of chin. His eyes, blue and clear as a mountain lake, and set deep in bony sockets appeared capable of piercing a lead shield. When he stood up, his six-foot-three height gave him a quality of austere authority that could cow an epicurean into a seven-day fast.

"Before we go on to assign parts for the Brotherhood Week Service are there any other matters anybody wants to bring up?"

38

Robert's question yanked Kleinman back to attention. He raised his hand.

Robert's brow lifted in surprise. "Yes, Morris?"

Kleinman rarely introduced a motion or a project. He spoke up when asked and cooperated with the group to the extent he felt was prudent, but his reputation with this crowd was not that of a pace setter. Robert's mild surprise was shared by the other men; they gave the rabbi their full attention.

Kleinman kept to his seat. Rising to speak, he thought, would serve to complete his isolation. The appeal would call enough attention to the gulf separating them. He searched their faces for a sign that they anticipated his purpose in asking for the floor. There was no hint, no indication at all. Why should there be? To Jews it might be a matter of life and death. To them? It was distant, far from mind. Biafra was only half way around the world; those for whom he would plead . . . the distance was a universe apart. They waited for the rabbi to speak.

"Undoubtedly, you're aware of the position our government has taken in the United Nations vis-à-vis Israel," Kleinman opened behind a façade of self-assurance, as one taking up a cause so patently just that no vindication was needed. "The United States joined with Russia to unanimously condemn Israel. Again this valiant little democracy stands alone, deserted even by her friends. We expect expediency, self-interest, hypocracy in international politics. But we are clergymen, ministers of God. We owe allegiance to a law higher than self-interest. We owe supreme allegiance to justice. And justice was betrayed this week in the United Nations. To condemn Israel for destroying airplanes, machines that are replaceable, and to ignore the bombing of shopping centers in Tel Aviv, apartment houses in Jerusalem, the bombing of a plane carrying nearly one hundred passengers, is to mock the sanctity of human life. If that is justice, then justice has lost all rational meaning. I grant that the issues in the Middle East are complex and confusing, that they are not amenable to facile solutions. Israel is not entirely blameless. But on this issue, this raid, we as ministers should applaud. In the annals of war this is unheard of: soldiers on the attack taking meticulous care, at great personal risk, not to inflict casualities on the enemy. My country's condemnation of Israel frightens me, not only because of the kinship I feel with its embattled people, but because that one-sided condemnation represents a victory for idolatry. We grieve over the destruction of machines and tolerate the slaughter of human beings. Have we as a nation become so mesmerized by our technocracy that we can no longer perceive an ethical distinction between people and machines?"

Passion invaded Kleinman's presentation; the resolve he had made not to let his emotions run off evaporated before the injustices he heard himself denounce. "Once again, Jews were a hair's breadth from extinction. Genocide, and again the world is silent. No! The world condemns the victim." Fervor carried him to his feet. He looked to Robert, to the nine colleagues, ministers in Blueport. His voice pleaded for compassion, his eyes for understanding. "I ask that we, men of the cloth, men dedicated to truth, publicly and officially protest this blatantly unjust condemnation of Israel to our State Department."

Kleinman fell back to his seat, hoping against hope that he had vibrated at least one sympathetic chord.

Silence. Stone silence. The silence of the uncaring, of indifference. Fool! Fool! Fool! To expect help from this quarter. It is necessary that we drown in order for Him to be exalted.

As through a mist, Kleinman saw his neighbor's hand go up. Graham's voice was pleasant: soothing, clean, and sharp as a razor's edge.

"I respect your feelings, Morris. We all admire your sincerity. And I understand that Israel occupies a special place in your heart. That is what makes it difficult for you to see the other side of the coin. What of the refugees? What of those human beings made homeless by Jewish occupation of Palestine? What of their despair? Israel has amply demonstrated a marked capability to defend her interests. Someone has to rise to the cry of the defeated. I can't take a commando raid on a civilian airport as lightly as you do, Morris. Certainly it doesn't deserve our applause."

More silence. Embarrassed silence. Deadly silence. Canon John Robert broke the silence.

"It's getting late, men. Let's get on with the assignments for our Brotherhood Week Service."

Three

Sometimes her job bored Martha to tears. For days on end she might sit twiddling her thumbs, waiting for the phone to ring or someone to drop in and help make the long hours pass, Then inevitably came the deluge. Today Martha forgot she had thumbs. The flyer for the next week's congregational meeting was finished and ready to go. At the last minute, as usual, Stein, the Center accountant, had delivered the financial report. It had to be typed in triplicate for the executive meeting on Sunday. Mrs. Weinstock telephoned and bent Martha's ear for twenty-five precious minutes complaining of the ten-dollar increase in congregation dues. Patiently, Martha explained that rising costs made the increase necessary; it had been voted by the membership three months ago. Mrs. Weinstock would not be mollified. She and her husband had been on a picture-taking safari when the vote was taken; had they been home, they would have voted against the increase. Ways should be found to cut costs, Mrs. Weinstock insisted. She demanded to speak to the rabbi. Tactfully, Martha informed her that dues weren't the rabbi's department. If she felt so strongly, she should take the matter up with the president of the congregation.

At long last Mrs. Weinstock hung up, announcing that she had an appointment at the hairdresser and would, when she was less pressed for time, have a talk with Ira Cane. Martha lined up three sheets of paper, inserted two carbons and rolled them into the electric typewriter. She picked up Kleinman's article for the monthly bulletin and scanned the handwritten copy. The rabbi's articles were always interesting. Often they provoked a good deal of discussion, too much sometimes. Martha enjoyed reading the rabbi's column, once she deciphered his hieroglyphics. Kleinman wrote well, but he could use a crash penmanship course. Martha strained to make out the title of the article, "Searching For My Brother."

Martha's fingers flew over the keyboard. She got through the second paragraph before she sensed the visitor's presence. She glanced up and spotted him standing in front of the glass partition that divided her office from the long corridor. He was tall, somewhat heavy-set, with wide but stooped shoulders. His full head of gray hair and his thick, precisely trimmed moustache gave him a quiet commanding dignity. He wore a tailored black coat over a charcoal suit and held a black homburg in his hand. Martha's maternal instinct was awakened by the sadness in his blue eyes. Timidly, he rapped on the glass. Martha slid open the partition.

"Can I help you?"

"If I may, I would like to see the rabbi," the man said. His voice was pitched to a low bass. The thick German gutterals jarred Martha's memory.

"My name is Otto Hoffman."

Martha repeated the name to herself. Where had she seen him before?

"I am Otto Hoffman, from Hoffman Jewelers on Third and Main Street. You have been to my store several times, I think."

"Oh yes!" Mr. Hoffman. I should have recognized you. I'm sorry. How is Mrs. Hoffman?"

"Mrs. Hoffman is well, thank you. She is now in the store."

"She can manage the store by herself?"

"Oh yes! She is a better business man than I am."

"Don't belittle your talents, Mr. Hoffman. Last month my husband walked into your store to buy me a present. He walked out with a hundred-dollar watch. You must be a super salesman to make my Fred spend a hundred dollars. It was the most beautiful anniversary gift I ever got from him, and I'm married more years than I care to admit."

The sad eyes smiled. "I'm happy you like it. But I cannot take credit for the sale. It was Mrs. Hoffman who waited on your husband."

"Then I thank you both; you make a good team." Martha was pleased that she had made the man smile. I'll see if the rabbi is in."

Martha pushed back her chair and stepped out of the Center office. Crossing the hall, she stopped at a door diagonally opposite, on which was affixed a nondescript rectangular plate with Rabbi inscribed in simple block letters. Martha knocked. Hearing no answer, she rattled the doorknob; the door opened a crack. She poked her head in.

Kleinman sat at the end of a long narrow room behind a metal desk. On both sides of the desk, three-quarters of the way up to the high ceiling, open book cases were set flush against the dull white cinderblock walls. Every inch of space was crammed with books. To the side of the desk, three drawers of a four-drawer filing cabinet were fully open, revealing a bulging mess of folders. The one tiny window in the room looked out on a drab boardinghouse whose gables and turrets belonged to another generation. Martha winced at the clutter on Kleinman's desk: periodicals, magazines, sheets of paper on which he had scribbled notes legible only to himself and which she would no doubt be asked to decode, volumes piled one on the other, strewn every which way. The chaos before creation. How did he manage to find anything in that disorder? Yet manage somehow he did.

It's about time they got around to furnishing the rabbi with an office befitting his position, Martha complained to herself. He should have a decent study to work in. It's a crying shame that our rabbi has to receive people in this long dark box.

Kleinman was in the midst of transcribing notes for a folder; he marked the place in the large tome from which he was extracting quotes and looked up. "Yes, Martha. What is it?"

"There's a gentleman here to see you. Mr. Otto Hoffman."

"Otto Hoffman! From Hoffman Jewelers?" Kleinman looked puzzled.

"Yes," Martha said. "He seems like a very nice man."

"I'm sure he is. Did he say what he wanted?"

"No. He just asked if he could see you."

"What could Otto Hoffman want to see me about?" Kleinman speculated to his secretary. "All right. Have him come in. And please phone my wife; tell her very gently that I'll be late for lunch."

Kleinman pushed himself up as Hoffman entered. The proprietor of Blueport's fashionable jewelry store appeared reticent. He hesitated at the door.

"Do come in," Kleinman urged.

"I'm sorry to come without first making an appointment,"

Hoffman said. He took in Kleinman's desk, cluttered with notes and open volumes. "If you are occupied, I can perhaps come again when you are not so busy."

"That's quite all right, Mr. Hoffman," the rabbi reassured his timid visitor, motioning him to a chair. "I'm not unaccustomed to seeing people without prior appointments. Please make yourself comfortable."

The jeweler sat down, rigidly cradling his homburg in his lap.

"You wonder, I am sure, why I have come to see you," Hoffman started, appearing to gain confidence.

"Well, yes. I am rather curious," Kleinman confessed.

Hoffman paused as if to gather his thoughts, then said: "In memory of my daughter-in-law I wish to donate to your temple five thousand dollars. I have been informed by one of my customers, a member of your temple, that the congregation is calling for donations to furnish your chapel. If somewhere in the temple you would find a place to commemorate the name of my daughter-in-law, it would please very much my wife and I."

Kleinman's surprise made it plain that the offer was totally unexpected.

"Five thousand dollars is a sizeable sum, Mr. Hoffman. Forgive me, but I was under the impression that you are of the Christian faith."

Hoffman's reply was firm. "I am of the Christian faith."

"You are?" This time the rabbi got hold of his amazement before it became full blown. "I do not mean to offend, but would it not be appropriate for your daughter-in-law to be memorialized in a church of her own faith?"

"Yes. That is why I wish her name to be memorialized in a synagogue."

"Your daughter-in-law was Jewish?"

"Yes."

"When did she pass away?"

"I do not know exactly. It was, I suppose, about the same time as my son . . . some thirty years ago."

Years of counseling, of face-to-face confrontation with pain had honed Kleinman's sensitivity. In the somber visage of the man sitting opposite him he read a deep grief and a pressing need to unburden himself of a great sorrow.

"How did they die?"

"They died in Auschwitz."

The phone rang, breaking into Hoffman's anguish; Kleinman picked up the receiver.

"Evelyn Gross just called," Martha said in an unusually solemn voice.

"Yes?"

"Her mother-in-law died this morning."

Momentarily, Hoffman's trouble was pushed to the side. "Poor woman! Poor woman!" Kleinman sighed.

"Dr. Gross wants to schedule the funeral for tomorrow morning. Eleven o'clock . . . At Monahan."

"Monahan?"

"Yes."

"He can't bury his mother from Monahan's chapel!"

"From Monahan," Martha repeated. "Evelyn Gross was definite about that. She asked that you call back to confirm the time. You can reach her after two. She'll be home the rest of the afternoon."

Kleinman returned to the gloom of Hoffman. "Mr. Hoffman, I'm sorry, but I must leave now. The mother of a congregant died. I have to see to the arrangements. About a memorial to your daughter-in-law, I believe something can be worked out. Might I suggest that you put your offer and your request into a short note and send it to the Jewish Center office. The board will act on it at the next meeting."

"I will do so, Rabbi. To whom shall I address the note?"

"Address it to the president of the Jewish Center, Mr. Ira Cane."

"I thank you for your time, Rabbi."

Kleinman offered his hand. He waited for Hoffman to leave and reached for the coat tree.

Four

Death makes no appointments. Death does not schedule specific hours for Christians and other hours for Jews. Death arrives at its own pleasure, in its own good time. Jews, Christians—there are no special dates of departure.

Off to one side of the chapel in a small room festooned with multicolored foliage and bedecked with garlands and wreaths an elderly gentleman reposed in embalmed serenity under a white crucifix.

What could Kleinman do? Demand that Monahan hide his other clientele because a Jewish funeral was on this morning's roster? That would be unfair as well as useless. Clyde Monahan was not insensitive to Jewish feelings. He did his best to accommodate the rabbi. Within reason he succeeded. The main chapel had been cleared of Christian symbols. But there was a limit. Clyde couldn't be expected to re-arrange his whole mode of operation for Kleinman's benefit.

In the beginning Kleinman had been squeamish. Burying a Jew from a Christian funeral home, allowing Gentiles to prepare Jewish bodies for interment went against his grain. There was little choice: Blueport had no Jewish funeral home. The Jewish community was not yet sufficiently large to warrant one. M. S. Blaustein's funeral home was located in Brentville, twenty miles west, and his congregants objected to the distance. They preferred the convenience of Monahan. So Kleinman adjusted. In time misgivings evaporated. Clyde Monahan was a good man, experienced and decidedly helpful in those first benumbing moments when death snatched a loved one from a family. A call from the rabbi and Clyde was at the deceased's home within the hour, day or night, to remove the body. And he did his job with finesse; it might even be said, with compassion. And if the truth be told, Kleinman was not overly anxious to make the trip to Brentville, either. A service at Blaustein's, to which the rabbi on rare occasions was called, meant a forty-mile round trip, a morning and an afternoon shot. From Monahan's to Beth Olam Cemetery was no more than twenty minutes or so at a fast clip.

Moreover, Monahan spared Kleinman the awkward business of honorariums. The funeral director included the clergyman's fee in the charge to the family. And it was a substantial fee, too, more than Kleinman felt his services warranted. In fact, his conscience was pricked over the whole subject of honorariums. A congregant was entitled to a funeral service by his rabbi without having to leave a tip. That's why a Jew belongs to the synagogue, to feel free to call upon the services of his rabbi when he is in need of them. But, after a time, this scruple was anesthetized. Small fortunes were spent on caskets that would shortly be covered with dirt. So figure the family makes a contribution to the *yeshiva* education of a rabbi's son. It's a *mitzvah*. Mentally, Kleinman allocated funeral honorariums to a fund for payment of Jonathan's tuition at Etz Chaim Academy. A rationalization? Maybe. But Kleinman no longer objected to Monahan's funeral home. Not publicly, not privately.

Except for Mrs. Gross. Not for this orthodox woman Monahan's chapel. Not for this pious Jewish woman with whom he had visited and read "*Tehilim*." Not for the wife of

48

old Mr. Gross who studied *chumash* and Rashi; not for Gross, with a tall black *yarmulke* perched on his gray head, who asked: "Would the rabbi be so good to make a *mi sheberach* in *shul* for my wife?" Kleinman couldn't stand aside and allow this. No! Mr. Gross did not have ten years of experience in Blueport that would allow him to make the adjustment to Gentiles handling Jewish corpses. Mr. Gross wouldn't object to making a twenty-mile trip to a Jewish funeral home for his wife. Mr. Gross had ample time now. His mornings would be free, his afternoons free, his evenings. Free and empty. All that he had to keep him busy now was a memory, a memory of his life with Mrs. Gross. A memory of her final leave-taking from him.

Kleinman had done the best he could with Dr. Gross. He had pleaded, cajoled. He offered to hold the services in the Jewish Center, which was done only on rare occasions. Blaustein would prepare his mother's body in his Brentville chapel, after which he would bring her back to Blueport for the funeral service. That way no one would be inconvenienced, and his mother would be laid to rest, as she should be, by Jews. To no avail. Monahan was a patient of his; Gross felt obliged to patronize his funeral home. Then, too, friends would be coming the night before to view the body. Brentville was too far. Kleinman stressed again that Dr. Gross' mother had been an orthodox woman. She would not have wanted to be buried from a non-Jewish chapel. His father would be hurt. Dr. Gross was stubborn. He had an answer for everything. His mother was dead. She knew nothing anymore and felt nothing; she was only a memory, his memory, and he would not have that memory spoiled by the morbid orthodox practices he remembered from childhood. As far as his father was concerned, he was numbed by grief, so bewildered by his loss he wasn't aware of anything; he wouldn't know the difference. "Monahan has a casket cover embroidered with a Jewish star," Gross argued; "they'll drape it over the coffin to show it's a Jewish funeral."

Monahan had removed all Christian symbols from the main chapel. There wasn't a crucifix in the large room. The impropriety that remained to give offense was burial rites in direct violation of Jewish tradition, but Monahan was not to be faulted for that. He did as he was asked to do, what the family paid him for. And they did an expert job on Mrs. Gross. Her cheeks bore more color; she seemed more alive now than when Kleinman had visited her. She looked as if she had just dozed off, as if momentarily she would awaken from her nap sprightly and refreshed. And the casket! Kleinman was no connoisseur of furniture, but he appreciated quality when he saw it. In his house there was nothing to match that wood. A beautiful piece of furniture was going into the ground. Attic wood, polished to a mirror shine, with silver handles and lined in plush satin.

Kleinman delivered the eulogy. He spoke his words of comfort:

"Man is obligated to bless God in time of distress as he is in time of gladness. Had Sarah Gross continued to live, you know what that would have meant. Pain and suffering. As she had a loving heart for you, so must you have a loving heart for her. You are pained because you have lost a mother, a wife, a grandmother, a friend. But she has peace now; she has God. If pain must be endured, would not a loving family elect to shoulder it rather than watch a loved one endure it? . . . But there is more to comfort us; there are the precious memories that remain. Sarah Gross led a long life, a good life, a fruitful and blessed life. . . ."

Kleinman described the fullness of Mrs. Gross' years. He called on the family to remember that they were privileged to have this fine and noble mother, wife and friend with them so long. "The Lord has given and the Lord has taken." Kleinman prayed that God might console them in their bereavement and strengthen their faith in His ultimate goodness.

The chapel service over and the immediate family safely tucked into a limousine, Monahan coaxed the laggards into their automobiles. Kleinman climbed into the front seat of the hearse besides the driver; Monahan gave a prearranged signal and the hearse started to move, with the family limousine directly following. Leaving the interment part of the funeral for his assistant to handle, Monahan went back to the chapel to direct the last rites of the elderly gentleman still reposing under the crucifix.

The trip to Beth Olam went quickly. At eleven twenty-five, Kleinman had finished the eulogy. By twelve the procession of cars had reached the cemetery gates and began cautiously to roll through the narrow lanes toward the grave site.

Two hundred yards before reaching the family plot the head limousine carrying Dr. Gross and his father stopped. Headlights that had signaled a funeral cortège now clicked off in succession as the line of cars waited, their motors running and exhaust fumes trailing white clouds in the cold January air. The hearse continued on alone to the grave. Kleinman turned to see the distance growing between him and the family car.

"Why aren't the cars moving with us to the grave site?"

"This is a hold funeral," the driver, a squat, flat-nosed man, said.

"What do you mean, a hold funeral?"

"We hold the family back until the casket is lowered and they cover the grave with artificial grass. . . . Makes it easier on the family."

"Who told you to do that?"

"Dr. Gross."

Kleinman held back his irritation. No point in letting it

out on the driver; he was only following orders. The rabbi waited for the grave diggers to slide the casket from the hearse. He waited till they set it on the rolling cart. He waited till the men pivoted the casket in the direction of the grave. Then he planted himself solidly in front of the cart.

"This casket does not move till the family is brought up. And I want six pallbearers to accompany the casket to the grave."

"But Dr. Gross, he . . ."

"Don't but me. Just do as I say."

"I can't, Rabbi. Dr. Gross ordered . . ."

"I don't want any arguments. I will not go on with the service until the family car moves forward. I want the family at the grave site when the casket is lowered."

The hearse driver yielded. "Okay, Rabbi. Let it be your funeral."

The driver waved the head limousine to move on. The gap between the cortège and hearse closed again, and the cars emptied of their passengers. Kleinman called for pallbearers, bringing on a confused flurry by this unscheduled ritual. He waited until six men volunteered. They lifted the casket. Kleinman directed them to make seven stops as they walked to the grave. The family trailed after the rabbi. The grave-diggers paced alongside the casket worriedly eyeing the panting pallbearers. At the grave site the casket was surrendered to the gravediggers. Working swiftly and silently they carried it up a small mound and by means of two supporting straps let the casket settle to the bottom of the grave. Kleinman intoned the brief interment service while the bereaved husband, leaning heavily on his son and daughter-in-law, stared down into the open pit, his eyes dry and lifeless. Kleinman chanted the memorial prayer, picked up the shovel at his feet, bit into the mound of earth and dropped its half load onto the casket.

"Please form two lines," the funeral director said, marking

the end of the service to the friends clustered about the grave. "The family will walk through the lines for your consolation."

Evidently, this new assistant to Monahan was familiar with Jewish funeral rites. Another plus for Monahan.

Dr. Gross pressed his father's arm to turn him to the waiting limousine. The old man resisted.

"Wait till the grave is filled in."

"Pop, the gravediggers will fill it."

"Wait."

Kleinman retrieved the shovel and passed it to the nearest pallbearer, who took it and deposited his load of earth. The shovel went from hand to hand until the casket disappeared under the falling earth that slowly rose to ground level and formed a mound over the grave.

Unexpectedly, the old man stepped forward and from memory recited the long burial *Kaddish*; his voice low and hoarse. It was probable that only Kleinman, who was so close their faces almost touched, made out the words at the end. It was a farewell spoken in Yiddish by Mr. Gross to his wife.

"Goodbye, Sarah, my precious Sarah. I ask you to forgive me. You should have been buried like a *Yiddishe* wife and mother. But my heart . . . it was broken. Over it was before I knew anything . . . I promise, Sarah . . . A *Kaddish*; this you will have . . . I promise. . . ."

Five

Where in heaven's name was Eighty-three Gardenia Drive? Kleinman squinted through the fogged windshield into the cheerless murk, hunting in vain for the number. It seemed that the Manor Park people were loath to put numbers on their houses for fear that the need of such crass indentification would diminish their eminence. Every house in Manor Park was distinctive; the mailman knew who lived where, and it was expected that all and sundry could identify each estate with its illustrious owner. Well, he was no mailman; he had trouble remembering the names of his congregants so how was he going to remember where they lived? Twice this month Kleinman had visited the Gross mansion; twice he had missed it and had to backtrack, and it was in broad daylight. At night it was impossible.

Aha! There's the house! Kleinman remembered the sprawling mass of English Tudor. To a *mitzvah* God speeds his lost sheep. The cars lined up in the driveway assured him that this was the house.

Kleinman turned into the driveway and wedged his sedan between a Buick and a Lincoln. He slid across the seat to the house side, raised his collar and braced himself against the cold. A sudden north wind speeded him towards the entrance, two pillars framing a wrought iron glassed-in enclosure. Kleinman juggled the rustic knob. The door was unlocked as is customary in a house of mourning. He entered without knocking. A tall, muscular youth came through the arched vestibule at the end of the hall. His wide shoulders and thick neck suggested the driving power of a halfback. He wore tapered tan slacks, a turtle neck sweater, and, on his big feet, brown loafers. His cheeks, slightly puffed and flushed, were generously sprinkled with freckles. Upon recognizing Kleinman his long, grave face broke into a warm smile.

"Hello, Mel. You certainly have grown." Kleinman slanted his chin ceilingward to meet the young man's eyes. The youth towered over Kleinman by a full head. "It's been so long since I've seen you, I hardly recognized you."

Mel squirmed. "Well. You know how it is, Rabbi. School keeps me pretty busy."

54

"Yes, I know," Kleinman said. "But once in a while drop in at the synagogue so that I don't entirely forget what you look like."

"Okay, Rabbi. I promise." Mel grinned and spread a huge right palm against his chest in penitence.

"Let me have your hat and coat. Dad and Grandpa are in the living room with the others."

A full-bosomed blonde maid wearing a frilly white uniform swayed into the vestibule. She beamed a shy smile, took Kleinman's hat and coat from Mel, and hung them in a closet. The youth pointed to the right and waved his rabbi to precede him. Kleinman passed through the high domed vestibule.

Light, untroubled conversation greeted the rabbi as he entered the large vaulted living room. Shafts of orange and yellow flames leaped up and curled about two thick logs in the white brick fireplace, radiating a lusterous warmth and adding a festive touch to the plush room. Lester Stern, owner of the L & S Cadillac agency, sat on a blue terra cotta lounge, his ankles cushioned on an ottoman. Opposite Stern, on a white wool sofa, Charley Green and another man Kleinman didn't recognize made up a friendly threesome. They each held glasses from which they sipped intermittently. Stern and Green were engrossed in conversation. Dr. Gross sat next to Stern. To the rabbi's surprise Gross was wearing slippers. Snatches of the conversation between the Cadillac dealer and Green reached Kleinman.

"But let's say for argument's sake that you're right. Your car holds up better. Okay?" Stern was temporarily yielding a point. "Try and trade your Lincoln. Boy, will you take a licking."

On the other side of the room, the women were animatedly discussing a winter sale at Matilda's, a fashionable dress shop patronized by the in set throughout the county.

Except for the slippered feet, the covered mirrors, and the

forlorn old man sitting on a low stool at the far side of the living room it seemed like a pleasant gathering of friends, a Saturday night social. Conspicuous by its absence was any reference to the purpose that had brought the visitors out on this bitter winter night; the subject seemed to be studiously avoided.

Rabbi Kleinman stepped onto the deep piled gold carpeting and made directly for Dr. Gross, acknowledging the others by no more that a cursory nod. He selected a club chair next to the doctor and sat down.

"Again, Dr. Gross, I'm deeply sorry about your mother." Kleinman's reference to the deceased abruptly stopped conversation on both ends of the room.

"Thank you, Rabbi. I appreciated your help at the funeral service. You delivered a moving eulogy; I found your words very comforting. And what you said was very true. For Mom it's better this way. Had she lived on, there would have been only pain and suffering. . . ." Gross' brow wrinkled; he looked across the room at his father. "It's my dad I'm worried about now. He just sits like that without saying a word. I wish I could get him to say something, even cry . . . anything."

"I'll talk to him," Kleinman said. He crossed over to the old man. Mr. Gross' wisp of white hair was covered with the same tall black *yarmulke* Kleinman remembered him wearing on the first visit he had made to the Gross home. The bereaved widower hunched over his stool, sad and lost, staring unseeingly at the carpet, his hands hanging limply between his knees. Minutes ticked off with no sound. Solemnity filled the room. The company stayed silent. In a few short minutes, the rabbi's heavy disposition had effectively put a damper on the festive atmosphere prevailing before his arrival.

"Your wife was a fine woman, an *ayshis chayil*," Kleinman said to the old man. "You remember; a few weeks ago I visited with you and your wife? She was truly a good woman. I am very sorry for your loss."

Slowly, Mr. Gross lifted his head, as if awakening from a drugged sleep.

"I was very pleasantly surprised to discover your son's fine Jewish background," Kleinman said reaching further into the curtain of grief insulating and isolating the old man. "Your loss and your son's loss, I know, is great. I would like to hear more about your wife. Would you care to tell me about her?"

Life seemed to stir in the old man's listless eyes. A heavy sigh pushed through the thin, crinkled lips as if constricting bands deep within had opened and released a ponderous melancholy. And then he began to talk. He spoke of the deceased lovingly, caressing the memory of her. He described the long and good years they lived together, the joys and sorrows they shared, and he gave voice to the loneliness and depression he now felt. Yes, his son was a good man; the father was proud of his son.

"He is a good doctor. Not religious maybe, like I would want. But to cure, to heal. What greater *mitzvah* can a Jew perform? So you see, Rabbi, I have much *naches* from my son. But he has his own family to take care of; his own problems to occupy him." The old man shook his head sadly. "I understand now what the Talmud meant: 'He who loses the wife of his youth even the holy altar sheds tears for him.' Sarah was the wife of my youth. Not even my fine son can take her place."

Dr. Gross came over to the rabbi and his disconsolate father. Affectionately he put his arm to the old man's shoulder. "Poppa, you're tired. Maybe you'd like to go upstairs and lie down?"

Mr. Gross raised his eyes. "Yes, Gavriel. I am tired, but it's good for me to talk. . . . I feel not so terrible now. . . . A little of the heaviness is lifting." He returned to Kleinman and the memory of his Sarah. Reluctantly, Gabriel Gross went back to his guests.

Kleinman gave ear and the old man poured out his heart. One by one, after brief and awkward expressions of sympathy, the callers begged their leave. Kleinman stayed close to the old man as he dipped into the past to drain it of memories. Finally, he reached the end of his need to talk. His strained face dissolved into a relaxed exhaustion; the communication of his grief had lifted his burden enough to make him aware of fatigue. His lids fluttered, closed, and shut out the tiredness of his eyes. Gently, Dr. Gross raised his father from the stool he had insisted on sitting on throughout the evening. Mr. Gross forced open his eyes and looked appreciatively at Kleinman.

"Thank you, Rabbi. Thank you for listening to an old man's *tsuris*." The voice was thick, hoarse with emotion and fatigue.

Evelyn Gross took her father-in-law's arm and escorted him up the spiral staircase to the upstairs bedrooms. Slowly, step by step, with a tenderness that Kleinman would have hesitated to attribute to the outwardly reserved and distant doctor's wife, Evelyn Gross helped the old man climb the stairs. Dr. Gross and Kleinman were left to themselves in the large living room. Gross sank into the lounge recently emptied of Lester Stern. Kleinman dropped into the sofa next to the fireplace. For several minutes the men meditated. A tired flame pushed its red tongue through the embers as if seeking new life in its dim glow.

"I see a lot of dying in my profession," Gross said, finally. You'd think by now I'd be used to it. Accept it. Not be touched by it. Nothing of the sort. When it's someone you care deeply about, . . . that's when it hits; then it explodes over you, and no previous experience makes it any easier to take. Then you see death. . . . I mean really see it. Not a body, a machine that's simply stopped functioning. You see a life, a person that once could feel and think and love and be loved, gone forever."

"You've been most fortunate," Kleinman interjected, "to have had both your parents so long."

"Yes, I've been lucky I guess. This is my first personal loss. It's not easy to take. That first moment you're forced to face up to the reality of it, when it dawns on you that neither you nor your loved ones are immortal. When I discovered my mother had cancer," Dr. Gross continued, "I knew she was going to die, but I don't think I really accepted it, not until I saw her lowered into the grave and heard that first shovelful of earth thud against the casket."

Gross paused in his ruminations. The image of that painful moment diverted him.

"You know, I was mad as hell when you insisted that the family stand there at that open grave and watch the casket lowered. I had specifically instructed the funeral director to lower the casket and cover it with artificial grass before bringing my father to the grave. If it weren't for the fact that I didn't want to create a scene, I would have returned to the car and really let you have it."

"And now you feel differently?"

"Yes. I confess I was wrong."

"Why? What made you change your mind?"

"Why?" Gross contemplated Kleinman's question. "Because I realize now that if you had allowed me to have my way, I would have added to my father's pain. He wanted my mother to be buried according to tradition, and he was more aware of what was going on than I thought. But more than that . . . I also realize now that it's senseless to conceal death. You can't excise grief with artificial balm. The anguish is there under the phony grass. It's got to come out; better that it does come out at the edge of the grave."

Gross looked Kleinman square in the face. "Rabbi, I thank

you for all you've done. You've been a great comfort to me and my father. Tonight was the first time since the funeral that he spoke a full sentence. Most of all I thank you for not letting me tell you how to be a rabbi."

Kleinman accepted Gross' appreciation with silent intensity. A moment elapsed.

"I know how busy you are," Kleinman said. "So if you like, I can arrange for the *Kaddish* to be recited in memory of your mother."

"I'd appreciate that, Rabbi. . . . I know that my father won't be up to it. But for the first month, at least, I'll make it my business to get down to the *minyan* and say it myself. It's been a long time since I've been to a *minyan*. I'm not sure I can still follow the service. But I'll make every effort to be there. Not because I've suddenly become a believer, but out of respect for my father . . . my mother."

"I would be hard put to find a better reason to come to the synagogue than to honor parents," Kleinman said softly.

Kleinman pushed himself up from the spongy softness of the sofa. Gross followed, and the two men walked to the vestibule.

"I've been so self-involved," Gross said, "I haven't even asked you how you've been feeling."

"Not bad. I'm still producing enough acid down there for three rabbis and a cantor thrown in." Kleinman laughingly patted his stomach. "But I think the ulcer is under control. It's too bad I didn't know five years ago what I know today. When you learn to look at the world in perspective you come to realize how foolish it is to aggravate yourself over trivialities. Had I known this before, I might not have worked myself into such a state in the first place. But, you know, youth is wasted on the young."

"I suppose even rabbis need time to mellow," said Dr. Gross.

"Particularly rabbis! Particularly rabbis!"

"I'm happy to hear that you've arrived at such a sensible attitude towards life, Rabbi. I hope you can maintain your equanimity at the next Board meeting."

"I try not to let Board meetings get to me anymore," said Kleinman.

"Good," Gross replied. "And especially, the next one. Don't let it upset you."

Kleinman peered suspiciously at Gross. "Why? What do you expect to happen?"

"You don't think that letter of yours is just going to fade away unnoticed, do you?" There was admonishment in Gross' tone.

Kleinman shrugged off the question. "I had an idea it might spark a debate."

"Spark a debate! You electrified the town. You blew a fuse; a hundred fuses. The *Blueport Gazette* has a large and standpat readership in these parts, and that was a strong letter, to say the least. It made some highly placed citizens in Blueport mighty unhappy. You knew such a letter would brew up one hell of a storm. I don't understand why you did it."

"It had to be done," Kleinman answered firmly.

"But why you? You don't even have any children in the Blueport school system."

"True, I don't have any children in the Blueport school system, but I have a responsibililty to my congregants who do. And there was no one else to take up the cudgels."

"But you can't afford to get yourself all stirred up again."

Kleinman replied with studied blandness, "I'll be cool, calm and collected."

"Yes. On the outside. But inside you'll be eating yourself up." Gross shook his head as if despairing of influencing his rabbi to moderation. "Anyway, try not to worry. I've lined up enough votes to back you. There shouldn't be too much howling. Except maybe from Ira Cane."

"Ira Cane? Will he be at the Board meeting?"

"In all probability. He's back. He paid me a hurried *shivah* call just before you arrived."

"I'm surprised I haven't heard from him yet."

"You will, Rabbi, you will. He probably hasn't got wind of it yet. But when he does, as he undoubtedly will before next week, he's going to be mad as a hornet. He's particularly sensitive about that kind of publicity. It'll be like touching a live nerve. Expect an explosion from Ira Cane. I'll do the best I can with him this time. But Rabbi, please," Gross spread his hands in supplication, "I do wish you'd take a respite between causes. I don't think your stomach can handle it; I know mine can't. If you must crusade, why don't you stick with civil rights, or fight poverty, or be a peacenik. At least you'll have somebody on your side. On this issue you're up against practically the whole town; Jews and Gentiles."

The maid came through the archway carrying the rabbi's hat and coat. Kleinman's eye roamed her pretty face, travelled down the white neck to the high firm breasts. She handed Kleinman his hat and coat.

"Thank you miss," Kleinman said.

She fluttered dark demure lashes and glided from the room. Kleinman watched her oscillating hips until they receded and turned a corner. He looked up at Gross and nodded approval.

"Why should we worry about Board meetings when there are so many other attractive subjects deserving our attention?"

Gross chuckled at this unexpected human side to his rabbi. "Well, at least that subject won't churn your stomach in the same way Board meetings do."

Kleinman glanced at his wrist watch. *"Oy vey!* It's ten-thirty. Now I really have a worry to churn my stomach. I promised Beth I'd be home no later than ten."

Gross grinned, helped Kleinman into his overcoat and opened the door. "I'll see you at the Board meeting then, Rabbi."

"Yes. I expect to be there. And thanks for your help. I probably will need all I can get to contend with Ira Cane."

Six

Consciousness burst in on Ira. Ruth nudged his shoulder. Startled, he sprang up and found himself on the edge of the bed meeting his wife's troubled look.

"You were moaning something awful in your sleep," Ruth said anxiously.

It took Ira several moments to cross the boundary separating his nightmare from cognition. The window opposite the bed was partially open. A gust swelled the heavy white drapes; the draft captured one corner and pushed it forward. It appeared to Ira that the billowing material was surging toward him in a threatening white wave. As awareness reached deeper into his consciousness his panic subsided; it was just a dream. . . .

"I'm okay," Ira mumbled, "had a nightmare." He clenched his fist; opened it, wriggled his fingers as if to reassure himself that paralysis had departed with the dream.

The dawn sifting through the translucent drapes reflected dimly on Ira's face. Ruth studied the furrows creasing his high forehead. Worry lines had firmly entrenched themselves between the widely spaced brown eyes. Lately, the lines were

63

there all the time, contracting the once smooth brow and distorting the fine features that had from the beginning so attracted her. Ruth couldn't understand it. It made no sense; no sense at all. They had everything human beings could reasonably want. More . . . much more. Ira loved her; on that score she had no doubts. He sat securely on the top rung of the business world. So many avenues were open to him, to both of them. The whole wide beautiful world was available to them for the asking. There was so much of life to enjoy. Ruth reached out to stroke her husband's forehead:

"What's wrong, Ira?"

He brushed her hand aside. "I said I'm okay."

"Something must be bothering you to be giving you these horrible nightmares."

"Nothing's bothering me," Ira said unconvincingly. "A guy can have a nightmare once in a while. It happens all the time."

Ruth was not satisfied. "Not night after night. It's the second time this week you've awakened in a sweat. What is it you dream about?"

"It's not important," Ira tried to make light of his recurring dreams, but he was unable to conceal from Ruth the apprehension still gripping him. The residue of his nightmare showed in his tense face.

"Tell me," Ruth demanded.

Ira submitted, inwardly relieved at being coerced into unloading the nightmare to his wife:

"God, it's like a one act play, almost the same every time. There's this door. I try to open it; I don't know why. There's something on the other side I gotta get to. But I never make it. Sometimes the key doesn't fit, or I can't find the keyhole; mostly my fingers freeze. And then Purnell skips up the stairs, opens the door, and slams it in my face. Then Robert creeps up behind me like a corpse, and he does the same thing.

Somebody or something drags me away, and I fall . . . keep falling. Then I wake up."

Ruth edged closer to Ira, her concern heightened. "We both know what that door represents, don't we?"

"I told you it doesn't mean anything," Ira said irritably.

"Yes it does," Ruth insisted. "And it's all so fantastically stupid. How can you let something so trivial upset you like that? You're so wrought up about that idiot club. . . . Maybe you should have a session with Dr. Kaplan."

"Me! Go see a head shrinker? What, am I crazy? Don't worry; it'll pass." Ira shifted his weight on the oversized bed. "Those bastards won't get to me."

"They've already got to you, Ira. You're nervous, irritable most of the time. Losing sleep. And all for what? It's maddening."

"Yeah, I suppose you're right. But where the hell do they get the gall? To just ignore me like I was some beggar asking for crumbs. I put Purnell where he is. Who the hell was he? A lousy two-bit teacher. Now he's superintendent of the whole shebang. And Robert! When he launched his building campaign, he knew my address; now he forgets I'm alive. . . . Ten thousand I contributed to his church. What an ass! I could have put that money to better use. Those two bastards alone could get me in."

"But, Ira, what is so important about getting in? Why push so hard where you are evidently not wanted? It's not as if we have no place to belong. We have our circle of friends. Good friends."

"And your friends, Ruth, the ones you grew up with. What about them? Doesn't it burn you at all?"

Ruth perched cross-legged on the bed. She leaned against the velveteen tufted headboard.

"Honey, I'm not the first gal to make the discovery that her friends aren't exactly true blue. I don't deny I was disappointed. Yes, it bothered me at first; I admit to that. But I can manage to live without two-faced bitches for friends."

Ruth swung her legs off the bed. The gathering light reflected her thighs through the sheer negligée. Ira stared at the soft white buttocks. Even after all these years Ruth's body could make him forget his problems, if only temporarily. Right now he craved to touch her legs, caress them, lose himself between their warmth. He made a grab for her waist. Dexterously, she maneuvered out of reach.

"Not now! You've got to get up."

"Get up? Why? What time is it?"

Ruth flicked the switch on the table lamp sitting on her side of the rosewood night table. Ira squinted at the amber light that suddenly flooded the room.

"It's six-fifteen," Ruth said.

"Six-fifteen!" Ira protested. "It's still the middle of the night. Come on, honey, get back to bed."

"No. It'll take you at least forty-five minutes to dress, shave and have a cup of coffee. You'll just about make the morning *minyan*."

"The morning *minyan*? To hell with the morning *minyan*! Come on, get back to bed."

In answer Ruth retreated further, placing her balled fists on her hips in a stance that said firmly, I'm not available.

"Ira, before your mother died you promised her you would recite *Kaddish* faithfully every year on her *yahrtzeit*, and on your father's. And I promised that you would keep your promise, and I intend that both our promises be kept. Your parents deserve that much from you. To remember them once a year by going to the synagogue and reciting *Kaddish* is not such a great sacrifice. Next time you feel sexy come home early and we can play games. Now, please get up."

Ira was acustomed to having his way, but he knew better than to force himself on Ruth when she wasn't in the mood

66

to sport with him. That beautiful broad of his could be stubborn as a mule.

"Okay, okay." Ira yielded and threw off the quilt cover. "But I'll remember your invitation tonight."

Ruth warmed but kept her distance; she bent to pick up the robe she had draped across the chaise lounge before going to bed. The motion tugged her negligée up to the sphere of her buttocks. Ira stared longingly, barely staving off an overwhelming impulse to jump her right on the bedroom floor. Ruth slipped into the robe, wriggled her toes into her slippers, and stepped sedately out of the bedroom.

She's quite a dish, Ira thought. Twenty years of living together with the same woman, and she could still get a rise out of him just by bending over.

Yeah, she could bug him with her *minyan*, her Friday-night services, her fool candle-lighting ritual every Sabbath. She nearly snapped his head off the other day when he walked into the dinette puffing on a cigarette while she was lighting the Sabbath candles. Sometimes he had it to the hilt. . . . That's the meat side. . . . That plate's dairy . . . No. No. Not that fork; you'll make my kitchen *trayf*. . . .

It was a first class nuisance!

But having Ruth . . . it was worth putting up even with that crap.

Seven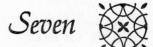

So far there were only four men in the Chaim Cohen Auditorium. The hands of the bald-faced clock hanging in splendid isolation on the bright yellow cinderblock walls showed seven twenty-five. Meyer Schwartz shuttled from chair to window and back to chair. He glowered at the clock, then at Mendelson calmly going about his self-appointed janitorial services. Irritated by Mendelson's unconcern, Schwartz pumped up a thunderous rasp from deep inside his throat, returned to the large rectangular window fronting Ocean Avenue, drew the curtain and snapped up the windowshade.

Schwartz was stocky and thickset. A little less than average height, he was built like a firmly rooted tree trunk; his arms seemed too long and his body too short for his broad shoulders. The tip of his bulbous nose, which switched to stoplight red when he was angry, as if his nose was the repository of all his excitement, almost touched his upper lip. Schwartz was the last of the charter members of the Blueport Jewish Center, founded some forty-five years before by a band of intrepid immigrants who had dared an ocean crossing once, then migrated again, from the tenement ghettos to the uncharted wilds far beyond the last familiar borough of the big city. At seventy-nine, Schwartz retained a spring to his step and was still active in synagogue affairs, a man not to be ignored or trifled with.

Schwartz squinted through the window at Ocean Avenue. Yesterday's snow had changed to a wet slush. A cold drizzle pelted the windowpane. Parked across the street, hubcap deep in ice water, was his ten-year-old Dodge. He surveyed the automobile from hood to rear bumper and concluded that it had outlived its usefulness. Maybe it's time to trade the jalopy in for a new model, he speculated; the car was getting old fast. Giving him trouble lately. Hard to start, especially on these damp cold mornings.

Augmenting Schwartz's dissatisfaction with his aging automobile was Epstein's new car, also visible from the window: a wide, low-slung Olds still carrying the dealer's price schedule. Epstein, who owned a furniture store on Main Street, was on the *minyan* roster for Monday mornings, and every Monday morning rain or shine Epstein could be counted on to show; it wasn't even necessary to phone him. So what if Epstein was an *am haaretz*, a Jewish illiterate; so he couldn't tell an *aleph* from a *beth-*, but the furniture dealer had a sense of responsibility. If the *machers* of the Jewish Center felt that kind of obligation, getting a *minyan* every morning wouldn't be like pulling teeth.

It's like this everywhere, Schwartz thought, finding consolation in the idea that Blueport was no different. There was no easy way; you simply had to make a pest of yourself; bang away on the phone, corner prospects and extract promises to give one morning a week. Either that or allow the synagogue to be without a *minyan*. And to Schwartz, a synagogue without a *minyan* was an insult to God.

Schwartz turned from the window and watched Mendelson in an unblinking frown. Mendelson was meticulously arranging the folding chairs in five precise rows. Three chairs to a row on one side of the room, an aisle down the center, and five precise rows on the other side. Wiry and beetle-browed, with a face like a pockmarked moonscape, Mendelson was the same age and height as the indomitable Schwartz, but built much more delicately.

"Somebody should teach them kids responsibility," Mendelson grumbled. "Every Sunday night they mess up the room. Wouldn't kill them if they took ten minutes of their precious time to put things back in place."

Schwartz had been listening to this complaint for six years, and he had not yet determined whether Mendelson was truly irritated or just enjoyed hearing himself grumble. If he had heard it once from Mendelson he had heard it a thousand times:

"It's the kids that count. We got to make the synagogue attractive for the kids. Old people like us with our old-fashioned ways have got to step aside for the new generation."

Like a broken record Mendelson already sounded; his *hokking* about the young generation and new ideas gave Schwartz a headache.

There was a character Schwartz would never figure out if he lived to be a hundred and twenty. And as far as Max Mendelson was concerned, he wished Schwartz a hundred twenty-three years of life . . . the extra three years so he shouldn't die suddenly. But *der alter* was of another age.

The two men saw themselves as antonyms; to the rest of the congregation they were synonyms. Cut of the same cloth; as alike as two herrings pickled in brine: both salty, cantankerous, stubbornly strident and unpredictable. When they believed there was a violation of the principles for which a synagogue should stand there was no hesitation and no soft peddling. The condemnation flew swiftly, caustically, and publicly—no matter the position or status of the culprits.

As to what constituted a violation of synagogue principles, Mendelson and Schwartz were rarely in accord. How could they be when they couldn't agree on what the principles were to start with. And their wrangling ran far afield of religion. Theology was thoroughly masticated, but included in their disputations were such worldly topics as politics, economics, the urban crisis, and a host of sundry matters. When they could buttonhole him, they would draft the reluctant rabbi to serve as a sounding board for their opposing views.

For thirty-seven years with hardly a break, Max Mendelson's world had been his little grocery store on Henry Street. It was an immaculate store, white-glove clean, everything in its place. Mendelson was a meticulous man with an orderly mind. He knew exactly where every can was, every box, every container. And he could reel off without hesitation the current price of every item in his well-stocked store. To his way of thinking, that was the only way to run a business. "You got to find a place for everything and know what it costs; a man should know his business inside and out."

For those thirty-seven years Mendelson did not step into a synagogue, except on two days a year. He allowed himself one day for Rosh Hashanah and one day for Yom Kippur. Not that Max Mendelson was a Reform Jew. On the lower East Side in those days one would have been hard put to it to even find a Reform synagogue. Mendelson didn't think about his Jewishness at all, but he did feel an obligation to attend synagogue on the High Holidays. However, he saw no point in observing two days of Rosh Hashanah. One day was enough; the second was only a repeat performance. Besides, he couldn't keep his store closed three days; he had Gentile customers who depended on him. . . . And Mendelson prided himself on being a responsible man in all that he undertook.

At the age of sixty-seven Mendelson sold his grocery store and retired to Blueport, where his elder son had established himself as a successful lawyer. After an absence of thirty-seven years Max Mendelson rediscovered the synagogue. The synagogue became his avocation and the daily *minyan* his personal project, particularly, the Chaim Cohen Auditorium in which the daily services were conducted. He arranged the chairs, stacked the prayer books and Bibles, folded the prayer shawls, kept a sharp eye on the *yarmulkes* and *phylacteries* with the same fastidiousness with which he had attended to his grocery store. Woe to the culprit who neglected to return a prayerbook to the shelves, or a *tallis* to the racks: "You want maybe we should hire a special janitor just to clean up after you?" He would charge at an offender. Or to the member who forgot himself and walked out of the room without

returning his skullcap: "What's the matter, you can't afford
a quarter to buy your own? Maybe the *shul* should hold
an appeal to buy you a *yarmulke*?"

Mendelson could be captious and carping, and most everyone in the Jewish Center knew it, many at first hand. Yet no
one raised an objection when his name was submitted for
Board membership . . . by Meyer Schwartz.

Mendelson allowed himself a momentary recess to glance
at Schwartz whose pacing was growing progressively more
agitated; he pretended ignorance of his colleague's perturba-
tion.

"What are you so nervous about? Something bothering you
maybe?"

"What bothers me," Schwartz replied sourly, "is you and
your chairs. If you spent more time on the telephone calling
members and less time arranging chairs, maybe we would have
people to sit on them."

"Calm down," Mendelson advised with infuriating serenity. He cocked his head, measured the space between rows
with a practiced eye and set a chair in its precise line. "You
shouldn't get so excited. You want maybe to get a heart
attack?"

"No, I don't want a heart attack," Schwartz retorted. "I
want a *minyan*." He directed a knobby finger to a middle-
aged man sitting in the third row. "This young man came all
the way from Rosewood to say *Kaddish* for his father."

"*Nu!* Let him say *Kaddish* for his father," Mendelson
suggested nonchalantly. "What's stopping him?"

Schwartz screwed his parchment-skinned face into a scowl.
"The empty chairs! That's what is stopping him. He can't
say *Kaddish* until we get ten men. Maybe you don't know
yet; we need ten men for a *minyan*?"

"And if he says *Kaddish* without ten men? You think the
walls of the *shul* will tumble down on our heads? Or maybe

God will stuff his ears?" Mendelson peered over his bifocals to see the reaction to that provocation. It came sharp and swift.

"I heard about your suggestion to the ritual committee that we give the ladies *aliyahs,* and I already know that you would like to count them into a *minyan.* Now, maybe we should count empty chairs too?"

The sarcasm left Mendelson undisturbed. "I am making only an implication. If the young man said *Kaddish* without ten men, it would not be such a catastrophe. Why must there be exactly ten men?"

Schwartz had learned to live with ignorance, and having a stubborn streak himself he could tolerate obduracy up to a point, but now he was confronted with a marriage of both, and it was too much. A fool and his folly are not easily parted. He was about to deliver this homily to Mendelson when the door opened, choking off the insult.

Kleinman trudged into the Chaim Cohen Auditorium; his steps were languid, as if it were the end, not the beginning of the day. He tended to be on the chubby side, and he filled amply the blue serge suit he wore, yet he seemed to sag in his clothes. A black knitted skullcap sat on his head. Its color emphasized the unhealthy pallor of his checks. Yellow pouches under both eyes announced another bout with insomnia.

"Good morning, Rabbi," Mendelson bellowed cheerfully.

"Good morning, Mr. Mendelson." Kleinman acknowledged the greeting cordially but with less volume. He turned to Schwartz. "Good morning, Mr. Schwartz."

"Good morning."

Noting Schwartz's lackluster response, Kleinman sensed that he had interrupted a warm discussion. Smiling feebly, he greeted Epstein and walked toward the stranger who sat quietly in the third row.

"I'm Rabbi Kleinman," the rabbi said, holding out his hand. Half-rising to accept the handclasp, the stranger introduced himself.

"My name is Fred Bass. I've got to say *Kaddish*. Do you think we'll get a *minyan*?" Bass looked around the room with misgiving.

"Yes, I'm sure we will," Kleinman said. "Though we may get started late. If worst comes to worst, we'll make a few calls."

Schwartz rasped from across the room, "That is not necessary. Mr. Mendelson says we don't need a *minyan*."

Mendelson turned his back on Schwartz. "It's nice if we could get one. But if not, would it be such a terrible sin if the man said *Kaddish* without a *minyan*?"

"No, it wouldn't be a sin," Kleinman said. "But it wouldn't have the same significance."

"Maybe you could explain to me why not, Rabbi?"

"Well it's rather involved, Mr. Mendelson. Why don't you join us at our adult study group. I'll discuss it with the class. Right now I'd like to put on *tallis* and *tefillin*."

Kleinman stepped to his lectern and opened a maroon velvet bag embroidered with a star of David. He removed the large cream-colored prayer shawl, faced the ark and draped the shawl about his head. He covered his face with the *tallis*, recited a benediction, then lowered it to his shoulders. Reaching into the lectern again he withdrew a smaller bag of the same color and texture. From the second bag he took out a pair of phylacteries. He wiggled his left arm out of his jacket, rolled up his shirt sleeve, baring his arm and wound the straps of the first cube around his bicep. Then he centered the second cube on his forehead, slid the empty pouches back into the lectern and began to intone the morning service.

"Well, why not?" Mendelson demanded of Schwartz, still looking for an answer.

"Because ten men make up a *minyan*," Schwartz said firmly, standing on the rock of tradition.

"So what if you don't have ten men?"

"So you don't have a *minyan*."

"So, if you don't have a *minyan*, still, why can't you say *Kaddish*?" Mendelson asked, going around full circle.

"Now look here, Mendelson," Schwartz went on like a man who feels a distasteful obligation to show infinite patience to a dolt. "You are a member of the Board of Trustees, right?"

"Right."

"You attend Board meetings, right?"

"Right."

"You know that for meetings to be official there must be a quorum?"

"Yes. I am aware that there must be a quorum for a meeting."

"Without a quorum the Board cannot conduct their business. Right?"

"Correct."

"And if they do conduct business without a quorum their decisions are not official."

"Agreed."

"So it's the same thing with the *Kaddish*," Schwartz triumphantly expostulated. "A quorum for services is ten men, and without ten men the *Kaddish* is not official. Do you understand now?"

Mendelson scraped his chin, immitating a disciple straining to comprehend the wisdom his master is expounding. Behind his silver rimmed spectacles his eyes twinkled impishly.

"Yes. Now, I understand perfectly. Every morning here in the synagogue we are conducting a Board meeting. And God . . . He is chairman of the Board."

Schwartz's nose turned red; his nostrils dilated violently, snorting in angry drags: "*Chutzpanik*!! You will burn. . . ."

The door suddenly pushed open, sparing Mendelson a vivid description of how he would spend eternity for his heresy. Three men walked into the *minyan* room, one following the other; the last, a short corpulent man in his sixties blocked the door, vigorously striking one palm against the other.

"*Boker tov, boker tov* to you all on this lovely damp miserable morning," the eighth *minyanaire* chirped in a rich baritone while standing at the entrance and counting heads. "Very good, we're almost there. Kirschenbaum is outside parking his car. He makes nine. One more and we're in business."

"Good morning, Cantor Rosenberg. Good morning Mr. Abrams; Mr. Miller. A good morning to you all. I am happy to see you." Mendelson's hearty welcome matched the *hazzens'* in exuberance. "Mr. Schwartz was so nervous we wouldn't have a *minyan*, he was having conniptions."

Mendelson swiveled to face Schwartz's scowl. "See, Mr. Schwartz, we got nine already, with Ira Cane we'll have a quorum . . . just like at Board meetings."

Schwartz ignored the added impertinence. The impudence of the old freethinker was just not worth any more of his attention.

"Don't count on Ira Cane," Schwartz said. "We better get on the phone and call somebody else."

Cantor Rosenberg intervened. "Don't worry, Mr. Schwartz. Ira Cane will be here."

"Look, Cantor! I know Ira Cane; I knew him when he was still Irving Cohen. He's not going to get up at this hour to come to a *minyan*."

"Well, maybe not on his own initiative," Rosenberg granted. "But his wife will make him come, whether he wants to or not."

"Nobody is going to make Ira Cane do what he doesn't want to do," Schwartz insisted.

"Ruth is not a nobody," Rosenberg retaliated. "She, let me tell you, is quite a somebody. I also know the Canes a long time. I remember like it was only yesterday when Irving, excuse me, Ira, I remember when Ira announced he was in in love and was going to marry Ruth. Oy! Was that the announcement of the year. Me? I wasn't so surprised; she was such a beauty. And she still is." Rosenberg smacked his lips to punctuate his approval then returned to Schwartz, audaciously waving an admonishing finger under the skeptic's nose. "Let me tell you, Mr. Schwartz! If Ruth wants Ira to come to a *minyan*, he'll be here."

Chuckling at the cantor's confidence in Ruth's prowess, Mendelson tramped to the window:

"Looks like you're right, Cantor. Here comes Mr. Ira Cane himself."

Ira parked his Cadillac in front of the religious school building, disregarding the sign: Synagogue Entrance, No Parking. He opened the door on the driver's side and stepped into ankle-deep slush. Slamming the door and swearing into the wind, he pulled his hat down and splashed through the cold drizzle. Icy water trickled down his ears and neck. He hopped over a rivulet and onto the sidewalk. Two full strides from the entrance his head came up to see Mendelson's face gawking through the window. The shades were up, the drapes drawn all the way, televising the Chaim Cohen Auditorium to every passing car. Mendelson and Schwartz had already donned *tallis* and *tefillin*. The others were in varying stages of preparation for the services. From where he stood, temporarily immunized to the cold rain, Ira also had an unobstructed view of Kleinman engulfed in a massive woolen *tallis* bending over his lectern and *davening* with a Hassidic sway, his head crowned by a giant black cube.

"Damn it!" Furiously, Ira burst into the building, shoved past the startled *minyanaires* to the window, yanked down the shades, shutting out the view from Ocean Avenue.

"Drapes! Windowshades! Cost us three hundred dollars,"

Ira spat at Mendelson. "Why do you think we bought them? You don't have to advertise the *minyan* to the whole street."

The tantrum made little impression on Mendelson. Coldly, he glared down his nose at Ira. "You are maybe ashamed of what we are doing here that you want we should hide ourselves?"

"Don't hide and don't advertise," Ira shot back." The *goyim* don't have to watch you *davening* away with your *tallis* and *tefillin.*"

Ira's sudden invasion had taken the other *minyan* members by surprise. They stood mute. No one moved to intercede. But now Mendelson's cold glare turned to anger.

"True the *goyim* don't have to watch, but if they do it won't hurt them, I don't think. I know if they watch, it won't hurt me. You are afraid maybe, Mr. Cane, it will hurt you?"

Open-mouthed, Ira groped for an answer; none came. He grunted an inaudible imprecation, backed off and left Mendelson standing at the window. Schwartz defrosted and handed Ira a skullcap, prayerbook and neatly folded *tallis.* Ira grumbled a thank you and slumped into a chair in the last row.

Schwartz shuffled to the reader's lectern to begin the service. On the way, he passed Mendelson and gave him a look that was almost friendly.

Eight

Ray Purnell's office befitted his position. A deep-piled kelly-green carpet, which he had personally selected, highlighted the richly panelled walls. Behind the simulated mahogany oval desk on the west wall hung a Diago landscape. A mural of Blueport at the turn of the century covered most of the west wall. The third wall boasted a stunning seascape. Three laminated diplomas on the wall as one entered proclaimed Purnell's academic credentials.

His office meant a great deal to Purnell. At times it served as a tonic to jangled nerves that were ready to split. On occasion, when frustration bit too deeply, he would close the door and tell Mary, his secretary, he didn't want to be disturbed for the next half-hour, and simply sat staring at his paintings and diplomas, contemplating the little empire he ruled.

But today, as he waited for Ira Cane, he was in too much of an uproar to think of anything but that God-damned letter. Indignantly, he reread the clipping; he chewed it over and over, and at each reading the gall of that son-of-a-bitch Kleinman became more bitter in his mouth. Ray Purnell's first impulse was to screw 'em all! You try to be decent, take the trouble of explaining your position. Does no good. Give an inch of ground and before you know it they're ordering you about on your own property. They own half the town already and more of them are piling in from the city every year. Now they're looking to break into the club, the one place they haven't yet infested. Well, so long as he had any influence, not one bastard would get in. But whatever happens at Pinetree, they had better keep their long noses out of his domain; no damn rabbi is gonna tell Ray Purnell how to run his school.

That was Purnell's first impulse. But rarely did Blueport's superintendent of schools yield to first impulses; he was too accomplished a bureaucrat to show all of his cards. Had he been the kind of man who allowed every feeling to surface, he wouldn't be sitting behind this desk today. To fit this chair required more than a few degrees; he had learned that early in the game. The Ph.D. he sweated for might have qualified him to mark papers, but to hold down this job he had to teach himself how to suppress his natural instincts to squash every criticism by a swift kick in the critic's ass. To be superintendent of schools in Blueport, to build the school system that he had raised up these last fifteen years, you needed to be a first class politician. You had to be adept at balancing one special interest against another. You had to be able to say no and make it sound like yes, or at least maybe. It necessitated an iron discipline to contain himself, and at times in order to prevent the lid from blowing he let out some controlled steam, but the caldron that boiled inside he managed to keep under effective restraint.

And under Purnell's aegis the schools in Blueport did grow —from two buildings housing five hundred students in its elementary and high school departments to twelve thousand youngsters in a complex of buildings that were the pride of Blueport and the finest in the county. Much of this growth was due, if he had to say so himself, to his powers of persuasion, to his talent for sugar coating some very expensive pills. While other school districts voted down budget after budget, Blueport advanced and built its superbly serviceable and architecturally aesthetic edifices. Nothing but the best would do for Blueport's children. It wasn't easy, Ray reminisced. Time and again he had been called down to justify his ambitious building programs by irate citizens who were presumptuous enough to call his judgment into question and who rebelled at the high taxes they were loaded with as a result of his ever-mounting school budgets. Mostly he got his points across and won the necessary increases.

And that required a paternal back-slapping pretense of concern for everybody's rights and problems, which became Purnell's forte. Also, over the years, he developed into an effective public speaker. He learned how to play on the mood of an audience like a maestro on a Stradivarious, projecting a homogenized down-to-earth no-nonsense style liberally sprinkled with spicy anecdotes and a needling humor that may have lacked finesse and stuck in the craw of some but nevertheless seemed to have mass appeal. He was a much-sought-after toastmaster at Blueport's rolling cycle of dinners, sponsored by one civic, social, religious, and fraternal group or another. . . .And so, for the most part, Blueport's citizens considered themselves fortunate in having Purnell's apparent dynamism charging their school system. For the most part. But not all . . .

There were flies in the ointment: a minority who did not think Purnell was the John Dewey of Blueport. Some disgruntled characters protested that teachers' salaries did not rise anywhere near as fast as Blueport's school buildings, and consequently the quality of education left much to be desired, the impressive plants notwithstanding. But that kind of carping cut no ice with Purnell. You can't have all of the pie in one gulp. At least Blueport's kids were not crammed into firetraps as they had been before he took over as superintendent. Yes. He had to cut out many a thorn in his side to bring his school this far. And now after pulling a one-horse school system up to this plateau by sheer ingenuity and personal drive, he wasn't about to let Jews dictate school policy. He wasn't constituted to take that kind of crap, and he didn't intend to. One way or another he was going to yank the rug from under Kleinman, and what better way to do it without stirring up a hornet's nest than by getting one yid to boot another.

Two short rings cut into Purnell's ruminations.

"Yes, Mary." Purnell fondled the buttons on his newly installed cream-colored phone.

"Mr. Cane is here."

"Very good. Show Mr. Cane right in." Purnell hoisted himself from the leather-cushioned chair and prepared a pose of benign amiability. The door swung inward. Mary, a heavy-breasted maid saying adieu to her thirties, showed Ira Cane into the room. Purnell smiled effusively and extended his hand.

Ira met Purnell's moist hand across the desk; he eyed the chair at the side of the desk but he remained standing, poker-faced and silent.

Ira was a touch shorter than Purnell, but his trim figure, his midwinter tan, and tailored pin stripe suit under a navy blue coat combined to give an impression of height and authority—at least in Purnell's mind. Actually, Ira's nerves played hop, skip whenever he found himself alone with Purnell. Ira didn't like the man; he knew that, but he couldn't figure out why Purnell put him so on edge. While vacationing down South, Ira had made more of a bundle in one land deal than Purnell would earn in the next five years. Ira controlled one of the largest banks in the country; he was chief stockholder of Antex Textiles, a firm employing over two thousand people. And yet this school teacher made him fidget.

"Glad to see you, Ira. How is Ruth?"

"Fine."

Ira's tone registered in Purnell's ear as unfriendly; however, he had been dealing with Ira too long to be so easily put down. No matter the effort, he intended to be gracious.

"Relax, Ira. Have a seat," Purnell urged. Ira complied, and waited for Purnell's next overture. The superintendent's big frame recalled to Ira Ray's past athletic prowess now interred under limp layers of flesh; the beer-barrel stomach seemed to have pulled down and swallowed his chest. Purnell dropped his weight into the chair and tilted it away from the desk to give himself more belly room.

"How did you and Ruth enjoy Miami?"

"We had a good rest."

Purnell decided to get down to business. "I appreciate your coming down to see me on such short notice," he said. "But you've been away over a month, and things have been happening in the interim." Purnell poked into his double chin with the back of his thumb; he smiled familiarly. "We've been minding the store. Holding the fort back home as best as we can. Can't allow our children's education to grind to a halt even though the Board of Education is gallivanting around the world."

"We don't expect it to grind to a halt," Ira retorted brusquely. "We know you're always on the line ready to carry the ball."

Purnell flushed at Ira's thinly veiled sarcasm. ". . . Ah . . . yes . . . Well. A problem has developed; as yet minor, but it could blow up and prove embarrassing to all concerned. And I think that you, as leading layman of the Jewish community, could nip it in the bud before it gets out of hand."

Ira's ears burned at the way Purnell dropped his voice when sounding the phrase, Jewish community. "What's the problem?"

"We've known each other for a long time, Ira. And you know how fair I've played it with all the faiths in the community. If I say so myself, I can take particular pride in the fine relationship I've had with the Jewish community."

Purnell rambled on, evidently determined to beat around the bush rather than answer Ira's question directly. Ira uncrossed his legs and drummed on his hat.

"In all the years I've served in Blueport as teacher and administrator," Purnell continued, "no one has accused me of partiality; I've imposed my friendship neither on you, nor upon that of my many other Jewish friends, nor, for that matter, upon my friends of any faith. I have never asked for or given special consideration."

"Okay, Ray. We Jews know that you've played fair and square. Get to the point."

"I will in a moment," Purnell said coldly. "I just want to give you the background."

"I know the background. We've both been living in Blueport most of our lives; so do me a favor and get on with it."

"All right. Four months ago I sent out the school calendar; it lists as you know all the holidays and important school events. Two weeks ago I get a call from Rabbi Kleinman; he asked to see me. I told him I'd be happy to meet with him; could he tell me what about? Maybe I could solve his problem over the phone and spare him a trip. Well, he said he just read the school calendar and was disturbed over the fact that this year it provided for an Easter vacation but didn't take into account your Jewish Passover."

"Rabbi Kleinman didn't want you to close the school all eight days of Passover?" Ira asked incredulously.

"Well, no," Purnell checked his annoyance. "Actually, the problem is that Easter and the spring vacation don't coincide this year; Easter comes much earlier. The calendar, therefore calls for an Easter holiday from Thursday, the twenty-third of March to Monday, the twenty-seventh."

"The rabbi didn't object to that?" Ira asked in puzzlement.

"No. It was the second break that caused ill feelings. The spring recess; it starts the seventeenth of April and ends the twenty-fourth."

"So why should that be a problem?"

"Because Passover begins on the twenty-fourth. Rabbi Kleinman was disturbed that I didn't move up the spring recess to include the first two days of Passover."

"That's not unreasonable. Why didn't you?"

"Look, Ira. You didn't know when Passover falls this year, and it's your holiday. How do you expect me to keep it in mind?"

Balls! Ira thought. That's what the bastard is getting paid for. To Purnell he voiced his objections more delicately. "Don't you get notified by the state of all Jewish holidays?"

"Yes. The office is notified, but I can't get personally involved in every administrative detail. It's a big school and I've got to delegate authority to my assistants."

"Why didn't they pick it up?"

"That's just it; they didn't. None of the department heads picked up the conflict. Not even Carl Rein; even he didn't mention a word about the Jewish holidays."

"Why should he? It's not Rein's job to tell you when to close the school."

"Rein's Jewish, isn't he? Passover is his holiday. He at least could have called it to my attention."

Purnell correctly interpreted Ira's silence as conceding the point. Emboldened, he returned to the offensive.

"Now the calendar has been out four months. Teachers and parents have made all kinds of plans. I can't change the schedule at this late date. Rabbi Kleinman should have spoken up sooner."

"Does the school send him a calendar?" Ira questioned.

Purnell stirred uncomfortably. "He doesn't have children in our school, so I don't think we send one to him."

"I suppose one of the kids' parents in our congregation finally caught the conflict and called it to the rabbi's attention," Ira speculated. "Okay, I'll go along that it's too late to do anything about it this year. Call the rabbi and reassure him that any kid absent because of Passover won't be penalized and that in the future you'll pay closer attention to the Jewish holidays. I'll see that the Center office sends you a schedule of the Jewish holidays marked for your personal attention. Also, I suggest you make it a point to send the school calendar to our office at the Center as soon as it comes out."

Ira started for the door.

"That's not all." Purnell motioned for Ira to wait and hear him out. Ira stiffened.

"I did assure Rabbi Kleinman that no Jewish student would be penalized for being absent, I even told him I would send a memo to all teachers not to schedule examinations on those days. Well! Instead of accepting that, he came out with a bunch of totally unreasonable demands. Your rabbi would like me to close down the school for the Jewish High Holidays; he asked that the school not schedule commencement exercises on Saturday. And he demanded that I reschedule our opening football game with Central High next fall. By pure coincidence, the game, which always is played on Saturday, happens to fall on your Day of Atonement. Now, I went to the trouble of writing a long letter to Rabbi Kleinman in which I explained the reasons for our school policy. I tried to make him understand that my decisions must be predicated on what is best for the total community, the majority of which is, after all, not Jewish but Christian."

Ira winced at the last observation but allowed Purnell to move on without challenge.

"You know I can't change the graduation exercises to Sunday. I need a rain day. We discussed this at a Board meeting at which you were present. And I can't change the football schedule; I don't make it up. The games are scheduled by the league. If I cancel out, the school stands to lose a lot of revenue, which we can ill afford to do."

"Okay." Inwardly, Ira fumed, but Purnell's rejection of every one of the rabbi's demands drew no opposition from him. "So, you wrote the rabbi a letter; so what do you want me to do now?"

Purnell rotated the clipping on his desk so that the right side of the type faced Ira. "This item appeared in the *Blueport Gazette*. It's signed by your Rabbi Kleinman." Purnell pushed the clipping toward Ira. "Here; read it."

Ira picked up the clipping and rapidly scanned the letter, flushing through his deep tan as he read. Purnell sat back, enjoying the sight of Ira turning livid.

Nine

Sandwiched between Jerusalem Avenue's wide tree-lined streets which hint of the opulence to the North, and the railroad tracks which skirt the borders of south Blueport's poverty, is central Blueport. Here live salesmen, engineers, white-collar workers, blue-collar workers, clergymen, aspiring attorneys, up-and-coming doctors, teachers, old-time Main Street retailers who missed their big chance to buy property now occupied by a monstrous shopping center that eclipses their little stores. The homes in central Blueport are no match for those in Manor Park, but neither are they to be compared to south Blueport's shacks. Within these *termini* there is considerable variation in style and cost. Barring a few exceptions, the houses nearest Jerusalem Avenue are at a premuim, and the demand for them is reflected in their price. The further south one lives, the closer to the tracks one buys, the less value and status does the house and its inhabitants have. As fortunes fluctuate, families move from one part of central Blueport to another; there is much shifting in this part of town. Occasionally, a family hurdles Jerusalem Avenue and buys into the coveted Manor Park, but this is as difficult and rare a feat as swimming the English Channel. It can be done and is done, but not often. Except for the up and coming doctors. They do climb the social and economic ladder with remarkable alacrity. Shortly after setting up practice in the swelling suburbs, the doctors move into the prestigious section and are welcomed into the golf and yachting clubs. Most other newcomers find passage exceedingly rough and rarely make it. What is not rare is the aspiration to make it to the other side. Even more prevelant is the manifestation of that hope; the envy of those who do not make it but are convinced that by all the rules of the game they should.

The drive to make the grade and the resentment of those who cannot be reconciled to the idea that their status is static is fed by the fact that the residents of Manor Park and central Blueport are not entirely isolated from one another as are the people in south Blueport. There are opportunities for social intercourse. In church and synagogue the democratic tradition of the Judaeo-Christian heritage asserts itself enough to allow the residents of the two sections to rub shoulders. The housewives of central Blueport bump into Manor Park matrons at the supermarket and discount houses—even the rich enjoy a good bargain. The Blueport school system is also a meeting ground for adults from both areas. At commencement exercises, school concerts, PTA teas there are further openings for communication. As for the youngsters at school, in addition to receiving a common education, cliques are made aware of each other, youths of different economic, cultural, religious, and racial stock sit next to one another and learn to appreciate the diverse types sheltered by Blueport's maternal embrace.

It was to central Blueport and to Blueport High School that Carl Rein, by chance or destiny, depending on the measure of order and sanity one credited to the governing forces controlling man's journey on earth, had come to settle and to teach. And Rein found a modicum of contentment. He was satisfied, he told himself often, with what he was doing and how he lived his life. The world is what it is and is not likely to be altered by his efforts, nor by anybody else's. Ecclesiastes had pronounced for Rein the final wisdom: "There is nothing new under the sun. There is no rememberance of the wise man more than the fool, seeing that in the days to come all shall be forgotten. . . . So let thy garments be white; live joyfully with the wife whom thou lovest all the days of thy vanity."

Carl Rein had lived in Blueport for four years with his wife and two children. He made no demands on the community; it made no demands on him. He drove each morning from his modest brick ranch—a six minute drive to school—and returned each afternoon to his wife and children satisfied that he had earned his keep and that his days were as useful and meaningful as the next man's; possibly more so, if use and meaning were at all apropos in describing any man's days.

Ocean Avenue is the most direct route to Blueport High, and Rein was not so neurotic as to detour because the Jewish Center of Blueport forced its attention on him, though he did admit to the unsettling push and pull the synagogue, any synagogue, had for him. One day the pull overpowered the push. He stopped at the curb and studied the synagogue bulletin board, his eyes going down the schedule of services till they came to the names of rabbi and cantor. Immediately, an image of Morris Kleinman clicked in his photographic mind. And he remembered. But he did nothing about the memory except look up Kleinman's address and drive by the house. Several times he was moved to pick up the phone and call, but he did not yield to this impulse, not even when Beth

Kleinman had sniffed out the fact that the Reins had settled in Blueport and repeatedly invited them over; not even then could Carl Rein make that short trip back to the past.

Rein championed no cause, he raised nobody's banners; his fatalism precluded personal involvement. Outside his classroom Carl Rein was no crusader. But facing students, his logic born of fatalism took flight. It was as if there were two Carl Reins. While the one on the outside proclaimed, "All is vanity," the one in class contradicted everything Carl Rein was on the outside. Rein was aware of this contradiction and accepted it, telling himself: as nothing is to be gained by fighting the world, so there was no use doing battle with his own paradoxical nature. He wasn't going to change himself either.

Rein was short and pudgy, but when he lectured, he hopped around the room like a rabbit on the run, across the width of the classroom, in front of his desk, behind his desk, up and down the aisle. Rein was the peripatetic professor par excellence; he liked to call his sessions dynamic dialogues. He goaded and challenged his students to examine their ideas, or, to be more accurate, their lack of ideas about anything not immediately touching their persons. When Rein's students entered his class in the fall, nine out of ten could not name their state senators; half-way through the semester they were ready to take over the country, and Rein thought it might be an improvement. Carl Rein was probably the only teacher in Blueport who could arouse enthusiasm among a restive senior class in a subject as vapid as political science. He understood his students, felt their confusion, repected their individuality, and his empathy earned for him their respect. And Carl Rein cherished that respect.

And because in class the crusading spirit in Rein dominated, he now found himself on the spot. He was confronted with a loaded proposal and he was the target, no doubt about that. With religious ferver he had hammered away at his favorite theme, the danger of censorship. Over and again he had emphasized how vital it is to give all points of view a forum for expression; suppress an idea because it is unpopular and you drive a nail into freedom's coffin. Staunchly, Rein had asserted that America's democratic institutions were capable of withstanding the most bizarre ideologies; the open market of ideas must decide the merit of an opinion. The right to dissent nourishes the life-giving blood coursing through the arteries of our free land. To his students he had stressed this theme with near obsessive repetition. And now his words were being flung back into his face. These youngsters, when they were so inclined, could be sharp; they were quick to spot a flaw in an argument and quicker still to zero in on an intellectual fraud. Rein's experience with youngsters had taught him this much: the unpardonable sin was hypocrisy. Once a fraud was unmasked he was effectively and irrevocably turned off. And now Carl Rein's intellectual integrity was being challenged.

His head cocked to one side registering disdain, Tom Purnell waited for a reply. The father's features were echoed in the boy's face. A large forehead. Eyes blue and empty. A nose straight as a die. Hair blond and cropped short. And a controlled sneer that communicated a self-assured smugness. Under the veneer, however, Rein read turbulence and instability. The class waited with Tom, tuned into the meaning behind the overtly innocuous proposal.

Rein was sufficiently familiar with Tom Purnell to know that this plea for fair play had not just popped into his head at this very moment. In all probability this proposition had been discussed in the cafeteria, in gym, in the halls, off school premises, wherever kids gather for their bull sessions. And if he, the only Jewish teacher in Blueport, threw cold water on the project, Tom would surely bring it to a boil. It wasn't Tom Purnell that troubled Rein; Tom's spite was so deeply ingrained that whatever answer Rein gave would make little difference to the swaggering youth. What did concern Rein was the effect a rejection would have on the rest of the class.

Thumbs interlocked behind his back, Rein paced the floor. Suddenly he veered to face the class and pushed Tom's question back at him.

"Why would you want to invite George Stonehill to speak to us? What purpose would it serve?"

Tom Purnell smirked. "Isn't that what you've been preaching to us; we should be open-minded, hear the other side?"

"Yes. That's true. But whose side does Stonehill represent?" Rein tried to glare Tom down; the boy remained unruffled.

"I wouldn't want you to think for a minute that he represents my side," Tom returned the challenge. He turned from Rein to weigh the class' reaction. His smirk broadened as he caught the approving glances of his coconspirators.

"But you got to admit, Mr. Rein, there are a lot of people who agree with George Stonehill."

"Do you know any?" Rein shot back. "Are they friends of yours?"

Tom held on to his composure. "Yes. As a matter of fact I do know people who agree with Stonehill. You might say some of them are friends of mine."

"What kind of friends do you have?"

"Oh, I have all kinds, I suppose. They're no different than anybody else's friends. Just average Americans."

"You mean to tell us the average American advocates genocide?"

Tom seemed to recognize his blunder. Adroitly, he ducked the question. "All I said was that my friends are average Americans."

"If you have friends who think like George Stonehill, they are not, thank the Lord, average Americans."

"Can't argue with you about what the average American believes," Tom answered, keeping his cool. You've been around longer than me, so I suppose you know more about the average American. But you won't deny Stonehill his day in court just because he doesn't represent the average American, will you? That would be contrary to all that you've been teaching us about democracy. Wouldn't it, Teach?"

Tom abandoned his role of pious supplicant and escalated to bold self-righteousness. "Two months ago you assigned us a reading in Karl Marx. Last month we heard a representative of the Socialist Party. So why not have Stonehill speak to us? He's in town. The administration at Lehigh University didn't interfere when the guys invited him to their school. Let's show 'em how liberal we are and give George Stonehill that forum you said everybody's entitled to . . . unless it's only commie rights we got to worry about."

While listening to Tom's monologue Rein fought an urge to grab the boy by the scruff of the neck and throw him out of the room. With enforced calm he asked Tom if he was through. Tom cocked his head to the other side and nodded. For several tense moments Rein contemplated the provocative arrogance pasted on the youth's face. Cross currents of hostility raced between student and teacher. The class waited on edge.

Rein delivered his answer in measured tones: "I wouldn't deny any rational man a forum for his ideas. But George Stonehill believes himself to be a reincarnation of Hitler. Given his way he would reopen his idol's concentration camps and finish what Hitler almost succeeded in doing. Exterminate an entire people: men, women and children. Hitler was a maniac bent on genocide. George Stonehill is a maniac. Unfortunately, insanity was not eliminated from our troubled world when Hitler committed suicide. There are still mad-men around. I do not feel it my duty to provide a forum for a madman."

Rein centered Tom in his contempt. ". . . even though he may be one of your friends. Now please take your seat and we will continue our discussion on the separation of church and state."

Ten

Ira Cane's attention strayed from Jack Sternberg's long-winded monologue to the Board members milling about the room. Satisfied that he had a quorum, Ira sliced Sternberg off in midsentence and brought down the chairman's gavel.

"If you'll cut the gab, the secretary can get on with the minutes," Ira said gruffly, demanding immediate compliance. Chafing, he waited for complete silence, then imperiously waved Martha on.

Martha refused to be rushed. Taking pencil in hand, she ceremoniously opened her notebook and thumbed through the pages. After a respectable interval she cleared her throat and began to intone the minutes.

Ostensibly, as in most synagogues, the Blueport Jewish Center was a democratically run organization. The president, four vice-presidents, treasurer, secretary and the fifteen trustees were duly elected by the membership at large. In practice, the Blueport Jewish Center was ruled by a clique that had perpetuated itself in office year after year. Ira had been Center president nine years. Three of the four vice-presidents had held their respective offices no less than seven

94

years, the fourth having been elected to replace Sam Harris
who had died two years before. Murray Gold, an attorney,
had been treasurer fifteen years; David Zatler, a relative newcomer to Blueport (he had moved to town eight years ago
and in a remarkably short time established a lucrative insur-
ance and real estate business) was secretary. Of the fifteen
trustees, eight had served at least three terms, and the others
from varying periods of six months to six years.

For as long as anyone could recall, no attempt had been
made to challenge the entrenched leadership head on. In
recent years, however, there were new faces at the semi-
annual congregational meetings. There was grumbling that
congregational meetings were a farce, that votes were
stacked, and that everything was decided on beforehand.
There were bolder voices which suggested that the synagogue
could stand an infusion of new blood and new ideas. Some
vocal newcomers even suggested that the synagogue might
benefit considerably if the old guard stepped down altogether. So far the disaffected minority had confined itself to
grumbling. With a quarter of a million dollar mortgage and
an annual budget of nearly two hundred thousand it required
money to cover the annual deficit, and the men at the top
were heavy contributors. The position of the old guard,
therefore, was still secure. But the handwriting was on the
wall. As the membership roster swelled, a larger base of support was being established, and as this came to pass, depen-
dence on a few angels was proportionally diminished.

In the meantime. Ira ruled the roost. He was the lay leader
of the Blueport Jewish community, and it was his responsibility, he believed, to decide on what was best for the Jewish
community, particularly on matters relating to non-Jews. He
had been raised in Blueport and knew its people first hand. It
had taken long, hard years to win a measure of Gentile recognition. More than once he had eaten crow to get even

this pittance. But he felt things were improving every year; in time there would be full acceptance. In the meanwhile, harmony prevailed between Jew and *goy*. Blueport had never experienced the religious dissension that tore apart some of the other towns until Kleinman stepped into the picture to provide grist for the anti-Semitic mill.

Ira was satisfied that the stage was well set to cut the rabbi down to size. To introduce the subject and get things started, Ira had lined up Jack Sternberg and Zatler. He had seen to it that they were well coached. Following Zatler, the floor would be open for discussion. Then he would put Purnell's complaint on the record. Ira was confident that the Board would vote to censure Kleinman and warn him to keep his nose clean and out of the public school system.

Martha droned on; the bored trustees listened, reconciled to the ritual. Ira fidgeted. Finally Martha closed her notebook and smiled coyly at Ira, waiting demurely for the compliment she felt he owed her for the reading. The door squeaked open to admit Rabbi Kleinman. Quietly, he slipped into the nearest vacant chair. The fleeting glance Martha caught of him made her put aside her unarticulated petition for appreciation. The rabbi's pallid, almost spectral face worried her. He seemed exhausted to the point of near collapse. He shouldn't have come tonight, Martha thought.

"Will someone make a motion that the minutes be accepted?" Ira snapped.

Martha turned back to Ira. His poker face showed no recognition of Kleinman's entrance. To her mind this was rude: Your rabbi comes in, you don't have to bow down, but it takes only a second to say good evening. Martha didn't care at all for Ira's discourtesy.

Jack Sternberg raised his hand. Ira recognized him.

"I make a motion that the minutes . . ."

"Good evening, Rabbi," Martha interrupted. "Glad to see you could make tonight's meeting."

Faces registering emotion from mild surprise to astonishment turned from Martha to Rabbi Kleinman and back to the chairman. If looks could kill, Martha would have fallen mortally wounded.

"Thank you, Martha," Kleinman said with a little embarrassment. "Glad to be here."

Little bothered by the chairman's visual bombardment, Martha answered Ira's muted glare with a honeyed smile.

Jack Sternberg raised his hand again. "I move to accept the minutes as read," he said, finally finishing his motion. David Zatler seconded.

The color of Ira's face gradually turned from red to Miami Beach tan. He recovered his composure and reverted to the role of efficient, self-assured chairman.

And Ira was strong at the helm. He was expert at propelling a meeting to the denouement he had planned. Meetings rolled on with few collisions and little of the friction that plagued many another Jewish Center. On issues where Ira was not committed he would permit debate just to liven things up a bit and give the membership a feeling that they did have something to say in synagogue policy. Rarely, however, did Ira Cane lose control of a meeting.

This evening was to be one of the rare exceptions when he did. Martha's little rebellion was an omen of what was to follow.

"Correspondence! Read the correspondence," Ira prodded.

"Is there any particular order you prefer I read the correspondence, Mr. Cane?"

"Just read, will you?" Ira ordered, his hackles rising. "Let's get this meeting on the road."

Serenely, Martha shuffled the sheets in front of her. Three

letters were read. The first was from the National Hebrew Academy, a seminary for the training of rabbis, teachers, and cantors. The seminary had sent its usual urgent plea requesting affiliated congregations to ante up their annual contributions.

"Always asking for money," Zatler grumbled for the benefit of all. "We can hardly carry our own budget."

Ira rapped the gavel. "Let's not discuss it now. We'll take up our contribution to the Academy under new business."

Martha went on to the second piece of correspondence. This letter was from the president of the Blueport Interfaith Council expressing his appreciation for making the "lovely facilities" of the Blueport Jewish Center available for the Brotherhood Service. Approving nods and smiles acknowledged the letter.

"So, I'm happy they like our synagogue," Meyer Schwartz said irritably. I will be even happier if next year they find lovely facilities somewhere else."

The Board's reaction was immediate and loud. Shock. Dismay. Meyer Schwartz was cuttingly denounced for his inhospitality to the noble cause of interfaith harmony.

"Okay! Okay! So I'm not ecumenical," Meyer Schwartz snorted. "I got a right to speak my mind."

Again Ira rapped the gavel. "Mr. Schwartz, please. You're out of order."

Schwartz screwed his face into an expression of undisguised disdain. But he held his peace and settled back in his chair for the time being.

The third letter was from the Metropolitan Synagogue Association asking the Blueport Jewish Center to send representatives to the forthcoming biannual convention. Martha read the letter. It evoked no comment.

"That's all I have," Martha said.

Ira reached into the inside pocket of his dark blue blazer

and drew out an envelope. "There's one more letter I got in this morning's mail. I know you'll all be happy to listen to this piece of correspondence." He appeared uncharacteristically jovial as he handed the letter to Martha.

Martha scanned the letterhead: her brows arched in surprise. She read on to herself. This time around Ira showed no impatience. He rather enjoyed the suspense his announcement had generated. For several moments Ira bided his time, then politely appealed to Martha.

"Would you, if it's not too much trouble, read the letter out loud? I think the Board would also like to know what's in it."

"Oh, I'm sorry, Mr. Cane. The letter is from Otto Hoffman, 'House of Precious Stones,' Five West Main Street," Martha read aloud:

" 'Dear Mr. Cane. I have been given to understand that a chapel in your temple is available for dedication. My wife and I are most concerned to perpetuate the memory of our daughter-in-law, Rachel Hoffman, who was of the Jewish faith. I would consider it a privilege to donate five thousand dollars for such a memorial.' The letter is signed, Otto Hoffman."

The reaction was as Ira expected. Ecstasy tripped across the room. Ernie Gruber, former used-car dealer and now owner of the Plymouth-Chrysler franchise, was awed. Ernie was devoted to the dollar, and running a close second was his enthusiasm for dirty stories. Both these loyalties served Ernie admirably in his business and evidently were no hinderance to his winning a seat on the synagogue Board. He lolled in the third row wearing a white and green jacket over a wide paisley tie.

"Five thousand smackaroos? Wow! That's a lot of cabbage," Ernie marvelled. "We sure can use it. For that kind of do-re-mi I wouldn't mind it if his daughter-in-law was an Arab."

Sy Wasser, sitting next to Ernie, agreed in principle. Ira permitted the happy chaos, pleased by the wide approval. Good! Ira congratulated himself; let 'em see it pays to cultivate the *goyim*. This would help his case when the other matter came up. Ira was ready to call the meeting back to order.

Suddenly, Meyer Schwartz's rasp cut through the clatter. He had bounded from his chair and was standing with his shoulders hunched over his barrel chest like an infuriated bull about to charge.

"Take money from a Nazi? For a *shul* in which I *daven?* Never!"

The Chaim Cohen Auditorium was plunged into a tomb-like silence over which Meyer Schwartz now presided. Standing alone, brandishing his fist in the smoke-filled room, he was Elijah returned to pronounce doomsday to the prophets of Baal. Gradually, the room came alive with low growls which picked up volume and grew to vehement denunciation.

Ira struck the gavel down hard, and in a rare burst of uncontrolled temper shouted, "Sit down, damn it! You're out of order."

Only a slight tremor marked Schwartz's immediate response. It was his nose that told the full tale. At first it paled, then the nostrils distended into wonderous pink cavities that swiftly turned scarlet. He bit at his upper lip. Ira watched transfixed as the menace within Meyer Schwartz pumped to the surface. Already he rued his impudence and wished he could call back his words.

"Sit down? Damn it? Out of order?" Schwartz bellowed the chairman's insult from his nose like a trumpeting elephant. "You *chutzpanik!* Before you were circumcised I was president of this *shul.* . . . You snotnose! To speak to me like that! Your father and me, we started this *shul;* built it almost with our bare hands. If he could hear you, in his grave he would turn over. You want to take a contribution from a Nazi for a *shul* and dare tell me I am out of order? You pipsqueak!" Schwartz's fists were like twin hammers pounding the air.

No one stirred. Not a sound disturbed the silence; it was as if time had jammed. The Board members seemed as much stunned by Ira's lamb-like passivity as the bitter assault itself.

Max Mendelson stood up, a picture of Buddhist serenity. His raised palm swayed breezily in an effort to cool the caldron. "Such terrible excitement! Israel can establish diplomatic relations with Germany, and he makes a *tarrarom* over a contribution. From a molehill, Mr. Schwartz, you are building a mountain," Mendelson calmly purred. "If the Jewish state is able to take reparation money from Germany, such a terrible sin it can't be for us to accept a contribution from Otto Hoffman."

Time started up again; the tension went out of the room. Several Board members applauded; the equation balanced perfectly in their minds. Hoffman and the Blueport Jewish Center on one side, Israel and Germany on the other. Ernie Gruber woke up and cheered, "Yeah, he's right." Ira, not by nature demonstrative, was ready to kiss Mendelson on both cheeks. When Schwartz had first proposed him as a Board member, Ira had been reluctant. But rather than listen to a lengthy dissertation on the qualifications for synagogue leadership he acceded, . . . and now he was thankful he did.

Schwartz scowled contemptuously at Mendelson then turned back to Ira. A cold calm had replaced his anger.

"I will not argue with you. I will not debate with you," Schwartz's measured phrases seemed punctuated with barbs of dry ice. "If you take money from this German, if you dedicate a chapel in our *shul* with the money of a former Nazi, I will not step into this synagogue again. I will, if I must, start another *shul*. I did it once, and I can do it again,

. . . and with me you can be sure will come at least thirty families. It will cost you a lot more than five thousand dollars. So you figure it out if it pays to accept this blood money."

Ira knew this mule of an old man was obstinate enough to go through with his threat and split the congregation. He vacillated, at a loss as to how to handle the crisis. Dr. Gross raised his hand. Ira recognized him.

"I think this is not only a financial question. There is a matter of principle involved. I should like to know if Rabbi Kleinman was apprised of this offer and what his opinion is."

Ira had not been anxious to publicize the fact that Hoffman's offer was originally broached to the rabbi; it wouldn't have helped his plans for tonight regarding Kleinman. Now he was prepared to share the honors.

"This whole discussion is out of order," Ira finally said. "All we're supposed to be doing now is reading correspondence. But if the Board wants to hear from Rabbi Kleinman, I'll call on him."

Kleinman rose to reply. "Yes. I'm aware of Mr. Hoffman's letter. He came to my office to discuss the donation. I'm not free to publicly discuss the full story behind the offer, but believe me it is a poignant tale. I suggest we make no decision tonight. Mr. Schwartz is a valuable member of our synagogue, and I appreciate the deep feelings involved in the whole question. I propose, therefore, that you table the matter until Mr. Schwartz and I have an opportunity to talk it over privately."

Ira jumped at this way out. "I think the suggestion is very good. If the Board agrees, we'll table the question to the next meeting."

The proposal won unanimous approval. Ira rapped the gavel. "The matter is tabled to the next Board meeting."

Kleinman sat down. Meyer Schwartz, morose and defiant

at the other end of the room, followed suit. Ira rapped his gavel again.

"Let's go on with committee reports. Treasurer's report please."

Murray Gold read the treasurer's report. Ira called on the respective chairmen to render their reports: building committee, youth, education, ritual, membership. The meeting now moved smoothly. Discussion of old business and new business was expedited. Ira returned to the helm. The virulent exchange with Schwartz had temporarily taken the wind out of him. For a while he had considered delaying the matter of the rabbi's letter until a more propitious time. However, now that he had retrieved control he decided that this was as good a time as any. And he had promised Purnell that he would get the Board to repudiate Kleinman's letter. Ira was anxious to let Purnell and the *goyim* in town know, as soon as possible, that Kleinman spoke only for himself and did not reflect, by any means, the feelings of the synagogue membership.

"Good and welfare report," Ira said, setting the strategy in motion.

As per plan, Jack Sternberg raised his hand. Ira recognized him. Sternberg heaved his fat rump from the chair. A half-finished cigar protruded between his index and middle finger. He tucked one thumb under his belt, tugged upwards and threw back his shoulders. After an appropriate clearing of his throat he addressed the chair: "Yes, I have something I would like to bring to the attention of the Board. Something that was embarrassing to me and can become a serious bone of contention in our fair community."

For emphasis, Sternberg lifted his well-chewed cigar to his heavy jowels and puffed twice.

"I am referring to a certain letter that appeared in the *Blueport Gazette* two weeks ago."

Kleinman bent forward, his lips pursed. His wan face betrayed his disappointment. So Jack Sternberg was to be the hatchet man. Kleinman's head swayed from side to side. By this time he should be inured to ingratitude, the rabbi told himself. The wrench in his stomach told him otherwise. Kleinman recalled the occasions when the Sternberg family had turned to him: Michael's *bar-mitzvah*, for which he had left a sick bed to officiate; Renée, a kind-hearted giving girl, who gave too soon and got herself pregnant three months before the wedding date, which her father might not have let her live to see, if Kleinman, at personal risk, had not interceded and done some quick calculations and rescheduling; and not more than a year after the doting grandparents arranged to name their beautiful, brilliant ray of sunshine at the Sabbath services, Jack Sternberg had called again to bury his wife's parents. Through the service Claire Sternberg was in shock, unable to comprehend what had happened. During *shivah* Kleinman had spent hours getting her to come to terms with the tragic accident.

"Rabbi, I don't know how we would have pulled through this tragedy without you," Jack Sternberg had said afterwards. "I'm eternally grateful. We'll never forget."

Wryly, Kleinman recalled Ecclesiastes: "Cast thy bread upon the waters, for after many days wilt thou find it again." Evidently, the sage did not take into account how short-lived are the memories of the world's Jack Sternbergs.

Now, Sternberg was brandishing the editorial page of the *Blueport Gazette* before the Board. "For the benefit of those who may have missed it, I would like to read the letter."

"Go ahead," Ira encouraged. "I think we should hear it."

Sternberg harrumphed again and read: " 'This year as in past years, our school administrators have displayed their usual disregard for Jewish rights. I recognize the problems involved in arranging the annual school calendar, and I appreciate that it is not possible to close the schools on every

Jewish holiday. However, I submit that it is grossly unjust and incompatible with our American democratic tradition to completely ignore the most sacred day of the Jewish year while being meticulous not to conflict with Christian holidays.

" 'This year the school will close for Easter and again for the spring vacation. Passover is ignored. And all that would be required to honor this important Jewish festival is to move the spring vacation up two days. The refusal of the school administration to accommodate can only be interpreted by Blueport's Jews as a deliberate slap in the face.

" 'Moreover, is it necessary to open the football season on Yom Kippur, the holiest day of the Jewish year? Must commencement exercises be held on the Jewish Sabbath, thereby precluding Jewish students who are Sabbath observers from attending their own graduation? Isn't it possible to schedule school concerts and other extra curricular activities, at least occasionally, on other days than Friday night or Saturday so that Jewish students could participate without violating their Sabbath?

" 'Good will and consideration could resolve these conflicts. The fact that the school authorities have made no effort to do so and have in fact consistently refused to accord even a minimum of recognition to the sacred days of the Jewish calendar indicates a sorry lack of good will. It is my hope that the ingrained American tradition of fair play will force our school administration to reverse their un-American prejudicial policies and show some respect and consideration for the Jewish citizens of our town.' "

Sternberg rolled the page into a tube and slapped the top end into his palm. He swept the room with a long glance, stopping short of Kleinman and returned to Ira. His cigar had shrunk to thumb size, and as he lifted it for a deep puff, its heat forced his right eye shut. For an instant the thought crossed Kleinman's mind that Sternberg decidedly resembled a cross-eyed sow.

"This letter is signed 'Rabbi Morris Kleinman,' " Sternberg honked. The identification provoked another coughing spell. After a moment of phlegm clearing Sternberg unrolled the tube, folded the page, tidily pressing the creases and proceeded with his commentary.

"Now, gentlemen! Like all good Americans I am a sincere believer in free speech. Furthest from my mind is the intention of bridling anyone. I wouldn't stop any man from expressing his opinion. But . . ." Sternberg hit hard on the "but," waited dramatically, then continued.

"The rabbi is not any man; he represents the Jewish community. When the rabbi speaks or writes, he speaks and writes for you and me. Now, who authorized the rabbi to write such a letter?"

Sternberg paused again, his hands spread out soliciting a reply. Hearing none, he answered himself. "I know I didn't, and I doubt anyone else here did."

Several Board members began to stir uncomfortably. Sternberg went on. "Let me tell you, this letter is resented by the *goyim*, deeply resented. Only yesterday I lunched with Lionel Patterson, . . . and you all know how much weight Patterson pulls in this town; he's warden of the vestry over at St. John; he's president of the Chamber of Commerce and of Blueport Trust. And Patterson is no anti-Semite. Some of his best friends are Jews, . . . and I count myself among them. He said to me, 'Jack, you'd better tone down your rabbi. This is a Christian town, and some important people have been offended by Rabbi Kleinman's letter. They're accusing the Jews of trying to de-Christianize the public school. They don't like it; it could trigger some nasty business none of us want.'

"Personally, I can't blame Patterson for feeling the way he

106

does, and I suggest we take his friendly advice," Sternberg said ominously. "I think we would be well advised to officially repudiate that offensive letter and disassociate ourselves from it completely. Furthermore, in my opinion, we should direct the rabbi to stop interfering in public school policy. There's enough to keep the rabbi busy in our Center without him looking for trouble with the *goyim*.

Zatler raised his hand. Ira waved him on with the gavel. Sternberg, infatuated by his eloquence, flourished his rear end like the rump of a prize cow and yielded the floor to Zatler.

"I agree with Jack," Zatler announced. "Let's face it, we Jews are a small minority in Blueport. We've got to live with the *goyim* and do business with them. We can't afford to antagonize the whole town. I go along with Jack. The Jewish Center should definitely disassociate itself from the rabbi's letter and demand that in the future he desist from making public pronouncements without first consulting the Board of Trustees."

Kleinman forced himself to sit quietly, thinking: "He that subdues his temper and guards his mouth and his tongue, keeps his soul from trouble." He reflected on this sound piece of advice from Proverbs. Perhaps, his silence would save his soul, but if he had to swallow much more of this effrontery his stomach would never make it.

"There are men whose words pierce like swords," he thought. The words coming from Sternberg and Zatlin were stabbing into his guts. The *chutzpa* of these men! Right to his face, as if he weren't here. It was not to be believed. Forewarned is supposed to be forearmed. Gross had warned him what to expect. "Set a guard to my mouth O Lord. Keep watch at the door of my lips," Kleinman pleaded silently for self-control.

But the consortium of Sternberg and Zatlin proved too much for Mendelson. Irately, he leaped to his feet. Usually his irascible disposition was mixed with a pinch of wry humor; now it was all patent anger.

"I think, maybe, you have all forgotten your manners," Mendelson inveighed without waiting to be recognized. "This is the way to talk about a rabbi? And while he is here in this room, listening to every word you are saying? You should be ashamed. All of you. You really think he wrote this letter to make trouble for us. He did it because he is our rabbi; that is his job. If you show no respect for your own rabbi, how do you expect the *goyim* to have respect for you? I think, Mr. Sternberg and Mr. Zatler that you should right now apologize to our rabbi."

Ira did not care for this new twist. The old man could sway the Board. Jack was too pompous and too crude and had pushed too hard. And asking Zatler to speak may have been a tactical error. He was a relative newcomer. It was one thing for the old-timers to criticize the rabbi, but it did seem presumptuous for Zatler to press for censure; he could create a backlash in the rabbi's favor. Contrary to his usual practice, Ira entered the fray.

"Nobody means to be disrespectful to the rabbi," Ira countered Mendelson's demand. "But that letter in the *Gazette* won't do the Jews in this town any good. We should disassociate the synagogue . . ."

Mendelson cut Ira off. "What's the matter, we're not citizens? We got no right to speak our minds? We should put a lock on our rabbi's mouth?"

"Mr. Mendelson is right," Sy Wasser said, usurping the floor. "I for one don't like this discussion at all. The rabbi is a citizen; he's got a perfect right to speak out. Besides, why shouldn't the school be reminded that Jewish children also attend?"

"I'll tell you why," Ira answered hotly. "Because there are a lot of Jews whose livelihood depends on the good will of the *goyim!* Ernie sells cars to the *goyim.* What's he going to do if they decide to boycott him? What of the Jewish merchants on Main Street? They may as well close their doors if the *goyim* stop patronizing them. . . . And what about you, Murray?" The lawyer had been sitting quietly throughout the meeting, trying to make himself as inconspicuous as possible. "You haven't said anything. You've been looking to be elected town supervisor, and this year you might make it. What chance do you think you'll have if they spread the word that Jews are out to Judaize the public school?"

Murray Gold squirmed as two dozen pairs of eyes swiveled in his direction. Damn! Why did Ira have to drag him into this? Political intuition cautioned Murray against taking a stand either way. Prior to the meeting Dr. Gross had solicited his support on behalf of the rabbi. Ira had tried to persuade him to join the opposition. The lawyer had deftly parried both attempts to entangle him in this mess. Murray gave himself a mental kick in the behind for not having sense enough to stay home and avoid this impossible dilemma.

"You're right, Ira," Murray finally rose to the chairman's prodding. He considered the problem like a judge, objectively weighing the pros and cons. "Some of us could be hurt if this thing gets out of hand. But Sy's got a point too. Occasionally we ought to remind the Gentiles that we also exist. Maybe the rabbi did come on a little strong, but I don't think we Jews should just lie down and let the *goyim* step all over us."

By this time even the pretense of parliamentary procedure had been abandoned. Ira was nonplussed by Gold's hedging betrayal. He had been certain that the meeting would go his way. The unanticipated opposition threw him badly. Temporary salvation came from an unexpected quarter.

"Nobody ever said it's easy to be a Jew." Schwartz's abrasive shout cut through the contention like Moses' rod parting the Red Sea. "We got to make a choice, both the children and the parents. It's either Yom Kippur or the football game. It's either keeping Sabbath and *yom tov* like a good Jew or playing in the school orchestra. I say we should make up our minds what we are and let the *goyim* do what they want. I know this is not easy, but to be a Jew you got to make some sacrifices."

Ira was amazed. If anything he would have expected Schwartz to stand behind the rabbi, particularly on this issue. The old man was an independent cuss; he really can cut through garbage; I shouldn't have antagonized him before, Ira thought.

And Schwartz's no-nonsense definition of what being a good Jew entails had a telling effect. The Board was impressed by the logic and even more by the fact that it had come from Schwartz. If an orthodox Jew like Schwartz believed that the synagogue and public school should go their separate ways, why should nonobservant Jews pressure the school authorities to honor Jewish holidays? This was the time to call a halt to discussion and move the question. It appeared that Ira was to get his vote of censure after all. He rapped the gavel, ready to call for a motion.

Dr. Gross stood up, his hand calling to be recognized. Ira hesitated, he had grave suspicions that what Gross had to say was not going to be helpful to the cause. But you just couldn't ignore a man like Dr. Gabriel Gross. Ira himself had urged Gross to accept membership on the Board. Gross had been reluctant; he had argued that his practice would leave him little time to be active. Ira, however, had persisted. Whatever time he could afford would be appreciated. No one was more aware of Gross' reputation both among Jews and Gentiles than Ira. So, despite misgivings, Ira felt compelled to recognize the physician.

"Mr. Schwartz, I agree that as Jews we are called upon to

make some hard choices which involve considerable sacrifice," the doctor said, "but I don't think that is relevant to the discrimination practiced by the public school authorities against our children. . . . And they are discriminating. And we shouldn't just sit back and let it pass. It's not just a simple choice between extracurricular activities and the Sabbath our children are forced to make. There's more to it than that."

Schwartz' brow knit in concentration; he sat down and tucked his chin into a cupped palm. There weren't many, particularly in Blueport, to whom Schwartz would defer. Dr. Gross was such a man.

"My son is to graduate high school this year," Gross continued, "and I would like him to be accepted by a first-rate college. I've been making inquiries, and I've discovered something that came as a surprise. Good grades alone are no guarantee that a youngster will be accepted by a first-rate college. Competition is so keen that admission boards have become very selective. They're looking for well-rounded students, not just the scholarly type. College admission boards give preference to youngsters who have participated actively in extracurricular activities during their high school years. It isn't, therefore, just a choice between Yom Kippur and football, the school orchestra or Sabbath services. These extracurricular activities can make the difference between our children being accepted or rejected by a good college. Perhaps even under such circumstances, a Jew should elect to observe the Sabbath and attend synagogue. I leave it for others to debate this point. But the public school has no right to force such a choice on my son or yours. I, for one, am grateful to Rabbi Kleinman for bringing the issue out into the open, and I applaud his efforts."

Gross stopped for a moment, glanced at Jack Sternberg, then went on. "Some of my best friends are Gentiles, and if they are offended by my rabbi's letter, well, then, I'll just have to look for other friends."

Dr. Gross sat down. The silence that followed was louder than the din heard all evening. Sy Wasser rose.

"If the chair will entertain a motion to adjourn, I so move." Murray Gold raised his hand. "I second the motion."

"The meeting is adjourned," Ira sputtered weakly. Kleinman didn't wait for the chairman's announcement. His face grim, the rabbi hurried to the door and left without speaking to anyone.

Ernie Gruber heaved a sigh of relief. Boy you'd think these guys've got their life savings wrapped up in the Center the way they go at each other." Ernie elbowed his neighbor. "Listen, Sy, I got a good story for you. I heard it the other day."

Sy wasn't in the mood for smutty inanities, but he was penned in, his escape blocked. He sat down again, resigned to suffer through. While the Board members drifted to the door animatedly discussing the evening's outcome, Ernie told his joke. It was about a raffle at the men's club. The first two winners in the drawing won two bottles of bourbon apiece. The third prize winner got a two-pound sponge cake. Ernie chortled. "So the guy blasts the MC, 'How come you put booze in the other packages and sponge cake in mine?' The MC gets pissed off and screams back, 'That's no ordinary cake, I'll have you know; that cake was baked by the *rebbitsen.*' The guy blows up, 'Screw the *rebbitsen.*' The MC looks the guy straight in the eye 'That, my good man, is the fourth prize'."

Ernie rattled like a merry cricket; his glee poured over Sy Wasser, gurgling up ecstatic chortles. He wound up for a full burst. The laugh never left his throat.

"You are a filthy-mouthed tramp, Mr. Ernie Gruber!"

His mouth open, Ernie stared down at the red-faced Mendelson. "You talk like from the gutter, and that is where you belong. Not in a synagogue; and on the Board yet!"

Mendelson lashed out furiously at the hapless raconteur. Somehow Ernie managed to close his mouth and scurry off like a whipped dog. Mendelson was left fuming to himself. He turned to Schwartz, who also had heard Ernie Gruber's joke.

"Such a man sits on a Board of Trustees of a synagogue! He votes, makes decisions on synagogue policy. You don't throw him out, you don't say a word. A dignified man like Otto Hoffman wants to make a donation and you threaten to resign." Mendelson shook his head to emphasize how the logic of it escaped him. "Will you please explain this to me, Mr. Schwartz?"

Schwartz's reply began in a whisper. "I don't like Ernie Gruber's jokes either, Mr. Mendelson. I don't care for Ernie Gruber altogether. You are right; he should not sit on the Board of our synagogue—of any synagogue. He has a filthy mouth; true. But let me remind you, Mr. Mendelson, his dirty mouth hurts nobody but himself. A *tzaddik*, Ernie Gruber is far from. This I know."

The whisper grew in volume and passion as Schwartz unravelled his emotions. "But one thing Ernie Gruber is not; he is not a murderer! His filthy mouth does not kill. The Germans, they were polite. They were dignified. They were clean, sanitary. So sanitary, they tried to sterilize the world by burning every Jew: men, women, children. Six million of us germs they got rid of. Yes. The Germans were polite. 'Please get into the shower,' they said to my parents, my brothers, my sisters. They even played music for them. A concert of murder, of hell. Give me to choose, Mr. Mendelson, and I choose Ernie Gruber sooner than a German. . . . And Otto Hoffman is a German."

Eleven

Tom Purnell studied the pattern decorating the wallpaper. He followed the floral design crisscrossing the faded paper in triangular clusters of three. Halfway down, the edging had crinkled and curled at the seams disclosing the pattern that in another day had graced the cheerless room. Tom wondered how many layers of wallpaper had been plastered on these ancient walls. His glassy stare dropped to the chemistry book resting on his lap. He tried to concentrate on the text, but the meaning of the letters and symbols eluded his grasp. He was unable to focus on them, to take hold of the phrases and absorb them into his consciousness. Lately, Tom had found it difficult to study; his mind refused to retain what he read. He gave up on the chemistry book and returned to a blank contemplation of the wallpaper. The squeak of the bathroom faucet intruded on the emptiness of his mood. Susan had come home fifteen minutes earlier. A loud bang on the front door and the sharp click of heels scampering up the wooden stairs had announced her arrival. Shortly, there followed a rustling of skirts and the sound of bare feet shuffling into the bathroom. Tom grew restive; the room felt hot and close. He shut the chemistry book with a thud, hopped to the narrow window opposite his bed, and pulled down the upper frame. The frayed blind flapped against the pane as cold wind gusted in from the dark starless night. Quickly, he closed the window and paced the length of the room, counting the number of strides. It took three to reach the window, and for some inexplicable reason three and a half to retrace his steps to the rickety bridge table that served him as a desk. Tom paced listening to the gush of water beating against the porcelain tub. The faucet squeaked again; directly the rapid tap slowly died away. Susan's padding sounded clearly through the thin walls. Tom's pace grew more agitated. He visualized his sister stepping from the tub, reaching for a towel and dabbing at her breast. He struggled to drive the image from his mind; the picture persisted. It was vivid and detailed: pink nipples rising from shaded buttons crowning her breast. Susan standing before the full-length mirror adjusting her brassiere. Susan turning and stretching for her panties hanging silken from the rack and waiting to be filled by her buttocks. Tom arrested his mental picture; it was this stage of his sister's undress that particularly aroused him: Susan bare, except for a bra, slipping into panties. Tom's breath came fast. He sat on the edge of the bed, unzippered his fly and groped inside his pants. A sudden spurt of activity coming from the bathroom diverted him from his crotch; he pulled his hand out and sprang from the bed into the hall. He hesitated at the bathroom door and tried the knob; it turned and swung inward. Just as he had sighted her in his mind, Susan stood at an angle in front of the mirror engrossed in her reflected image. She wore a blue terrycloth robe which hung loose and open; her legs were slightly parted. Tom's stare lingered on the pubic mound showing through the open robe, then lifted to her breasts. Susan had cupped her breasts in her hand, pushing them forward as if measuring their size and firmness. To Tom his sister's breasts seemed to radiate a pink heat. Tom's heel scraped against the tiled floor. Susan pivoted sharply to the sound.

"Why the hell don't you knock!" Susan's scream jolted Tom from his trance-like scrutiny of her body. She pulled the belt to her robe with an angry tug.

"Can't I have any privacy, even in the bathroom?"

Tom pretended innocence. "If you don't want visitors, why don't you lock the door?"

"You know damn well the lock's broken."

"Okay. I'm sorry; I apologize. No need to get excited. We've seen each other in the nude before." Tom exposed his teeth in a wide, fraternal grin. "After all, we're brother and sister."

"Look, Tom! We're not kids anymore. I know you've been peeping every chance you get. You got to stop it. It's not right anymore."

"Aw, you're imagining things."

"I'm not imagining! You got to stop it."

Tom shrugged. "How come all of a sudden you're so modest? It wasn't so long ago you asked to see my pecker."

"Shut your dirty mouth."

"It's no dirtier than when you asked."

"Tom, we're not kids anymore."

"You said that already."

"Well, we're not." Susan's eyes narrowed. "Leave me alone. If you got hot pants, go find yourself a girl."

Tom's smirk was wiped clean by Susan's derision. He struck back. "You got yourself a boy, I hear, a Jew boy. The word is out. You and Stanley Cane have been shacking up."

"None of your damn business what I do, or who I do it with." Susan's contempt burned deep. Tom backed away a little from the heat.

"Maybe it's not my business. But why the hell do you have to pick a Jew boy?"

"I like him; that's why."

"You're dumber than I thought, if you think Stanley Cane wants you for anything else than the pussy you're putting out."

"Whatever Stanley Cane wants me for and what I give him

is none of your damn business. I repeat; you leave me alone. If you can't get yourself a girl like any normal guy, go jerk off."

The lashing contempt found its mark. Tom turned livid; his nostrils flared. He lifted his fist menacingly.

"I'll scream if you touch me," Susan warned, holding her ground. "I'll scream so loud the whole town'll hear me. . . . They'll put you away . . . you nut!"

Tom's hand stayed suspended in mid-air; the color of his cheeks drained to colorless tallow; his eyeballs looked like glazed twin marbles. He backed away out of the bathroom into the hall. He veered and raced into his room, slamming the door behind him. He flung himself on the bed. The pillow caved in fluffing about his face and muting his low-pitched macabre wail.

Twelve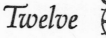

Stanley gunned the motor awaiting the click of the red light. Synchronizing almost perfectly with the shift to green, the red Mustang shot straight ahead, its tires squealing at the sudden strain of rubber pushing against asphalt. The forward lurch whiplashed Mel Gross into the backrest.

"Where's the fire?" Mel groaned, soothing his aching neck.

"Under the hood, man! Under the hood," Stanley Cane chortled. "This machine has got spirit. It's raring to go; can't hold her back."

The speedometer nudged to sixty in a two-block spurt past a plainly marked sign: Town Of Blueport Speed Limit 25 Miles Per Hour. Stanley slackened the accelerator; the needle

moved downward. He pressed on the pedal again; the speedometer held at forty-five.

Behind the wheel, Stanley Cane was in his element. The
souped-up engine responded to his touch as if it were an
extension of his body. An automobile both excited and
soothed Stanley; it was something he could love because he
understood and trusted it. There was no subterfuge to an
automobile; it went where it was supposed to go and did what
it was told to do. A machine was impartial; it had no preju-
dices and held no secrets. Behind the wheel Stanley felt
secure, though he could hardly articulate why. Not even to
himself.

The red Mustang continued on to the east end of Jerusalem
Avenue. Suddenly, Stanley hit the brake. Mel sucked in his
breath; his body stiffened, reflexively bracing itself for the
looming catastrophe. Stanley swerved into Fourth Avenue.
The car screeched into a wide right turn, careening on two
wheels, barely missing an oncoming pick-up truck. The car
settled back on its four wheels. Mel exhaled in slow, choking
gasps.

"Buddy boy, I don't want to hurt your feelings, but they
tell me I got a bright future ahead of me. The way you're
pushing this chariot I may get to miss most of it."

"Brother, you got no faith; that's your trouble," Stanley
chuckled. "Trust me, boy, and I will yet lead you to the
promised land."

Yielding to his friend's fear, Stanley slowed the car down
to the posted speed limit. The two youths drove through
Blueport's business district heading north towards the bay.
Mel peered through the windshield at the bleak, inhospitable
streets. Here and there a solitary pedestrian leaned into the
biting wind. Mel switched the heater to high.

"I sure hope the promised land you're heading for is

warm." Despite the added flow of heat, Mel drew up the collar to his overcoat.

"More than warm, son, more than warm." Stanley's supercilious grin hinted at pleasures ahead if Mel would dutifully follow his lead. "Where I'm taking you, it's downright hot."

Mel affected deference. "Wouldn't be offending you, if I asked you where?"

"Not at all friend. Not at all," Stanley obliged. "I got us a date with a couple of friendly females. Eight-thirty at Cap'n Sharkey's."

"When did I appoint you my matchmaker?"

"A good friend doesn't wait to do a pal a favor," Stanley purred, ignoring the irritation in Mel's tone. "It's about time you got your horizons broadened. And I got just the broads to do the job."

"I don't know. The crowd that hangs around Cap'n Sharkey isn't my style. Going there is asking for trouble. Why don't we see what we can pick up at the Center? There's a dance on tonight."

Stanley gave him a look of paternal exasperation. "Man, I don't know why I bother with you. I try to do you a favor; line up two sure pieces. Instead of appreciation I get a hang-up."

"What's wrong with the girls at the Jewish Center?"

"What's wrong with the girls at the Jewish Center?" Stanley mimicked. "Nothing's wrong with them. They're great to have for sisters. Maybe to do the *hora* with and take to the Jewish Museum. But man! if you want to enjoy life, you got to break outta the virgin circuit."

"Okay, Stan, don't get yourself in an uproar. Let's see the big deal you cooked up."

Mel settled back in his seat, resigned to letting his friend set the pace for the evening's activities.

Aside from the public school, which collected Blueport's youth under one roof for a few hours of education, the town boasted several offbeat establishments where young people could gather. For the most part, these unofficial youth centers were located on side streets off the Blueport Marina. In season the marina burst with boats of all sizes and shapes, but at this time of the year the boat basin was deserted. Most of the stores catering to the summer crowd were closed, but a few taverns stayed open out of season and catered to teen-agers. Here, the youth of Blueport could assemble without parental interference and charge up the monotony they bewailed was their lamentable lot in the square world.

Under the auspices of sympathetic tavern keepers who asked only that the cash registers ring and that their clientele refrain from razing the premises, suburbia's youth practiced their own style of integration. The police looked askance at the lively diversions these borderline establishments offered, but so long as parents didn't complain, the police were content to keep the taverns under surveillance and be remembered at Christmas for their forebearance. Occasionally, a drunk teen-age driver smashed up a car. Once in a while a sweet sixteener known to frequent the taverns found herself pregnant. Several parents, curious about the glazed eyes of their children, took time out to probe further and learned that their progeny were high on mind-expanding drugs they had acquired at the taverns.

Thus far, however, the town had been fortunate. No drunken or drugged teen-ager had been killed or had killed anyone; no riots had erupted to blot the good name of Blueport. The occasional tremors were hushed by publicity-shy parents and kept out of the newspapers. Since there was no direct evidence that the taverns were responsible for youthful aberrations, and the tavern keepers, when in doubt as to whether a customer was of age to be served hard drinks, made a show of demanding a driver's license or draft card, the police were cooperative. Youthful offenses were dispatched with discretion, and the taverns continued uninterrupted and unmolested to fill with perfect inpartiality the void in the existence of Blueport's advantaged and disadvantaged youth.

About thirty cars jammed the gravel covered parking lot. With expertise, Stanley maneuvered his Mustang into an empty space and shut off the ignition. In high spirits he drove a playful fist into Mel's shoulder.

"Arise and shine, friend. Heads up; we have arrived." Mel made no response.

"What's the matter, boy?" Stanley inquired condescendingly. "You still want the Jewish Center? If that's your scene, I'll turn around. Let it not be said I forced you into manhood. Don't want to be accused of giving you a trauma. . . . You may never recover."

"Okay, big man!" Mel put on a sportive façade. "Lead me to your hunting grounds. Let's see what your kind of broads have to offer."

"That's the spirit, friend." Stanley slapped Mel's thigh approvingly. "Let's go."

The boys slammed the car doors and raced toward the joys of Cap'n Sharkey's. Stanley reached the entrance first; he pushed his weight against the heavy pitted door. It rattled open.

"Enter our house of pleasure," Stanley made a fop's bow and invited Mel to precede him.

Mel crammed into a square vestibule illuminated by one naked bulb screwed into a low-hanging ceiling. Stanley pulled the door shut and jauntily pointed the way to an oblong room, its ceiling only a foot higher than the vestibule. The room was large enough to accommodate about a hundred people and appeared filled beyond capacity. A bar spanned three-quarters of the room's width. About twenty youths, several of whom Mel recognized from school, were crowded in front of the bar. The standees squeezed between ten stools fighting to get the bartender's attention; their boisterous demands for service blended with the rest of the shouting into one deafening clamor. A garish purple haze suffused the dimly lit room. Smoke rose in thick spirals and hovered over the bar. There were several private booths whose occupants were barely visible. A steady procession moved from the booths to the bar and back. Long haired youths, some bearded, meandered about the room in groups of two's and three's hurling friendly imprecations at one another. A constant cacophony welled up from the postage-sized dance floor where squirming couples bumped, jerked, flexed, and pivoted to the discordant bleats of a band while onlookers clapped their tumultuous approval.

Stanley paused at the entrance; his eyes searched the room. "There they are," he pointed to the bar. "They're waiting for us. Let's go meet the broads."

The boys elbowed their way through the noisy crowd. Stopping at the dance floor, Stanley grinned at a couple flailing the air with intricate body and arm twists.

"Hi, Bob," Stanley saluted over the racket. "The place sure is jumping tonight. Eh, buddy boy?"

The dancer interrupted his gyrations, glanced at Stanley, nodded, and went back to his partner. It seemed to Mel that his friend had just been rebuffed. If it was a snub, Stanley did not interpret it as such; with his usual aplomb, he continued to steer Mel towards the bar. Through the haze Mel made out their dates sipping tall glasses and snapping their fingers and rumps in tune to the wild rhythms. Two youths, their backs to Mel and Stanley, hemmed the girls in on either side. One youth was mapping the rotund bottom of the maiden to the right. She emitted a screech and playfully slapped his wrist. He laughed and moved his hand up to her breast. Stanley edged in close to the bar. The girl having her buttocks and breasts fingered brightened him with a smile. She was attractive, Mel conceded, in a flashy, unpolished way. She wore a very short miniskirt that showed off to advantage her long legs and thighs. Full breasts pushed roundly against a tight orange sweater. Her nose was small and tilted at the tip. Her eyes were large, blue-green, thick with mascara, and heavy with lashes. She had long auburn hair that fell to her shoulders. Her mouth, painted a pale pink, beckoned sensuously.

"Girls! Here we are. Your ticket to a night of pleasure," Stanley announced. "Mel, meet Cathy Blaine. Didn't I tell you she's a beaut? And this . . ." Stanley gestured gallantly to the lovely blonde at Cathy's side. "This is my baby doll, Susan Purnell."

The broad-shouldered youth whose hands had been creeping from Cathy Blaine's buttock to bosom and back again twisted his body in a slow-moving arc and looked disparagingly at the new arrivals.

"Well, well, Marty! Look what's come slumming to our part of town . . . the children of Israel, son of money bags and son of medicine man." Tom Purnell flung his greeting with scalding contempt.

The chatter and horseplay about the bar subsided in ebbing waves. Stanley stood speechless, at a rare loss for words. Mel's face reddened; he made a move toward Tom, hesitated, and stepped back unnoticed. The silence attracted further quiet and spread through the room. A crowd began to gather at the bar. Susan slipped off the stool and hooked her arm into Stanley's.

"Don't pay any attention to him," she said. Stanley remained at the spot as if held by invisible chains. She tugged at his arm.

"Come on, Stan! We'll go find us a booth. Don't let him ruin our night. He's got a mean, prejudiced mouth." Susan tossed her head scornfully at her brother.

Tom Purnell stiffened. "Me prejudiced?" He thumbed his chest in hurt innocence. "Susan! How can you accuse me of being prejudiced?"

Tom turned and complained to the skinny, pimply-faced friend at his side. "Marty, my own sister, my own flesh and blood calling me prejudiced. What do you think about that?"

Marty Simpson shrugged his thin shoulder blades, grinning inanely and running his fingers through long locks of dirty brown hair which curled under his ears. Tom whirled back to his sister.

"Not only am I not prejudiced, baby sister, I'm really a great liberal. In fact, Stanley my boy, I'm glad you came tonight." Tom's glance swung to Stanley. A mannered courtesy honeyed his words. "I've been hoping to bump into you. I got a petition I'd like you to sign. Didn't expect to meet you this end of town. . . . Let's see . . . maybe I got it with me." Tom reached into his checkered blazer and fumbled for a moment.

"Yeah! Isn't that luck for you? I got it with me. Been carrying it around just in case I run into other liberals like me."

Tom pulled out a yellow sheet, waved it at Stanley and began to read: " 'We, the seniors at Blueport High, believe that an informed citizenry is essential to a democratic society and can obtain only when free speech is encouraged—regardless of the point of view. Bearing this principle in mind, which our teachers have impressed upon us, the seniors have voted to invite George Stonehill, a nationally known figure, to address our class. We respectfully petition that Mr. Stonehill be permitted to speak in our school."

Tom shoved the sheet at Stanley. "Here, great liberal, sign it."

Stanley shifted weight from one foot to another. Tom pressed on, adding mockery to Stanley's discomfiture.

"Oh! Maybe the great liberal didn't bring a pen with him. . . . Guess he didn't expect to do any writing; had other things on his mind tonight. Eh, Suzy girl? Grinning lewdly, Tom patted his crotch. "Anybody got a pen for the great liberal?"

Marty held out a pen. Tom thrust the paper under Stanley's chin. Stanley's arms hung limp and useless.

"What's the matter, great liberal? Don't you believe in free speech? You Jews are all the time hollering about equality. Your rabbi likes to write letters how we don't give you people a fair shake. Come on, now. This is your big chance to show us Gentiles how liberal you are."

Stanley remained inert. Sniffing disgust, Tom played to the audience jamming the bar. "Looks like the great liberal forgot how to sign his name."

Susan made another try to budge her date; she tugged at Stanley's sleeve. He stayed fixed and dumb. Slowly, Tom's brow inched upward, creasing his forehead with what seemed a new and better thought. "Wait a minute!" Tom plucked the sheet from under Stanley's nose. "Maybe your pal would like to sign?"

Tom shoved the petition at Mel Gross who had stayed inconspicuously in the background.

"Maybe you're a great liberal?"

Thus far silent and peculiarly uninvolved, Mel stepped forward. "Okay. Let's see it." Mel held out his hand. "I like to read what I sign."

Surprise spread across Tom's face. The petition dangled between his thumb and forefinger. Mel hooked the sheet from Tom's light grip and began to read, ignoring the buzz around him. Stanley seemed to shrink to half size, as if afraid to breathe too hard lest it draw attention back to him. Mel finished, turned the paper to its blank side, and studied it carefully, as if to make certain there was nothing he might have missed. He folded the sheet, meticulously ripped it in half, then in half again.

"Here's your petition back." Mel offered the pieces to Tom. "Shove it up your ass. If you can't get it up all at once, try pushing it up piece by piece."

Abruptly, the buzz stopped. The silence solidified around the two youths, who had become actors in a play that had suddenly taken on an unexpected twist. Tom stood dead still. Mel opened his hand; yellow scraps floated downward. He toed the fragments and ground them with his heel, as if stubbing a cigarette. Color rushed back into Tom's drained face. He pulled his right hand backward to shoulder height, fists clenched like tight rocks. Mel readied himself for the attack, his guard up. The gallery gave its undivided attention to the impromptu floor show, waiting with bated breath for Tom to spring his punch.

"Cool it, son."

Steel fingers ringed Tom's wrist.

"I don't want trouble here. You got differences, settle 'em elsewhere."

Tom struggled to wrench free of the bartender's bear-like hold. The vise tightened.

"You start a fight here, Tom, and I'll blackball you from these premises permanently."

Tom opened his fists; his arms and body slackened. "Okay, Sharkey. Let loose. I won't start anything here. I'll finish this my own way."

Sharkey let go; he adjusted the spotted apron hugging his huge girth and returned behind the bar as if nothing had happened. Mel lowered his guard, contemptuously glaring Tom down. For a moment there was a tense pause as the antagonists took each other's measure. Mel ignored Tom and turned to the wide-eyed Cathy, who had not moved a hair.

"You want to join us, Cathy?"

Cathy hopped off the stool into Mel's arms; admiration sparkled in her eyes. The couple held hands, nudging into the crowd. The circle opened, respectfully clearing a path. Cathy slithered through, her buttocks bouncing. As she glided past Tom her bottom saluted him with an extra bump. Susan yanked Stanley's sleeve, pulling him out of his trance and almost off his feet. Temporarily squashed, he let himself be led by Susan's firm hand. The foursome retired to a secluded booth at the far end of the room. An electric guitar struck a chord, and Cap'n Sharkey's reverted to normal chaos.

Thirteen

Adamantly, Beth thrust the heavy sweater at her husband. "Put it on; it's cold outside." Grudgingly, Kleinman slipped his arms into the sleeves. Beth hovered like a hen mothering its brood. Obediently, Kleinman buttoned up under the searching eye of his wife. A fragile rebellion sputtered.

"Nu! So I put on the sweater. So now it's warm outside?"

Beth showed small appreciation for her husband's wit. "I hope your sermon isn't as stale as that joke. Now put your jacket over the sweater, and don't forget the scarf."

"But you got me so bundled up, I can barely move," Kleinman protested.

"No buts. Just take the scarf. I don't want you coming down with another cold."

Tucking the scarf deep down into his sweater, Kleinman stretched for his coat in the hall closet. Beth watched him struggle to introduce his arm into the sleeve. The aperture was too narrow for the bulky clothing; the sleeve folded into the elbow. He tried again, this time clutching the cuff with his arm up into the sleeve. He repeated the process with his left arm, then with spasmodic jerks that resembled the hopping of a frightened rabbit, he fought to pull the coat over his sweater, jacket and scarf. Beth cupped a hand to her mouth; a giggle sprayed through her fingers.

"Here, let me help you with your overcoat," she offered.

Kleinman made a wry face. "Who'll help me coming back?"

"I'm sure you'll manage somehow," Beth said, tugging at the coat.

"Thanks for your confidence," Kleinman said, pulling down the brim of his black felt fedora. "Well, if I collapse under the weight, I can just double over and roll down to the synagogue; fortunately, it's downhill. But how'll I get back home?"

"Very funny," Beth brushed off the facetious remark and changed to another subject. "I don't think I'll get to services today. I want to stay with Jonathan; he's still coughing badly. I wish you didn't have to walk on a bitter day like this; you don't look too well to me, either."

"Don't worry, dear," Kleinman reassured. "The exercise will do me good." He wobbled to the door. "I'll probably be late coming home. This Sabbath is Sammy Gold's *bar-mitzvah;* the services may take a little longer than usual."

"Oh, that's right," Beth fingered her lips. "I forgot all about it. Make my apologies to the Golds. I hope they understand."

"There probably will be so many people, they won't notice," Kleinman said. "If they do, I'm sure they'll understand."

Beth tilted her cheek, Kleinman strained to bend and kiss it; his clothing was a stiff bundle of resistance. He brushed her forehead with his lips and opened the door to the vestibule. A north wind whistled under the spacing of the storm door, gusting winter into the house. Beth shivered at the cold and at the thought of her husband walking over a mile in the raw weather to the synagogue. Kleinman unhooked the latch to the storm door, stepped out, and quickly pushed it closed; he waved and stepped into the cold. Feeling the wind, he was grateful that Beth had insisted on the sweater and scarf; the layers of clothing didn't seem burdensome at all now. Beth stood at the door, watching him pick his way down the snow-covered path until he turned a corner and disappeared from view.

In good weather Kleinman didn't mind the walk; in fact, he enjoyed it. Walking to the synagogue on Sabbaths and holidays was just about his only exercise, and on nice days he looked forward to the leisurely stroll.

By now, the rabbi promenading down Jerusalem Avenue was a familiar sight in Blueport, particularly to parishioners heading for the shopping center, beauty parlor, beach, golf course, or whatever activities Jews reserve for Sabbaths and holidays. Some even suffered a passing twinge of conscience, though the qualms were never so sharp as to divert the offenders to the synagogue.

The shortest route to the synagogue was via Jerusalem Avenue, by way of West Main Street, which was the outer edge of Blueport's business district. To get to Ocean Avenue, the rabbi had to pass several stores owned by members of his congregation. Lenny Davis owned North Shore Carpeting.

The proprietors of the furniture and appliance stores were also good dues-paying members. As a matter of fact, most of the retailers on Main Street were his *balebatim*. When Kleinman was new to Blueport and took his maiden walk to the synagogue, the sight of the commercial bustle sorely disturbed him. Seeing his congregants do business on the Sabbath was unsettling. Not that Kleinman had secluded himself in an ivory tower before his election to the Blueport Synagogue. The rabbi was not naïve; he was aware that American Jewry paid little heed to Judaism's sancta. Still, it was one thing to know it as a distant critic, and another to be in the middle to see his own congregants, who were his responsibility, live their lives oblivious to the law to which he had dedicated his life. Their delinquency, he couldn't help feel, was his failure. That first autumn in Blueport, Kleinman shunned Jerusalem Avenue and walked to the synagogue by way of Birch Lane, a residential street. It added a quarter of a mile to his walk, but he avoided the sight of the Sabbath commerce.

When the lovely Indian summer turned damp and winter arrived in earnest, Kleinman returned to the shorter route. He did his best to ignore the Sabbath violators; he walked as if bridled, looking to neither the right nor left. But it was not always possible to speed past the offending sights. Storekeepers with time on their hands waiting for the early customers would spot the rabbi go by and shout a friendly hello. Sometimes, when business was unusually slow, they came outside to ask a question or just to make conversation. Before three seasons were out, Kleinman had made a gradual accommodation. (Strange how easily one adjusts to the mores of the multitude. At first he was so distraught, he ran rather than face it. The pain downgraded to mild discomfort; the discomfort to resignation.) He couldn't change anything, so he accepted. Kleinman even found himself rationalizing for the Sabbath violators. It was not by choice that his congregants worked six days a week. Surely, they would much prefer closing Saturdays. But they had to make a living; this is the system in America, and they were enslaved to it, like everybody else. What could they do?

"Lord, give us the courage to change what we can, the strength to accept what we cannot, and the wisdom to know the difference."

But, oh, how rare is that wisdom, to know the difference. And rarer still is the courage to question one's motives for making adjustments. In frank moments Kleinman wondered whether his gradual acceptance was due to a realistic resignation to facts that couldn't be changed, to sympathy for the hard lot of his retailers, or to less certitude about the value of those beliefs to which he had once been unequivocally committed. He had come to this town as a young enthusiastic rabbi eager to deepen the commitment of Blueport's Jews to the law. Now, ten years older, if not wiser, self-doubt gnawed at Blueport's rabbi; he no longer found it possible to escape the disturbing truth that his effect on Blueport was far less than Blueport's effect on him, that the messianic dreams he had harbored were just that—dreams. And as he walked to the synagogue, his head bent into the edged wind that slashed his face and swirled snow into his tearing, near-blinded eyes, Kleinman felt the cold penetrate further into his body and deeper into his convictions. Did his refusal to drive a car on the Sabbath really constitute such a significant religious act? Did it really make any difference to man or God? Rabbi Morris Kleinman questioned and walked on.

"*Baruch Hashem*, thank the Lord," Kleinman mumbled as he turned the corner into Ocean Avenue. He was breathing hard now, his breath showed in white puffs. He pressed into the wind that whipped furiously against his eyes and face,

as if it were making a final effort to drive him back. Kleinman pushed past the Hebrew school building. Through lids
almost frozen closed, he noticed that the shades in the Chaim
Cohen Auditorium had been pulled up, the drapes drawn.
Above the portable ark, the Eternal Light sparkled through
the window: Mendelson's retort to Ira Cane. That old codger
had to prove that he bows to no man's tyranny. If his lips
weren't nearly frozen, Kleinman would have smiled. He hurried by the Hebrew school to the grandiose synagogue building which housed the main sanctuary. Climbing the marble
steps as quickly as his years, weight, and wind allowed, he
pulled at the heavy oak portals framed in hammered bronze
and bounced into the vestibule, stomping his feet and rubbing
his nearly frostbitten face. Sensation returned to his numbed
limbs in slow waves. He stood for a moment gratefully savor-
ing the warmth flowing into his body.

The vestibule opened into a spaciously luxurious lobby.
Rubbing his shoes on the doormat before stepping on the
deep piled wine-red carpet, Kleinman crossed the lobby to
his dressing room. A large number of coats lined up on
hangers caught his attention as he passed the cloakroom. He
stopped for a quick count. Twenty. This was unusual. He
hadn't expected the Golds this early. Services began at nine
on Sabbath mornings, and the ornate clock on the mahogany wall showed eight forty-five. It was a rarity for the *bar-
mitzvah* family to arrive at the start of services, much less
fifteen minutes early.

Shrugging at the mystery, Kleinman continued to the
dressing room, peeled off the outer clothing Beth had loaded
on him and donned his robe. A mirror was attached to the
narrow metal cabinet. Kleinman studied the drawn face looking back at him; he was alone in the room, yet he found it
hard to accept the image staring back at him as his own face.
It was someone else, looking over his shoulder, someone older,

whom the years had lined and grayed. Resigned finally to the idea that it was his face, he adjusted the high three-cornered black skullcap to fit snugly on his head and reached for the silver-embroidered prayer shawl hanging on the rack. A knock interrupted his pontifical preparations.

"Come in," Kleinman answered. Meyer Schwartz burst in.

"Good *Shabbes*, Rabbi." Schwartz' bellow was slightly under par.

"Good *Shabbes*, Mr. Schwartz," Kleinman said, showing his surprise. Ordinarily, Schwartz and Mendelson arrived about eight-thirty. Mendelson would check to see that the prayerbooks and bibles were neatly stacked; Schwartz generally spent the half hour before services studying the commentaries to the scriptural reading assigned for that Sabbath. A visit by Schwartz before services meant something was amiss.

"Is there any problem?" Kleinman asked.

"No," Schwartz said. "But you should know what's in there."

"What do you mean, what's in there?"

"I mean we got fourteen men in the *shul*. With Mendelson, me, the cantor and you, we got eighteen. But we still got no *minyan*. So if you start now, you should know we can't say *Kaddish*."

"With eighteen men we still have no minyan?"

"No! With eighteen men we still have no *minyan*," Schwartz insisted enigmatically.

"But why?" Kleinman searched Schwartz' sphinx-like visage for a clue. "Nobody changed the law; we still only need ten men for a minyan as far as I know."

"We need ten Jews for a *minyan*," Schwartz pounced. "The fourteen men inside are *goyim*, and we don't count a *goy* into a *minyan*. Jewish *goyim* we have to count, but *goyisher goyim* we don't count yet."

"But how do you know they're not Jewish?"

"I know because when they came in Mendelson handed them *siddurim, chumashim, yarmulkes,* and *talaysim.* They took the *chumashim* and *siddurim,* and when Mendelson told them that in a synagogue men must wear a head covering, they put on the *yarmulkes.* But the *talaysim* they wouldn't wear.

"From experience I already know," Schwartz continued, "when a man walks into a *shul* and refuses a *tallis,* he is either an orthodox unmarried Jew who knows the law that only married men are required to put on a *tallis,* or he is a *goy.* The people in there don't look to me like orthodox Jews. So, what else are they? *Goyim.*"

"Well, I suppose you're right," Kleinman's brow uncreased. "To tell the truth, when I saw all those coats hanging in the cloakroom, I was surprised. I thought the Gold family had come early."

"The Gold family come early?" Schwartz dismissed that possibility out of hand. "I'll be surprised if they get here before the Torah reading." The old man pushed his *yarmulke* to one side and scratched his white mane. "What I don't understand is what these people are doing here so early. Who are they?"

"Most likely they're friends of the Golds," Kleinman speculated. "Murray Gold being in politics has many Christian friends. Probably he sent them the usual *bar-mitzvah* invitation. And when a Christian gets an invitation to a religious service that calls for nine o'clock, he comes at nine o'clock. Christians aren't aware that a Jewish nine o'clock means ten. I feel for them; what they also don't know is that the service lasts almost three hours."

What lay in store for the *goyim* wasn't going to disturb Schwartz' Sabbath. "Well! If they don't know, they'll find out soon enough," he snorted.

Kleinman was mildly distressed. "I would prefer that when our people invite non-Jews they suggest to their Gentile guests to come later. It's senseless having Christians sit through a three hour service that has no meaning for them."

Schwartz' eyes narrowed suspiciously. "Rabbi! If you are maybe suggesting again that we cut the service shorter, I refuse to take the hint."

Kleinman raised his palms defensively. "No such thought even crossed my mind. A bargain is a bargain. You don't object to abbreviated services and the organ on Friday night, and I won't suggest changes in the Sabbath morning service." Kleinman dropped his hands and chuckled. "I appreciate your advising me about our guests. I promise not to recite *Kaddish* until I count ten familiar Jewish faces. Okay?"

"Very good. Then I think we should start."

The two men left the dressing room; before entering the sanctuary Kleinman stopped at the door. "By the way, Mr. Schwartz, my sermon today may be of special interest to you; it has a bearing on that matter of Otto Hoffman. After services I'd like to talk to you about it." At the mention of the jeweler's name Schwartz' face clouded; he nodded. Kleinman let the subject drop for the time being, not knowing whether the nod was an acceptance or rejection. He entered the sanctuary and walked down the center aisle. Schwartz waited till the rabbi ascended the pulpit, then followed, passing Mendelson, who was arranging the prayer books and Bibles on a high shelf in the rear of the sanctuary. He strode to his pew, eyes straight ahead, to avoid visual contact with Gold's punctual invitees, picked up his large woolen *tallis*, threw the ends into a double fold over his shoulders, and sat down.

"The congregation will please turn to page 38 and rise for the opening prayer." A diffused echo in the near empty sanctuary returned Kleinman's announcement. Cantor Rosenberg skipped to the reader's lectern, tweaked his turning fork and intoned the opening phrases of the "*Ma Tovu.*"

"How goodly are your tents O Jacob; your dwelling places O Israel. O Lord, through Thine abundant kindness we come into Thy house, and reverently do we worship Thee in Thy holy sanctuary."

Kleinman concluded the translation and sat down on the red velvet pulpit chair. Cantor Rosenberg continued to chant the service in Hebrew. From his seat in the second pew, Schwartz complimented Rosenberg's baritone with his own sing-song rasp. In the rear, Mendelson stacked prayer books and prepared for the late arrivals. The early arrivals sat in awkward silence.

How odd; how strange is Jacob's sanctuary today, Kleinman paraphrased the opening lines of the service to himself. Jacob's children are a puzzle; their sanctuary an anachronism, and the ways of their God an enigma. A *bar-mitzvah* service in a synagogue begins with fourteen Gentiles and their wives . . . and four Jews.

To Kleinman's happy surprise, the Gold family arrived at nine fifteen. Eleven male regulars were already present and plowing through the "*P'sukey D'zimra,*" oblivious to the Gentile visitors sitting solemn and stiff-necked in the rear pews. Murray Gold headed the family procession. He paused to greet his non-Jewish guests, then continued to the first pew, almost directly under Kleinman's lectern. Mrs. Gold followed, with Sammy a nervous stride behind. Mrs. Davis, sweetly diminutive and white-haired, immediately sat down. Murray Gold's wife allowed herself the luxury of posing momentarily in the aisle, plump and mink draped, before dropping with studied dignity next to her mother. Mr. Davis tugged his *tallis* from a satin bag brocaded in silver, coiled the upper half over his face and head and recited the benediction. The short prayer concluded, he sat down and without hesitation opened the *siddur* to the correct page and joined in the service. Kleinman took note of the large woolen *tallis* worn by Mr. Davis—magnificent with a beautiful *atarah*, six rows of flat silver squares sewn flush against the upper half. Kleinman also recognized the telltale yellow tinge to Mr. Davis' *tallis*, a sure sign of age and use.

Murray Gold slipped on his *tallis;* it was much smaller, silk with thin lacey fringes, snow-white, fresh, clean, and apparently worn as often as a full solar eclipse. Kleinman was no longer surprised by the skeptics, the professed agnostics in his congregation whose parents were orthodox Jews. But acknowledgement of the fact afforded small comfort. . . . Where did the fault lie? What had the fathers done wrong that left him striving with a generation lost to Judaism?

Perhaps it was no one's fault, Kleinman conjectured. Perhaps, it was an inevitable sequel to an age that had played havoc with all tradition. The lament of his teacher, the late professor Gershon Einbeinder, Professor of Mysticism at the seminary, came to Kleinman's mind: "Modern man has re-enthroned the mythological gods of materialism," Professor Einbeinder had written, "and the Jewish vision of the transcendental has also been beclouded by the transitory. Twice daily, the fathers affirmed the perfect unity that structures the universe; their sons fracture creation with the cultus of a reincarnated paganism. God once looked at his people through the clear panes of a window—the Lord saw and was perceived. Now the God of Abraham, Isaac, and Jacob peers through a lattice. He beholds the vacuous frenzy of his children while they pronounce his demise."

The guest of honor squirmed between his parents, sporting tight pants, a plaid jacket, and a loud tie, and nervously clutching his *Haftorah* booklet. Two days before the *barmitzvah*, Kleinman had met Sammy to review the service; the rabbi was awed by Sammy's *Haftorah* booklet. Isaiah had been thumbed through to near illegibility. The binding was broken, pages creased and loose. Notes were inked between the lines, scrubbed on margins. If Sammy and his peers and their parents could be induced to take Jewish education as seriously as they did a one-shot *bar-mitzvah* service, American Jewry would in no time raise a generation of scholars such as it hadn't been blessed with in all of its history. But there was no use bewailing today's Jewish values. It could be and, indeed, used to be worse. At least, most candidates for *bar-mitzvah* were exposed to four or five years of Hebrew, Jewish history, and tradition. Not long ago it was common practice for parents to present their prodigies at the age of twelve and a half and demand, "Here, Rabbi, make a Jew out of him." So things were improving; perhaps, his successors, the next generation of rabbis, would succeed in restoring the significance of this day to children and parents.

The sanctuary began to fill up quickly, with well over two hundred people seated before ten o'clock. Ira and Ruth Cane arrived at nine-forty-five. Ruth was invited to sit in the third pew as a guest of the Golds. Ira stepped to the pulpit and slouched in the president's chair next to Kleinman. Ira seemed especially sour. Considering the circumstances, however, his defeat at the Board meeting with Murray Gold a sorry disappointment, Kleinman understood the flaccid "Good Shabbes" he got from Ira and gave him credit for coming at all. This much could be said for the president of the Jewish Center: he held on to a grudge, but it didn't keep him from fulfilling his duties.

Sol Harris, chairman of the ritual committee, ushered the Golds to the pulpit. Kleinman waited for the celebrants to approach the ark. Solemnly, the Golds faced the bright red glow of the Eternal Light, Murray to the right, his wife to the left, and Sammy between them. Kleinman addressed the father first:

"You will now recite the declaration of release."

"*Boruch sheptarani mey onshi shelazeh*," Murray Gold confidently proclaimed the rehearsed formula.

"You are no longer accountable for the religious acts of your son; his deeds of omission or commission. From henceforth the responsibilities of our common heritage shall be his to carry. I ask you both now to recite the '*sheheche-yanu.*'"

The Golds responded in unison: "Blessed art Thou O Lord, King of the universe, who hast kept us alive and sustained us and enabled us to reach this sacred moment, the *bar-mitzvah* of our son." The last phrase brought a tear to Mrs. Gold's eye; she dabbed at it with a white laced handkerchief.

"Samuel, you will now recite the blessing for the *tallis*. And as your parents drape the *tallis* about your shoulders it shall symbolize that you accept the responsibilities and privileges of Israel's faith, law, and tradition."

Sammy recited in a loud clear voice, his earlier jitters gone: "Blessed art Thou O Lord our God King of the universe, who hast sanctified us by his commandments and instructed us to don the *tallis*."

Murray and his wife, each holding a corner of the white and blue striped prayer shawl, draped it around their son. Murray took his wife by the arm and escorted her back to their seats.

Rabbi and *bar-mitzvah* boy stood alone before the ark. Sammy climbed the two steps to the velvet curtain and tugged the satin cord. The *parocheth* opened to reveal six Torah scrolls encased in elaborately embroidered velvet and rayon and crowned with silver vestments. The congregation lifted its voice, and the ancient refrain from Numbers spiralled from the pews in a crescendo of song.

"*Vayehi binsoa ha-aron* . . . and it came to pass, whenever the ark was to journey forth, Moses would say, 'Arise O Lord and let Thine enemies be scattered; let them that hate Thee flee from before Thee'. Out of Zion shall go forth Torah, and the word of the Lord out of Jerusalem."

Fourteen

Ray Purnell flung off the quilted cover and twisted his beefy frame into a squat. He inched to the edge of the bed, dangling one leg and groping for his slippers with the other. His big toe touched the cold wood of the floor.

"Damn! Where the hell are those slippers?" His heel brushed against the felt. He plucked the slipper out from under the bed with his toes, carefully avoiding contact with the frigid floor. The left foot searched uncertainly for the mate; it found the slipper a little to the left. "These floors get damn cold in the morning," Ray muttered. Elissa had been pestering him to carpet the master bedroom, but he had spent fifteen hundred for the living room carpet last year and another thousand to refurnish the living room. How the heck did she expect him to do more on his income? He was no millionaire. Ray rubbed his eyes, ran his fingers through his receding hair-line, scraped his beard, scratched several times under his armpits. He pushed himself towards the bathroom, bleary-eyed and heavy-lidded. He tried the knob; the bathroom was locked.

"I'm in here, Dad," Tom's voice was muffled by the flushing toilet.

"Hurry up," Ray growled. "I gotta get in."

"Be out soon as I can," Tom shouted over the swoosh of of rushing water.

"Might as well go downstairs to wash up; that kid'll be in there another twenty minutes combing his hair," Ray muttered grouchily to the door. "If I could afford it, that's what I'd do—build another toilet upstairs."

Ray padded the length of the dingy corridor past Susan's room. Her even respiration came through the partially-opened door. Wonder what time she got in? He peeked into the room, his paternal instinct fleetingly asserting itself. Heck! What difference does it make? Suzy can take care of herself. Ray limped downstairs to the foyer bathroom. Elissa was hovering over the stove, making coffee, her back to him.

"Good morning, Raymond," Elissa called without turning. "You want me to start your breakfast?"

Raymond! Besides Elissa, the only one in Blueport who ever sounded his name in just that tone was priggish Miss Spencer, his teacher in the fourth grade. Peculiar how images blurred by the passage of long years are brought into sharp focus by the right catalyst. And Elissa had a way of conjuring up old maid Spencer in Ray's mind. Jet-black hair tied primly into a bun that touched her pinched shoulder blades. Body sparse and frigid, standing on spindly legs, two pogo sticks supporting a pole. Ray rankled at the resemblance. His wife's low-pitched, mannish voice grated on Ray's ears, particularly after her soporific performance the night before. Ray was no sex athlete, and he didn't expect acrobatics, but with the response he got from Elissa, he might as well take vows of abstinence; he was mated to a psychological celibate. The pity of it was he could do nothing about it, not in his position. He had to walk the straight and narrow; he couldn't afford to philander, even though opportunity knocked in the well-loaded pants of Jo Anne Prentiss, whom he had hired six months ago to fill a vacancy in the language department. Ray was sure that extra wiggle whenever they passed in the corridor was meant for him. More than once he was tempted to throw caution to the winds. But it wasn't worth it . . . risking a career for a piece of tail.

"Didn't you hear me?" Elissa turned demandingly to her mute spouse.

Although she leaned to the thin side, Elissa was by no means unattractive. Her large, dark eyes were set wide apart. The nose, a trifle long but ruler-straight, added a touch of the exotic to the sharp contours of her face. Her lips were pale and full. A dimple softened the square chin. Her breasts, small and firm, showed a cleavage over the low-belted bathrobe. Unlike Jo Anne Prentiss, Elissa's slender height evoked no fantasies. Elissa's was a more subtle sensuality, a promise held out to someone who had the finesse to realize its potential.

"Yes, I heard you," Purnell snapped.

"Then why don't you answer?" Elissa's dark eyes flashed.

"Good morning, good morning," Ray said through gritted teeth. He preferred to avoid a bout if possible, but his ego still smarted from Elissa's bored submission to his nocturnal lovemaking. "I'm tired in the morning; you're exhausted at night. So we're even."

Elissa ignored the barb. "I'll have your breakfast ready in twenty minutes."

Ray slammed into the bathroom and turned the faucet on full blast. Fifteen minutes later he emerged clean-shaven and tranquilized.

"The coffee is ready now, dear," Elissa said agreeably, blotting out the previous belligerence. "Do you want to join me?"

"Okay." Ray accepted the armistice. He was determined to have a quiet Saturday morning.

Elissa poured coffee and set a platter of assorted Danish pastries in the center of the table. Ray slumped into his chair, sinking his head down to meet the cup. He hooked a finger through the ear and raised the hot coffee to his lips. Elissa winced at the rolling slurp. Balancing the coffee precariously in one hand, Ray stretched across the table for the platter with the other. He grabbed a Danish, bit into it, and munched. Avoiding Ray's eyes, Elissa watched him chomp through breakfast. She selected a Danish, broke off a piece, and chewed fastidiously. Lifting her cup, little finger hooked, she sipped softly, then daintily returned the cup to its saucer.

"Raymond!" Elissa interrupted Ray's second grab for the platter.

"Yeah!" Ray's hand froze over a prune Danish. Elissa disregarded Ray's unspoken recommendation to let quiet reign.

"I think we should have gone to the *bar-mitzvah* services."

"What for?" Ray completed the grab for the Danish, anticipating, feeling trouble brewing. Whatever went on in Elissa's brain, once it found a voice it rarely failed to irritate him.

"Because we were invited."

"So what! I get invited to a lot of places I don't go to."

"We're going to the dinner tonight. Don't you think it would have been proper to go to the services?"

"Look, Elissa! Because I agree to eat their food and drink their liquor doesn't mean I'm obliged to join in their clap-trap."

"If you're willing to eat their food and drink their liquor, you should be willing to go to their synagogue to see their son's *bar-mitzvah*."

"Elissa!" Ray pronounced his wife's name as if it brought a sour taste to his mouth. "I like the food and whiskey Jews serve, but not so much that I'm going to subject myself to the garbage they serve in their synagogues."

"That's a despicable thing to say."

"Well, that's the way I feel about it."

"But why? How do you know what goes on in a synagogue? You've never been inside one."

"You don't have to be inside to know what goes on. What do you think they do? Mumble endless rituals in Hebrew. Call themselves the Chosen People, and derogate what Christians believe."

Delicate lines crossed Elissa's pale forehead; her mouth curled scornfully. "Not only are you a bigot; you're a hypocrite. Since when have you become a defender of the faith? When was the last time you went to mass? You haven't been inside a church since we were married, except at your mother's funeral. And I was surprised you went even then."

"That's got nothing to do with it," Ray sputtered. "I just don't like synagogues."

"But how can you like or dislike something you've never experienced?"

"Do me a favor, Elissa. Let's drop the subject," Ray's request was not a plea, but a warning. "We're going to the dinner; that should be enough."

Elissa cradled her cup, contemplating its steaming contents. She raised her eyes and searched Ray's face.

"Tell me, Raymond, why do you resent Jews so much?"

"What the hell!!! You ask me to join you for breakfast, and serve me an inquisition!"

Elissa's pale cheeks flushed. "I asked you a civil question. There's no need to shout."

"I'm not shouting," Ray struggled to temper his anger. "All I want is a quiet breakfast, without you hounding me about Jews. I got a bellyful of them these last few weeks as it is."

Elissa looked quizzically at Ray. "What do you mean? What happened?"

"The *Blueport Gazette* is your favorite reading material, isn't it? You read it cover to cover every week, don't you?"

144

"Yes, I like to read the papers thoroughly." Elissa let the sarcasm go by.

"Well! Didn't you read the letter to the editor by their rabbi?"

"You mean Rabbi Kleinman?"

"Yes, I mean Rabbi Kleinman. Whom do you think he was attacking? Yours truly. Me. Your loving husband. To add insult to injury, I asked your good friend Ira Cane whether Kleinman's letter represented the views of the Jewish community. The bastard assured me Kleinman wrote the letter on his own. He guaranteed he'd get the synagogue trustees to officially repudiate their rabbi's letter and make him retract. I'm still waiting. . . ."

"Why would Ira make such a promise?" Elissa interrupted. "It would be terribly embarrassing to their rabbi."

"Terribly embarrassing to their rabbi?" Ray exploded. "What do you think his letter was to me?"

Ray glowered at Elissa, enraged. "But you don't have to worry about Rabbi Kleinman, dear, loyal wife of mine. There's not going to be a retraction. Apparently Jews stick together. . . . Except for Ira Cane. He'll sell his mother for that one thing he wants more than anything he's got."

Although she shrank from Ray's low-keyed hate, Elissa asked, "What is that?"

"To get into Pinetree. And so long as I'm a member, that bastard is gonna be blackballed, along with all other Jews. Money bags Irving Cohen alias Ira Cane can screw his rabbi, screw his synagogue, screw himself, but he's not gonna get in. Not if I can help it."

Elissa stifled her disgust, rose, and lurched to the refrigerator. She groped inside; the refreshing chill cooled her revulsion. Passably composed she returned to Ray carrying a container of milk even though the one on the table was still almost full.

"Good morning, Dad; hi, Mom!" Tom hailed from the foot of the stairs; he stood between the kitchen and the foyer. Elissa looked up, concerned lest he had overheard Ray's obscene outburst. Well, it didn't make much difference; his bigotry saturated the house. There was no hiding it. She tried to shelter her children from their father's boorish influence, but it was impossible. Ray's venom, his bigotry, was more than she could handle or counteract. Tom walked over to his mother and dutifully pecked at her cheek.

"What's for breakfast, Mom? I'm hungry as a bear."

Morosely, Ray acknowledged Tom's presence and went for another cup of coffee. Elissa forced a smile at her son.

"Sit down. You can start with orange juice," Elissa directed. "It's on the table."

"How about some bacon and eggs?"

"Give me a chance to make it," Elissa snapped. "You just came down."

Ray glanced over the edge of his newspaper. "What time did you get in last night, Son?" he asked nonchalantly.

"Oh, it wasn't too late."

"Not too late!" Elissa charged in. "I didn't get to bed before two, and you still weren't home. Where were you?"

"Out with the fellows."

"Out where?" Elissa demanded.

"Oh, come off it, Mom. I don't have to give a detailed account of where I go. I'm almost eighteen."

"You went to Cap'n Sharkey's, didn't you?"

"So what if I did?"

"I told you, I don't want you there. You're bound to get into trouble associating with that crowd."

"Let him alone, Elissa," Ray intervened. "He's a big boy now. Natural for him to sow a few wild oats before they clamp the ball and chain on him." Ray gave his son a conspiratorial wink.

146

Tom joined his father at the table. The aroma of frying bacon wafted from the stove and filled the kitchen. Elissa served Tom but found a variety of excuses not to return to the table. She no longer felt up to suffering her husband anymore this morning. Even Tom irritated her more than usual; he gulped his food as if the seven years of famine were to begin within the hour.

"Take it easy, Son," Ray chuckled. "We'll need a crane to get you out the door."

Tom glanced at Elissa out of the corner of his eye. "You know how it is, Dad, us growing boys need all the vitamins we can get."

Ray watched his son fondly. The brief moments Ray spent with Tom gave him pleasure. Ray was proud of Tom, of the boy's tall, lithe frame, his clean Anglo-Saxon features, his muscles rippling under shirtsleeves. His son's virility and supercharged impetuosity carried Ray back to his own college days. It couldn't be more than yesterday that he had played fullback at Blueport High. He remembered it all so vividly—there wasn't much that could stop him once he broke through the line with that old pigskin under his arm. . . .

"Dad, I'd like to ask you something."

"Go ahead, Son. What's on your mind?"

"You know Eddie Thompson? He's in my class."

"Yes. I know the Thompsons. Fine stock. Eddie comes from a good family."

"Well, Eddie's older brother goes to Lehigh University. His brother told him about this guy George Stonehill. The fellows at Lehigh invited him to speak . . . oh, about three, four months ago. At first the administration kicked up a fuss, but finally they backed down and allowed him to speak to the students. Eddie said his brother thought Stonehill an interesting character. There was a question and answer period after the talk, and the guys lashed into him; you know Lehigh has a lot of Jewish students. But Stonehill, Eddie's brother said, kept his cool and handled himself neat. Anyway, they had a great debate, and everyone benefited by the give and take."

"So, where do I come into the picture?" Ray rattled his paper impatiently.

"Well, a few guys thought it might be a good idea to invite Stonehill to speak to our senior class. They got together, discussed it and elected yours truly to ask Mr. Rein, our government teacher, what he thought of the idea."

Tom's report cut into Elissa like a knife edge. The brazen insolence! She pictured the scene: Tom standing up in class, simulating naïve innocence, suggesting to Carl Rein, a Jew, that he invite a rabble-rousing anti-Semite to his class.

"So what did Rein say?" Ray asked.

"Rein didn't go for it at all. He nixed it and gave me a hard time for even suggesting it."

Climbing indignation roused Elissa from her silence. Ray's noncommittal attitude struck her as tacit approval of the whole rotten project. Her husband's nonchalance infuriated Elissa even more than Tom's impertinence.

"What did you expect Mr. Rein to do? Agree to invite that Nazi to spout hate to his class? Where do you get your gall?"

Tom gaped at his mother with lamb-like innocence. "Gee, Mom, what are you sore at me for? It's not my fault the fellows at school picked me to be their spokesman."

"But you didn't object, did you?" Elissa sizzled.

"No, I didn't object. Why should I? I mean, we get all kinds of kooks speaking to us. That's what Rein's been preaching to the class all year; we should hear every side of an issue in order to be qualified, intelligent voters able to make intelligent decisions. Why should I have objected?"

"You must admit he has a point," Ray said.

"No! He has no point! There is a difference between a

controversial speaker and a fanatic who publicly defends Hitler's genocide."

"I think it's worse allowing a communist who advocates the overthrow of American democracy to speak to a class. These commies are paid Russian agents; they're dangerous. Stonehill is a crackpot; he has no real following. What harm can he do?"

"Look, Mom. . . Dad," Tom intervened, his tone saccharine. "I don't want to start a fight between you. Maybe we ought to forget the whole thing. Anyway, I gotta go now. Have an appointment with Eddie at ten thirty. Want to study for a math test with him."

"Yes," Elissa agreed, her eyes flashing wrath. "We had better forget the whole thing."

Tom scraped his chair away from the table. He started for the alcove, hesitated, then faced his father again. "Before I go, Dad, I'm obliged to tell you. The fellows got up a petition. About thirty guys signed it. They asked me to show it to you. It's to allow George Stonehill to speak at the . . ."

Elissa's glaring rage arrested her son's ploy. Tom shielded his face in mock fright. "Don't get excited, mom! I'm not telling Dad what to do. I was asked to present the petition to him; I accepted the job. I just want to be able to tell the guys I carried out my assignment."

"Okay," Ray chafed, weary of the bickering. "Show me the petition."

"I can't show it to you now."

"Why not?"

"I haven't had a chance to get all the signatures again."

"What do you mean, again? Did you lose it?"

Tom slipped his hands into his back pocket, and swayed on the balls of his feet. "No, I didn't lose it. Gee, I'm not that irresponsible."

"So what did happen to it?"

"Well, as I said, I had the petition with thirty signatures on it. Then I came across Stanley Cane and Mel Gross—they're both in my senior class. Neither of them had signed the petition. I figured I'd ask them to sign. I handed the petition to them. . . ." Tom screwed his face as if trying to recall the exact details.

"Yes, go on," Ray urged.

"Cane took the petition from me," Tom proceeded. "And before I had a chance to stop him, he tore it up."

"Who tore it up?" Ray demanded.

"Stanley Cane tore it up," Tom repeated the lie with a straight face.

"And you let that runt kid get away with it?" Ray sputtered, incredulous that his son was so faint-hearted.

Tom shrugged. "Well, me and a friend were with a couple of girls. I didn't want to start a riot. Besides, it's no problem getting the guys to sign another petition. Especially after I tell 'em who tore it up."

Ray's puffed jowls flushed crimson. "All right, Tom. You make up another petition and bring it to my office. I'll give the matter further thought."

"Okay, Dad. As soon as I get the guys to sign it."

Tom pulled his hand from his pocket and covered his face, but not before Elissa caught the triumphant smirk. Hastily, Tom retreated to the hall closet, yanked for his windbreaker, and stepped out of the house.

Elissa struggled to control the tempest raging within her. She stared wordlessly at Ray. He picked up the newspaper lying at the edge of the table and rustled the pages to the sport section, oblivious to the hurricane about to erupt.

"The man is a psychotic rabble-rousing Nazi," Elissa's ire sliced the silence. "How can you even think of allowing George Stonehill to spout his poison in your school?"

Ray slammed the paper to the table. Up to a point he was master of his emotions, in control of the violence lying just beneath the surface. The point had been reached.

"You're damn right, it's my school. I built it to what it is. Who the hell are you to tell me how to run it? Now you listen to me, and listen to me good, Elissa," Ray mouthed his wife's name contemptuously then spat out his anger in a rising crescendo. "For five years I've had to put up with that bastard Irving Cohen on my Board of Education. Then I get a rabbi telling me when to close my school. Then the bastard's bastard tears up a petition signed by a class of Christian kids that my son is supposed to show me. If that's not enough, now my Jew-loving wife tells me whom I can't invite to my own school. I've had about all the crap I can take! I'm going to run my school as I damn well see fit."

"Run my school as I damn well see fit," Elissa mimicked. "You're not fit to run a school! You never were."

"Shut your skinny, priggish, sexless face!!!"

Elissa's cheeks, normally pallid, turned ashen. Accumulated rage pressed against her chest; bottled-up anger uncorked. It twisted and curled and pushed up to her throat, billowing and clamoring for release. Her eyes blazed demonically.

"You're sick, Raymond. You're sick, sick as Stonehill." The wrath inside burst forth. "I don't know what makes a Stonehill sick, but I know what's twisting your mind. You rotten bastard. Ira Cane. You hate him for what you think he took from you. You stupid fool! You never had her. Not for one minute."

"What the hell are you talking about, you bitch?"

"You know what I'm talking about. That's what's been eating up your rotten guts all these years. I thought I could make you forget her. It's no use. . . . It never was. You won't face the truth; you weak bastard. You could never face the truth about what you really are. A nothing, a zero. And she knew it. She never could stand you. I know; we were friends. You always were coarse. Vulgar. Foul-mouthed. She was too refined for you. I thought I could change you, so I took you in on the rebound. But it's no good. Once a pig, always a pig. You ruined my life with your twisted hate, and you've turned your son into the same bigot you are."

Ray stared open-mouthed, absorbing the bitter invective flowing unchecked. From a placid, self-possessed, dispassionate woman, Elissa had been transformed into a raging, uncontrollable shrieking hysteric. Unexpectedly, she lunged at Ray. Small clenched fists pummeled, flailed wildly, beating against his head, his neck, seeking his eyes. Sharp nails dug painfully into his neck.

"Face it! You lousy, rotten filthy bastard! Face it! Christine is Ruth now. Even if you could raise Hitler from the grave and incinerate every Jew, she wouldn't have any part of you. She despises you. . . . She always despised you. . . . She always will."

The blows rained down savagely; Elissa was a woman run amuck. Ray broke through her wild battering fists, grabbed both her arms, and curled thick, powerful fingers around her wrists, holding them rigid with his right hand. His left hand snapped forward, smashing backhand into Elissa's face. She buckled to the floor, doubled over at his feet, sobbing and whimpering. Blood oozed from one nostril and trickled down in a crimson line, cutting across her swollen lips to her chin.

Fifteen

Endlessly, like an infirm snail, the line filed past the rabbi; his arms pumped mechanically. Upstroke . . . downstroke . . . up . . . down . . . "Good *Shabbes*, Rabbi . . ." "Enjoyed your sermon, Rabbi." "Inspiring service, Rabbi." "Good *Shab-*

bes . . ." Faces blurred into hands. Which fingers his, which to the teeth grinning by? A three-hour-fifteen-minute service . . . took too much out of him. Would his legs hold out? Weak . . . Finally, the end in sight; thank God!

Though it was not traditional, before heaven ordained his *makkeh*, his ulcer, Kleinman had introduced the custom of the rabbi standing at the door to greet congregants; and no matter how long the line, he enjoyed the personal touch, particularly when he had preached well, and the Sabbath greetings were liberally sprinkled with praise for his sermon. Blueport's rabbi devoured applause like any performer. Ice clinking in a double shot of scotch at the *Kiddush* was also a delight to contemplate, and after the Sabbath salutations Kleinman would quickly doff his pulpit regalia and hasten downstairs. But all this was long ago when he still had the stamina of youth and health, and was allowed to wash down the sponge cake with something stronger than grape juice. Today he was too weary to even think of going down. He had to rest . . . just a few minutes. The rabbi surrendered to fatigue, falling into a light doze. A tap on the door chased his pleasant catnap.

"Come in." Kleinman shuddered to full wakefulness.

A short, stocky Negro entered. His face was as dark as a starless night. Perching on his head at a dangerous angle was a white *yarmulke*. He wore a polka dot bow tie, white shirt starched cardboard stiff, and navy blue pants pressed to a knife-edge crease. He marched authoritatively towards Kleinman, a tall glass in one black hand and a napkin in the other.

"I warmed up some milk for you, Rabbi."

"Warm milk?" Kleinman grimaced. The Negro held out his offering.

"That's what the *rebbitsen* said. When she gives me orders I don't ask no questions; you better not neither. Also toasted up a couple slices *challa*."

"All right, Bill. Thanks. Just leave it on the desk. I'll drink it in a few minutes."

Bill eyed Kleinman anxiously. "You okay, Rabbi?"

"I'm fine, Bill. Just a little pooped."

Bill handed Kleinman the *challa* and white napkin. The rabbi broke off a piece, recited the *"Hamotzi"* and chewed. Silently, Bill stood by watching; he pressed the warm milk on the rabbi. Kleinman agreed to several sips, then looked up at the frowning Negro.

"Do me a favor, Bill. Tell Mendelson I'll be a while coming down and to go ahead without me. Cantor Rosenberg can make the *Kiddush*."

Bill inspected Kleinman's tired face. "Why don't you skip this one altogether, Rabbi? You look beat."

"I'll be all right. Just tell Mendelson to go ahead. If the Golds ask for me, tell them I'll be down in a little while."

"Okay, Rabbi. You need anything, I'll be downstairs. Got to help my wife serve the *Kiddush*."

Bill Morely was the custodian of the Blueport Jewish Center. Two finer people than Bill and Eunice Morely would be difficult to come by. Even rarer was a Negro as knowledgeable about Jewish customs as Bill. He knew more about synagogue protocol than the president of the congregation, though in this instance that wasn't saying much. The couple had been working for the Center eight years now. Bill was sixty-four, and Eunice admitted to somewhere in the upper fifties. The two had become indispensable to Kleinman, particularly since his illness. Often the thought occurred to Kleinman that those two would make ideal Jews: their consideration and compassion had been cast in the crucible of suffering. Perhaps that's the catalyst his own people lacked. Success, prosperity, was hardening the Jewish heart. But suffering (Kleinman always circled back to the same conclusion) does not guarantee to inculcate sensitivity to another's pain. It would be interesting, though Kleinman sometimes found himself speculating, if a dozen black Jewish families moved into Blueport. What would be the reaction of his congregation? How would his liberals receive a dozen black Jewish families? *Ad nauseam* his liberals grumbled, "It's time the rabbi and the synagogue caught up with the times." Their homes were pig-*trayf*; the religious school taught *kashrut*. Kleinman preached about the sanctity of the Sabbath; they thought the whole idea of the Sabbath and of sanctity was medieval. The rabbi confused them and their kids; what's worse he creates conflict between home and synagogue; he's still living in some European *shtetl*.

A dozen Negro families applying for membership in the Blueport Jewish Center—that would provide his liberals with a real conflict. It was one thing to discriminate against a Negro. The Jew found it easy to fall in with the prejudice of the larger community. Negroes are uneducated, lazy, immoral, prone to violence. Negroes depress property values. But for one Jew to discriminate against another! That kind of bigotry does not yield to rationalizations so readily. Yes! A dozen Negro families. That would be a beautiful conflict for his liberals to take home. Or does their crusade to make the synagogue conform to the twentieth century stop at that point?

Bill turned to leave. "By the way, Rabbi. Mr. Schwartz was looking for you. Shall I tell him you're up here?"

"I'll see him when I get down. . . . No wait," Kleinman remembered his conversation with Schwartz prior to the service. "Please tell him I'm in my dressing room, and ask him to come up after he's made *Kiddush*."

"Okay, Rabbi." Bill walked out of the room.

Kleinman finished the milk, alternately sipping and chewing on the *challa* while trying to recall the joys of scotch and spiced hors d'ouvres that once were his reward for laboring through a *bar-mitzvah*. Gradually, strength ebbed back into his enervated limbs. Slapping his thigh, he hung up his robe and *tallis*, which he had carelessly strewn on the desk, and packed his pulpit skullcap into a cardboard box. He turned to the rap on the door.

"Good *Shabbes*, Rabbi."

"Good *Shabbes*, Mr. Schwartz."

Kleinman, familiar with the varying nuances of Schwartz' moods, detected a singular cordiality in the rasping voice. The grizzled features came close to a smile. Schwartz was pleased about something, which was as frequent as rain in the Negev.

"I didn't see you downstairs by the *Kiddush*, Rabbi. You are feeling all right, please God?"

"I'm fine, Mr. Schwartz. Thank you. Just a little tired."

"Well, you got a right to be tired. That was a long service. And one of the longest sermons I ever heard you give on a *Shabbes*. But I must tell you, it was a real *Shabbes davening*." Schwartz kissed his fingertips. ". . . *Geshmack!*"

Experience had conditioned Kleinman to live with Schwartz' criticism. Approbation coming from the old man was unsettling. Kleinman didn't know how to deal with it, so he just listened.

"And let me say also . . . your sermon? Maybe it could have been a little shorter. But good! Very good! I heard even the *goyim* talking downstairs how they liked it. I enjoyed very much how you interpreted the Joseph story. Very nice the way you made the application, how Joseph forgave his brothers. You gave it to them good . . . those three-day-a-year Jews; always criticizing the synagogue, always finding fault with religion. Only the bad they remember; they forget all the good things religion has accomplished. Yes! Very well put, Rabbi. I must tell you to your face."

Sensing possibilities in Schwartz' kudos, Kleinman squeezed into the opening. "Thank you, Mr. Schwartz. I'm delighted

my sermon made a favorable impression on you. Perhaps it
helped make you see the matter we discussed at the Board
meeting in a new light?"

"What matter?" Schwartz failed to make the connection.

Kleinman closed the circuit for the old man. "The matter
of Otto Hoffman."

The light still failed to go on. "What has that got to do
with your sermon?"

Kleinman flicked the switch himself. "It has a great deal to
do with my sermon. That's what I was trying to say. It's such
a waste to spend our lives bearing grudges, hating. Refusing
to forget and forgive."

The light darkened Schwartz' half smile, bringing back his
familiar scowl. "Rabbi! There are things that cannot be forgotten, things that it would be a sin to forget. Should I forget
that six million Jews were murdered by the Nazi butchers?"

"No, Mr. Schwartz," Kleinman said. "That must never be
forgotten. You are correct; it would be a sin for Jews to forget their martyred people. Still, Mr. Schwartz, we are *b'nai
rachamanim*, children of a merciful God. And we are supposed to imitate his mercy."

Kleinman felt his weariness returning. He sat down and
motioned Schwartz to a chair; the old man declined. Pressing
his hands to his temples, Kleinman looked up at Schwartz.
"Otto Hoffman was not a Nazi. True, he did not speak out,
he did not raise his voice against the horrors. Perhaps he
should be condemned for his silence. But let us remember
what our sages said: 'Do not judge your neighbor until you
are in his place.' Who can really say he would have had the
courage to stand up to Hitler in those terrible times? It is not
for us to judge Otto Hoffman. God has already passed judgment on him. Mr. Schwartz, I have heard his tale, and I tell
you, the sentence has not been light."

Schwartz' stony posture gave not a hint of softening.

Sharp, angry lines pulled his mouth taut. "Nothing can be compared to what the Nazis did to our people. Nothing! I condemn them. I hate, and I shall always hate, every German. Five brothers, *talmidey chachamim*, they butchered; two of my sisters and their eight children, more deserving to live than me they all were, the Nazis slaughtered. No! I will not forget. I repeat to you the words of our *Torah: 'Zachor es asher asa l'cha Amalek*,' remember what *Amalek* did to you." Schwartz smashed fist into palm; the pupils under his beetle brow dilated with hate. "Blot out the memory of Amalek from under the heavens. *'Lo sishkach.'* And I will not forget, Rabbi. Not in my lifetime. No, I will not let Otto Hoffman buy my hate for a few dollars; not for a million dollars. I wish to keep it. I wish to go on hating him and all that is his."

Kleinman felt himself being inundated by the torrent of hate pouring out of the old man; he kept silent, waiting for the bitter arraignment to run its course. Then slowly, speaking as much to himself as to Schwartz, he tried to work through his own conflicting emotions.

"Believe me, Mr. Schwartz, I also cannot forget the horror they inflicted on our people. The enormity of our tragedy is beyond calculation. Great centers of Jewish learning wiped out. Anguished cries of the tortured! Children led to gas chambers. These voices will never be stilled. I was a chaplain, Mr. Schwartz, and I saw for myself the aftermath of that bloodbath. Sometimes I close my eyes, and after all these years I still see the mountains of corpses stacked one on the other; corpses the Nazis didn't have time to burn. . . . And the living corpses, staring with eyes of the dead."

Kleinman held on to Schwartz' anger; he hoped to win his confidence by allying himself with it, then piercing it with an appeal to their common tradition. "I, too, cannot forget that horror. But, Mr. Schwartz, I am as you, a descendant of Avraham *Avinu*, and I must remember . . . we are both obliged to remember what our Torah tells us about the father of the Jewish people. How he, a mere mortal, confronted the creator of heaven and earth, how he pleaded with God to spare Sodom and Gomorrah. How he argued with the Lord, daring to question God's justice. Do you remember what Avraham said to God, Mr. Schwartz? 'Shall the judge of all the earth not do justly? If there are fifty righteous people in the midst of the city, will you sweep away the righteous with the wicked?'

"Imagine that, Mr. Schwartz! Avraham arguing with God to spare two perverted cities. And when God agreed to his terms, having the *chutzpa* to bargain: If there are forty, thirty, twenty, ten? And God agreed to that as well."

Fighting to bend the old man to his words, Kleinman became captive of his own emotion; his voice quivered. "Shall we, Mr. Schwartz, forget the mercy taught us by our father Abraham and remember only our hate?"

Kleinman's impassioned plea, his biblical references did nothing to lessen the old man's rage. In deference to the rabbi's position Schwartz fought to restrain himself, but the disgust he felt that a rabbi should rise to a Nazi's defense showed and distorted his features.

"Permit me to remind you, Rabbi, of one of your own sermons." Schwartz's posture was still correct, but antagonism chilled his words. "You said, and I am quoting you, Rabbi, 'The key to Abraham's plea is the phrase, *b'soch ha-ir*, in the midst of the city.' Abraham, you said in your sermon, believed that if there were fifty righteous men in the midst of all that wickedness, or forty, or ten, working, struggling to eradicate the evils, then maybe the city could be saved. But if the righteous sit on the sidelines with their hands folded, not caring, doing nothing to put an end to the horrors that surround them, such righteous people are of no use. For such empty righteousness Avraham would not have intervened, would not have expected the *Ribono Shel Olam* to spare Sodom and Gomorrah. These were your words, Rabbi. This is what you preached only a few weeks ago."

Over the years, Kleinman had developed a healthy respect for Schwartz. He was an inflexible fundamentalist, a traditionalist who would not budge. But he was sincere, and his intellect seemed to grow keener with age. In a battle of ideas, the old man was a formidable adversary. It was true; Kleinman did preach that sermon. Schwartz had quoted him almost verbatim. Once in every while this happened. An ordinary sermon, on an ordinary Sabbath. Words, thoughts he had himself forgotten, recalled to him, weeks, months, sometimes years after he had preached them. Uncertainty intruded into the rabbi's stance; still he could not capitulate to such hate.

"I'm pleased you recall my sermons so well, Mr. Schwartz. Nevertheless, that interpretation does not give us license to nurse our hatreds, to take indiscriminate revenge on every man who has associated with transgressors. The Talmud relates that Rabbi Meir was once angered by highwaymen who had waylaid him. He cursed them and prayed that they die. His wife heard the curse and demanded that he retract. 'Pray better, my husband,' she said, 'that the robbers repent. For when sins cease there will be no more wicked people.' Rabbi Meir heeded his wife's words. He prayed that the highwaymen repent. And they did."

Kleinman searched the old man's face for even a minor concession, some compromise. None was forthcoming. The features remained hard as steel. "Mr. Schwartz, I make no claim on behalf of Otto Hoffman's innocence. I do not justify his silence. He is guilty of not rising to fight the devil, but so are many others, besides Germans. There is no evidence that Otto Hoffman personally committed atrocities; he was not personally involved in Hitler's insanity; he was not a member of the Nazi party, and for the guilt he does bear, Otto Hoffman has paid dearly. . . . I know."

"Rabbi, I'm only a layman, not as learned as you. I am not competent to debate with you Bible or Talmud. But also I cannot forget my dead. I cannot forgive."

Schwartz lost control; the fury could no longer be contained. Hot anger made his voice tremble. His gnarled fist slammed into the desk. "And I will not *daven*. I will not be a member of a *shul* that takes one dollar from a German!"

Kleinman bounded from his chair and faced Schwartz at eye level. He looked into the old man's leathered countenance. He looked and saw the scar tissue, the pain of memories that would not fade, and immediately he checked his own anger at the stubborness of this rock who would not give.

"Mr. Schwartz," Kleinman sounded the name softly. "Apparently, I can't change your mind about Otto Hoffman. But let me remind you of a contribution made to the synagogue by one of history's first anti-Semites, a contribution we have readily accepted. All of us. You! Me! Every Jew that ever puts a *siddur* in his hand and davens. Each day we begin our prayers with his words: '*Ma tovu ohalecha Ya-akov, mishkenosecha Yisra-el*', how goodly are your dwelling places O Israel. And who wrote this prayer, Mr. Schwartz? Who contributed it to the synagogue? Balaam, a pagan prophet who set out to curse Israel and ended up by blessing us. . . .

"Good *Shabbes*, Mr. Schwartz. I must go down to the Gold *Kiddush*. They are waiting for me."

Sixteen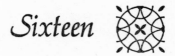

Canon John Robert followed Kleinman's knight with amused surprise; he boomed a demand for an explanation. "What's gotten into you, Morris?"

Kleinman hunched over, chin cupped in his hands, his eyes glued to the chessboard. "Oh, I just decided to experiment with a new opening."

The priest's brow wrinkled, pulling his eyes into a squint. "You, Morris, are experimenting with something new?"

Timidly, Kleinman met Robert's skepticism. "Why John, I'm really not that conservative now, am I?" Correctly divining what Robert's answer would be, given a chance, Kleinman jumped in with a reply. "I'm not averse to trying something new . . . occasionally."

With a curt wave, Robert brushed off the image of Kleinman in the adventurer's cloak. "In the five years we've been playing chess, Morris, you've opened with your queen's pawn eight out of ten times; the other two, you open with your king's pawn. Suddenly, out of the clear blue you spring a knight opening on me. I got a sneaking suspicion you bought yourself a book on chess openings . . . you did, didn't you?" Robert's finger stabbed accusingly. Laugh lines cornered the priest's mouth, betraying his glee at the cat and mouse game.

"Well . . . yes . . . as a matter of fact I did buy a book on chess openings." Kleinman stammered his *mea culpa* like a child caught with both hands in the cookie jar. "But you drove me to it. I was frustrated. I know I can handle you across the board. It's the openings, that's where you trounce me. . . . So I bought a book on chess openings. There's no law against it, is there?"

"No, I guess not. I suppose that's why they're published." Robert released a chuckle and moved his pawn to queen four with the self-assurance of a man who might have written the chapter on knight openings.

"Okay, Morris. Let's see how your investment pays off."

Kleinman squeezed the tip of his nose, contemplated Robert's move, then answered by a fianchetto of his king's bishop. Robert countered to queen's bishop three. Without hesitation,

Kleinman moved his pawn to queen's knight three. The Episcopalian minister tucked a finger into his stiff collar.

"Morris! Evidently, you've not merely bought a book on chess openings, you must have been up nights memorizing all the sequences. Is that cricket?"

"All's fair in love and war, and chess is war on a checkerboard. Now you won't take me on the openings. The game will be won or lost across the board."

"'Looks like this is going to be one long, tough war." Robert peeled off his collar and bent over the chessboard, the self-confident humor smothered in deep concentration.

Father Robert's stately home stood on the crest of a gently sloping knoll surrounded by an acre of lawn. The house overlooked Spring Glen Creek, which fed into the Great North Bay. Robert's love of chess was exceeded only by his passion for boats. In his youth he beat to windward and raced in many a choppy sea, and even now, well into his sixties, the minister's boat was one of the first to be taken out of drydock in early spring. On the tenth anniversary of Robert's call to St. John, his congregation, knowing of their minister's love for the sea, purchased an old Spanish style house in the Spring Glenn section of Manor Park, remodeled it from cellar to attic and presented the keys to the Roberts at a gala ceremony. With the keys came a thirty foot sloop.

The room in which the contenders sat, engrossed in the black and white chessmen, was panelled in dark mahogany. Heavy off-white drapes, tinged with rose, framed a wide picture window overlooking the patio, its flagstone floor now covered with snow. Red and pink flames flared from two logs crackling in the fireplace; their hot glow illuminated the Persian rug, heightening its rich multicolored tones. Snowdrifts hitting the fogged pane accentuated the quiet warmth of the room.

"Check!" Robert pronounced the warning to the king; his bishop stood at the corner of two diagonals, one leading to Kleinman's king, the other to his castle. Robert straightened up and rubbed his back; his deep set eyes reflected satisfaction. Kleinman chewed on his lips; his eyes crisscrossing the board. They stopped at Robert's black queen; the frown changed to a smile. He lifted his knight and set it between his king and the threatening white bishop. Kleinman sat back to await Robert's answer. The priest made no move to counter the threat to his queen; he seemed temporarily to have lost interest in the battle.

"Morris, I meant to tell you," Robert intruded into the quiet, "Ira Cane applied for membership at the Pinetree Country club."

"So." Kleinman gave his attention to the chessboard, congratulating himself on slipping through the trap.

"So, they'll reject him. Purnell's adamant on that subject. He'll do all in his power to keep Pinetree closed to Jews."

Kleinman pulled his gaze from the chessmen and looked at Robert. "Tell me, John. Perhaps you understand. Why is Purnell such an anti-Semite? Take away this inexplicable aberration, and he's an intelligent and capable administrator. What have we Jews ever done to earn his displeasure?"

"Purnell's anti-Semitism isn't entirely inexplicable, Morris. There's an explanation."

"What explanation?"

"Well, I'm not qualified to make psychoanalytical diagnosis, but it appears to me that Purnell's anti-Semitism is a product of a long-festering bitterness towards Ira Cane."

"Why should he dislike Ira Cane so much?"

"It all started a long time ago," Robert said. "With Ruth Cane."

"Ruth?" Kleinman wondered. "What does she have to do with it?"

Robert chewed the tip off a long fat cigar. He snapped the fin of a fish-shaped statuette; a flame spurted from the mouth end. Robert touched the snub nosed end of the cigar to the flame and inhaled deeply, letting the smoke out in slow rings. He offered the box to Kleinman; the rabbi, recalling his last ulcer attack, shook his head.

"Ruth is a convert to Judaism," Robert said, sending a second puff to chase the first. "I suppose you know that."

"Yes, I'm aware of it," Kleinman said.

"Before Ruth married Ira, she was one of ours, a member of my church," Robert stared meditatively at the widening rings of white as they floated ceilingward. "As a matter of fact, her family was one of the founders of St. John back in the late eighteen hundreds. I remember Ruth well. At the time, she was Christine. She attended our Sunday school, sang in the choir. Christine was a charming child, and she blossomed into a beautiful woman. The Purnells were also old stock, charter members of St. John. Not as well to do as the Harrisons. . . . Harrison, that's Ruth's maiden name."

Kleinman interrupted. "You mean the Harrisons, of Harrison Shipping, are Ira's in-laws?"

"Not by choice, Morris, not by choice. You can be sure of that." Robert smiled wanly at Kleinman's open-mouthed astonishment. "It surprises you, doesn't it? You think it's only Jewish parents who suffer traumas when their kids bring home the good news. When Emory Harrison was finally let in on the secret, he near flipped his fedora. He did everything possible to dissuade Christine. Warned her, threatened to disown her, never speak to her. Melinda Harrison tried to make Emory accept what he couldn't change. Melinda knew her daughter, and she knew that no amount of bullying would put her off. And Melinda Harrison preferred gaining a son-in-law, even if he was Jewish, to losing a daughter. Not the old man; he never made the adjustment.

"It had been taken more or less for granted that Ray would unite the Harrison and Purnell clans. But it didn't turn out that way; Christine had other plans. Looking at it with the wisdom of hindsight, it really wasn't so extraordinary. In those days, the few Jewish families in Blueport were most cordially welcomed. There wasn't even a sniff of anti-Semitism, I suppose because there were so few Jews. The Jewish kids attended school, mingled freely, were even invited to parties . . . though their parents rarely allowed them to accept. There was no Jewish problem then. As I recall, Ira—Irving Cohen at the time—and Ray were buddy-buddy. In those days they used to cruise as a duo all over town, including church dances. That, incidentally, is where Ira met Christine, at a church dance. Anyway, Christine and Ray never clicked. He was wild, unpredictable. She, just the opposite; sensitive, not shy but modest.

"And one day it happened. The kids stopped asking questions, stopped trying to mollify their parents. They just took off and eloped. Christine converted; she became Ruth, a Jewess, and the Cohens had no choice but to accept the marriage. Emory Harrison never really did. Most chagrined was Ray. Evidently, he had entertained the illusion that he was first on Christine's list. It was about that time that Ray became very much aware that his erstwhile buddy was Jewish. I suppose the embarrassment of that loss still lacerates him. That and Ira Cane's phenomenal financial success. What else does he have to convince himself that he is not a nonentity, but to keep Pinetree closed to Jews and Ira Cane out?"

A hush settled over the two men, underscoring the sound of logs crackling low in the hearth. Robert stretched for the poker leaning against the red brick and stoked the embers; rejuvenated flames danced from the floor of the fireplace.

"Well, Morris?" Robert returned to Kleinman. "Do you want me to act on Ira's application? I could force the issue.

If I speak out, the membership will have to listen. Ira could be the wedge to open Pinetree. Do you want me to try?"

"John! Pinetree's policies are of no concern to me."

"But they ought to be, Morris."

"Why?"

"Because they're excluding your people."

"It's a big county. My people can play golf somewhere else. In fact, they have a pretty fancy club of their own in Brentville from what I hear."

"You're not overly anxious to get Pinetree open to Jews, are you, Morris?"

"Candidly, no. Where Jews play golf is not uppermost in my mind. There are more important issues over which to crusade."

Robert refused to drop the subject. "I think, Morris, you're mistaken in taking the discriminatory policy of Pinetree so lightly."

Kleinman became brusque. "I'd like to play chess; it's your move."

Gliding over the rabbi's irritation, Robert relentlessly pursued the subject. "Aside from the social snub, Pinetree's exclusion of Jews is a distinct business disadvantage. Do you have any idea how many deals are made on the fairways?"

"You don't see many of my people on welfare, do you?" Kleinman snapped. "They're doing quite well, despite the handicap." Tempering his pique, he looked curiously at Robert. "Tell me, John, why are you so interested in opening Pinetree to Jews?"

Robert jumped to the challenge. "For one thing, I believe bigotry is out of order. Also, I think both Christians and Jews have much to gain by open lines of communication. Our people should be exposed to one another not only at formal brotherhood services or in business, but socially. More contact between our faiths would benefit all of us."

"There's no dearth of social contact between Christians and Jews. I'm simply not interested in Pinetree. It's your move, John. Let's play chess."

Robert persisted, stalking his prey with infinite patience. "I'm disappointed in you, Morris. I do believe you want to keep your people in splendid isolation. There's an ecumenical spirit abroad blowing fresh winds; aren't you at all interested in encouraging this new liberalism?"

Kleinman wearied of the chase; he pounced on the hunter. "John, you fancy yourself quite a liberal, don't you? And me, I don't know where you put me. Actually, I don't know myself to which camp I belong. But if you're really concerned about our interests, I'll give you a list. Get the missionaries off our backs, cut out the Christianizing in our public schools. Use your good will to rid the school of Christmas plays, Easter pageants, the "nondenominational" Protestant prayers. Have Purnell arrange football games and concerts and commencement exercises on days other than our Sabbath. Schedule some of the school's extracurricular activities on Sundays."

Robert stiffened; he looked offended. "You know I can't do that. After all, the school is more than ninety-percent Christian. I would be remiss in my duty as a minister of the Gospel to ignore the opportunity of exposing thousands of Christian children to Christian ideals."

Chess was pushed to the rear of Kleinman's mind; he moved to tear down Robert's declination, thrusting aside tact. "John, you're absolutely right. This is a Christian town, it's a Christian country, and we Jews are a minority. And we get more than enough exposure to Christianity from the cradle to the grave. Do you have any idea how the Christmas spirit blasts at the Jewish ear? Its thunder is deafening. And not only Christmas, but Easter, and all your holy days and holidays. Christ is all around us: on radio, television, movies, in the air we breath. We couldn't escape exposure if we tried.

So don't push me about my people getting too little exposure to Christian ideals.

"But just give this some thought, John." Kleinman pounded on the table; Robert watched in alarm as the chessmen jumped and fell back to position. "What kind of exposure to Judaism do Christians get? What do your people know about the faith that gave birth to Christ? I don't mean the kind of knowledge they'll get by playing golf with an Ira Cane at Pinetree. I mean authentic Judaism, from authentic sources. Why, your people believe that 'love thy neighbor as thyself' originated in the New Testament; do they know that it was first stated in Leviticus, in the Testament to which your theologians have condescendingly appended the adjective, 'Old'?

"I've conditioned myself not to wince when a Christian uses the word, Pharisee. To you, it's a pejorative. To us the Pharisees were scholars and saints. How many of your people, and I include priests and theologians who should know better, denigrate Judaism's phenomenal legal structure? Do they know, or have they even made an attempt to understand the purpose of Pharisaic legalism, which was to protect the orphan, the widow, to raise the poor, to establish a just society, to instill in the Jew a reverence for life? I admit we are top-heavy with ritual legalism, with laws that are superfluous to the ultimate ideal. But the church was no laggard either in the fine art of building complex structures of ritual irrelevancies, of theological absurdities. Has the church finally decided how many angels fit on the head of a pin? There is as much legal debris in the church as there is in the synagogue, if not more. Tell me, John, are your people and your children exposed to these truths?"

Not once throughout the passionate polemic did Robert flinch. Stoically, he absorbed the frontal assault, waiting for Kleinman to calm down. The priest's face still showed a paternal condescension, but the eyes seemed to have relented.

Which expression reflected Robert's inner feelings, Kleinman was unable to determine; perhaps both did.

"It may come as a surprise to you, Morris. I've been giving what you just said much thought long before I heard it from you today. As a matter of fact, I had a project in mind I wanted to discuss with you; this is as good a time as any."

Robert's cryptic answer piqued the rabbi's curiosity; his belligerence shifted to interest.

"I would like to send groups of teenagers from my church to the synagogue," Robert said. "Perhaps they might be given a tour of the synagogue building. See what the inside of a synagogue looks like. Sunday mornings would be convenient for us, if that fits in with your schedule. I'd like you to speak to them, explain the symbols, answer questions I know the kids will have."

Kleinman lit up at the idea. "Sure, John. That's an excellent thought; I'd be delighted. Any Sunday you say. Just give me about a week's advance notice so I can clear my calendar."

Robert showed pleasure at the speed with which Kleinman accepted his suggestion. The rabbi turned apologetic. "Sorry, I got carried away. . . . Now let's play chess."

"Okay! Just one more thing, Morris." Robert's matter-of-fact tone camouflaged the bomb he was about to drop. "The thought occurred to me. . . . You ought to become a member of Pinetree."

"John! I do believe you're getting senile."

The ministers' eyes twinkled merrily. "I'll remind you of that remark after I trounce you, your book of chess openings notwithstanding. But, seriously, why not? Every clergyman in town is offered an honorary membership. You're a bona fide clergyman. *Ergo*, you're entitled to membership in Pinetree."

"Don't be assinine, John. Where do I fit in a restricted

country club? A Jew, a rabbi yet? Where do you dig up these ideas? To make it more ridiculous, I wouldn't know which end to hold a golf club."

"You could learn. Every golfer has to start sometime. And you'd be amazed how much steam you work off on the fairways. Many a time I visualize one of my elder's faces on the ball as I tee off. Besides, the exercise would do you good; that spare tire around the middle could use some trimming."

Robert's eyes traveled downward, halted at Kleinman's midriff, then returned to his face; Kleinman was shaking it from side to side, amused and amazed at the outlandish proposal. But Robert was not to be deterred, under his deadpan features was serious intent. "I make you an offer, and I would consider it an insult if you turn me down. Ten lessons from my pro. He's a Scotsman, but still a fine chap and a good instructor. In no time you'll be making par and birdies."

"The only birdies I know have wings. Come off it, John. I can't accept, and you know it."

"Why not?"

"Because I don't belong at Pinetree."

"Yes, you do. You're a clergyman serving in Blueport. Just about the only one who hasn't been offered a membership. I can't force you to accept. But I'm determined that it be offered you."

Kleinman's wry amusement was turning to exasperation. "Oh, go ahead, and do what you want."

"I will, and I really believe you ought to accept. Unless you're worried that your faith will be shaken by socializing with us *goyim*."

"That's not funny, John."

"I apologize. I shouldn't have said that. But I think it's a great idea. Rabbi Morris Kleinman, member of Pinetree Country Club. Some eyebrows are gonna shoot right through their scalps." Gleefully, Robert swatted an imaginary ball as he contemplated the picture. "It could prove to be most educational."

"All right, John." Kleinman looked down at the chessboard. "I said my piece; now you move yours."

Seventeen

"Pay the man, Beth."

"But he was only here twenty-five minutes."

"Was the stove working before?"

"No."

"Is it working now?"

"Yes . . . but . . ."

"No buts; is it working now?"

Beth was not to be put down so easily. "But when I called him he said a service charge is seven dollars."

"So, he billed you the service charge plus eighteen dollars for labor."

"A dollar a minute?"

"You don't like the prices, don't call him again. But you've got to pay. Send him a check. Today. It's a month since he fixed the stove." Kleinman waved the bill under Beth's chin. "The Torah plainly says: 'The wages of a hired man shall not be withheld even until the morning.' "

"Baumgarten is not a hired man; he's the boss. And he's got more money than you'll ever see. . . . To charge his rabbi a dollar a minute; he should be ashamed."

Kleinman's patience was rapidly running thin. He reminded himself of the talmudic admonition: "A home where a man loves his wife as himself and honors her beyond his own person shall be blessed everlastingly." But some wives have a knack for trying their husbands' souls beyond endurance. And Beth had an infuriating genius for turning an argument on its head and boring a hole in his learned quotations. "You don't like his prices you don't call him again; but you pay him," Kleinman repeated the order with all his masculine authority.

"Okay, it's your hard-earned money," Beth abdicated gracelessly. "But I'm going to call the Better Business Bureau."

"Call whomever you like, but mail the check today."

Kleinman, triumphant though bruised, marched to his study to prepare for tomorrow's Bible class. He was cogitating over the problem of how to explain Jacob's struggle with an angel to a group of housewives ranging in age from thirty to sixty-five and in education from high school to one woman with a doctorate when he heard the door chime and a moment later Beth's squeal.

"We have a guest, Morris," she called. "One of your dear *chaverim*, an old friend has finally, finally decided to honor us with his presence." The sound of galoshes blurped into the study, followed by animated pleas.

"*Chatati, pashati;* I have sinned, I have transgressed; I beseech your forgiveness."

Kleinman peeped into the alcove. All he could see past the end of a wide china closet was one short leg of the mysterious stranger and a piece of posterior that held forth the promise of a generous portion to come.

"You don't deserve to be forgiven," Beth scolded. "Four years you're in Blueport, and not once do you have the courtesy to pick up a phone and call. I invite you to my house; not only don't you come, but I get a note back like it was in the refrigerator overnight, 'Sorry, due to other obligations . . .'

This is the way to answer an old friend?" Beth shivered at Rein. "Give me one good reason why you have avoided us; maybe then I'll forgive you."

Forsaking Jacob's battle with the angel, Kleinman rose to arbitrate this more immediate skirmish. The target of Beth's ire, standing meekly in the gray alcove light, turned as Kleinman entered. More than a decade had passed between encounters, but recognition was instantaneous.

"No! It can't be. It is," Kleinman exclaimed. He ran to grab Carl Rein's hand and pulled him into an embrace. "*Shalom aleychem! Shalom aleychem!* It's wonderful to see you."

Still enthusiastically pumping Rein's arm, Kleinman scowled at Beth. "A long lost *chaver* comes to our house, and you can't resist giving him a lecture for not coming sooner."

"Well, why didn't he come to see us in all this time?"

Kleinman glowered. "He didn't come because he didn't come."

"He didn't come because he didn't come," Beth mimed in a talmudic chant. "Now that's an answer to expect from a scholar."

Kleinman abandoned the debate; he released Rein's hand. "Carl, I apologize for my wife's behavior. Long ago I resigned myself to the fact that the last one able to control a *rebbitsen* is a rabbi." Rein made a feeble gesture of conciliation. Gently, Kleinman pointed him towards the living room.

"Sit down, Carl. Relax. She's got a terrible bark, but she doesn't bite." Kleinman turned to Beth. "Now that you've given your lecture, maybe like a good *rebbitsen* should, you'll show some hospitality and bring our guest something to eat and drink?"

"Please don't bother," Rein said hastily. "It really isn't necessary."

"Not necessary? Don't bother?" Kleinman looked offended. "In the four years you've been in Blueport, you haven't stepped into my house, and now you turn down my hospitality?"

Beth grinned roguishly. "So! Who's lecturing our honored guest now?"

Kleinman clung to his dignity. "All right, *rebbitsen*. That's enough! Go defrost something from the oven. . . . I mean the freezer . . . or wherever you modern *baleboostehs* get your instant dinners from."

Beth marched into the kitchen, pleased at having had the last word. Kleinman drew a chair opposite Rein. For a few minutes the men sat pensively.

"So, how are Sonya and the children?" Kleinman asked. "Saul, I read in the *Gazette*, was a Merit finalist, geniuses like the old man."

Rein smiled. "We're all fine, Morris. Just fine."

Kleinman drew a deep breath. "It's been a long time, Carl. You bring back some old memories."

"You sound like Methuselah," Rein grinned.

"You know, Carl, that's not a bad metaphor. It very aptly describes how I feel. As a matter of fact, not more than a year after I was *bar mitzvah* Rav Moshe Shtein already predicted that we would have a lot in common; Methuselah and me." Kleinman looked up to see if the name registered. "You remember Rav Shtein, don't you?"

"Remember Rav Shtein!" The exclamation left no doubt that the Rav was not forgotten. "What did you do to deserve that commendation?"

"Well, on one of those not infrequent occasions that my mind wandered from the *Gemara* we happened to be studying," Kleinman reminisced, "Rav Shtein asked me to recite. To my grief, I had lost the place. It was amazing . . . Rav Shtein could spot me daydreaming with his back turned; almost as if he had a built in radar receiving signals from my brain." Kleinman recalled his old teacher's prescience with awe. "I still shudder at those eyeballs piercing at me through his bifocals. 'Kleinman,' he screeched, brandishing that sawed-off cane he was never without right under my nose. 'You are like Methuselah. He lived nine hundred years, and when he left the world, all the *Torah* had to say about him was that Methuselah lived nine hundred years, and he died. If you live to be a thousand, Kleinman, you will amount to nothing and accomplish nothing." Kleinman pitched his voice high to better imitate Rav Moshe Shtein's prophecy. " 'You, Kleinman, will always be an *am haaretz*, a dunce.' "

Rein leaned back and merrily joined Kleinman in reminiscing about their boyhood escapades at the *yeshiva*. "You and Rav Shtein didn't get along too well, did you?"

"We had our differences," Kleinman conceded.

"Differences!" Rein chortled. "That's the understatement of the year. I still carry a picture of M. S. racing after you with that cane." Rein slapped his thigh, laughing as if the chase was still on. "I remember him cornering you at the door; you making that desperate leap to unhook the latch and barely escaping the old rav's clutches."

"Yes, I got the latch open in the nick of time. But he caught me on the next one and laced into me double." Kleinman massaged the back of his hand, laughing with Rein at the old bruises and old memories. Their laughter crested and ebbed. Kleinman looked questioningly at Rein.

"But you, Carl. You were the *masmid*, the scholar from a family of scholars. If anything, you should have become the rabbi, and I the rebel. How did it happen? What made you turn your back on it all?"

Rein's face clouded. "I suppose, if you were to retrace the route I've gone, you could say it began with '*bittul Torah*.' "

"What do you mean?"

"You remember Rav Margol?"

"Yes," Kleinman said. "Our *rebbe* just before we graduated to the *mesivta*. I think we were sixteen at the time."

"That's right. We were studying a *Mishnah* in the tractate *Kiddushin*. If I remember correctly, it was toward the end of the first chapter. The *Mishnah* states that, 'He who performs one precept will be rewarded, and his days will be prolonged.'" Rein spoke slowly, burrowing for thoughts long interred. "The *Gemara* goes on to debate that conclusion. In another context, the sage Rabbi Yaakov had asserted that wherever the reward for a *mitzvah* is stated in the Torah, it refers not to this world but to *Olam Habah*."

"Yes, I vaguely recall the discussion," Kleinman interjected. "Haven't looked at that *Gemara* in years, I'm ashamed to say; been too busy rabbinating."

"Rabbi Yaakov then cites Deuteronomy chapter five to prove his point. That verse commands, 'Honor your father and mother,' and it promises, if the *mitzvah* is obeyed, 'it shall go well with you, and your days will be prolonged.'" Rein thrust into the talmudic discussion, one thought stimulating another; his delivery gathered momentum as his agile mind retrieved forgotten texts. "Rabbi Yaakov cites another verse where the reward for obedience is explicitly promised; chapter twenty-two, also in Deuteronomy. There the *Torah* enjoins the Jew to spare the mother bird when taking her young. 'Thou shalt let the dam go, and the young mayest thou take for yourself, in order that it may be well with thee, and that thou mayest prolong thy days.'"

"It's fantastic how you remember the details of that *Gemara* after all these years. I've always been in awe of your photographic memory," Kleinman marvelled. "The passage comes back to me now. Rabbi Yaakov then relates an incident which refutes the *Torah*'s promise of reward for good deeds. He tells of a father who bids his son to ascend a loft and bring down fledglings nesting there. The son obeys, climbs the loft, sends away the dam before taking the young. On the way down, the boy falls and is killed. Rabbi Yaakov demands, 'Where is this man's happiness, and where is his long life?' This proves, Rabbi Yaakov concludes, 'Man's reward for good deeds is to be found not in this existence, but in paradise.' "

Kleinman was pleased with himself. "See, Carl. With a little assistance, I, too, can remember. . . . But what has all this to do with *bittul Torah?*"

For a moment, Rein withdrew into himself, as if he were struggling with more than a text, as if with the talmudic sages he had dredged up other memories.

"*Bittul Torah,*" Rein finally said, "was what Rav Margol screamed when I questioned the conclusions drawn by that *Gemara.*"

"That's strange; it wasn't like Rav Margol to discourage questions. He was the one who trained us not to take any opinion in the *Talmud* for granted. What conclusion did you question?"

"I questioned Rabbi Joseph's conclusion," Rein said; Kleinman's vacant stare indicated that he had pulled too far ahead. Rein slowed to give his friend's memory a chance to catch up. "Rabbi Joseph is the sage who maintained that if Acher would have known of Rabbi Yaakov's interpretation, that man should expect reward for good deeds only in paradise, he would not have sinned."

"Acher?" Kleinman pondered the name. "The Other, a euphemism for Elisha Ben Abuyah, the renegade rabbi."

"That's correct," Rein prodded. "Acher, Elisha Ben Abuyah, was one of four sages who entered pardes, the garden of mystical speculation."

"Yes, I remember that tale." Kleinman quoted the legend: "Four entered *pardes;* Ben Azzai, Ben Zoma, Acher and Rabbi

Akiba. Ben Azzai died, Ben Zoma went mad, and Acher became an apostate. Only Rabbi Akiba emerged whole. That story is a warning to all those who seek to penetrate forbidden mysteries, who demand the key to the way God runs his world."

"Yes, it is," Rein agreed. "And I suppose, I've long felt an emotional kinship with Acher. I admired him for having the courage to enter *pardes*, and I pitied him because of the raw deal he got from tradition.

"At any rate," Rein said, picking up his original thought, "the *Gemara* in *Kiddushin* recalls the tragedy that triggered Elisha Ben Abuyah's apostasy. He had witnessed the martyrdom of Huspit, who was tortured to death during the Hadrianic persecutions. When he saw the tongue of this great scholar dragged along the dirt by swine, he cried out in anguish: 'The mouth from which flowed pearls of wisdom now licks the dust.' After beholding his colleague's martyrdom, Elisha Ben Abuyah rejected God. Rabbi Joseph maintained that had Elisha Ben Abuyah known of Rabbi Yaakov's assertion that the righteous are rewarded only in another life, he would not have rebelled.

"Well, after class, I went over to Rav Margol, as I often did," Rein continued softly, "and I told him, perhaps a little too bluntly on reflection, that I don't agree with Rabbi Joseph at all. I said that it probably would have made no difference to Elisha Ben Abuyah; even if he had known of Rabbi Yaakov's interpretation, he would have rebelled."

Rein paused. "I can still see Rav Margol go into shock at my audacity. After the rav came to himself enough to ask me why I felt as I did, I answered, "Anyone who thinks about good and evil has got to have better answers than Rabbi Yaakov, which I don't think is an answer at all.' The temperature in that room dropped quickly. 'Rein,' the rav said to me, steaming, 'You will become an apostate like Acher. To dwell on such subjects is a sin. It is *bittul Torah*; a waste of precious time that you should better devote to subjects your mind can handle.' For the first and last time Rav Margol shouted at me, practically screaming at the top of his lungs. I just turned my back and walked out on him."

The involved recapitulation began to tell on Rein; sorrow and fatigue were written on his face. Kleinman's silence encouraged him to continue. "At the time, I was only dwelling on the subject, I was obsessed with the question of why the righteous suffer. A month before my falling out with Rav Margol I overheard my parents whispering about Saul. My brother hadn't been feeling well; he was losing weight and complaining of abdominal pain. They took tests and when they finally did an exploratory it was too late. They just closed him up. . . . Six months later he was gone. . . . I loved Saul. . . . I needed better answers than *bittul Torah*. Rav Margol couldn't provide them, so I quit and searched elsewhere."

Until this point, Kleinman had listened sympathetically. At the last allegation, however, he shook his head. "Come now, Carl. I can't believe that one episode with Rav Margol was enough to make you turn your back on God. You were too sharp, too knowledgeable, to expect final answers to such questions."

"Sharp or not, that started it off," Rein insisted. "From that moment I became obsessed with precisely the subject Rav Margol condemned as *bittul Torah*. I went to college. Studied philosophy, psychology, comparative religion. Before long, the whole foundation supporting my beliefs just crumbled."

"But, Carl," Kleinman objected. "I also went to college. I took the same courses. Sure they shook me up. They weakened some of the certainty, took out some of the smugness, but my faith wasn't shattered. I was forced to re-examine ideas I had once accepted as axiomatic. Still, nothing I was exposed to in college contradicted the basic truths of Judaism. My faith didn't provide all the answers, but, surely, neither did our professors. Descartes couldn't even prove he existed by a syllogism, so how do you expect to comprehend God's ways by intellectualizing? That's not the whole of it, is it?"

"No. That's not the whole of it. Do you want to hear it all?"

"If you want to tell me," Kleinman said softly.

Rein hunched forward, fidgeting with his cufflinks, clasping and unclasping his hands. "After college I went on to graduate school. That's where I met Sonya. My wife doesn't come from a family of scholars. In fact, what Sonya knew about her religion could be put on the back of a postage stamp. Sonya was just a bright Jewish girl with whom I fell in love. She was lonely; I was lonely. We decided to get married, and that's where the agony began. . . . You see, Sonya was a divorcée. At eighteen she married another kid of nineteen, and the two of them weren't ready to set up housekeeping. The marriage lasted less than a year.

"To make a long story short, Sonya's ex enlisted and was reported a POW. Civilly, she was divorced, but the idea of a *get* had never dawned on her; she didn't even know what the word meant. So, unless the enemy was prepared to set up a court of Jewish law so that Sonya's ex could give her a Jewish divorce, Sonya was an *agunah,* in limbo and prohibited from remarrying. At the age of twenty-one, Sonya wasn't ready to accept that kind of status. I didn't want to lose her. We got married by a justice of the peace."

"But you knew the *halakha;* you knew the law," Kleinman exclaimed, as if his objection could undo what had happened more than two decades ago. "You knew the consequences."

"Yes. I knew we would be considered adulterers and our

children bastards, forbidden forever to any pure-bred Jew. I knew the *halakha*." Rein's tone became abrasive. "But knowing the law is one thing, and being on the receiving end of an unjust antediluvian tradition is another. I was in love, impetuous. I thought eventually my family would come around and accept the civil divorce and my marriage as legal."

"You must have realized your father could never accept it," Kleinman protested.

"I said I was in love; young, impetuous. Did you expect me to just forget about Sonya? Lose her?" Rein's questions were accusations, as if Kleinman were responsible for the Jewish divorce laws. "Well, my father didn't accept. We had a son, made a *bris;* my father wouldn't come; he wouldn't step into my house. It tore me up—a grandfather not coming to the circumcision of his grandson! I decided not to *bar-mitzvah* Saul."

Rein's bitterness made his voice low and cutting. "Now that you've heard my story, Morris, let me ask you a personal question. What would you do if my daughter, the *momzer*—that's what she is according to the law, a bastard— would ask you five or six years hence to officiate at her marriage to a *halakhakally* pure Jewish boy, maybe your own son, you can never tell. What would you do, Morris?"

Rein drummed his fingers on the armchair, waiting for a reply. He studied the wan face, saw the consternation written in the troubled eyes and regretted having pushed so hard. The question was rhetorical. Rein knew the answer. Kleinman must either renounce the viability of *halakha*, or repudiate his own reason, his compassion. Till now the divorce laws had been no more than academic debating points. Suddenly all these problematic niceties were clothed with flesh and blood. The problems lived; they breathed. They affected the children of a friend.

The accordian partition screening the kitchen folded open,

Beth emerged, smiling and wiping her hands on the hem of a gay pink and blue apron bordered with white frills. Her eyes darted from mute host to voiceless guest.

"Have you two been sitting here all this time just looking at each other? Don't you have anything to talk about after all these years? Come on now, wake up; refreshments are being served in the main dinette. Maybe that will help start your mouths moving."

Rein bounced from gloom to cheer. "*Rebbitsen* Kleinman, My mouth has been moving too much, I think." He sniffed exaggeratingly. "That aroma coming from your kitchen, what is it? It smells like *Gan-Eden*. What delicacy have you prepared for this repentant sinner?"

"Permit me to answer on behalf of my wife," Kleinman joined in the new mood. "That aroma signifies that you are about to partake of the house specialty, cheese blintzes. My *ayshis chayil*, my woman of valor, has many talents, and outstanding amongst them is her cheese blintzes. I've considered giving up the rabbinate and opening a chain of cheese-blintz counters around the country.

"I can just see it. Her name in lights, the length and breadth of the nation: Blintzes by Beth." Kleinman waved a wide arc with both arms.

Beth interrupted her husband's dreams. "Stop talking so much nonsense, will you please, and sit down before my blintzes get cold."

Waving his hands in protest, Kleinman remonstrated, "First we are criticized for not talking, now for talking too much. A woman of valor I have found, but where is there to be found a woman that a man can please?" Kleinman escorted his chuckling guest to the dinette. The oval table was covered with a bright red table cloth. In the center, a heaping platter of crisp browned blintzes was companion to a cream pitcher filled with thick sour cream.

"Sit down, Carl," Kleinman beckoned Rein to a chair and slipped on a black skull cap.

"Got one for me, too?"

"Certainly," Kleinman said. He twisted to a long, low buffet within arm's reach and withdrew a bright red *yarmulke*. "Here you are, Carl. This one matches the table cloth, my booty from the last *bar-mitzvah*." He offered the platter; Rein took a blintz. Kleinman urged another on him and took three for himself. Scooping a full tablespoon of sour cream, he heaped it on his plate and skillfully dismembered a blintz, sawing it lengthwise and crosswise with his fork; he speared the cleanly cut slice and dipped artfully.

"Won't you sit down with us, Beth, and give us the pleasure of your company?" Rein pulled out a chair for his hostess.

"You two go ahead and eat," Beth said. "I'm just going to prepare coffee and cake. I'll join you in a few minutes."

Voraciously, the two men attacked the platter. They ate silently, each retreating into his own thoughts. After a third helping, Rein sat back, smacking his lips, His face boasted a newly acquired white moustache.

"Excellent! A dish fit for a king." Rein dabbed at his lips several times. "Long will I remember this delicious repast. You're right, Morris. You could package these *blintzes* and make a fortune." Kleinman smiled.

Beth reappeared, balancing an urn in one hand and a seven-layer chocolate cake in the other. She had exchangd her apron and shift for a smart wool knit suit; the flat shoes had also been replaced by high heels.

"Are you going out in this weather?" Kleinman said.

"Yes, dear. I have a Sisterhood Meeting. Rose Wasser called to remind me. I'm to deliver the invocation tonight."

"I didn't hear the phone ring."

"You men were so engrossed in those blintzes you wouldn't

have heard a fire alarm." Beth swung to Rein. "I'm sorry I've got to run. Help yourselves. Give my love to Sonya. And remember, Carl! I expect to see both of you . . . and soon. . . . Goodnight all!"

Kleinman pushed the cake towards Rein. "My wife's sudden entrances and exits take a little getting used to. Here, help yourself."

Rein cut into the cake, slicing off a small piece and pecking at it meditatively; his mood seemed to have picked up its earlier intensity.

"You know, Morris, I . . . I really had been on the verge of calling you a number of times. Somehow I just couldn't get the phone off the hook."

"No need to apologize," Kleinman said. "You're here now. Beth and I are pleased to have you."

"You both have been very gracious." Rein hesitated. "I feel like a cad, but I must confess there was an ulterior motive to my visit today."

Kleinman smiled knowingly. "The thought occurred to me that you might have some reason for popping in out of the blue other than old times' sake."

Rein grinned sheepishly. "I may have a photographic memory, but you, Morris, seem to have an uncanny talent for reading a man's mind. Maybe that's why you became the rabbi, and I the *apikoros*."

Kleinman accepted the contrast without comment.

"These last four years have been relatively good years for me," Rein continued. "I've enjoyed my work; Sonya is happy. It's a nice community, a good place to bring up children. Lately, though, I've been smelling anti-Semitism. At first it was a whiff. Now it's becoming a stink. When the school scheduled the opening football game on Yom Kippur, I figured it to be an honest error. Then exams were scheduled on the first days of Succoth. This, too, could have been nothing more than coincidence. After all, the school is preponderately Christian, so why should Jewish holidays be on the administration's mind? But when I saw the make-up tests, I began to wonder. They were way out of line, far tougher than the original, and several of our bright kids who had stayed out came through poorly. It bothered me; no matter how far a Jew strays, anti-Semitism rankles. But there was nothing I could do; the kids were given make-up exams, and I couldn't prove anything. I held my peace and went about my business teaching government.

"Two months ago I heard a rumor that the seniors wanted to invite George Stonehill to speak to their class. I discounted the rumors as scuttlebutt. It was inconceivable that the school would give that psycho a stage to perform on. The invitation was no rumor, . . . and the inconceivable happened: someone at the top consented. I've heard Stonehill speak. He's a candidate for the men with the white suits, but his is a crafty madness. To give the devil his due, the man is an effective, persuasive demagogue. He could very easily stir up the latent anti-Semitism in the school. I know those kids; they're ripe for trouble. I went to Dr. Purnell hoping to persuade him to cancel the talk . . . even though I had reason to believe that the project was initiated by Tom Purnell, his son. Well, Dr. Purnell was not too subtle about where he stood. He made it quite clear that I should be grateful for the privilege of teaching in Blueport High, and if I would like to continue, I had better stick to my knitting."

Kleinman was no stranger to Purnell's character. But this was outrageous. Kleinman's stomach, relatively quiescent these past weeks, warmed up. The thought of that bigot in charge of the education of thousands of students fueled his insides. Rein continued, oblivious of the fires he had started up in his friend.

"My first impulse was to resign; pack up and leave. After

thinking it over, I changed my mind. It would be reprehensible to abdicate without putting up some resistance. I decided to see you. The president of your congregation carries a lot of weight with the Board of Education. Possibly, pressure from on top would persuade Dr. Purnell to call off his mad dog."

As Kleinman reflected on Purnell's latest fiat, his rage began to subside. This time the superintendent of schools had gone much too far. Purnell had climbed out on a limb; perhaps with Rein's help he could saw it off.

"Do you think it's wise going over the head of the superintendant of schools? Whatever Purnell is, he's not dense. He'll put two and two together, and it'll add up to Carl Rein."

"That doesn't trouble me," Rein said. "We've simply got to stop Stonehill from infesting this town. I know him, and I know my kids. Bringing George Stonehill to Blueport would be like striking a match to a gasoline can."

"All right, Carl. I'll speak to Ira Cane." The grandfather clock chimed the half hour.

"It's eight-thirty. I've been here nearly two hours." Rein patted his stomach and pushed back his chair. "Delicious, Morris! Thanks for the refreshments and conversation; I'm beholden to you for both. It was good getting this delectable repast into my system and letting some of the frustration out."

The two men ambled to the foyer. Kleinman handed Rein his hat and coat. "I'd like to ask you something, Carl. If you think I'm out of line just say so."

"Go ahead. If you get too personal, I'll tell you where to get off."

There was no break in Kleinman's solemnity. "Our discussion before, it troubles me."

"You don't have any reservations about standing up to Purnell, do you?" Rein said.

"No. It's not Purnell. He's not the first anti-Semite we've

had to contend with, and I'm afraid he's not to be the last. It's the other matter we were talking about that disturbs me.

"Carl, you've collided with rigid *halakha*, and you've been hurt. So you elected to live outside the tradition. Tell me honestly, Carl, have you solved any of the mysteries of good and evil now that you've discarded God and Jewish law?"

Rein put on his coat slowly. The erstwhile *yeshiva bachurim* stared at each other. In both pairs of eyes there was earnest searching and turmoil.

"No, Morris. I haven't found the answers," Rein conceded. There was sadness and resignation in his tone, but not surrender. "I'm still plagued by the old questions. Good and evil, suffering and injustice. But you tell me candidly, Morris. You've stayed on the inside. Have you resolved them?"

For a moment Kleinman let the challenge hang between them unanswered, then thoughtfully he replied. "No, I haven't. You've disencumbered yourself of God and *halakha* and have resolved little if anything. I'm still carrying the yoke of the law and have fared no better. I think neither of us have resolved the problem of good and evil, because neither of us can come to terms with the injustices we see and experience. And I firmly believe that this inability to reconcile ourselves to them, our compelling drive to fight injustice even if it means challenging God himself, is something we have inherited with our *Yiddishkeit;* it is part of being a Jew. Our laws and traditions have woven a loathing for evil and injustice into the warp and woof of the Jewish soul."

"You're probably right, Morris. You're probably right. No one can completely divest himself of the past."

"Especially a Jew, Carl. Especially a Jew . . ."

Eighteen

Heavy snowplows armed with monstrous scoops had worked feverishly through the night, but the sidewalks were still an obstacle course with little more than narrow paths cut through the high drifts. Mounds of dirty gray snow piled flush against the curbs protruded into the streets in mountainous humps. Kleinman skipped over a pool of running slush and started across Main Street. The crisp white snow that had covered the streets during the night was now a dirty sludge beneath the skidding tires and sliding pedestrians. Kleinman weaved through bumper-to-bumper traffic that crawled along Main Street. Raising his collar against a sudden gust, he hopped gingerly onto the sidewalk and hurried for the entrance. The building, which Kleinman had passed countless times but never been inside, sprawled the length of Spruce street; although not the tallest, it contained more square feet of office space than any other in town. It was also one of the oldest, with ornate curlicues and sculpture in bas-relief that burlesqued the baroque excesses of the early 1900's. Kleinman strained at the iron fretted glass door; it opened to a complaining creak. He entered a dimly lit vestibule and trudged up a long flight that fed into a labyrinth of narrow winding corridors flanked on both sides by offices. His heels thumped heavily on the wooden floor, receiving an answering echo from the other end of the corridor. He stopped at 30–B and searched the opaque glass door for a name. There was nothing to indicate who, if anyone, occupied the office, only a number and a thin shaft of light from under the door. Kleinman pulled a scrap from his pocket and checked the number noted on the paper. Nervously, he mashed the scrap into a wad, vacillated a moment, drew his shoulders together as if girding for battle, then rapped firmly on the glass. Steps on the other side advanced towards the door; it opened wide.

When Kleinman had squeezed into the small, unpretentious hallway of Three Spruce Street he had felt mild surprise. The sight of Ira Cane's office made his preconceived notions spin wildly altogether. He had anticipated stepping into a spacious suite lavishly furnished, where some trim, modish receptionist would announce him over an intercom to a private secretary who would, after a respectful wait, usher him into the inner sanctum.

Poised before him instead, was a heavy-set, large-boned middle-aged giant in a blue knit blouse and matching skirt. the hemline of which almost touched her thick ankles. Glancing around the heavy-breasted matron, Kleinman took in a half dozen filing cabinets stacked against the naked walls. Except for the cabinets and a desk set at right angles to a window overlooking Spruce Street, the room, which was no more than an oversized closet, was bare. A wooden partition rising from floor to ceiling inset with translucent glass screened an inner office.

"Yes? Can I help you?" The high pitched lilt sounded incongruous coming from the burly Amazon.

"I'd like to see Mr. Cane, please."

"Do you have an appointment?"

"No."

"Mr. Cane is very busy. If you would state your business and leave your name, I . . ."

"I'm Rabbi Kleinman, Mr. Cane's rabbi," Kleinman impatiently cut in.

"Oh?" The lilt rose a quarter of an octave. "I'll tell Mr.

Cane you're here. I'm sure he'll find time to see his rabbi."
She moved to the screened cubicle.

"What is it, Lucille?" Ira's voice came through the screen
sharply.

"Rabbi Kleinman is here to see you."

A cracking noise that sounded like a chair smacking into a
wall followed the announcement. As if by magic Ira suddenly appeared besides Lucille, his face grim and unfriendly.

"Good morning, Ira." Kleinman's greeting was cordial, but
he made no move to enter.

"Good morning." Ira's frigid response contained no welcome.

"Something has come up that I'd like to discuss with you,"
Kleinman said. "If I could have a few moments of your time."

"I can't see you today, Rabbi. I'm busy." The rejection was
dry and curt. "Whatever it is, I'm sure it can wait until next
month's Board meeting."

"If it weren't important, I wouldn't intrude on your valuable time," Kleinman persisted. "As president of the Jewish
Center, I think you might spare your rabbi a few minutes."

"I don't need to be reminded of my obligations to the
Jewish Center," Ira retorted acidly. "My contributions to
the synagogue are generous enough. I can't spare the time;
I'm too busy."

The rabbi hesitated, as if considering whether it was worth
his while answering. He surrendered to the preacher in him.
"The measure of a man's generosity is the extent to which he
gives of what he treasures the most, not values the least."

Ira winced at the bite in the aphorism but continued to
block the door.

"But I didn't come to sermonize to you, Ira. If you can't
spare me any of your time, I'll handle the matter myself."
Kleinman turned to leave.

During the exchange, Lucille had been standing with her mouth slightly open. Suddenly, she sucked in a loud gulp, the lower lip caving in and vanishing under a row of widely spaced teeth. Her massive brow lowered in contempt.

Ira capitulated. "Okay, Rabbi. Let's see what's so all-fired important."

Kleinman had a powerful urge to get out and slam the door in Ira's face, but the promise to Rein harnessed his anger. He allowed himself to be led into the cramped inner room. Ira gestured for the rabbi to be seated.

"Lucille," Ira called over Kleinman's head. "What time is my appointment with Murray Gold?"

"Eleven-thirty," Lucille said. "But Mr. Gold called while you were on the phone. He said he'd be delayed about a half hour."

"Okay. Let me know as soon as he arrives."

Lucille compressed her bulk into the cubicle and closed the door. Ira glanced at his wrist watch.

"I got fifteen minutes, Rabbi. What's the problem?"

Kleinman plunged directly into the reason for his visit. "A faculty member at Blueport High informed me that George Stonehill was invited to speak to the senior class. Stonehill is an anti-Semite. He shouldn't be permitted to address high school students. The faculty member suggested that I ask you to use your influence as a member of the Board of Education and intervene to cancel Stonehill's scheduled talk." Kleinman spoke in clipped tones; he was coldly phlegmatic and indifferent, as if he had come merely as an agent and was little concerned with the response.

"Why didn't your faculty member complain through channels?" Ira snapped.

"He did," Kleinman said. "He went to Dr. Purnell. Dr. Purnell refused to do anything about it."

"So, your faculty member decided to go over the head of

the superintendent of schools," Ira's voice was scornful as he phrased the words faculty member. "Well, Rabbi! I'm glad you came after all. Now there'll be no misunderstanding between us. Even if I could stop this Stonehill from speaking, I wouldn't lift a finger. Why should I? This is a free country. The school has a right to invite anybody it chooses, and no one has any business interfering, least of all the rabbi of our Jewish Center."

"Thank you for your time, Ira . . . and your opinion." Kleinman's tone was empty of emotion: he rose to leave. "As I anticipated, I'll have to handle the matter myself."

The reply detonated Ira. He sprang up to face Kleinman; his chair swiveled a full turn, rolled backward and smacked against the wall. Ira's eyes showed a steel fury. "If you get yourself involved in a public controversy with the high school administration and embarrass the Jewish community again, I promise you, Rabbi, I won't rest till you're on the way out as spiritual leader of the Blueport Jewish Center! No matter the cost."

"Ira," Kleinman said wearily, "I think the cost of remaining spiritual leader of the Blueport Jewish Center is rapidly becoming prohibitive for me."

Kleinman turned, leaving Ira fulminating to his back, yanked at the door, and departed angrily from the cubicle.

"Pardon me, Rabbi!" Kleinman sidestepped to avoid collision; Lucille's knuckled fist, poised to rap on the door, was no more than three inches from his nose. Her flustered breath blew warm on his face.

"If you'll allow me to pass?" Kleinman said soothingly.

"Oh, yes. I'm sorry, Rabbi," Lucille apologized again and removed her huge girth from the threshold. As she cleared the door, Murray Gold's squat figure came into view. He was sitting on the edge of Lucille's desk with a black attaché case on his lap.

"Hi, Rabbi," Gold's warm greeting was mixed with surprise.

"Nice to see you, Murray," Kleinman said, pushing past Lucille. How's your wife and the *bar-mitzvah bachur?* I haven't seen Sammy since the *bar-mitzvah*."

"You know how it is once the kids are *bar-mitzvah*; they get busy with school, and a million other activities." Gold slid his rump off the desk. "But we're all fine . . . Are you through with our great leader?"

"He's all yours," Kleinman said sourly. "I'm finished with him."

Gold smelled the vinegar in Kleinman's reply. He shrugged. "Well, take care of yourself, Rabbi. See you."

"Send my regards to the family," Kleinman called. He nodded farewell to Lucille, and let himself out.

Gold squirmed past the secretary into Ira's office and settled into a chair. He attempted to maneuver one leg over the other; his knee came into painful contact with the metal edge of the desk.

"Either your office is shrinking, or I'm expanding," Gold whimpered, rubbing the throbbing joint. "It's getting harder for me to squeeze in here. I wish you'd get yourself a larger place."

Gold opened his attaché case, pulled out a folder and laid it on the desk. "Here are the closing papers, Ira. No problem, it's all legal. You donate the house to the Center; the Center credits you with a forty thousand contribution, I doubt you'd get twenty-five in today's market. So, the deal costs you nothing, and the Center doesn't have to build a new house for the Kleinmans. In fact, we might even get fifteen thousand for the old dump."

"A house for the Kleinmans?" Ira sat down, tapped a cigarette on the desk, lit it, and blew out an angry puff. "I'd like to give him his walking papers."

"That was no social call then, I take it," Gold said, pointing his thumb towards the outer office.

"No, that was no social call. Every time I see that character he manages to get my dander up. I'd add another five thousand in cash to get him sacked."

"It wouldn't be that simple, Ira. The rabbi is very strongly entrenched in Blueport. There's a lot of people who wouldn't go for it. Kleinman's picked up a lot of friends over the years. Even the *goyim* have taken a shine to him, it seems."

At the mention of *goyim* and Kleinman in friendly association, Ira instantly came alive. "What makes you say that?"

"Well, one of my clients, whom I just saved from ten years in jail for tax fraud, is on the membership committee of Pinetree. Yesterday I went to his house to get his signature on some papers. The guy was celebrating; he had a little too much and told me like I should feel greatly honored that the committee voted to give Rabbi Kleinman an honorary membership in the Pinetree Country Club."

"What did you say?"

"I said that our rabbi is now a member of the Pinetree Country Club. . . . What's the matter Ira? You look kind of pale."

Nursing a tantrum, Kleinman stomped into his study. Waiting for him was a note from Martha, written in her tidy cryptic scroll:

"Gone bank make deposit also lunch. Be back 1:30. Canon Robert called. Wants talk you. Will stop by 12:30. If miss each other call him at home. Martha."

It was twelve-fifteen; the morning had been a disaster. His own lunch could wait. He wasn't hungry anyway, and maybe Robert could lift his depression. Kleinman pulled a Bible from the shelf and sat down to wait. He flipped open his notebook and scratched a few notes, studied his scrawl, then petulantly ripped the page out of the book and tossed it into the waste paper basket. He made another start, with no more success. He was too upset. Ira had put him into too destitute a mood to think straight. He riffled through the Bible: Genesis, Exodus, Leviticus. The pages snapped past his thumb. Numbers—a verse jumped to mind. The verse and its implications had been lying, percolating in his brain, vague and undefined, ever since Carl Rein had brought him the news of Stonehill coming to Blueport High. Suddenly, the uncertainty lifted. For the first time he saw clearly; he knew exactly what he had to do. He had been fighting this battle stupidly all the way. You don't plead with the devil, you don't strike bargains with him, and you don't play by his rules, by any rules. You play to win, if you want to keep your soul. After days of vacillating and turbulent introspection the rabbi felt the relief that comes with the decision to act.

A knock announced John Robert and twelve-thirty almost at the same time. Kleinman went to open the door.

"A happy noon to you, Morris," Robert said cheerfully. "Glad you waited."

"Hello, John, come in." Restively, Kleinman pointed Robert to a chair and fell into his seat.

"What's the matter, young fellow?"

"Oh, nothing."

"Something is bothering you; I can tell. You got that harassed look; you know, like when I trounce you three in a row, and you can't wait to get back at me."

"Is it that obvious?"

"It sure is."

"Well, it's not chess; it's the congregation. Sometimes they can damn well drive you up a wall."

Robert reached across the desk and gave Kleinman a fatherly pat on the back. "Let an old timer give you a bit of advice on how to handle a troublesome congregation."

"Go ahead," Kleinman said, looking jaded. "I can use some sage experience."

"All you got to do is outlive them," Robert grinned. "Don't quit; just outlive them, as I did. Eventually, the trouble makers simply fade away."

"I didn't think you had them in your church."

Robert let out a long whistle. "Oh, we got our bundles, too; I can tell you, brother."

"Well, I have no intention of quitting. I will admit, though, there are times when I wonder whether the game is worth the candle."

"It is if you believe you are doing the Lord's work."

"I like to think I am," Kleinman said. "But sometimes I get the impression he's lost interest."

Robert's face turned coldly austere. "The Good Shepherd is always concerned about his sheep."

"You're right, John. I suppose we all need a talking-to occasionally; the job gets a little rough at times."

"The Lord's work can be difficult."

"And lonely," Kleinman added. He clasped his hands over the desk. "Now, what did you want to see me about?"

"Oh, yes. I almost forgot what I came for." Robert dropped the stern front. "This character the kids have invited to speak down at the high school . . . I suppose you've heard about it. What's his name? . . ."

"George Stonehill," Kleinman jogged Robert's memory, reining his own anger. "Yes, I've heard about it."

"Do you want to put the pressure on to get him cancelled?"

Kleinman began to answer, reconsidered, and held back. He looked down to the verse from Numbers he had printed in bold letters before Robert's knock: **"Behold it is a people that dwells alone, and is not to be reckoned among the nations."** He underlined the quotation with heavy pencil marks.

"No, thanks, John. I think I'll handle this my own way."

"Okay, but if you need help, call me," Robert said and quickly dropped the subject, "Remember, we have a game on Monday."

"Right!" Kleinman smiled for the first time. "You'll get another run for your money."

Robert saluted and left the study.

Nineteen

Casually, Mendelson sauntered into the Chaim Cohen Auditorium. As soon as he stepped into the room he was struck by the sober overtones. Conversation was hushed; the usual jollity before Ira's rap for order was conspicuously absent. The mood in the room augered serious business ahead. Mendelson spotted Schwartz and squeezed between two chairs to a vacant seat next to him. He tipped his spectacles down to the beak end of his nose.

"You think, Mr. Schwartz, if we should call for a special *minyan* on such short notice, we would get a fine attendance like this?"

"Everyone's turned out for this special meeting because we got a very serious matter to take up."

"All of a sudden the *minyan* is not so important to you like Board meetings," Mendelson gibed. "What we take up at the *minyan* is not so serious to you anymore, maybe?"

"Sit down, Mr. Mendelson," Schwartz commanded. "The president is calling the meeting to order."

"So, the president is calling the meeting to order. A *gontzeh megillah!*"

A no-nonsense scowl came from Schwartz; he was in no mood to joust tonight.

"My, my! Everybody is so serious. So all right. I'll sit down."

Ira rapped sharply for order. His opening was more brusque and imperious than usual. "Since this is a special Board meeting, we'll dispense with the reading of the minutes."

Ira was determined. No more kid-glove treatment; to hell with tact and political maneuvering. Tonight he was going to have done with it once and for all.

"Our contract with Rabbi Kleinman is due to expire the thirty-first of July. I want the Board to vote that we don't renew it, and I want approval to look for another rabbi."

Insofar as Ira was concerned the matter was settled. The function of the Board was to rubber stamp what he had already decided. For a moment, the room was silent.

"With all due respect to you, Ira, and what you've done for the Jewish Center, I think we're entitled to an explanation." Underneath Sy Wasser's conciliatory tone was unmistakable rebellion.

"I'll give you an explanation if you need one," Ira said in a voice that made it clear he felt no obligation to explain, but would, nevertheless, condescend to elaborate. "Kleinman's long been a trouble maker; now he's gone too far. The high school invited some character to speak to the senior class who doesn't meet with our spiritual leader's approval. So what does he do? He doesn't ask anybody. Doesn't consult with the Board. All on his own, our rabbi goes ahead and writes a letter to every parent of the senior class, on Jewish Center stationery yet, implying that the superintendent of schools is a bigot; that the principal of the high school is no better; that Blueport's school system is ridden with anti-Semites, and that the American thing to do is for the parents to call a strike in protest and keep their kids out of school until the administration cancels the talk. This town is predominantly Christian, and Rabbi Kleinman just doesn't give a rap how he compromises the Jews. He's made us taste bad in Blueport." Ira cut himself short; he searched the room. "Dr. Gross. You must have gotten this letter, too. What's your opinion?"

Gross kept to his seat. His reply was hesitant, barely reaching the chairman. "Yes, I received the letter. . . . I must confess it was intemperate."

Bolstered by Gross' reluctant support, Ira said, "That's it, then! There's nothing more to be said. Will someone make a motion that Kleinman's contract not be renewed?"

Dutifully, Sternberg raised his hand. "I so move, to . . ."

"Wait a minute," Murray Gold interrupted. "It's not that simple. Before we vote, we better consider the fact that the rabbi has tenure. He's been with the congregation now . . . how long?"

"Going on eleven years," Schwartz volunteered. "More than three times longer than any other rabbi we've had."

"Thank you, Mr. Schwartz." Gold returned to Ira. "According to the rules of the National Rabbinical Council, if we unilaterally decide not to renew the contract, we are obligated to pay severance. One month's salary for every year he's been with us. Now that would amount to a pretty penny. . . . Roughly, I figure it to be about twelve thousand dollars."

Ernie Gruber piped up from the rear. "Wow! For that kind of dough, Kleinman would probably change from rabbi to monk."

Jack Sternberg was not amused; he puffed hot and shouted across the room through his chewed up cigar: "Who's the National Rabbinical Council? This is not the Catholic Church. In our religion we got no Popes, and we don't have to take any orders from a rabbi's union. If they don't like the way our Jewish Center does business, they can return our annual contribution to the Rabbinical Seminary. In my opinion one month's severance pay would be more than generous."

"The Council may refuse to send us another candidate," Murray Gold countered. "What do we do then?"

The problem did not daunt Sternberg. "So, we'll apply to some other rabbinic group or advertise for a rabbi in one of the Jewish papers. I'm sure there are plenty of free-lancers who would be happy to come to Blueport. We pay a pretty good salary."

Approval fanned out, swelling and amplifying the tumult. The vice-president's bid for independence from the National Rabbinical Council had touched a responsive chord. Ira made no effort to bring the meeting back to order.

"Mr. President! Mr. President!" Dr. Gross shouted for the floor in an uncharacteristic outburst. Still chewing his cigar, Sternberg glared across the room at the irate physician. He sat down without further comment. All eyes shifted to Gross. "This is not a meeting anymore. This is a prearranged public hanging, out for the rabbi's neck."

"Now, just a minute," Ira protested. "Whatever will be decided tonight will be decided democratically."

"How can anything be decided democratically in this chaos you've allowed, if not encouraged."

Ira turned purple at the open accusation. "You've got something to say, say it."

"Thank you! It's kind of you to let me speak," Gross said sarcastically.

"I'm compelled to agree, as I stated before"—Gross forced calm into his voice—"that the rabbi's letter was out of order. And I still think the rabbi to be wrong. Free speech is a basic right. No matter how obnoxious the views of any citizen are, he has a right to express them, especially when he has been invited to do so. The man in question we all know is an anti-

Semite of the most vicious kind. Nevertheless, I believe there may even be some merit to the invitation. It's better, I think, that our young people be exposed to the harangues of this bigot within the controlled situation of a classroom. At least there the bigot can be challenged by rational minds. Again, I repeat, in my opinion Rabbi Kleinman is wrong in trying to deny this man his right to speak."

Gross paused to concentrate his argument. He stood tall and impressive, his developing logic arresting attention. "But free speech is a two-way street. If I argue the right of an anti-Semite to express his opinions, I'm not about to take that right away from my rabbi. An anti-Semite has a right to spout bigotry, and Rabbi Kleinman has a right to pen letters if he so chooses. There's nothing criminal in what he did; injudicious, maybe, but no more."

The doctor's convolutions were beginning to worry Ira; the son of a gun was shrewd. First sympathy with the cause, then the twist in favor of the rabbi. Perhaps Murray was right; Kleinman had many friends in Blueport. Had Ira overestimated his own strength and underestimated Kleinman's? No! Ira reassured himself. This town was too small for the two of them, and he was not the one who was going to have to pack his bags for a one-way trip to somewhere else. Not after that idiot thing Kleinman had done. To tell the truth, it was difficult to understand what had prompted him into such a blunder. It contradicted all that he knew of Kleinman's character. But there was no mistake. As hard as it was to believe, it was true; Ira had checked it out. Even Schwartz had stumbled on it and felt himself betrayed.

"Now, as to the rabbi's contract," Gross continued, "after giving much thought to the relationship between this congregation and Rabbi Kleinman, it appears to me that since we are at such odds, it may be better for the both of us if we part company. Personally, I believe the rabbi will be elected to another pulpit sooner than we will be able to find a replacement of equal calibre and integrity. Men like Rabbi Kleinman are not in large supply. Be that as it may. I don't deny the right of this Board to refuse to renegotiate his contract. If that's what we decide, fine. I'll go along, regretfully. But the majority rules. However, if we do not renew his contract, we are under a moral obligation to give him severance pay in line with the standards set up by the National Rabbinical Council. When we applied to the Council for a rabbi, there was an implicit understanding that we would abide by their rules. And one of those rules is tenure. I concede it may be better for Blueport that we terminate the contract and think in terms of electing a rabbi more flexible to our needs. But Rabbi Kleinman has served us more than ten years, and we are obligated to honor our agreements written and understood and give the rabbi the severance pay due him, one month for every year he has been our spiritual leader."

Gross sat down. Quiet reigned. No one asked for the floor. Sternberg nervously chomped on his cigar. The doctor's argument was compelling, and he appeared to have scored; Kleinman did have at least as much right to propagandize as Stonehill. Even Ira was visibly impressed. He mused over the logic, not overjoyed with it but resigning himself to the idea. It didn't pay to antagonize a man with Gross' broad influence over the issue of severance pay. What the hell did it matter if Kleinman was paid off to get him out of town? What was money for, if not to get what you want or get rid of what you don't? The important thing was to send him packing.

"Okay! I'm agreeable," Ira deferred. "We'll give him the full severance pay you claim he's entitled to, and if our budget doesn't allow for it, I'll increase my contribution to the Center accordingly. It's settled." Ira raised the gavel.

"Just a minute," Mendelson's voice stopped the mallet before it completed its downward swing. He stooped in the aisle, one hand resting on the back of Schwartz's chair.

"Would you mind waiting until a motion is introduced?" Ira let the gavel descend slowly to hit the table with a dull click. "Then you can have the floor."

Mendelson refused to yield. "Yes, Mr. Chairman. I would mind. Because even to introduce such a motion is a disgrace, and I want to give my opinion before it is made."

Dissent tumbled from the rear. This time Ira put it down quickly. "You got a right to your opinions, Mr. Mendelson, and you can give them to us after the motion." He banged hard on the table, brusquely ordering Mendelson to sit down.

The crack of the gavel unleashed Schwartz; he sprang to Mendelson's side. "It wouldn't hurt you, Ira, if you showed a little respect to a man twice your age. Maybe you could learn something."

The old man was obviously incensed at the discourtesy shown to Mendelson, but there was a lackluster quality to his bellow. The familiar fire and brimstone was missing. His challenge to the chair was relatively mild, suffused with a weary disappointment rather than defiance. Ira, however, was not prepared to chance an explosion. He remembered the last one and did not relish the thought of a repeat performance.

"Okay, Mr. Mendelson. You have the floor," Ira yielded. Schwartz sat down heavily, as if, for the first time, he felt the weight of his years. Mendelson glanced curiously at his friend, then addressed the chair.

"I have experience with men like Stonehill, Mr. Chairman. I remember how they used to stand on street corners when the Nazis were butchering Jews in Europe and tell the American people they should do the same thing to us here. More than once my store window was broken by young boys, whom those *momzerim* incited. Believe me! I was plenty

204

scared then, and I tell you, such men are still dangerous. Instead of sitting here talking about sending our rabbi away, a testimonial you should be making in his honor for trying to stop this *meshuggener* from poisoning the minds of young boys and girls. Yes! A testimonial he deserves for everything he has done for this synagogue, and for all the Jews in this community! Rabbi Kleinman has courage and honor." Choking with emotion, Mendelson was forced to stop momentarily. His hand, still clutching the back of Schwartz's chair, began to tremble.

"I realize I'm not a very important man in this synagogue," Mendelson found his voice after an awkward silence. "Big contributions like some of you make, I cannot afford. So maybe it makes no difference. But if this motion to send away Rabbi Kleinman comes to the floor, I resign immediately. I cannot stand to listen to my rabbi being insulted. He deserves not your insults, but your praise."

The trembling in Mendelson's hand moved up to his arms and shoulders; he appeared exhausted by the intensity of his passion. Ira studied the reaction of the Board in the stillness that followed. Sternberg shifted uncomfortably. Sy Wasser sat with his head bowed toward his feet as if his neck had frozen him into that position. Even Ernie Gruber had no wisecrack to suit the occasion. There was an unusual reticence to speak, an unnatural withdrawal into the quiet. Mendelson's emotion-charged defense of Kleinman had had an impact even greater than Dr. Gross' recondite presentation.

Affecting ignorance at the unpleasant task forced on him, Ira prepared to drop his bomb. "I didn't want to bring this up. I hoped it could be avoided. After all, Kleinman is a rabbi. But you leave me no choice. You say Kleinman has honor? Principles?" Though Ira's rhetorical query was in response to Mendelson, he was looking directly at Schwartz.

"What do you say to that, Mr. Schwartz, you agree?"

The old man cast his eyes to the floor. "I don't know! I don't know!"

"You can't say whether the rabbi has honor? Principles?"

"No, I can't say anything." Schwartz lifted his hands to his face as if to ward off Ira's cross examination.

Mendelson stared unbelievingly. "Why don't you answer him?" he almost screamed his question.

"I'll tell you why he won't answer you, Mr. Mendelson." Ira glanced at Murray Gold. Murray nodded. "Because Mr. Schwartz knows the rabbi is a hypocrite."

Mendelson staggered as if hit by a heavy weight. "You should be ashamed of yourself," he shouted with what seemed to be his last ounce of energy and fell to his seat.

Gross jumped up. "What right do you have to make such a statement?"

Sy Wasser stepped into the fray, anger splashing red across his face. "That's going too far, Ira. You may not fancy the rabbi, but he's always been honest and forthright, maybe too much so."

Schwartz sat impassive, withdrawn from the recriminations hurled at Ira. The old warrior's hunched posture bespoke tired resignation.

"Forthright? Honest?" Ira derisively tossed Wasser's words back to him and the Board. "Then tell me how do you explain our honest and forthright rabbi, who is fighting to rid the world of anti-Semitism, at our expense, how do you explain his becoming a member of a country club that wouldn't allow any one of us to step foot in the place?"

The bewildering news stunned Kleinman's indignant defenders into silence. "That's right! Murray can verify it. Our esteemed spiritual leader, self-proclaimed champion in the battle against bigotry is now a member of Pinetree Country Club. And if there is any doubt about my facts, ask Mr.

Schwartz; nothing happens in this town that passes by Mr. Schwartz."

No one bothered to ask; it wasn't necessary. The defeated expression on the old man's haggard face was answer enough.

Twenty

Ira steered his Cadillac between the two brick posts positioned at the driveway entrance. Cautiously, he negotiated the treacherous road; it had been cleared early that morning, but the wind had returned drifts onto the winding path, and driving up the incline was hazardous. Dusk was already dimming the white sheen covering Manor Park's gentle slopes. The sun, like Ira, seemed prematurely tired and ready to pull in the day. It hung low behind the sprawling L-shaped ranch, half an orange ball that projected its enfeebled radiance on the Great North Bay, making the icy water shimmer like beaten silver. Ira flicked a switch under the dashboard, beaming an invisible signal to the garage; the door lifted noiselessly into its sheath. He inched into the garage; the door dropped quietly behind him. Wearily he went into the house, headed straight for the bar, poured himself a jigger, and clinked an ice cube into the Scotch. Taking a long swallow and still holding the half-drained glass he trudged through the green reception hall. Brushing past the huge formal dining room, Ira parted the accordian doors and peered into the adjoining dinette. Ruth was setting the plastic topped dinette table. She was dressed in skin-tight slacks and a jersey top.

"Hi," Ira rotated the Scotch in his glass, nursing the pleasant thought of pulling her slacks down right then and there.

"Good evening." Ruth's welcome home was not encouraging.

"Where's Nancy?"

"She's away."

"I thought her day off is Tuesday."

"It is. She had an appointment with the doctor this afternoon, so I told her to take the rest of the day."

"So, you're chief cook and bottle washer today," Ira tried to sound like the sympathetic husband.

"I don't mind," Ruth said. "Stanley won't be home tonight; it's just the two of us."

"You mean, we're alone?"

"Yes! We're alone."

"Now that's nice for a change," Ira grinned lasciviously. Setting the glass on the table, he ambled over to Ruth and amorously circled her waist, gently pulling her towards him. She broke loose, turned her back, and walked wordlessly to the formica-topped kitchen cabinet.

"Hey, honey! I'm home," Ira fretted. "How about paying some attention to your loving spouse?"

"I'm preparing dinner," Ruth said frigidly.

"I get the feeling tonight I'm gonna be served a hot dinner with cold shoulder," Ira complained. "What did I do wrong now?"

Ruth swung around. She looked at Ira, frowning; her blue eyes flashed a warning. "I spoke to Beth Kleinman today."

"Yeah? What did she have to say?"

"She told me what happened at the Board meeting."

"So, Kleinman sent his wife to cry on your shoulders?"

"He didn't do anything of the kind! I met her at the hairdresser's. We both use the same girl to do our hair. Beth has the appointment before me. Sometimes she waits, and we go for lunch. I could tell the minute I saw her something was wrong—she was trying to avoid me. I insisted she wait. It took me all of lunch to drag it out of her. That was a rotten thing you did, calling the rabbi a hypocrite. You, of all people. You're the one who can't sleep nights because they won't let you into that lousy country club."

Ira scooped the glass from the table and drained it. "That's different."

"Why is it different?"

"Because I'm not a rabbi, and because I don't search under my bed for anti-Semites. Every other day he's denouncing the *goyim* as bigots, or sounding off about assimilation. Then he goes and joins a restricted country club. Yeah! I'd say he's a hypocrite."

"He never joined Pinetree. That was your version."

"What do you mean, he never joined Pinetree?" Ira railed. "I happen to know for a fact that the membership committee voted to accept Kleinman's application to the club."

"Well, your facts are all twisted," Ruth said positively.

Ira wavered at her certitude. "How are my facts twisted?"

"The rabbi did not apply to Pinetree," Ruth said belligerently. "Beth told me how the whole thing came about."

Ira lifted the glass to his lips, tilted it, then remembered it was empty. He slapped it to the table, lit a cigarette, and squinted through the smoke at Ruth's deepening scowl.

"Rabbi Kleinman and Canon Robert have a weekly chess game. They happen to be good friends, despite what you say about the rabbi considering every Gentile to be a bigot. All the clergy in town are invited to play at the club. It was Robert who recommended the rabbi. As you are well aware, Robert has some influence in Blueport. So the committee gave the rabbi an honorary membership. There's as much chance of Rabbi Kleinman using that membership as you being appointed deacon in Robert's church."

"Okay, so I was wrong about the application," Ira conceded.

"Okay, so you were wrong?" Ruth said, infuriated by his bland confession. "You pressure the Board to fire the rabbi, and all you have to say is, 'Okay, so I was wrong about the application." She struggled to hold back the rising tide of indignation. "Tell me, Ira, what is there about the rabbi that makes you dislike him so? What do you have against him?"

"He rubs me the wrong way," Ira said tartly.

"But why, Ira?" Ruth's question was almost a supplication. "He's conscientious, dedicated to his profession. The Temple has done very well since he's been here. The membership likes him. Even the non-Jews respect him. Beth is a doll. Why are you set on forcing them out?"

"If Kleinman had stuck to his job and kept his nose out of the public school, he could have stayed on for life as far as I was concerned. But no! Not him! He wasn't satisfied with being rabbi of our synagogue. Only last week he was in my office asking me to go over Purnell's head to cancel out the invitation to this guy Stonehill, because he doesn't approve. I warned him to mind his own business.

"But nothing stops our rabbi! He went ahead anyway. Didn't give a damn about what I said, or the trouble he would start. Where the hell does he get his damned nerve, calling for students and parents to strike the public school? . . . and calling Purnell a bigot?"

"But Purnell is a bigot; you know that better than anyone else," Ruth said vehemently. "And an invitation to a warped mind like Stonehill is our rabbi's business. He would be remiss if he did nothing to stop that anti-Semite from spewing his hate into our kids' minds."

"Look, honey, it's over and done with. Finished. The Board voted not to renew Kleinman's contract. Okay. He'll get a job with some other congregation."

Catching Ruth's surging anger, Ira stopped his own steam. He stretched for her waist and tugged her close. "We're not letting him go empty-handed. He's gonna get a nice fat check as a going-away present. We'll all be better off. Now let's forget about it." Ira pulled her tighter, one hand climbing into her slacks. "How about us flying South for a week of sun and sand? We'll get away from it all. Get a new perspective on things."

Ruth pushed him off, disdainfully rejecting his amorous advances. "Maybe you need a new perspective on things, Ira, but my vision is very clear. You pressured the Board to force the rabbi out in order to get in the good graces of Ray Purnell. Isn't that it? You're hoping he'll put in a good word for you at Pinetree, aren't you?"

Ira extended his arms in a plea for conciliation. "Ruth, you shouldn't get involved in this. It really is none of your affair."

"It is my affair," Ruth insisted agitatedly. "I'm involved. We have a son in the school. We live in the community. When an anti-Semite tries to turn the country against Jews we're all affected."

Ira gestured futilely. "I don't understand why anti-Semitism sets you off so. After all . . ." The thought was aborted before it found a voice.

"After all, I what?" Ruth pressed.

"Nothing! Forget it."

"No! Go on, Ira. Finish what you meant to say," Ruth goaded.

"Don't push, Ruth," Ira held back his own smoldering fury.

"After all . . ." Ruth persisted, ignoring Ira's plea to call a halt. "I wasn't born into the tribe. Isn't that what's on the tip of your tongue?"

"I didn't say that."

"No, not with words. It's written all over your face."

"Ruth you're treading on thin ice."

"Maybe I am. Maybe I'll fall in. Maybe we'll both fall in and be washed clean."

"Stop it, Ruth," Ira grabbed at her wrist; her contempt and rage made him release his grip.

"No! I won't stop it." Her tone was thin and slicing. "That's why I appealed to you in the first place. That's why you married me. Wasn't it? Because I was a *shiksa*. That's what you would have liked me to remain, Irving Cohen's *shiksa*. That's why you resented my trying to live like a Jew. That's why you kicked up such a fuss over my keeping a kosher home, as if it were such a great sacrifice on your part. That's why you discouraged me from going to temple. Even ridiculed me for lighting candles. You wanted to keep me a *shiksa*. Laying me gives you that feeling of being in with the *goyim*, doesn't it?"

Ira reeled at Ruth's savage attack. The fortress he had structured, which had provided him refuge, as uneasy as it was, swayed precariously. Ruth's cold rage coiled around his armor; it divined the chinks and crevices, entering, penetrating. He felt himself painfully exposed.

"Please, Ruth. Psychoanalysis is not your forte." Ira felt himself slipping, coming near to panic.

"I don't have to be a psychoanalyst to see through you!" Ruth's wounded pride and bruised ego blinded her to the debacle she was inviting. "You've been sending signals for years. It shows in everything you say and do. Your obsession to get into that stinking country club. Your irrational dislike of Rabbi Kleinman, whose only crime is that he faced up to Purnell's bigotry and is trying to keep an anti-Semitic lunatic from infecting this community. Your ridiculing me for trying to make this a Jewish home. I don't have to be a psychoanalyst to understand what I mean to you. I'm your *shiksa*. Well! To hell with you. I'm fed up. If you want a *shiksa* so desperately go out and find one. I'm a Jewess!"

Involuntarily, Ira's right arm elevated; the back of his hand poised over Ruth's head. She stood her ground, glaring in icy defiance.

"Go on, Ira, hit me!" Ruth thrust her flushed face upward, daring Ira, challenging him to complete the swing. "Beat your wife. That will qualify you for membership at Pinetree. Both of us, a *shiksa* and her *shaygets!*"

Ira's arm descended, froze. Suddenly, he pivoted, hurtled from the room, and slammed the portico door. Ruth dropped weakly into a chair. The roar of a car engine turning over reverberated angrily through the house, drowning out Ruth's muffled sobs.

The skid screeching in from the driveway reached her only vaguely. Then, all she could remember was the nightmarish crunch of the impact, the crash of metal ramming into concrete.

Twenty-one

Another *Shabbes;* another sermon to prepare. How many had he preached since coming to Blueport? Kleinman cogitated in the quiet of his study. Figure an average of two a week, no preaching in July and August. That still leaves about eighty-four a year. Close to nine hundred in ten years. Then there were the festivals and holidays, the eulogies, unveilings, and wedding talks. Testimonials and memorial services, lectures and special events. Messages in the synagogue bulletin. All in all, about three thousand sermons, speeches, lectures, and messages. A plethora of words.

Not too many more now, his days in Blueport were numbered. Soon he was to change trains. Another pulpit, another community. Ira Cane had won. Kleinman was convinced that Ira's was a pyrrhic victory. What Ira craved—acceptance, self respect—would continue to elude him. And the congregation unfortunately was the loser, caught in the crossfire of a man falling over himself to grasp a mirage and his rabbi trying to educate Jews to distinguish between illusion and reality.

Thoughts of the enforced parting dispirited Kleinman; it was like saying adieu to family. Several youngsters nearing *bar-mitzvah* were children of couples he had married. Another few years, and these kids would themselves be ready to stand under the *chuppa*. To officiate at the marriage of young people whose parents he had united in marriage . . . yes, that would have been a fulfilling experience and undoubtedly to the parents as well. His presence under the *chuppa* would have imparted a sense of continuity and added another dimension of meaning to those rites of passage. Such is the happy dividend accruing to a rabbi who manages to hang on and to a congregation that helps him. Too bad he would not be here to share with them in those joys. Kleinman indulged his self-pity.

As rabbi, he had become intimately involved, often entangled in the lives of his parishioners. He shared their *simchas*, their sorrows, and their secrets. For ten years he listened to their plaints and problems. Most of them picayune, petty, but many legitimate and critical. To some he represented an outworn irrelevant tradition; to others he epitomized all the wisdom embodied in the Jewish heritage. And it was the latter image that troubled him most. Their trusting naïve endorsement served to exacerbate his growing sense of inadequacy. He was called upon to dispense counsel in exigencies that demanded far more wisdom than he possessed. How often had he stood impotent before the questioning gaze of a child in pain, of a young widow. How many times had he looked down in mute frustration as the open pit claimed its note long before it was due. "Dust thou art, and to dust shalt thou return." But why a child? A bride? A young mother, a father in his prime? Why to dust even before one has lived? It had taken many agonizing tragedies and much excruciating introspection before he gained insight into the healing power of simple silence, before he discovered the comfort a sympathetic ear can bring and the strength that flows to a troubled soul from one who listens with sincere concern.

But his departure from Blueport was not to be all black. In this cloud there was literally a silver lining. True, his ego was deflated at the involuntary change in venue. Nevertheless, in some ways Ira had done him a favor. Kleinman was assured by the Seminary placement office that he need not be concerned. He had top priority and would be the first to be considered for any congregation available, and several important ones were pending. Evidently, his record at Blueport was impressive. Ten years! No rabbi before had come close; either they had given up the congregation as hopeless or were forced out as he now was. None had lasted more than three years, most less. So, he had no worry about being elected to another pulpit. And the severance pay, almost a year's salary, was more money than he ever had at any one time. Now he and Beth could take that long hoped-for and often postponed trip to Israel. Yes. He should write Ira a thank you note.

And a new congregation. New people, new challenges— that was also something to look forward to. Maybe it's better for both rabbi and congregation to make a change after ten years. You look down to the same faces, speak to the same crowd week after week, go through the same routine day after day, month after month for ten years, and you can't help but fall into a depressing rut. The change of scenery was beginning to look good. And Beth, too, would adjust. She was becoming more amenable to the idea and was already planning which movers to use, even though they still had no idea where they might be going.

To get back to the sermon. He was still rabbi of the Blueport Jewish Center and had a sermon to preach tomorrow night. What should he speak about this Sabbath? He flipped to Exodus, looking for an idea . . . the breakthrough to freedom . . . but only the beginning of a long, arduous trek to nationhood. Through the harsh desert without and the confusing wilderness within before the promised land would be sighted. A ravaging devastating trip. And the towering figure urging them on in alternate bursts of love and wrath. Slaughtering the neophytes who backtracked to Baal, yet daring oblivion to demand forgiveness for his people from the awesome power they had provoked. This was the one man who might have been deified by the Jew.

Kleinman paid silent tribute to the intuitive genius of the tradition in concealing for all time the burial ground of Moses. If his sepulcher were known, there was no doubt but that it would have been venerated as a shrine. He, who consigned to fire the golden calf, ground it to powder, and cast its ashes to the winds, would himself have been raised as an idol. Had men discovered Moses' burial place, they probably would now be hawking souvenirs and picture postcards at his grave. Yes, there was profound wisdom in forever screening from men the grave of this monumental emancipator and lawgiver.

Kleinman's thoughts roamed freely. Fascinating to consider, he mused that this spiritual giant, God's first missionary, shrank from his assignment. Moses hesitated, vacillated, insisted that he was unequal to the task. He simply didn't want the job. Reluctantly, only after much prodding, to the point of angering the Lord, did Moses agree to be God's spokesman before Pharaoh and Israel.

Kleinman searched the first chapters in Exodus. He shuffled through the thumbworn pages, stopped, peered intently at a verse, and shook his head in amazement, as if he were seeing it for the first time.

"And Moses said to the Lord, 'Please O Lord! I have never been a man of words, either in times past, or now that you have spoken to your servant. I am slow of speech and slow of tongue.' "

This man—who had broken the shackles of a slave people, led them out of bondage, molded and consolidated an amorphous rabble into a cohering nation, and pulled from heaven the secret of angels a revolutionary concept of God, man, and the universe—this man was tongue-tied! Kleinman recalled the *Midrash* that described Moses as a stutterer. And a good thing he was, too, the thought struck Kleinman. If Moses had been as glib as some of our modern spiritual leaders, Pharaoh, in all likelihood, would have overtaken the Hebrews and whipped them back to the pyramids while Moses was orating to the Red Sea. Yes. That's a good title for a sermon. Kleinman found his inspiration . . . "The Eloquent Stutterer."

Suddenly, the phone's sharp ring burst uninvited into Kleinman's meditations. He picked up the receiver.

"Your wife wants to talk to you," Martha said.

"Put her on."

Beth's voice skipped over the wire between breathless gasps. Kleinman became alarmed.

"What is it?"

"Ira! He's been in an accident. Ruth just called. She's frantic. They quarreled. Ira ran out of the house and smashed up in the driveway. She's at the hospital. North Oaks. Go over right away, Morris. She's all alone and blaming herself for the accident."

"I'm going."

"Call me as soon as you know anything."

"Yes."

In one bolting motion Kleinman slammed the receiver, grabbed his coat, and bounded from the building. He raced to his car, his coat open and flapping in the gale, oblivious to the cold moist wind sweeping down Ocean Avenue.

The odor was familiarly pungent to his nostrils as Kleinman hurried down the corridor. A nurse wearing her angelic cap and harried face pushed an oblong cart on rubber cushioned wheels. Strapped to the wagon, a woman lay supine and apathetic between green hospital sheets. Kleinman had walked these halls for ten years and had seen patients wheeled to operating rooms times without number. Yet these sheeted bundles being carted to surgery never failed to send a dismal chill down his spine.

Kleinman followed the turn in the corridor and stepped into the waiting room. Ruth was alone; she sat rigid on a cushioned bench, staring blankly at the green wall. Her puffed, bloodshot eyes were as bleak as the dismal weather outside. The tension and fear playing over her features stirred Kleinman to pity. He bent, took her hands in his, and caressed the long, trembling fingers.

"Oh, Rabbi! I almost killed Ira. I almost killed my husband," Ruth sobbed; tears ran untended down her cheeks.

"How badly is he hurt?" Kleinman tried not to show his own fears.

"I don't know. I haven't been able to see him; he's still in surgery," Ruth answered between tight, pulsing cries. Suddenly, she wrenched her hands from Kleinman and brought them to her face. A tall figure clad in a green surgical gown with a surgical mask dangling from his neck hurried towards them. Dr. Gross smiled.

"He is a very lucky man to even be alive, but he'll be okay."

"Thank God!"

"He'll be limping for a few months. He smashed his knee cap, but we should be able to rebuild it almost as good as new."

"Can I talk to him now?" Ruth's brimming eyes implored.

"You may look in on him if you want, but I gave him a sedative; he's sleeping now, Ruth." Gross noted with concern the pyramiding after-effects of her ordeal. She seemed near collapse, as if only the tension of waiting to hear had held her up till now.

"I suggest you go home and get some sleep also. You'll be able to talk to Ira in the morning." Gross pulled off his cap; he loosened the string to the surgical cap, letting it fall into his hand. "I leave Ruth in your care, Rabbi. See that she goes home directly and gets some rest."

"I will," Kleinman promised.

"Ira will be fine. You'll have him home inside a week." Gross patted Ruth's hand. He left and disappeared at a turn in the corridor.

"Come, Ruth, I'll drive you home." Kleinman held out her coat. She stayed bolted to the bench, staring up at him with wet eyes.

"What am I going to do, Rabbi?"

Kleinman let her coat fall back to the chair; he sat down beside her. "Do you want to tell me about it?"

"We quarreled. It was horrible. I was horrible." Ruth shivered. "But, Rabbi, I couldn't help myself. After Beth told me what Ira did to you at the Board meeting, I saw red. He had no call . . . no right."

Kleinman showed annoyance. "Beth shouldn't have involved you. She shouldn't have said anything to you."

"She couldn't help herself . . . just as I couldn't. To see you torn apart like that! How could she keep it in?"

"None of this would have happened if she hadn't involved you in our problems," Kleinman insisted.

Ruth shook her head. "It's not Beth's fault. This was a long-overdue battle. It had to explode sooner or later. . . . I love him, Rabbi, but I don't understand him. I try; I tried all through our marriage, but I just can't." Ruth looked up at Kleinman with barren, desolate eyes. "Why doesn't he want me to live like a Jewess? Aren't I a Jewess, Rabbi?"

"Of course you are, Ruth," Kleinman said, confused by her doubt. "Why do you even ask such a question?"

"But he doesn't want me to be a Jewess," Ruth wept with dry eyes. "I did everything I could to make a Jewish home for my family. I really did. But he made it so hard for me. And I must have something to believe in. Maybe Ira can live without believing. Maybe he's strong enough. But, Rabbi, I c n't. I must have a religion."

"It's that bad?" Kleinman sympathized.

"It was awful, just awful." Ruth shuddered as if touched by a cold hand. "I told him he married me because I was a *shiksa*, that he wanted me to stay a *shiksa*. In all the years we've been married he never lifted a finger, but today he was ready to hit me. He almost did. Then he ran out of the house and nearly killed himself. . . ." The tears which apprehension and fear had blocked now spilled out in a rush. "Oh, Rabbi! What am I to do?"

Kleinman heard her out, patiently waiting for the hurt and guilt to run its course, appreciating that she had to vent her feelings but recognizing that she must be made to understand that her husband, too, had deep needs.

"Ruth! Hear me out carefully, and try to follow what I'm going to say to you." Kleinman looked into the tear-filled eyes, lovely even in their despondency. He pulled at her attention, hoping to quicken to insight the love he knew she still felt for Ira. "There are many reasons why a man and woman marry, many things that attract two people enough to make them want to share their lives as husband and wife. Essentially, it is need—the expectation of fulfilling certain needs, needs of which we are often not even consciously aware. One deep need Ira has, and I emphasize one because his love for you goes beyond any one thing. One of his needs is to be accepted by Gentiles. And as a Gentile who loved him, you fulfilled an important need. This is no reason to feel hurt or resentment. There are far stranger impulses that drive a man and woman to seek fulfillment in marriage."

Ruth stared uncomprehendingly. "You want me to forget I'm a Jewess?"

"I didn't say that, and I didn't mean that."

"What did you mean?"

Kleinman became stern, appropriating for himself the role of a father figure, who after reason fails falls back on parental authority. "I mean, don't resent Ira for what he feels, and don't interpret his need as a denial of love for you as a person. Be a Jewish wife and mother as you have been all these years. Continue to make a Jewish home for your family. But don't condemn Ira because he still sees you in the light of his own need. Show him that you, who were once a Christian, elected to live as a Jew and found truth and beauty in Judaism. Eventually he will be convinced that you are a Jewess for no other reason than that you want to be. When that time comes, he will be able to live with himself and with you, as you really are. You, Ruth, must convert Ira. From a sense of worthlessness to self-respect."

Kleinman held out his hands; his face softened. "Come, Ruth. We'll look in on Ira, then I'll take you home. It's been a long hard day for you."

Twenty-two

Approximately one hundred strong, Blueport High's seniors queued into the oversized lecture hall. The high-domed, brightly-illuminated room was built like an amphitheatre.

Ten tiers of laminated desks, each desk provided with its own folding chair padded in a cool mauve fabric descended to the bottom of the semicircular bowl at the base of which was a platform and a lectern flanked by six chairs. Sloping upward from the floor half-way to the ceiling, two giant windows afforded a panoramic view of the athletic field, now topped by an unwrinkled layer of snow. Beyond the field a threatening nimbus floated under the sun, casting a dark shadow over the frozen bay.

Prattling garrulously, shoving, and playfully jostling one another, the students scrambled for seats. Suddenly, as if on signal, the tumult broke off. Adam Kent, principal of Blueport High, pushed through the door. He stretched tall and sinuously, the crown of his black toupee almost brushing the lintel. Pivoting his string-bean torso, he beckoned at two men in the hall to enter and follow him.

Carl Rein watched with undisguised disgust as Kent escorted them down the aisle to the podium. The man immediately behind the principal, striding with an erect martial gait, was about forty of medium height with wide, powerful shoulders. His square chin exuded confidence. The nose was long and straight. Widely-spaced eyes, high forehead, and closely-cropped hair graying at the temples lent his ruggedly handsome features an air of resolute intelligence. He was dressed conservatively in a two-button pinstriped suit. His black pointed shoes were polished to a mirror-like sheen.

Trailing third like a marionette marching in cadence was a pimply-faced youth, slightly built and barely older than the seniors about nineteen or twenty. Rein hadn't expected a tea party, but this apparition took him by surprise. It wore black jackboots and a brown tunic tucked into a wide black belt, which was fastened by a heavy, silver buckle. The bicep of the robot's left arm carried a black band bordered in silver. In the center of the band a white square highlighted a crimson sword, its cutting edge serrated. The red hilt of the sword formed an inverted cross. A billed cap set at a smug angle over the thin face bore the same insignia. He toted a red attaché case in his right hand. To Rein, the uniform, the walk, the stance, all screamed, "Heil Hitler."

"Mr. Stonehill," Adam Kent invoked his guest's name as if it were holy, "this is Carl Rein, head of our social science department." Smiling benignly, Stonehill offered his hand, a hugh bear-like paw with manicured fingernails. Rein stared down at the visitors as if they had come with the black plague. Stonehill's hand hung suspended and empty. His smile flattened, freezing on his face. He let his hand drop slowly, only a slight tremor curbing the edge of his mouth reacted to Rein's disdainful brush-off.

"The class is yours," Rein said dryly. He hopped from the platform, leaving the principal to the care of Stonehill and his robot-like partner. Kent's unhappy grimace followed Rein as he scaled the tiers to the top row and sat down. Muttering apologies, Kent showed the guests to the chairs on the platform. He rose to the lectern, cleared his throat several times and scanned the audience.

"Today, boys and girls, we will demonstrate to you, not merely by words but by deeds, how democracy works," Kent proceeded to wave the flag of country and Blueport High. "Your class petitioned the school administration to permit a man of highly radical views to present his side. After due deliberation, the faculty in consultation with Dr. Purnell, our superintendent of schools, decided that exposure to diverse points of view will enhance your appreciation of the democratic process, which is the basis of our American heritage."

Pompous and patronizing, and oblivious to the yawning, shuffling, and chair-scraping, Kent droned on. Tom Purnell, seated in the fourth tier, three desks to the right of Mel

Gross and Stanley Cane, showed his elation. He turned and gave a snickering glad hand to the boys. Stanley's eyes locked onto Kent's Adam's apple, which bobbed up and down. Mel Gross slouched in his chair, his long legs extended, ankles crossed under the desk, a picture of indifference to Tom Purnell's sneer and Adam Kent's tedium.

"It is for this reason that the faculty and administration have agreed, and I believe wisely, to invite our guest to present his point of view to us," Kent went on ad nauseam. Finally, he concluded his apologia and dissertation on democracy. "This, of course, does not imply that we endorse the opinions of our speaker today. I trust you will give him your respectful attention. Following the address the floor will be open for questions. Boys and girls! I give you Mr. George Stonehill, who will speak to you on the subject, "Dangers to America Today.'"

George Montgomery Stonehill rose smartly to a scattered burst of applause. Adam Kent sat down and settled back comfortably. Stonehill positioned himself in front of the lectern and stood motionless, only his eyes shifting from side to side. Several moments passed. Students and faculty gave their full attention to the podium. An anticipatory silence filled the room. The sense of expectancy and drama mounted. Stonehill's opening was abrupt.

"Fellows and girls! You're to be congratulated for inviting me."

Stonehill downshifted to studied modesty. ". . . not because I'm so special, or there's anything great about me. No! I'm just an average citizen. You're to be congratulated because you want to hear the truth spoken by an American who loves his country, and you had the guts to say so."

Having captured his audience, Stonehill lowered his voice as if he were speaking off the record and taking the students into his confidence. "And let me tell you, it's getting harder for any American who believes in America first even to get a chance to speak. . . . That's why I congratulate you for inviting me."

Stonehill's tone was calm. He spoke without histrionics. Yet there was an intensity, a flair to his posturing that pushed his presence forward, demanding and getting attention. He crossed his arms, relaxing over the lectern, and modulated his voice to convey sincere man-to-man talk.

"I'd like you to chew on this, men. And you are men. Your country will soon be calling you to defend these United States of America. Now, I ask you, men, why is a large and powerful nation like ours having so much trouble with the gooks in Vietnam? We should be able to stomp on them, crush them like the ants they are. No reason why we couldn't have polished them off in a week without losing so many of our fine, red-blooded American boys. Why couldn't we beat the gooks in Korea? Why did we have to settle for a stalemate there? We got the power; our boys have the guts. Nobody can deny that. Nobody knows it better than the gooks." Stonehill allowed himself a contemptuous chuckle for the benefit of all the gooks in the world who had felt the might of American manhood.

"If any proof is needed of our power, well, just remember what we did to the Germans. We bombed, pounded them without mercy. We demolished their cities. We pushed them to their knees. We wouldn't settle for anything less than unconditional surrender. And Germany was not a country of illiterate gooks. Germany had a mighty military machine, one of the best in the world. How come we pulverized Germany, and we can't beat the gooks?"

Stonehill paused to give his audience a chance to account for this enigma he had brought to their attention. No one offered an explanation. He continued: "The reason isn't too hard to figure. If you're willing to face facts. And we better face them, or one day we'll turn around and find the gooks running our country. I'll tell you why we couldn't beat the gooks in Korea . . . because the commies in this country tied our hands. We can't beat them in Vietnam, because the same traitors won't let us. . . . And we near blew Germany off the map because that's what the American commies wanted us to do. There's no question about it. Anyone with his eyes half-open can see the truth, that is, if he wants to. Commies have infiltrated our government on all levels. They play the fiddle, and Washington dances to the tune. Soon the commies will have all of Asia under their heel. Then they'll be ready to take us. Our boys could still check the commie hordes from overrunning the world, if they were allowed to hit the enemy with full power. But the commie traitors in Washington are tying up our air force. Our brave boys are being stabbed in the back by their own government." Stonehill paused again. His hard gaze scaled the tiers of the lecture hall, surveying the audience he had bagged.

"Don't think for a minute that the communist conspiracy is a myth. It's no fairy tale, fellows and girls. When Khrushchev said the commies would bury us, he wasn't kidding; he meant every word."

Stonehill slammed his fist down to the lectern. "They're shrewd, dangerous, those commies, and they got us boxed in good!"

Stonehill moved to the side of the lectern. He clenched his right hand and waved it over his head. "And who are these commies? How come they were able to get such a stranglehold on our government?"

The questions were thrust at the students in quick, staccato phrases, dramatizing the ominous disclosure he was about to make. Rein sat in the rear, chewing on his lips. He knew what was coming; he had heard it before. Rein wanted to scream, to strike out and bash the man's face in. It was not easy to sit still for this demagogue. But they had studied all the possibilities, he and Morris, and it was agreed: Rein would not allow himself to be provoked. He was not to dignify Stonehill's diatribes by even attempting a rebuttal. Rein was to do nothing, say nothing. His job was to record it all. Later they would take action. He checked the tape recorder; there was enough tape on the spool for another hour. He turned up the volume knob.

"Just give this some thought, friends. Who started the commie movement?" This time Stonehill answered himself without pause. "Marx! Lenin! Trotsky! That's who." Stone-hill's eyes narrowed to sinister slits. The steel gray pupils glinted under half-closed lids. . . . "And what do they all have in common?"

Rein braced himself.

"They were all Jews!"

Throughout Stonehill's discourse, Kent had been sitting comfortably relaxed, his hands clasped over his abdomen, his pointed chin tucked into his chest. At the mention of "Jews" he stiffened. The brow shot up towards his toupee. He opened his mouth. For an instant it seemed that Adam Kent was about to cut off the speaker. Then the moment fled. The brows dropped back; the mouth clamped shut. Adam Kent reverted to neutral observer.

"Now, I know there are some who call me a bigot. They say I'm an anti-Semite and that I'm prejudiced." The equanim-ity with which the assembly absorbed this encouraged Stone-hill to push on, confident that they were ready and eager to hear more. "If you take the trouble to look up the word in any good American dictonary, you'll see that prejudice is defined as, 'bias or opinion held in disregard of facts that con-tradict it.' Okay I'm willing to let the facts speak for them-selves. I'll lay the bare facts on the table, and you judge for yourselves, . . . and I got plenty of facts. I can prove that

Jews are behind the communist conspiracy. . . . I'm not saying all Jews. I don't hate Jews, as some who don't really know me claim. Most Jews are okay."

The harsh threat of Stonehill's tone relented for a moment then picked up renewed malice. ". . . Or they would be if they could get out from under the thumb of their leaders, their rabbis. But they've got to do as they're told. That's their religion. If they could be left alone, they might be good, useful citizens, patriotic Americans like you and me. But their synagogues and rabbis won't let them. I know. I've researched the Jewish religion, and I've learned a good deal about what they believe in."

The darkening sky visible through the windows behind the speaker's platform fulfilled its threat. A freezing rain dropped onto the athletic field. The rain tapped against the glass, sending rivulets zigzagging across the panes. Fat flakes of wet snow slid down the glass. Inside, the lecture hall was a snug, cheerful contrast to the dreary weather without. Stonehill went on to unmask his villains.

"Jews follow a peculiar ritual on Passover night, which is laid out in detail in an odd book they call *Haggadah*. Now, this Passover book is crammed full with tales and songs of how the Egyptians were battered by the Jews. It describes how the Jewish God avenged the Jews and heaped horrible plagues on the helpless Egyptian people. One of these plagues killed so many Egyptian babies that the Nile turned into a river of blood. When Jews read this story at their Passover service, they dip their fingers into wine, which is supposed to symbolize Egyptian blood. Now, I know that they never used real blood as they were accused of doing by the Church during the Middle Ages. Jews are forbidden to eat or drink anything that has blood in it. That's part of their dietary laws. But the cup of wine they drink at their services does symbolize their bloodthirsty hatred for the Egyptians."

At first, Stonehill's uninterrupted venom had filled Rein with fury. It required all his self-discipline to control himself. Gradually, despite his rage, he began to marvel at the skill with which Stonehill manipulated his audience. Adam Kent, the faculty, the students were mesmerized. Adroitly, Stonehill distorted Jewish beliefs and practices. There were kernels of truths to his lies. The lunatic had accumulated a smattering of facts about Jewish tradition, and he used these nuggets ingeniously to stab at the Jews. He took facts out of context, slanted them, turned them inside out. With deft expert strokes, he portrayed the Jew as a dissolute monster. Stonehill was a demagogue par excellence. Dangerous; vicious beyond expectation.

"And don't think it's just Egyptians they hate," Stonehill continued. "No! They got no use for any of us Gentiles. They believe they're the Chosen People. That idea is part of their religion also. They despise the rest of us. They even have a special name for Gentiles, *shekatzim*, which means lice, vermin. That's what they believe; they have a divine right to rule the world, and communism is the way they're going about it. Adolf Hitler exposed their scheme. That's why he decided to deport them. And that's all he had in mind. The rest of all the malarkey, about concentration camps, Jews rounded up for gas chambers, crematoria? All bunk. Lies. Sure, some Jews resisted, and a few got killed. But the rest? Mass murder? Genocide? All Jewish propaganda!"

Throughout his lecture which went up and down in pitch and volume but managed to stay on the sane side of an hysterical harangue, Stonehill moved in a small circle around the lectern. Now he paced the width of the platform. His tone became animated, strident. "And let me tell you! Jews have the sharpest propaganda machine in the world. Especially in this country. They control the press, radio, television.

Jews run Hollywood, the publishing houses, most of the mass media. That's how they put the pressure on the politicians in Washington, and that, by the way, is how they were able to push the Arabs out of Palestine. Those poor Arabs, some of them Christians too, were living peaceably on their land, bothering nobody. Along came the refugee Jews, asking for sanctuary like they did in this country. The Arabs, they're a good-hearted people, hospitable, simple folk. So they give the refugees some land to settle on. Before they know what's coming off, those shrewd refugees own the country. Now the Arabs are refugees, chased off their own land. The Jews couldn't have done this on their own. After all, there are fifty million Arabs to a couple of million Jews. But they managed to get the United States to do their dirty work for them."

Stonehill quickened his stride, pacing in widening arcs around the lectern. Suddenly, he veered, turning full face to the assembly. "We've got to wise up before we lose our country. We've got to get rid of the commie traitors infesting our government . . ." The speaker's metallic gaze fanned out over the heads of the students, ascended the tiers and came to rest on Rein. He balled his right hand and smashed it into the lectern. ". . . and corrupting our schools!"

Arms rigidly extended, Stonehill raised his palms to shoulder height. His right index finger swept across the platform, pointing to the students. "And it's up to you to make sure that the gooks and the commies don't take over our country, our children, our sisters. You are the future of this nation. We depend on you!"

Stonehill slackened his arm; its *seig heil* menace receded. He tramped around the lectern to the edge of the platform, one hand thrust into his pocket. "Well, I've had my say. I thank you for permitting me to lay the facts on the table. I haven't pulled any punches. That's not my style. Let the chips fall where they will, I always say, . . . 'Now it's time you do some of the punching.'

"Before you do," Stonehill turned to Adam Kent, smiling ingratiatingly, "with Mr. Kent's permission, I'd like to distribute some literature for you to read at your leisure."

The principal of Blueport High nodded affirmatively.

"Thank you, Mr. Kent," Stonehill said. He gestured to his partner, who had been sitting like a statue all through the hour. "My associate will pass out the literature."

The sallow, pinch-faced robot stepped off the platform carrying his attaché case and marched to the first tier with an exaggerated military strut. Opening the case, he pulled out several packets and handed them to a freckle-faced youth who passed them along the line. The robot continued up the second tier.

"Okay. I'm ready for questions."

There was no response. Stonehill waited, at ease and smiling. His amiable grin solicited questions. Still no response. Only the rhythmical tap of sleet against the windows. A hand shot up in the third tier center.

"I have a question."

Mel Gross' bid for the speaker's attention set off an excited murmur in the seats immediately around him. He straightened his slouch; one hand inclined toward Stonehill, the other casually fingered a pencil. Stanley Cane's head jumped up as he recognized who was asking for the floor. He had been sitting with eyes lowered, sedulously avoiding the stares of his classmates, which he felt were burning a hole in his back.

"Go ahead, son, ask your question," Stonehill prompted pleasantly.

"My question is . . ." Mel pressed his palm against the desk and pushed himself up to a standing position. A slight commotion stirred the room as students and faculty in the other tiers searched and discovered the owner of the voice.

Then quiet. A chubby blonde with red, puffed-out cheeks sitting one tier in front, craned her neck for a better look.

"My question is," Mel repeated, "Mr. Stonehill, why don't you shove your fat face into the toilet and flush it? You're full of shit!"

The cheeky blonde clutched her ample bosom, sucked in a mouthful of air, and held it. Stonehill's amiable smile disappeared. The blood seemed to drain from his face and concentrate in his thick, bullish neck. His lips pressed tight in a grim line. Knotted veins in his temples stood out like blue cords. Astonishment pasted Adam Kent to his chair. In the rear tier, Rein crouched halfway between sitting and standing, unable to move either way. Stonehill's crony was stretching to pass out a packet of "wisdom literature" to a pretty brunette in the fifth tier. The packet fell from his hand, bounced to the floor, and scattered under the chairs. No one moved to pick up the pamphlets. Disbelief clamped every mouth in the room. Time ground to a halt.

"Shut your trap, Jew bastard!"

Heads bounced from Mel Gross to the fourth tier where Tom Purnell was standing, his eyes blazing venom. Mel turned slowly as the age-old epithet was spat out to his back. He faced Tom's rage, calm almost nonchalant.

"I know who my father is, prickhead. Tell me, which pimp screwed momma Mary?"

Purnell exploded. He vaulted the space between them and flung himself at the blasphemer.

"Christ-killing Jew bastard!"

Mel sidestepped and smashed his fist into Tom's face as he came hurtling down. Tom emitted a painful gasp and dropped between the chairs. Contemptuously, Mel appraised the doubled-over figure. Tom lifted himself to his knees. Red bubbled from his nostrils. Suddenly, he leaped. His hands grabbed for Mel's neck, squeezing with all the power that hate could muster. Mel's right fist slammed sharply under Tom's armpit, deep into the fuming boy's chest. The hands relinquished their stranglehold. Tom buckled to the floor, gasping for air.

The tableau melted into pandemonium.

Twenty-three

Alternately patting and rubbing his midriff, Kleinman studied the bulge protruding below his chest and scowled.

"I don't mean to be critical, dear, but your dinners are not helping my figure. I've put on fifteen pounds in the last six months. Maybe you should cut down on the starch?"

Beth stood midway between the table and the dinette entrance, avidly scanning the heavy print in the *Blueport Gazette*.

"I'd like to have my old trim handsome figure back again, honey," Kleinman said stroking his belly affectionately. Beth moved to the table, oblivious to her husband's complaint.

"Did you hear what I said, dear? I'm getting too fat. You should go easy on the calories."

Beth groped for the chair. Her hand found the rounded top and glided the rest of her into the seat. "What is it, dear?"

"I said your oatmeal has lumps in it like rocks. I chipped two teeth on the lumps."

Her reply floated back as if from another planet. "If your teeth bother you, dear, why don't you go to the dentist?"

Kleinman leaned forward. Only the upper half of Beth's forehead showed over the newspaper. He pressed down the front page. Beth glared.

"That's rude, Morris."

"It's rude to read at the table. Particularly, when your husband is trying to talk to you."

"I'm sorry," Beth apologized but held tight to the paper.

"You'll be sorrier if you don't put that paper down. You're liable to find yourself reading one fine morning: 'Husband sues for divorce. Complains wife reads at table and pays no attention to him.' What's in there, anyway, that's got you so absorbed?"

"The riot in the school last Friday."

"Well! Well! Well! So it did make the news after all. Good!" Kleinman's hand jumped across the table for the paper. "Let me see it."

"Uh–uh . . ." Beth shook her head. "You said it's not polite to read at the table."

"Don't fool with me, Beth," Kleinman said sternly.

Unimpressed, Beth refused to relinquish her hold. "I'll read it to you, dear," she said sweetly. "That will give you a chance to pick the lumps from your teeth." Juggling the paper under his nose, she delivered the headline: "Hate was the subject at Blueport High on Friday."

As she moved down the column, Beth quickly abandoned the comedy, reading on in increasingly grave tones: " 'Nationally known bigot George Stonehill, in an address to the seniors of Blueport High, said that communist Jews are conspiring to seize control of the country. The speech ended in a student riot. Police were called in and arrested forty students. Ten seniors were treated at North Oaks Hospital for injuries. Damage to the school is estimated at $8000. Carl Rein, social science teacher at Blueport High, who recorded Stonehill's speech, said that he and Rabbi Morris Kleinman of the Blueport Jewish Center tried to dissuade the school authorities from allowing Stonehill to speak. They were told to mind their own business.

" 'At an interview in his study, Rabbi Kleinman was asked by this reporter if he would accept the school's invitation to answer Stonehill. The rabbi said that any attempt to answer a bigot is an exercise in futility; he insisted that the school authorities had created the problem by giving an anti-Semite a forum to spew hate. It's now the school's responsibility to undo the damage, if they can.' "

Beth put down the paper and waited for her husband to react. He seemed little disturbed. In fact, he was surprisingly calm.

"Don't you think you have an obligation to refute Stonehill's diatribe and not just sit back on your rear so smugly?"

"Is that the way to speak to your husband?" Kleinman feigned deep hurt. "A rabbi, yet?"

"This isn't funny, Morris. You can't just let Stonehill's remarks go unchallenged. You should speak to the seniors."

"I will, dear, I will. All in good time." Kleinman rose and gave Beth a nip on her cheek. "In the meantime the fire under Purnell is good and hot. I don't want to cool it just yet. Let him simmer a little."

"I hope you know what you're doing, Morris."

"I do the best I know how, honey. And then I leave the rest to God." Kleinman bent over and nibbled on the other cheek. "Thank you for the oatmeal. It really wasn't lumpy. I just wanted the pleasure of your company. I've got to go now. I have several appointments."

Beth raised a petulant face. "I wish I could spend one Sunday morning with my husband."

"That's the penalty for being a *rebbitsen*," Kleinman said airly. "You can't have only privileges you know."

"What's the privilege?"

Kleinman grinned. "Me, of course."

Beth ignored the repartee. "When will you be back?"

"Oh. I expect about one. Then, I promise on my honor, I'll make the supreme sacrifice and drive into the city to visit with your parents."

"All right. One o'clock. I'll be ready and waiting."

Is there any balm to mitigate the grief and guilt this man has carried for decades, and will continue to bear, a man whose mind must stumble with memories too awful to contemplate? How does one tell him that there are those who would have him suffer through eternity without absolution or peace? Kleinman would much have preferred not to be the courier of this message. He felt that no matter the words he chose or the alternate suggestions he offered, he would be sending Otto Hoffman forth with another stone to weigh him down and drive him further into despair.

"Mr. Hoffman, your offer is very generous. I want to thank you. The Board of Trustees considered it carefully and were most impressed." A light brightened Otto Hoffman's troubled eyes. "There was much discussion by the Board members. But . . ." Kleinman faltered. The light in Hoffman's eyes dimmed. ". . . the Board would prefer to reserve the dedications for members of the synagogue and their families. . . ."

Kleinman wanted to apologize, to ask forgiveness for his lumbering, clumsy attempt to cushion the insult. Hoffman anticipated him.

"Rabbi Kleinman, I understand the feeling of your Board members. I cannot forgive myself; how can I expect that they should forgive me? I am sorry to have troubled you." Hoffman started to rise.

"Please, Mr. Hoffman, a moment more of your time," Kleinman petitioned for a further hearing. There were occasions when candor was more merciful than the evasiveness demanded by tact. "There are amongst us, Mr. Hoffman, those who will not forget, who will never in their lifetime divest themselves of their hate. Though I do not share their intractability, I do understand their feelings, and I cannot find it in my heart to condemn them. They have much suffering to remember. Nevertheless, your daughter-in-law was a Jewess. She never, as I understand it, renounced her faith?"

"By no means," Hoffman said. "In fact, I have reason to believe that my son had converted to Judaism."

"Then your daughter-in-law's memory should be perpetuated in our synagogue. I have a proposal that might interest you." Hoffman rearranged the homburg on his lap and sat back to listen. "My study could be dedicated to your daughter-in-law. It would take less than half of your generous offer to furnish it top to bottom. And in a way it might better serve to perpetuate your daughter-in-law's name. There's more traffic passing through my study than in the sanctuary, I'm sorry to admit."

"This would not be objectionable to your congregation?"

"I have already proposed it, and the Board consented. After ten years of service to the congregation, they owe me that much."

"I accept," Hoffman jumped for the proposal. "You will please keep my full check. Use it for your study and give the remainder to any charity you choose. A rabbi's study! Yes. I think that would be a fitting memorial to my son's wife."

"Thank you, Mr. Hoffman. If you approve, I will have the plaque inscribed: 'Rabbi's Study, dedicated to the memory of Rachel Hoffman.' Since we don't know the precise day of her death, we will designate a day you select as a day of memorial. What we call the *yartzeit*."

"Yes, I am familiar with the expression," Hoffman said.

"On the *yartzeit*," Kleinman explained, "we will light a memorial and offer a prayer in her memory."

"Please understand, Rabbi . . ." Hoffman hesitated. "I offer this donation not to ease my conscience but that the name of an innocent Jewish girl cut off in the bloom of youth be remembered by her people."

Hoffman's pathos was profoundly moving to Kleinman. He searched for something comforting he might say to assuage Hoffman's self-flagellation. Nothing original came to mind. The phone scrambled his thoughts. He lifted the receiver.

"Rabbi, it's ten-thirty," Martha's reminder came over loud and strong. "The class from St. John. They're waiting for you in the Chaim Cohen Auditorium."

"Oh, yes!" Kleinman clapped his forehead. "I almost forgot. Tell Mr. Anderson I'll be with him in five minutes." He started to return the phone to its cradle. Midway he checked himself and brought the phone back to his mouth.

"Martha!"

"Yes, Rabbi."

"Is there any heat in the sanctuary? The boiler went out over the weekend. We had to use the Chaim Cohen Auditorium for services."

"Bill started it up about an hour ago," Martha said. "But it'll take at least another hour before the sanctuary warms up."

"The coldest day of the year, and the boiler goes out." Kleinman fretted. "The youngsters will just have to keep their coats on." He put the receiver down and extended his hand across the desk. "I want to thank you for your generosity, Mr. Hoffman. I'll order the plaque. When it is ready and inscribed, I think a dedication service in memory of your daughter-in-law would be proper. I'll call you when the plaque arrives."

"Thank you, Rabbi. I'm truly grateful for your understanding."

Kleinman pulled gently from Hoffman's smooth-skinned hand. "I'm sorry, I must hurry. I have a group of youngsters waiting for me to take them on a tour through our synagogue." He reached for his coat. "By the way, Mr. Hoffman, these youngsters are from St. John. That is your church, if I remember correctly."

"Yes, it is," Hoffman looked surprised.

"About a month ago I arranged with Canon Robert to show his Sunday school classes our synagogue. It would be a pleasure to have you join us."

"Thank you, Rabbi. This would be most enlightening for me. I have never been in a synagogue."

"Come then, Mr. Hoffman. You are cordially invited to join our tour."

Kleinman stretched again for his coat. He put one arm into the sleeve, twisting and contorting to find the other. Hoffman came to his assistance.

"Thank you, Mr. Hoffman. It seem the years are passing me by. It's hard for me to put on my own overcoat."

For the first time since their meeting a smile routed the sadness in Otto Hoffman's eyes. "You are still a young man, Rabbi. Yes. If I may be so bold, still a young man with much to look forward to."

Twenty-four

Don Anderson, director of St. John's Sunday school program, shortened his stride to permit Kleinman, who was taking two steps to his one, to close the gap between them. Anderson walked tall, his cheeks ruddied to a healthy pink

by the cold that still held Blueport in its relentless grip. He
seemed to absorb energy from the biting gusts that made
Kleinman grit his teeth and shrink deeper into his upturned
collar. Otto Hoffman followed, defending his homburg
against the flailing wind. Behind the three adults, some forty
teenagers filed out of the religious school building, stamping
their feet, beating gloved hands together, puffing white
clouds in the arctic blasts. Spurred by the cold, Kleinman
raced up the marble steps, wrenched open the massive gilded
oak doors and gestured vigorously for the crowd below to
follow him into the synagogue building. Anderson sprinted
up the stairs, taking them two at a time. St. John's adolescent
delegation trailed their teacher into the lobby and formed a
quiet semicircle around Kleinman. He tried to put them at
ease.

"Mr. Anderson. I was looking forward to giving you and
your class a warm welcome. But it looks as if the elements
have conspired against me. It's just about the coldest day of
the year, and to my embarrassment, the boiler rebelled over
the weekend. Don't think we always have trouble with our
heating system, only in the winter."

"No problem, Rabbi," Anderson cheerfuly assured Kleinman.

"The boiler is working now," Kleinman said. "We should
have the sanctuary comfortably heated within the hour. So
please, do keep your coats on for the time being."

The group clustered around Anderson still somewhat ap-
prehensive but curious to see the sanctuary in which Jews
worship.

Kleinman felt envy as he caught the rapport between Don
Anderson and his class. There was a friendly yet not over-
familiar relationship between students and teacher. Smiling
inwardly, the rabbi speculated that he might just teach Anderson Hebrew and offer him double what he was getting

at St. John. That should make his ecumenical-minded partner, Canon John Robert, very happy—filching his best Sunday school teacher to prepare *bar-mitzvahs* at the Blueport Jewish Center.

The youngsters inspected the dark panelled, red-carpeted lobby. Gradually, their curiosity won over the nervous diffidence of being in a synagogue and meeting a real, live rabbi face-to-face.

"Before we go into the sanctuary," Kleinman addressed the group, "I'd like to explain our custom of wearing a head covering. It probably harkens back to the days when Jews lived in the Middle East. To walk bareheaded in that hot sun was to invite sunstroke. Consequently, one wasn't considered fully dressed unless one wore a head covering, and no one would think of entering his temple without being fully dressed. In any case, men cover their heads as a mark of respect when they enter the sanctuary. Ladies are not required to wear a head covering, provided they're single. Since none of you girls are married, I assume, all you have to wear is your hair. You'll find skullcaps over there in the right hand corner."

Anderson reached into the deep receptacle and removed a fistful of *yarmulkes*. He put one on his head and distributed the remainder to the boys. They donned the caps to the teasing quips and giggles of the girls.

"We're ready to go in," Kleinman announced. "As you walk down the aisle, please look at the symbols on the stained glass windows. I'll explain them later."

Kleinman opened the doors and led the line into the sanctuary. The silent pews glowed in the flood of color of soft reds, greens, and yellows pouring through the stained glass panels. Midway down the aisle he stopped and pointed to the vaulted roof above the walnut-grained ark.

"Happy are they who dwell in Thy house," a verse

from Psalms, was inscribed in gilded letters across the width of the overhang. Kleinman interpreted the quotation to the class.

"Though we believe that God's presence is everywhere, and he can be worshipped almost anywhere, we consider the synagogue as God's house. It is in the synagogue that we Jews worship him as a religious community."

The class followed Kleinman down the aisle and sidled into the pews, filling the first four rows with a little less clatter than is usual for teen-agers. Otto Hoffman seated himself in the fifth row, his homburg resting on the cushioned pew and a white *yarmulke* on his head.

"Now let me explain the symbols on the panels; then I'll give you a chance to ask me questions." Kleinman directed their attention to the panel in the far left hand corner of the sanctuary, on which was etched a yellow *shofar* in a field of blue. "That is a ram's horn, the well-known Rosh Hashanah trumpet. The ram's horn is sounded on the Jewish New Year to commemorate the great sacrifice Abraham was prepared to make at God's behest." Kleinman turned to the class "Anyone know what the sacrifice was?" The question was met by silence.

"Come on, class, don't embarrass me in front of the rabbi," Anderson prodded from the third row. "You know the answer. We studied the Old Testament last year."

A dark-haired girl raised her hand coyly.

"Would you please give me your name?" Kleinman asked. "My memory isn't too good but I'd like to get to know you as best I can."

"Bonnie Sommers."

"Yes, Bonnie. What was the sacrifice?"

"Isaac! Abraham was ready to sacrifice his son, Issac."

"Right. And did he go through with it?"

"No. At the last moment God stopped him."

"Correct. This was a test to see how far Abraham's loyalty went. But God does not want human sacrifice. So, a ram was substituted. It was a dangerous experiment, safe only in God's hands. On Rosh Hashanah, which is our day of judgment, we ask God to judge us favorably. Not because we always deserve it, but because of our ancestor, Abraham, who was prepared to offer his beloved son to God. In a sense we trade on Abraham's merit."

Although the boiler had been working for almost two hours, it had not yet raised the temperature appreciably. The teen-agers snuggled into their coats and pressed together to capture body warmth from each other. Anderson, seated in the aisle pew of the third row seemed comfortable, oblivious to the cold. In the fifth row, Otto Hoffman barely moved. He appeared to be listening, but there was a distant look in his grave eyes, as if he were seeing more than was in this room, beyond this space and time.

"This is an illustration of a *Seder* plate." Kleinman motioned the class to the fifth panel, almost directly overhead. It rose on the far left wall to the height of the arched roof above the Ark. A silver plate with six cupped depressions, each hollow inscribed with silver lettering, stood out in the colored glass. "The *Seder* plate is our table centerpiece for Passover. You might be interested to know that the Last Supper was a Passover Seder. Does anyone know what Passover commemorates?"

A dark-complexioned youth, the collar of his fur-lined cardigan turned up, raised his hand. "I'm Frank Rogers," the youth indentified himself. "That's when God killed all the first-born males of the Egyptians and passed over the Hebrew houses."

"That's true. But that isn't all the holiday celebrates. Passover is important to us because it commemorates the exodus from Egypt, our ancestors' release from bondage. The symbols of the *Seder* plate represent some of the food we eat at the *Seder* service. They're what you might call memory aids. To help the Jew recall and feel what his ancestors experienced as slaves. For example, bitter herbs are eaten to remind us of the bitterness of slavery. I don't have time to go into more detail. Suffice it to say that Passover is a lesson, an exercise in freedom. An expression of Jewish devotion to liberty."

A youth in the third row sneezed. Kleinman glanced at his watch. The class had been patiently attentive for half an hour. He was impressed by their interest.

"I really am sorry we couldn't get the building heated in time for your visit," Kleinman apologized again.

"Don't worry about us, Rabbi," Anderson said merrily. We're doing just fine. Clean, cool air won't hurt us, will it class?"

A resounding rejection of the very idea that they were chilled to the bone rolled over the pews, followed by a wild beating of arms across chests, collars pulled over ears, hands digging into pockets for warmth. Kleinman chuckled and pointed to the rear of the sanctuary and across the aisle.

"The next panel illustrates the two tablets on which the Ten Commandments were inscribed. The eighth panel"— Kleinman picked up speed—"represents the Burning Bush, the bush that was not consumed. That's what we could use here today to heat up the place." Kleinman's aside provoked loud agreement; he shifted back to low gear. "Is there anyone who recalls what great mission began at the Burning Bush?"

A cherubic, dimpled doll in the fourth row raised her hand. "Nancy Falco," she sang her name. "It was Moses' mission. God revealed himself to Moses at the Burning Bush for the first time and asked him to go back to Egypt to get the Hebrews freed."

"Very good, Nancy. This class is well-versed in the Bible.

"The ninth panel, as you can see, depicts a silver goblet. We call it a *Kiddush* cup. From the Hebrew word *kadosh*, holy. Traditional Jews usher in the holy days with wine; it is our way of sanctifying the Sabbaths and festivals."

Kleinman moved on to the final panel. "This is a picture of a *Torah* scroll. The *Torah* is the most revered Jewish book. It contains the Pentateuch, the first five books of the Bible. After I answer some of your questions I'll show you what a Torah looks like close hand. Okay. I'm ready for questions."

Anderson took off his coat and laid it across his lap. Most of the class was now sitting with coats unbuttoned. The temperature had climbed to the fifties, blunting the edge of the chill. By the silence, Kleinman recognized that though the timidity of their first encounter with a rabbi had somewhat abated, the youngsters were still reluctant to question him.

Anderson broke the ice. "While my class thinks up what to ask you, I have a question. Is there any significance to the fact that there are ten panels? I understand that in order for Jews to pray there must be ten men present."

Kleinman considered a moment before replying. "Actually, it isn't necessary to have ten men present for a Jew to worship. As I said earlier, Jews believe God is omnipresent; he is everywhere. One Jew or a thousand may pray to him, and they may do so almost anywhere. However, it is true that ten male adults are required for formal public worship, and certain prayers are recited only when there is a quorum of ten male adults. It's quite possible that the architect in planning the sanctuary windows did have that in mind. I don't know for certain."

A hand went up in the third row. Kleinman acknowledged a petite freckle-faced girl with flaming red hair.

"I'm Mary Anderson."

Kleinman's baffled stare darted from the winsome redhead

to Anderson's dark-complexioned features. The Sunday school teacher chuckled. "Yep. That's my daughter, Rabbi. My wife's a redhead." Kleinman smiled.

"Go on, Mary. What's your question?"

"Why do you have to have ten for a quorum? Why not eight or twelve or fifteen? What's special about the number ten?"

"That's a good question, Mary. The fact is, we don't know the real reason for the choice of number ten; we can only speculate. The historical origin of the tradition is probably lost in antiquity. But the rabbis did validate the tradition from a well-known biblical story.

"The source is Genesis, chapter eighteen. God reveals to Abraham his intention to destroy Sodom and Gomorrah. Do you recall Abraham's response?"

"Yes," Mary said. "He pleaded with God to spare the cities."

"Right," Kleinman confirmed. "Then he goes on to argue with God. He calls upon God's justice not to destroy the righteous with the wicked. Then he has the nerve to bargain with the creator of heaven and earth. Remember, Abraham starts out with fifty. 'Will you destroy the cities if there are fifty righteous men? If there are forty?' At what point does Abraham stop?"

"I think it was ten," Mary said.

"It was ten. And that is one source the rabbis of old found to validate the tradition of ten for a quorum."

"I see." Mary wrinkled her cute nose. "If you can't find ten men in a community to pray to God, it's not worth saving. Is that the idea?"

"I . . . I . . . wouldn't put it that strongly, Mary," Kleinman faltered on the short curve of her conclusion. "But I would agree, if a Jewish community can't find ten men to worship God, it is in spiritual trouble."

Mary pondered the answer, nodded in agreement, and sat down. A tall attractive girl with unusual self-assurance rose from the second pew. Her long billowing tresses curled down to the small of her back. Her gracefully tapering fingers hovering close to her shoulders called attention to the swell of her breasts.

"I'm interested in the wine goblet that Jews drink from on their Sabbaths and festivals about which you spoke earlier."

"Would you please give me your name."

"Susan. Susan Purnell."

"Yes, Susan. What is your question?" Kleinman's face did not show the surprise he felt.

"Does the wine you drink at your services have the same significance as the wine in the Mass?"

"How do you mean, the same significance?"

"I mean, is it supposed to contain the blood of Abraham, or Moses, or God. Like the wine in the Mass is supposed to be the blood of Christ?"

"No! There's absolutely no analogy, absolutely no connection," Kleinman hurled back the answer with more vehemence than he had intended. For a moment the comparison had stunned him. Small wonder Christians had been so easily persuaded that Jews drink blood on Passover; they've been doing it symbolically every Sunday for centuries.

Susan Purnell was undaunted by the rabbi's strident note. "Then what is there about the wine that gives it the power to sanctify your Sabbaths and festivals?"

This time Kleinman gave himself a moment to collect his wits. He erased all pique from his voice. After all, his own congregation had ridiculous notions about Jewish ritual. Why should this Christian girl be expected to know better? Actually, she had good reason to make such a comparison.

"It's the Jew, by his observance, who sanctifies the holy days," Kleinman said after a long pause. "Not the wine.

Wine is a symbol of joy. We drink wine to show our pleasure in welcoming these holy days into our homes.

"There is a Passover ritual which in a negative way demonstrates this point. At our *Seder* service, when the ten plagues God inflicted upon the Egyptians are recited, some wine is poured from the goblet. This is to show that no man's cup of joy can be filled while someone else suffers, even though he be an enemy. And the Hebrews had good reason to think of the Egyptians as enemies." Kleinman studied Susan's reaction. "Do you understand what I'm trying to say?"

"Yes, Rabbi. Thank you." Susan sat down slowly. Her smooth brow was wrinkled, and the blue of her eyes betrayed an inner perplexity, as if she were baffled by still-unresolved contradictions.

A beefy youngster with a face as rotund as a pumpernickel lifted his heavy bulk from the fourth row and raised his hand.

"Yes, young man," Kleinman acknowledged the portly youth.

"My name is Charles Niebling," the boy volunteered. The voice, a high pitched squeak almost set Kleinman to laughing. "My friends call me Charley Nibbles."

Charley stroked his belly, happily interpreting the chuckles of his classmates as approval. "I seen this picture once of a statue of Moses. The head had horns on it. Do Jews believe that Moses had horns?"

Guffaws burst from the front pew to the rear. Charley's head swerved on the axis of his neck as far as the barrier of flesh allowed. He stood for a moment totally bewildered, his embarrassment unfurling in crimson layers. Then he went limp, as if utterly demolished. He dropped back into his seat. There was a thud as buttocks and pew met.

"Charley! That's a good question!" Kleinman's response punctured the derision. "There's a very interesting tale to

248

how that picture of Moses came to be." Kleinman turned to
the class. "The picture that Charley saw is the result of a
mistake made by a great biblical scholar of long ago."

Charley perked up. As the mocking laughter faded, won-
derment then delight crisscrossed his face. Kleinman surveyed
the change of mood. Satisfied that Charley Niebling, plucked
from the abyss of mortification, felt himself vindicated, the
rabbi started on his explanation:

"Those horns on Moses can be traced back to an error
made by St. Jerome, who translated the Bible into Latin. His
famous translation is known as the Vulgate. Even before St.
Jerome's time (he was born around the year 340) there were
already a number of well known Greek translations of the
Bible. But St. Jerome felt that those earlier translations were
not accurate. So, he decided to do one himself based on the
original Hebrew texts. St. Jerome, however, did not know
Hebrew. But that didn't stop him; he was a determined man.
He went ahead and took Hebrew lessons from a Jew. After
he had mastered Hebrew, St. Jerome spent fifteen years trans-
lating the Hebrew Bible into Latin. The Catholic Church
thought so highly of St. Jerome's work that in 1546, the
Council of Trent authorized it as the official bible of Roman
Catholicism. But even St. Jerome, as brilliant and dedicated as
he was, made mistakes. And one of his mistakes led to Moses'
horns.

"When Moses came down from Mt. Sinai for the second
time (The first time, you may recall, he found the people
worshipping a golden calf and he shattered the tables he had
received from God), the Bible relates that as he approached
the people with the second set of tablets in his arms the Hebrews drew back in fright. To quote the verse in Exodus: 'His
face sent forth beams of light.' Now the text uses an unusual
word for light, *keren*. This Hebrew word is a homonym, a
word with two meanings. *Keren* means shafts of light. But

it also means horns. In Exodus: 34, *keren* is to be translated as a beam of light. St. Jerome erred and translated the verse as: 'His face sent out horns.' Medieval artists, including Michaelangelo, were misled by St. Jerome's error, and in their paintings and sculptures of Moses, they depicted him with horns. This error even gave rise to the belief that Jews have horns. What Charley probably saw was a picture of the famous statue of Moses sculpted by Michaelangelo. How's that for a blooper? Just goes to show how careful a scholar must be in his work."

Kleinman glanced at his watch again. It was almost twelve. He had promised Beth to be back by one. The hours seemed to fly whenever he was in front of a class. And the youngsters from St. John had been particularly stimulating. But he had better make time, or he wouldn't hear the end of it . . . and rightly so. Even a *rebbitsen* is entitled to a piece of her husband. . . . And he felt unusually tired . . . a peculiar kind of fatigue; it began with a twinge under his left armpit, no more than a pinprick, and expanded to a tight band around his chest.

"Mr. Anderson," Kleinman called. "I've got to be on my way by twelve thirty. Before we go, I'd like to show the class a *Torah*. If there's time after, I'll answer more questions."

"Fine, Rabbi," Anderson said.

Kleinman walked up three carpeted steps to the massive free-standing Ark. The doors were stained in dark walnut. Its handles, one on each end, were triangular knobs of silver. Kleinman rolled the doors open, disclosing the plush curtain underneath. Two embroidered lions stood upright, each with one paw on a bell, their tails curling. Lions and bells flanked the tablets in the center of the curtain. Inscribed in gold lettering on the tablets were the first two words of each commandment. A crown of gold, intricately gilded with loops and curlicues, perched on the head of the tablet. Three bright yellow stars of David on the upper border arched over three branches luxuriant with three green leaves. The lower brim of the curtain was edged with fine velvet lace of midnight blue. Kleinman tugged at the satin cord. The tassled end escaped from his fingers. He caught the swinging endpiece and pulled again. The curtain resisted his tug a second time.

"Finally got the boiler going, now the curtain's stuck," Kleinman grumbled. "Sometimes it'd be the better part of wisdom to go back to bed and start all over again."

"Can I help you, Rabbi?" Anderson offered from his pew.

"I'll get it open." Kleinman put both hands to the cord and pulled down hard. It yielded part way to his straining. "There it is! That could have been embarrassing. The rabbi, not able to get to the *Torahs* in his own synagogue!"

The tight band pressing around the rabbi's chest widened; what had earlier been a twinge under his arm turned to noticeable pain. Ignoring both, he slid the curtain open the rest of the way, giving the class a full view of the seven *Torah* scrolls. Each *Torah* rested in its own velvet-lined compartment. They were attired in mantles of satin and velvet and wore silver breastplates with silver bells and delicate silver loops. He reached into the ark, lifted a scroll from its seat, carried it to the reader's lectern and laid it down gently. After stripping it of its vestments he covered it with a velvet cloth and invited the students in the first two rows to come up to the pulpit. They hesitated, each one reluctant to be the first.

"Come on, class! Look alive," Anderson encouraged. They filed up briskly at his urging. Kleinman removed the velvet covering and rolled the scroll open to the width of the lectern.

"What you see before you is the text of the first five books of the Bible." Kleinman skimmed the silver pointer across a column. "It is written in Hebrew, on parchment, exactly as it has been for centuries. This *Torah* is about two hundred years old." The scroll's antiquity evoked wide-eyed wonder from the group. "Reading a *Torah* scroll is rather difficult because it has no vowels, periods, or commas. To make it even harder, each word has a musical note, a cantillation of its own and that, too, must be memorized by the reader. So you see, reading a *Torah* scroll during a service requires a great deal of training."

Susan Purnell peered in awe at the scroll. "Are boys required to read the *Torah* at their *bar-mitzvah?*"

"It isn't a must," Kleinman said. "But I'm proud to say that most of our boys do read a portion."

Susan shook her long blonde tresses, evidently impressed. Kleinman directed their attention back to the scroll.

"Notice the minature crowns on the letters. The scribe who wrote this scroll must have been a great artist. See how clearly the lines stand out, even after all these years."

"Do you mean to say that this whole thing was written by hand?" a skinny, tow-headed youngster asked in astonishment.

Kleinman nodded. "The *Torah* must be written by hand with a special kind of quill and made-to-order ink. The parchment must be from a kosher animal, like a lamb or sheep. Furthermore, if there is one error, if one letter has been rubbed out, the *Torah* may not be used at services until the error is corrected."

"Wow! That makes it rough on the scribe." The awed youth whistled. "Those *Torahs* must be worth a lot of money."

Kleinman agreed. "Yes, they are. But to a Jew, a *Torah* scroll is priceless."

Bill Mosely speared his shovel into the snow. . . . Only a few more scoops and he could get back to buffing the auditorium floor. He had left off when he realized that the old delivery truck wouldn't be able to get through. Pulling a pack of cigarettes from his windbreaker, he struck a match, cupping one hand over the flame, and caught the light on the first try. It was cold, a cold relentless winter. And this weekend, the worst of all, the boiler breaks down. Spend half a million dollars putting up a building and can't get a reliable heating plant. Bill impugned the probity of the whole damn building trade. They take your money, scram to the Bahamas, and leave you to shiver. Too bad about those kids picking just this Sunday; the first half hour they must've froze their fannies. Well, kids could take cold a lot better than an old black man from Mississippi. . . . By now it should be nice and cozy inside. . . . The electric heater! He had forgotten to turn it off. Lately, remembering was a problem. Good thing, though, he had remembered that old heater in the basement; he hadn't used it for years. It took the bite out the freeze while he was working the auditorium floor.

Bill inhaled a final drag on his cigarette and was about to flick the butt when he heard the first cracking sound. It detonated like the snap of a bullwhip. A second crash followed. Then the tinkle and crunch of glass shattering. Clutching the shovel, Bill raced toward the sound. He made the corner in time to spot a leather-jacketed youth swinging a can at the lower-level window. Bill came on fast, brandishing the shovel and bellowing like a wild boar. The boy swerved to avoid Bill's wrathful charge; he lashed the can through the window and slammed into a blue sedan idling at the curb. Bill rushed the car, screaming blasphemies. Someone seated in the back rolled down the rear window. Bill ducked as an empty whiskey bottle whizzed by his ear. The sedan lurched forward, its tires screeching as the back wheels dug into the hardpacked snow. Bill stood at the curb whipping the wind with his shovel. He cursed at the fast disappearing car, remembering curses he hadn't used since boyhood down on the farm. Bill was mad as Lucifer, mad and confused. Who the hell were those bastard kids? He had seen Negro churches smashed up by the men in the white sheets, burned to the ground. But a synagogue? By white boys? Never expected such trouble in this town. Bastard kids!

Bill trudged over the bastard's footprints to check the damage. Jagged rainbow-colored slivers protruded from the sill like a mouthful of broken teeth. A gust twisted down Ocean Avenue, picking up drifts and spinning snow into the auditorium. Carefully, Bill edged closer to the casing and peered through the wide hole of what had been a stained glass window.

He smelled it immediately but sniffed again to confirm what his nose already knew. Smoke! Curling and belching flame from the overturned heater. The stage curtains billowed to the wind, caught sparks, and ignited in an orange burst. Red and blue tongues of flame lapped at the tables and chairs. Bill ran for the entrance, his brain pulsating fear. . . .

. . . *The kaleidoscopic assortment of precious stones catches the overhead light and sparkles like stars on a clear, moonless night. Otto Hoffman slides the glass doors closed; they move silently on smooth bearings. He stands, admiring the colors, almost alive in their glittering beauty. From outside, a commotion intrudes on Otto's rhapsody. He tears his eyes from the display case to the street. A crowd is gathered, babbling in clusters under the window. Their prate is frolicsome, a holiday spirit is in the air. Traffic is backed up for a block. Happy laughter floats into the store. Otto is curious. He dons a light coat and steps out into the brisk evening air. Dusk drops its shadows earlier now on Bergerstrasse, in the late fall of 1938. Business people, office workers, shoppers on their way home, stop to join the revelry. The circle expands.*

Otto threads his way to the inner edge. He looks down at the pavement and smiles at the sight. Three men on their knees. Two are elderly, their dirty beards matted and disheveled. Baggy suits hang loose on their emaciated bodies, like ill-fitting burlap. The third man is younger; he is beardless. His clothes are even more ragged. The three men clutch stiff brushes. They scrub the cobblestoned street. An officer supervises their labors, towering over them, tall and official. His boot tips toward the bucket; he barks orders. The Jews dip their brushes into the bucket. A cutting smell stings Otto's nostrils. He winces and draws back. The blonde Aryan's lips curl disdainfully. The Jews scrub. Their hands are red, raw. Blood is crusted on the cracked skin of the younger man. One elder falters. His knees buckle. He falls prostrate. The younger man crawls to his side. Gently, he raises the old man. The crowd jeers, hoots, mocks. They are entertained. They demand an encore. The officer stands arrogant and immaculate in his tailored uniform. A swastika encircling one arm proclaims his teutonic virility, and that of the crowd. He prods the Jews, jabs at them with the butt of a club, eschewing contamination by contact. "Move faster, Jew," he orders. "Scrub harder." The cobblestones of Bergerstrasse must shine tonight. The young Jew looks up. His humiliation meets Otto Hoffman's smile. The wan eyes fasten on Otto. They are watery, dark like a deep, endless ocean that hides unknown mysteries in its depths. Otto's smile freezes. The eyes pull; they draw dread from Otto. He cannot turn off the haunting eyes. The suffering face pierces into Otto's memory. . . .

Otto wrenches himself from the past. He looks up to the pulpit. Kleinman speaks of Jewish reverence for the *Torah*. The first group is about finished. In a moment the second will be summoned to view the scroll; Otto's legs will refuse to carry

him. He already knows they will refuse to do his bidding.
Perspiration wets Otto's collar; his fingers clutch the pew.
Otto's eyes are blank. They see not what is up front . . .
but what is behind.

*The officer raises his boot to kick the young Jew. The
Jew unlocks his eyes from Otto and returns to the brush and
the cobblestones. But the look lingers. It accuses. It denounces
and stabs.*

Otto closes his eyes to chase the image. It burns under his
eyelids. He shuts them tighter. . . . Screams tear into Otto's
ears. His head snaps to the source of the shout. A black man
stands at the synagogue doors; his face is a dark frenzy.

Smoke! Otto tastes acrid smoke. The black man darts
down the aisle. His arms flail the air; his frenetic dash holds
terror. Otto cannot sort out the past from the present. What
was merges with what is. Horrors separated by decades
coalesce. Fire fuses with fire. . . .

*Flames spurt skyward, illuminating the night, painting it
in hues of red and yellow. Heat billows up in undulating
waves. Shapeless figures scurry into the flaming building.
Two emerge. In each arm they carry velvet-covered scrolls.
They scamper from the burning synagogue. Firemen stand
at their engines. At ease. Sheets of fire shoot from windows
sprouting monstrous red tongues. Thick curds of gray, mass
and surge into the orange sky. The firemen aim their hoses.
Water jets forth. Not at the burning synagogue. At the comic
figures hugging the scrolls. They hop, skip, and jump to
avoid the onrush of water. The firefighters laugh. A stream of
water finds its target. It scores one, then two. The dancers
are bowled over; The scroll falls to the wet ground. It un-
rolls into the swelling puddles. The hilarity expands. It is con-
tagious. Otto catches it. He spreads it to the street, to the
city, to all of Germany. The firemen now aim their nozzles
at the gutted synagogue. Someone darts from the crowd. He*

*stomps an open scroll. Laughing maniacally, he grabs it by
its charred handle. The parchment rips. He flings the half
left in his hand into the flames and dashes away from the
heat. . . .*

Anderson vaults the distance between his pew and the pulpit. He thrusts the teen-agers towards the door. The pews in
front of Otto come alive with frightened children. They
dash past him, the girls screaming. Their shrill cries propel
Otto from the nightmare of the past to the horror of the
present. Kleinman scoops up the scroll on the lectern and
gives it to the black man. The rabbi twists to the Ark and
pulls to remove another. The black man takes the second
scroll and rushes the door with arms filled. Hoffman catapults
from his seat to go to the rabbi's aid. Kleinman is tugging
more scrolls from the ark. Anderson takes two and scrambles
after the black man.

"Mr. Hoffman! Here. Quick!"

Kleinman bends into the Ark again, straining at the weight
inside. He maneuvers another scroll out, breathing hard. Otto
takes it from him. Kleinman's arms go for the next *Torah*.
They do not emerge. The rabbi stiffens and reels toward
Otto. Pain contorts the rabbi's face. He clutches at his chest.
His eyes roll; the pupils disappear into the white. He crum-
bles like an empty sack folding into itself. A pulpit chair, its
velvet padding singed, topples and grazes Kleinman's temples.
Otto rushes to his side. He straddles Kleinman's prostrate
body, grasps the heavy chair with his free hand, and flings
it across the pulpit as if it were furniture in a doll's house.
He kneels, still holding tight to the scroll, and cradles Kleinman's head in his right arm. The dark hair is mottled by red
blotches.

"Rabbi Kleinman!" There is desperation in the hoarse
voice. He calls again; he implores. Otto lifts the rabbi with
his free hand and fumbles for the pulpit steps. They give

257

way. One foot goes through to the ankle. Flames lick at the
Ark curtain. The heat paws at Otto's face. He holds fast to the
rabbi and cannot let go of the scroll. A supporting beam over
the Ark crunches loose. Otto wrests his imprisoned leg free.
Blood stains his torn trouser leg and reddens the exposed
calf. Otto carries his burdens down the center aisle. A crimson trail follows his limp. Behind him, the Ark totters and
crashes into the lectern. Flames reach out and feed greedily
on the pews. Dimly, Otto hears sirens wail. He pushes at the
synagogue portals; they resist. He lunges at them with his
shoulders; they give way and swing open. Vaguely, Otto
perceives the crowd massing across the street. Gray-coated
figures sprint up the steps and take Kleinman from him. Arms
lead Otto down to street level. Through the haze and stench
of smoke, he sees the rabbi carried off on a stretcher. His
head swims. He reels, sways. His arms are empty of rabbi
and scroll. Fire engines. Hoses endlessly coiling, vomiting
water. Flames . . . *Bergerstrasse* . . . Ocean Avenue . . .
*Bearded skeletons scrub the streets . . . The beardless one
locks on to him with death's eyes. . . . The cobblestones
bleed! Rachel, forgive me. Frederick, my son!*
   The mob roars with laughter. . . . The mercy of darkness . . .

Twenty-five

In the last three days Captain William P. Reagen hadn't slept
five consecutive hours. And it showed. His square shoulders
drooped, circles bagged his eyes, which he could barely
keep open. Outside his office, a mob of reporters crammed

the small anteroom, pumping the desk sergeant. Their jabber
screeched through the door like baboons gone berserk. They
were howling for specifics. Was it arson? Any leads yet to
the blue sedan? The driver? Was there a blue sedan, or
did the custodian dream up the car to cover his own sloppy
negligence? Questions! Questions! He had given them three
statements already, and they still weren't satisfied. Damn
those newsmen! When you're looking to publicize the po-
licemen's benefit, you can't scare up a reporter nohow. Now
they come on like the plague, hounding the department.
Don't give a man a chance to do his job. And if you do throw
'em a bone, they put meat on it, spice it up, and feed their
own blown-up version to the public without regard to the
consequences.

Hell! He wished he could trace that blue sedan. Two days
now Doyle's been hunting, and he wondered if he hadn't
sent the detective on a phantom chase. But that fire spread
fast. Too fast, according to Fire Chief Kreiber. Even if the
heater had overturned, it shouldn't have flared up so quick.
Not unless there was something flammable to feed it. Arson?
Hard to believe. Not in Blueport. Never had this kind of
trouble before. And forty kids from St. John were in that
building. God! That could have been a tragedy. Carelessness?
Maybe an act of God? The whiskey bottle! Did it come from
the blue sedan, or Morely's hip pocket? It was a cold day;
he'd been out shoveling snow. Maybe he quaffed a pint to
warm up. But Morely was no sot. Been with the synagogue
eight years. No!! Morely was a reliable black. Reagen's instincts backed the custodian's story. But who the hell in this
town would . . . ?

Captain Reagen's door opened a crack. Patrolman Clyde
Thompson popped his red head in.

"Captain! Fred Downing's out there fightin' the reporters
off. Should I let him in?"

"Of course, let him in, stupid," Reagen yelped over the din clashing into the office from the anteroom.

"Okay, Cap! Just wanted to make sure." Thompson ducked out of the doorway.

Blueport's corpulent little mayor, his face puffed and excited, shoved through the jam. Ignoring the squall, he slashed his way to Reagen's office, pushed the lanky patrolman to one side, and barged in. A red checkered scarf was dangling from his neck down to the last button of a heavy suburban coat. Thompson shut the door from the outside; the clamor dulled but still battered at the door. Reagen rose from behind his desk. The mayor stormed at him, waving a newspaper as if ready to toss it on a pyre, preferably one that had Captain William P. Reagen on its stake.

"Did you see this morning's paper?"

"Yes, I read it."

Downing screamed the headline anyway: "Rabbi Morris Kleinman suffers heart attack while rescuing scrolls from burning synagogue. Captain William P. Reagen suspects . . ."

Reagen interrupted. "Now hold it, Fred! I never made that statement."

"The reporter said he was quoting you," Downing waved the paper accusingly.

"Misquoting is more like it."

"What the hell did you say?"

"That I don't know for sure. That's all I said. That damn reporter asked me if I believed Morely's story. I said I'm reserving judgment until all the facts are in."

"But you said arson cannot be excluded. You intimated it was arson. That the fire was of suspicious origins and bears further investigation."

"That's routine," Reagen defended his statements to the press. "I don't exclude anything until the full report comes in."

Downing spurned the captain's explanation. "You tell the reporters the fire is of suspicious origins, you put out an alarm for a blue sedan with three white teen-age passengers. . . . This is a small town, Bill. People get excited quick. Your 'suspicious origins' have stirred up the devil and put us on the spot. Somebody's head is gonna have to roll. There were forty Christian kids in that synagogue building; ten of 'em are in the hospital with serious burns."

Reagen's patience was wearing thin. "I know about the kids. There's also Rabbi Kleinman."

Mention of the rabbi fueled Downing's excitement. "Yeah! And that doesn't help the situation any. The Jewish boys are hollering bigotry. They're blaming his condition on the fire. Damn it! He couldn't have picked a worse time to have a heart attack."

Reagen's glare bore down hard on the mayor. "Maybe he wouldn't have gotten one if not for the fire. Maybe he would have gotten it ten weeks or ten years from now. If he had heart trouble, that fire didn't help any."

Downing relented. "I didn't mean it the way it sounded. But they're hitting me from all sides. Your doubts and 'suspicious origins' to the press have pushed Ray Purnell on my tail."

"What's Purnell got to do with it?"

Downing's jowls reddened like ripe tomatoes. "Since you put an arson bug in our citizens' heads, the hindsighters are blaming him. They're saying it happened because he allowed Stonehill to speak at the high school. As it is, the riot last week must have made him feel that he's sitting half-ass-out. Now you've really put him on the line."

"Nobody's accusing any of the high school kids. I never publicly made any such connection."

"They're making the connection without your help. If Morely is telling the truth, who else were those white boys in the car? Who else are you looking for but high . . ."

The sudden ring of Reagen's phone startled the mayor. He

clutched the ends of his scarf, hanging on with trembling hands. The captain snapped the receiver to his ear. "What? Who? Certainly I'll speak to him." Reagen covered the mouthpiece with his palm. "It's the County Supervisor's office. Now I'll hear it from McCain."

Reagen went back to the phone; his forehead wrinkled deeply, his thick eyebrows angled downward, almost touching one another at the bridge of his flat nose. "We're doing everything we can, sir. . . . Yes . . . We're just as anxious to get to the bottom of it. . . . No, I can't be sure. . . . Maybe there is a connection . . . though I doubt it. Yes, if you say the FBI has jurisdiction, we'll certainly cooperate. . . . Yes, sir! As soon as we have anything more I'll let you know immediately." Pensively, Reagen dropped the phone. The mayor, already an agitated bundle of nerves, came near hysteria.

"Well, what did he say? What did McCain want?"

Doubt clouded Reagen's square-jawed face; he seemed unsure of himself. "There's been a rash of church and synagogue fires throughout the county. Nobody's been hurt till now and not much damage, so they've been able to keep the lid on. They were afraid publicity would encourage the crackpots, so they kept it quiet. Looks like the lunatics have moved over the county line into the suburbs, and we got the biggest blast. I guess we had to get the city's troubles sooner or later."

"You mean they suspect this isn't just a local affair?"

"That's what McCain's boys think. They feel professional agitators are out to fan religious and racial hatreds. They're afraid more's on the way."

As the problem magnified in scope and the orbit of responsibility for Blueport's crisis broadened to county- and city-wide proportions, Fred Downing's hysteria abated in reverse ratio. The hot potato was to be shared, maybe taken from his hands completely. Well! He wasn't one to insist on monopolizing trouble. He looked at Reagen with a new calm.

"You'll have to cooperate with the FBI."

"I'll cooperate with anyone that'll help me wrap this up. Just so long as we . . . " A timid knock interrupted.

"Come in," Reagen answered. Thompson shuffled in from the suddenly quiet anteroom.

"What happened to the reporters?"

"I guess they gave up." Thompson bared his teeth up to the molars. "Most of 'em just upped and left."

"Well, what do you want?"

"Doyle is outside. He's waiting to see you."

The captain's eyes flashed. "Send him in." He turned to the mayor, who now seemed to be at ease with himself and the world. "We may have the answer now."

The announcement did not make Fred Downing happy; he tensed.

Though he was a big man whose bulk suggested he would have an elephant's step, Mike Doyle glided into Reagen's office on a whisper. He was about forty-five, with a stolid face, thinning steel-gray hair, cynical lips, and skeptical eyes that looked out at the world as if it were all a lie.

"We found it," Detective First Class Mike Doyle announced.

"How?" Reagen asked.

"Checked every car coming in. Don't know what the school buses are for. Seems to me every kid in town's got a car. Must be three thousand cars in that parking lot."

Downing's glare shifted from the detective to the police captain, gathering distraction as it moved from one to the other. "You said the high school kids weren't involved."

"Had to check out all the possibilities."

The mayor's whine gave Reagen a touch of nausea. He shifted back to Doyle. "You sure it's the right one?"

263

"No doubt about it, Cap. A blue Chrysler, like Morely said. He remembered the last two plate numbers. Zero, one. That was the year he was born, 1901, he thinks." A faint smile brushed Doyle's cynical mouth.

"Whose car?"

Doyle hesitated; his eyes swung to Downing. Reagen signalled for him to speak up.

"Purnell. Tom Purnell was the driver."

Downing's face turned a sickly white. Reagen whistled between his teeth.

"You sure, Mike?"

"Yep! Didn't take much to get it out of him. The kid is scared. Admitted he was driving. I got him outside. Want me to bring him in?"

"Hold off, Mike. We gotta step soft on this one."

"Why step soft, Cap? He admitted he was driving the car."

"Any explanation?"

"Yeah! He's got an explanation. Says he went to pick up his sister. She was one of the kids went to visit the synagogue."

"You don't buy it?"

Doyle flicked that possibility off the list. "They came by chartered bus, and the bus was supposed to bring them all back to St. John."

"What about the window and the paint can? Was that Tom Purnell?"

"Don't think so. Purnell swears it was his buddy, Frank Simpson, who smashed the window and threw the can in. Says he tried to stop Simpson. I believe it was Simpson who threw the can."

"But you don't believe Purnell tried to stop him?"

"No, Purnell would hang anybody so long as he doesn't swing with 'em."

"What makes you so sure about Tom?"

"I asked him where Simpson got the can from. Purnell said he had it in the car trunk. How'd Simpson get the trunk open unless Purnell gave him the key?"

"But why'd they do it? It doesn't make any sense."

"I don't know why, Cap. In fact, I don't think they know why. They were boozing it up all night. Simpson's parents are off on a cruise, and the kids had the house to themselves. Figured they'd extend the festivities, and they picked the synagogue for a blast. They didn't mean to burn it. That was an accident. But they did intend to do some decorating. And I'm ready to bet my rating that the instigator was Tom Purnell."

Downing plumped weakly into a chair. "Poor guy!"

Reagen jumped to Downing's wail. "What poor guy?"

"Ray. Ray Purnell. This is gonna break him for sure."

Twenty-six

Rein pulled hard on the doorknob, venting his frustration on it, as if the glass door were responsible for his misery. A blast of warm air rumpled his hair as he stepped from the cold into the overflowing lobby of North Oaks Hospital. Anxious families and friends waited for visiting hours to start. Nurses paraded back and forth with starched efficiency. A loudspeaker blared for Dr. Brian Stacey to come to obstetrics. Rein pushed through the bustle, his own face a mask of worry. A sign in white lettering in a field of blue read Maternity Ward. He turned and went in the opposite direction, following the arrow pointing to the west-wing elevator.

Bitterly, he ruminated over life's enigmatic contrasts: the same flash that lights our instant in infinity brings birth and death; the identical arc of eternity vaults man's afflictions and his joys, his happiness and his heartache. Here, under one roof, squalling infants make their entrance into the world while the dying rasp their departure. Rein dredged for the words of the High Holyday liturgy: "Who shall live and who shall die? Who shall attain the measure of man's days and who shall not? Who shall perish by fire and who by water? Who shall be tranquil and who shall be at ease?"

Until the ax falls no one knows which head will roll, Rein had long ago concluded. Not because the answer is hidden, but because there is no answer. It's all a mad senseless insane accident. That is the curse of the rational mind. Unless it surrenders to delusion, it can concede only irrationality.

Rein hurried to the elevator, reaching it as the doors were gliding shut. A trim nurse put her hand to the doors. They popped open. Rein thanked her; she smiled prettily, straightening a misplaced auburn curl under the white-winged cap. The elevator lifted smoothly to a soft hum. Out of the corner of his eye, Rein studied the bright-eyed passenger. Here was life, health, youth, ministering to the sick, surrounded by pain and seemingly untouched. Rein wondered that the suffering she saw daily was not reflected in her attractive unlined face. Was she still too young? Too new to her job? Or did nature in its wisdom raise a mental barrier that stopped the cries of the ailing at the outer fringe of awareness?

Above the doors an arrow on a crescent shaped marker settled on Three. The doors opened. At eye level, as he stepped out, the blue and white sign Intensive Care Unit chilled Rein's groin, giving him the sensation of a filled bladder. He followed the arrow to the end of the brightly lit corridor. On this floor, the movements and pace of both

266

nurses and doctors were hushed, as if here, life and death hung in such precarious balance that inadvertently, one might by an irreverent whisper tip the scales.

Rein turned into the waiting room. A tall, slender youth stood on the threshold peering apprehensively down the hallway. A door closed softly. Muted clicks of a woman's high heels sounded in the corridor. The youth tried to squeeze past Rein. They bumped shoulders. The boy apologized. Rein followed his worried look.

The ashen face he saw was hardly recognizable as that of Beth Kleinman. Dark rings puffed her parched cheeks. Her eyes, the eyes Rein remembered as always sparkling with a touch of the roguish, were without life.

"Oh, Carl!" Beth said heavily. He could sense her struggle for control.

"How is Dad, Mom? The boy came between him and Beth.

"He's a little better, Jonathan. Dad's holding fine."

The boy showed his need for reassurance, but there was little conviction in his mother's voice.

Jonathan was a head taller than his father. But the father's features, Rein noted, were there. The same high forehead and wide span between the somber eyes. Thick dark hair and a nose a trifle too long, with wide flaring nostrils. A dimple he had obviously inherited from Beth softened his chin.

"I don't think I've met your son," Rein extended his hand.

"Oh, I'm sorry, Carl," Beth apologized. "This is Jonathan. Jonathan, this is Carl Rein, an old and dear friend of your father. They went to *yeshiva* together."

Jonathan clasped Rein's hand tightly. "Glad to meet you. Dad spoke of you a number of times. He likes to reminisce about *yeshiva* days."

There was a maturity about the boy that impressed Rein.

He could be no more than eighteen, a year younger than his own son. Saul was bright, but still childish in many ways. This youth carried himself like a man. Was it the *yeshiva* training, or had he suddenly been plunged into manhood these last few days? Beth dropped wearily onto a chair. Rein sat opposite her. Jonathan walked across the room and stared vacantly through the window at the dimming sky.

"Carl! I can't believe it. I just can't get myself to believe it. We thought it was just an ulcer. And he was feeling much better lately. Could it have been the fire? We should have left Blueport long ago. It was too much for him. They were tearing him apart. . . . I don't know. . . . You read about such things happening . . . to someone else . . . some far-off place . . . not to you."

"What do the doctors say?"

"They say it was a massive coronary. He looks so weak. . . . He also has a slight concussion. But that's the least of it. It's the heart! They're afraid . . ." Beth sobbed into her hands.

Rein touched her arm. "Is he awake?"

"Yes, I think so."

"Shall I go in?"

"Dr. Gross is with him. But go in anyway. Morris asked for you several times. He seemed very anxious to talk to you."

"I won't stay long."

Beth nodded. Her eyes brimmed; the tears flowed freely. "He's in room 318." She blew into a tissue.

Jonathan pulled away from the window, saw his mother in tears, and came to her side, protectively laying his arm around her shoulders.

The picture of mother and son wrenched at Rein's gut, evoking old memories of his mother in a hospital room, awaiting the inevitable. They had been graced with more time. For six months they had watched Saul waste away.

When the end came, it was an act of mercy. This was sudden, less time for suffering. Which torment was preferable? An academic question to the sufferer and his loved ones.

Rein averted his gaze from the private grief between mother and son, and walked out of the waiting room. He stopped at 318, hesitated, then tapped on the door. It swung inward. A tall, broad shouldered figure clad in a green gown blocked the entrance.

"Are you Mr. Rein?" Dr. Gross was grim. It was plain that this physician's concern went beyond professional interest.

"Yes."

"The rabbi has been asking for you. I promised him I'd allow you in. He's very weak. Don't stay more than a few minutes."

Rein nodded. Gross stepped aside, holding the door open for Rein, and left.

A table lamp shed a dim light on the bed next to the window. There was a slight stirring under the sheet as Rein entered. He brushed against the foot of the bed and choked back a gasp at what he saw. Kleinman's head was bandaged. The pillow was not much whiter than the face it cushioned. One arm lay limp under the cover. An inverted bottle hanging overhead fed a yellowish liquid into a coiled tube taped to the other hand.

"Not a pretty picture, am I?" Kleinman smiled feebly. Rein stepped around to the head of the bed.

"I never admired you for your looks, Morris." Rein forced a grin. He pulled a chair to the bed.

"I'm glad you could come, Carl. I . . . I wanted to talk to you . . . tell you something." Kleinman stumbled, as if what he wanted to say was dimming in his mind. Rein dipped closer to the bed.

"Morris. Perhaps, I should come back later or tomorrow, when you feel a little stronger?"

Kleinman tried to turn his head to Rein. The effort proved too much. "No. Please stay . . . may not have a chance again." He held back a moment, closed his eyes, opened them, and, by sheer will-power it seemed, drew strength from some inner reserve. "It's strange . . . couple of years ago I developed pain in my stomach. Thought it was cancer and panicked. Had to take tranquilizers. Even went to a psychiatrist. Now it looks as if the *Ribono Shel Olam* is truly calling, and I feel no fear, no fear at all. In fact . . . feel an odd peace. Don't misunderstand, Carl. I want to live . . . Regret . . . may not see Jonathan grow up, marry. Become a grandfather. Jonathan's a good boy. Have you met him?"

"Yes, Morris," Rein said. "He's a fine boy. He looks a lot like you. A better-looking copy, though."

Kleinman's eyes seemed to laugh. "Yes, I would like to be around a little while longer. But there's no fear now. Regret, but no fear . . . strange."

"I'll go now, Morris. You've got to rest. Conserve your strength. I'll be back tomorrow."

"No. Please stay," Kleinman pleaded. "I have something to tell you. Tomorrow . . . tomorrow may be too late.

"I've been thinking a good deal about that talk we had at my home. Remember? When was it?" Kleinman withdrew his free hand from under the cover to touch his brow. "It was just a few weeks ago."

"Yes."

Unexpectedly, Kleinman's voice gathered volume. He managed to twist his head. Rein was startled at the sight. The eyes staring up at him were like twin lights in the sockets of a corpse.

"You forced me to think about something I've pushed out of mind. . . . From this position you can't do much else but think. . . . Carl, we all have our doubts. If I were God I'd run this world differently. No question about it; so much of His creation doesn't make sense. No sense at all. But one can be a Jew, a good Jew, despite the doubts. I found I could doubt and still remain a rabbi . . . maybe even a better rabbi. There's a smugness in certainty that stands in the way of truth." Kleinman's head rolled back. He lay flat on the bed, his face pointing up to the whitewashed ceiling. "But, Carl! There is an intelligence behind the enigma, the paradoxes. An intelligence that transcends our reason, that our minds, bounded by logical rules, can't apprehend. . . . Strange, how I can feel it now as never before. I'm sure this world of ours is not just a mindless accident."

Rein leaned over the bed, so close to Kleinman he felt the hot breath of his labored breathing. "Why, Morris? What makes you so sure?"

"Because there is something. It would have been so much simpler for there to have been nothing." An urgency powered Kleinman's voice, as if he had been saving this last reserve of energy to spend on what he wanted to pass on to his friend. "But there is something. There is existence, more than existence. There is love, friendship, family. There is human intelligence. The mind, as limited and fragile as it is, is a marvel, a mystery beyond its own comprehension. The greatest insanity is to believe that all this is only an accident. Yes, Carl. Somewhere there is an explanation to our questions. . . . Please God, He is the answer."

Rein stroked his *chaver's* free hand. He pressed it and started to rise. Kleinman made another effort to turn to Rein. His head lifted a fraction and fell back.

"One more thing, Carl . . . I almost forgot . . . the reason I wanted to talk to you." The voice was losing clarity and growing fainter. "About that question you asked at my house."

Rein moved his ear closer to the bed. "Which question, Morris?"

"Just before Beth's blintzes calmed you down. Remember?"

Rein felt himself on the verge of tears. "Yes, Morris. I remember."

"I thought about it and thought about it. And the answer is yes. I would officiate at your children's marriage. I'd be happy, proud to. Because someone a couple of thousand years ago laid down a law, doesn't mean we're forever bound to it. God's will is sifted through the minds of human beings. Man interprets His will. Two thousand years ago it was interpreted one way. We can interpret it another way. God's will is immutable. We can't change that, but we can change our interpretation of it. Yes, Carl. I would officiate, and give my blessing to your children."

"Thank you, Morris. Coming from you it means much. I'll always remember."

Kleinman's head rolled back. His eyelids fluttered once, then closed. "So tired . . . so tired . . . *Laych B'shalom*, Carl."

At his brother's death, Rein could summon no tears. For the first time since childhood, he cried. Slowly, he backed away from the bed, pulled a handkerchief from his pocket, wiped his eyes, turned a final lingering look toward his *chaver* and walked into the corridor.

Twenty-seven

Majestically, the rust-red steeple stabbed into the swollen puffs of clouds spiralling between earth and sky. St. John's summit was the highest point in Blueport. To Canon John Robert, its spires were meant to pierce heaven itself, to touch

God's throne. The clap of its huge bells clanging their summons to the faithful, "Come ye and worship in God's house," was a joyful music. To his ears, those mellifluous notes were an overture to a heavenly symphony orchestrated by a church that had a direct line to the divine conductor.

For the first time, St. John's senior minister felt certainty slipping. The line had been severed; contact was broken, and the opus had become a dirge.

John Robert parked the Buick in the space reserved for his car, slid wearily out, and tilted his head skyward, sensing as never before the unbridgeable chasm between the spire crowning his church and heaven's lowest stratum. Isaiah's admonition to all Temple builders hit Canon John Robert with full force: "The heaven is my throne and the earth my footstool; where is the house which ye may build unto me?"

These last few days had reduced John Robert's steeples, his spires, his church, and most of all, John Robert himself to true size, microcosms in an unfathomable infinite macrocosm. He was tired beyond feeling. For forty years he had ministered to his parish, convinced he was serving God and truth, certain that one road led to salvation and that road passed through the church. Now that he neared the end, doubts and contradictions riddled his conviction.

Robert trudged up the incline to the church entrance. The heavy portals, suspended on perfect bearings, obeyed his touch and swung open easily. Passing through the domed vestibule, he stepped into the narthex and contemplated the carved walnut screen separating the vestibule from the great nave. The tracery was filled with antique glass; its twelve divisions bore shields of twelve apostles worked in lead silhouettes. Robert's brooding gaze wandered to the north window above the balcony. On its variegated glass surface the master artist had interpreted the Christian virtues of faith, hope, love, justice. His eyes dropped from the window to the pulpit. At his behest, rough logs had been brought from the Holy Land to furnish the altar. Olive wood from the Garden of Gethsemane and the Mount of Olives, and cedar wood from Mount Lebanon. Did all this grandeur make any difference to the main task of implanting Christian virtues in the minds and hearts of his communicants? Or, as he was agonizingly being compelled to concede, had the physical church so occupied his thoughts, these stained glass windows so beclouded his vision, that he had lost the church of the spirit and betrayed his calling? The very majesty of St. John, which he had so admired, now flaunted its splendor at him with accusing fingers.

Torpidly, Robert worked his way down the aisle of the great nave. Halfway down he stopped. A slender figure, silhouetted by beams of light from the fenestrated grandeur above, drifted to the altar rails. Robert watched her hesitate at the altar, solitary and miniaturized in the church's vastness. Her legs flexed to kneel. She went down part-way, then stiffened, as if unable to make the full descent. Almost a hundred feet separated Robert from the woman, but there was something disturbingly familiar about her. Though weighed down by fatigue and depression, he closed the distance between himself and the altar, pulled by a potpourri of sensations he could not yet define. The woman turned as if she had been expecting and waiting for him.

"Why?" His question was communicated less by word than by gesture. An in that pithy word-gesture was mirrored bewilderment and embarrassment.

"I had to come. I had to find out."

"Find out what?" The voice that had thundered certainty from the pulpit to the last pews could now scarcely be heard.

"Who I am? What I am?"

"And did you find out, Chr . . . Ruth?" Robert arrested an instinctive impulse to deny her Jewish name.

"Father! I'm so mixed up, so confused."

"But why did you come here to find an answer?"

"I don't know, Father. I don't know." Ruth's breast heaved with the ache of her conflict and confusion.

"My child! My dear, troubled child!" Robert opened wide his arms, once again the eager missionary leaping at the first opportunity to return this lost straying soul to the bosom of Jesus. Then he remembered . . . and guilt and shame engulfed him like waves at high tide. Abjectly, he let his arms fall to his sides.

"He was such a good man, Father. Such a good man. Sincere. Dedicated. Kind. He pleaded with my husband to keep that bigot away. If Ira had only listened, this wouldn't have happened. . . . Ira wouldn't listen. Ira betrayed him. . . . The whole congregation betrayed him." Ruth buried her face. Muffled sobs sifted through her fingers. Ruth raised her head.

"Father! Why did they crucify their rabbi?"

"Don't condemn Ira," Robert said with heavy heart. "He's the least to blame. Don't condemn the congregation. They really didn't understand what they were doing. . . . None of them really understood."

There was a curious faraway look to Robert. His face pointed to the crucifix above the altar, but his eyes quested for that which was beyond images. Ruth sensed the struggle raging within the priest.

"Rabbi Kleinman wanted Stonehill to speak at the high school," he said grimly. "Yes, Ruth!" Robert persisted in the face of the astonishment he read in Ruth's eyes. "Rabbi Kleinman went to Ira knowing full well your husband would never agree to pressure the school. If the rabbi had wanted to stop Stonehill, it was simple. I offered to help him. All I had to do was pick up the phone, call Purnell, or the chairman of the Board of Education. That would have been the end of it. And Rabbi Kleinman knew that. But he refused my help. He insisted on handling the matter by himself."

Robert's words pounded at Ruth's temples. The revelation was beyond her ability to grasp. Disbelief furrowed her brow.

"Yes, Ruth. It's true. Publicly, the rabbi made a show of protesting Blueport's school policies. But I know he really wanted little changed. He once challenged me to stop Christianizing the public schools. Protestantizing, as he phrased it. He knew very well I would not and could not take up his challenge. And he didn't want me to. I see that now."

"But why? What you're saying doesn't make sense."

"It made sense to Rabbi Kleinman. You see, Ruth, he believed that if you scratch a Christian, you will find us all anti-Jewish underneath. Not anti-Semitic, but anti-Jewish. He believed that by force or guile our ultimate aim is to convert every Jew. And he worked to expose our intent to his people. To show that Christianity was still a threat to Judaism and that the Jew could survive this threat to his faith only by minimizing his contact with the source of that threat. Rabbi Kleinman realized that open defiance of the ecumenical spirit would be futile. His people were too taken by the liberal winds blowing from Rome. They believed the Church had finally conceded Judaism's right to exist on its own terms. Rabbi Kleinman was skeptical. No! Rabbi Kleinman knew that it was a lie. But he couldn't come out and say so. He would have been ground under, labeled as a reactionary. So, he gave us enough line to demonstrate we are still fishermen out to hook Jewish souls.

"And he found the Church a most effective membership committee on behalf of his synagogue, and he used us to the fullest advantage. Every time a Jewish child came home from school singing of Jesus in the Manger, parents to whom Jewish education was furthest from mind panicked to join the synagogue and enroll their children in Hebrew school."

Ruth shook her head, furiously denying what she was hearing. "No, it can't be true! You're accusing Rabbi Kleinman of being a bigot himself, of bringing all this heartache on himself."

"Don't judge hastily, my child," Robert entreated. "It isn't Ira. It isn't the Jewish congregation, and it isn't Rabbi Kleinman who must carry the guilt for what has happened to our town. I've been forced to look into my own heart and my own conscience. And there, Ruth, is the stain."

An oppressive stillness descended from the upper reaches of the great nave. The silence was so thick that Ruth felt she could touch it. High above St. John, the struggling sun had briefly pierced the brooding mass of a low-hanging cumulus and sent a feeble beam through the window over the chancel, diffracting the light into rainbow colors. Orange-red touched the right foot of Christ on the Cross. The segment of spectrum spread over the contorted body, bathing it in a fiery glow.

"When Rabbi Kleinman went to see Ira, he knew in advance that Ira would refuse him. And when I volunteered my help, I knew the rabbi would not accept. Yes, I knew Rabbi Kleinman wanted Stonehill to speak. I was aware of his purpose—to polarize the two communities, Jew and Christian. To clarify once and for all where everyone stood. Yes, I knew. . . .

"I should have taken the bull by the horns," Robert said painfully. "I didn't because I, too, wanted Stonehill to speak. The rabbi's motive was to expose our fraudulent embraces. He miscalculated. Even he did not gauge the full measure of hostility lying just beneath the surface that such a racist could release. And the rabbi paid dearly for his error. But I! Why did I want Stonehill to speak? I've asked myself a thousand times. Free speech? Principles? No! It wasn't in defense of freedom that I held back from interfering. I can't fool myself. If an atheist had come to blacken the church, I wouldn't have just offered help. I would have shouted! I would have demanded! And Stonehill never would have stepped foot in Blueport! Why didn't I scream out? I don't know whether Kleinman succeeded in exposing our true designs to his people, but he succeeded all too well in exposing me to myself. I am a bigot, a hypocrite, and my part in precipitating this tragedy weighs the heaviest."

Robert's penance bewildered and embarrassed Ruth. This was no ordinary man humbling himself; this was Canon John Robert, whom she had once regarded as God's emissary, as near divinity as any mortal could be. And the memory hurdled time and conversion, and moved her to turn again to him for answers she desperately needed.

"I still can't accept what Ira . . . what the congregation, did. They humiliated their rabbi. I've seen it happen before. Why do they abuse their religious leaders? Demean their synagogue . . . themselves? Why, Father?"

Strong gusts in the overcast sky collected the billowing clouds into a uniform mass of gray and closed the holes through which the sun had briefly shone. The golden sunbeam which had brushed Christ on the Cross paled, Robert strained to see the image in the gathering dusk, but could see only the bare outlines of God's Son. He turned slowly to face Ruth's question.

"I've wondered about that, too, Ruth . . . a long time. I think Jews are in the throes of an agonizing reappraisal of their most fundamental doctrines. Auschwitz demolished their faith in a just, merciful God. For Abraham's descendants this is a traumatic, painful experience. It was they who first conceived the idea of a universal ethical God. The Jew is per-

turbed, distraught, though he may not be consciously aware
of the reason for his distress. And he is striking out at the nearest, most vulnerable target. Unconsciously, he blames the rabbi
and the synagogue. And the indictment is not entirely un-
justified. I've seen it in Rabbi Kleinman's eyes. I've heard it
in his words. Faith is burning feebly even in their religious
leaders. They are floundering . . . all of them. . . . The
Jewish nation is in the midst of its greatest spiritual crisis. . . .
They are hurting. . . ."

Robert spoke flatly, without inflection, as if he were ex-
temporizing to himself more than clarifying enigmas for
Ruth. In midsentence his stoop straightened. He stepped towards Ruth and reached for her with his arms, long and thin,
like two arms of a giant candelabra.

"Ruth." Robert whispered with reverence the name to
which she had converted. "Ira is a good man, a good man with
a problem. He is your husband; he needs you. Your help. Go
back and help him. . . . Return to the faith you chose."

"They're so confused, mixed up, and you tell me to go
back?"

Ruth felt his fingers press into her shoulders. They hurt,
but she almost relished the stinging pain.

"Don't deprecate their confusion, Ruth. A holiness per-
meates the turmoil besetting them. A holiness I have just
begun to perceive. The Jewish people have been through this
wilderness many times. Abraham's wandering shaped his belief in one God. Israel lost in the desert came forth with the
Ten Commandments. In pagan Canaan the Jew produced
prophets. While suffering his first exile, he laid the foundation of the synagogue. Again and again the Jew rose from the
ashes, and like the mythical phoenix flew to even greater
heights of spiritual and intellectual insights. *Talmudism,
Hasidism,* mysticism . . . and now, Ruth, they're at it again.
What will come forth this time no one can predict. But this

I have learned . . . learned from Rabbi Kleinman. Without realizing, he taught me my most important lesson. . . ."

Robert's grip loosened; his body slackened. The leonine head that had briefly found its full height stooped back to humility.

"All through my ministry I believed that Jesus Christ provided the solution to every human problem, that faith in him automatically resolves every mortal dilemma. But that is not what faith is all about. It's taken a lifetime to divest myself of this infantile trust. By his very doubts, Rabbi Kleinman opened my eyes to a deeper truth. Faith, my dear Ruth, is not an answer to all our questions. Faith is a challenge to all our paltry answers. Faith is the compelling urge to accept the challenges, the drive to ascend, despite them, because of them."

Gently now, Robert held Ruth at arm's length. He looked longingly at her lovely face. He looked and saw the infant he had baptized, the little freckled girl to whom he had given communion. He had put the Host to her tongue, His Blood to her lips. He had watched her blossom into this beautiful woman. Robert bent down and brushed her forehead with his lips.

"Never did I dream that I would be capable of saying this. Go back to your husband, Ruth, your family, your religion. The Jews are a Chosen People. Chosen perhaps against their will. But Chosen to carry God's message to man. He will not abandon them. God will send them and you light to dispel the darkness. . . . Go back, Ruth."

Robert stepped away from her, opened the communion rail, passed through and stood wordlessly under the crucifix, hands clasped to his chest, he dropped to his knees. Ruth turned her back to the genuflecting priest. Silently, she walked down the long aisle and out of the church of St. John.

Twenty-eight

Patches of frozen sod peeked through *Beth Olam's* snow-capped landscape. Evenly spaced pines and firs spread their ice-encased branches like monstrous ribs. Thawing winds contesting mid-winter's icy hold whistled between the waist-high monuments. Overhead, a sparkling noon sun burnished an almost cloudless sky. Limousines and a long line of private cars parked bumper to bumper snaked around the entire cemetery block choking off Ararat Lane. A thousand people had overflowed the synagogue which was still charred and blistered from the fire. They had stood in aisles, spilled into the lobby from the auditorium. And they all rode the cortège, following at a threnodial pace behind the hearse for the twenty-mile trip to the cemetery.

In life, Morris Kleinman attracted little more than a *minyan*. In death, he pulled the community together and filled the Blueport Jewish Center. They came en masse from all quarters—longtime friends, past foes, Jews, Christians. And officiating was his casket, draped in black under a scarred pulpit, charging this final service with the concentrated power of a thousand sermons, a thousand liturgies.

Walking in hushed lines, the mourners pressed up the slope and assembled in concentric circles around the grave site. Beth held tight to Jonathan, flanked by her aged parents on one side and Carl Rein on the other. The coffin hovered over the open grave, held in place by two straps. A burly, ruddy-faced gravedigger, dressed in baggy dungarees and windbreaker, flicked a lever on the lowering device. The

281

casket swayed laterally, then began a slow descent to the bottom. A second worker came to his assistance. They straddled the yawning pit. One at the foot, the other at the head, worked the straps out from under the casket and pulled the last physical link joining the coffin below to the world above. Beth sobbed into her hands. The workers carted off the straps and mechanism. Jonathan tightened his grip on Beth's waist.

Cantor Rosenberg intoned the *"El Malek Rachamim,"* entreating God to gather the deceased under the "wings of the divine *Shechinah*." The limping cadences looped and trilled their soulful lament around the monuments and mourners. Jonathan stepped forward to recite the burial kaddish. He began firmly: *"Yisgadal v'yiskadash shmey rabbah . . ."* Beth's lips moved silently with his. Towards the last phrase, "May there be abundant peace from heaven and life for us and all Israel," his voice cracked. For an instant a vacuum seemed to suck the *élan vital* from the air. Jonathan inhaled and finished. He stepped back in line and entwined fingers with his mother. Breath returned to the living.

Schwartz picked up the shovel lying partially covered by a carpet of artificial grass. He scooped earth from the mound at the side of the grave and let it fall. The dirt thudded against the casket. Beth whimpered. Tears trickled down Jonathan's cheeks. Schwartz handed the shovel to Mendelson. He swung into the mound reluctantly and slowly dropped his contribution. The shovel passed to Rein. It felt cold and hostile in his hands. He wanted to push it away, to smash it against the stone monuments and run. "Old Traditions" stirred, gluing his fingers to the handle. He twisted the shovel into the mound, tilted it over the grave, let its half load slide to the bottom and passed the shovel to Sy Wasser.

Looking grim, Dr. Gross stood at the inner rim of the circle with his wife and watched the shovel go from hand to hand until the casket disappeared under the earth. Murray Gold stepped to the mouth of the grave and dropped a shovelful. He returned to his place beside his wife. Directly behind Murray, Ira Cane moved from Ruth's side. Slowly, he limped to the grave, bent painfully to pick up the shovel, his left leg stiff, and let fall the last shovelful.

The funeral director unfurled his green carpet over the the grave and called for parallel lines. Jonathan steadied his mother. She lingered for a final look, steeled herself, and passed between the rows. Beth's parents and Carl Rein followed. Whispered consolations in English, Hebrew, and Yiddish trailed the bereaved. A tall, bowed figure stepped out of line, blocking the narrow path. The procession halted.

"Beth . . . what can I say? There aren't any words to carry what I feel." John Robert spread his hands helplessly. He staggered. Two men rushed to his side. He motioned them back. "There aren't many years left for me, Beth, but those I have will be filled with the memory of your husband. I cherished his friendship. He meant so much to me . . . how much, I didn't realize until it was too late . . . too late. . . ."

A rueful smile crossed Beth's face. "Yes, Canon. It is too late. Isn't it? . . ."

The two men helped Robert back into line; he faded into the crowd of family and friends. A black-clad chauffeur assisted Beth and her parents into the limousine. Jonathan slid into the jump seat. Slamming the door, the chauffeur wedged behind the wheel and sped off. The crowd of mourners broke and people scattered to the parked cars.

Schwartz and Mendelson remained at the grave site, standing somber guard while the gravediggers with quick, experienced strokes stabbed into the dwindling mound to complete the filling in. The sound of earth thudding against earth vied with revving engines.

Dragging his heels, Schwartz shuffled away from the

grave. Mendelson hung back, probing the elevation of earth mounting the gravesite with a rebellious melancholy. Lifting watery eyes skyward, he brandished a gnarled fist at the clouds. He turned and caught up with Schwartz.

The two men plodded to the gate, their heavy steps testifying to the years that seemed to have suddenly aged them. They walked silently, each wandering in his own maze. The stillness hanging over the cemetery was punctured by clanging shovels as the gravediggers, their task completed in Ararat Lane, tossed the implements of their trade into the back of a pick-up truck and moved on to another section of Beth Olam.

Mendelson interrupted the brooding quiet. "I don't understand! I just don't understand! How could He allow such a thing to happen?"

Sinuous gray clouds floated between sun and earth. The landscape darkened. A north wind portended the end of the brief thaw.

"I don't know how or why God does what he does, Mr. Mendelson. Long ago I stopped trying to understand God's ways." Schwartz directed his words to Mendelson and his eyes to the overcast sky. "I know only we got to arrange for a *minyan* at the *rebbitsen*'s house so the rabbi's son can say *Kaddish* for his father."

"*Kaddish*? What good will that do? What does it all really matter?" Gloom, defiance, sorrow cluttered Mendelson's rebellion.

Schwartz stiffened. His jagged profile flashed the old fire. It blazed but a moment, then died as quickly as it had been ignited. His body slackened.

Immediately it had slipped, Mendelson regretted his irreverence. It was thoughtless. Nothing had been gained by scoffing at tradition. Only giving more pain to a friend. He wished he could retract his heresy.

"It matters, Mr. Mendelson, it matters," Schwartz chanted

hoarsely. His sing-song seemed to come from far off. "You remember when you asked the rabbi, may his soul rest in peace, why we need ten men for a *minyan?*"

"Yes, I remember." Mendelson tried to fathom the connection.

"He said you should come to his class. I was interested, so I went. And I learned something about the *Kaddish* I didn't know." Schwartz paused to recapture the day and the lesson. "Yes, I learned much from Rabbi Kleinman. True, he was a little too much the modern American rabbi for me. At my age it is hard to understand these changes . . . all these new ways. But I respected him; he was a *talmud chacham*, a scholar and a pious man in his own way.

"The rabbi pointed out that the *Kaddish* does not make mention of the dead. It just praises God. He called it by a fancy name. A doxology. *Nu!* Except for the fancy name, I already knew that. For this I didn't have to come to his class. Then he asked: 'Why especially when someone dies should we praise God with a *minyan?*' His answer gave me to understand what the *Kaddish* really means."

Mendelson forgot his remorse; he listened closely. "The rabbi said, in every man there is a *tzelem elohim*, there is in us a part of God. When a man dies, a bit of God leaves the world. The Divine is diminished. To return that holiness to the world is the purpose of the *Kaddish*. But that is too big an assignment for any man to accomplish by himself. For such a holy task is needed a congregation of Jews—a *minyan*."

The sun wiggled through a break in the clouds. A faint glow limned the gloom etched in the faces of the two octogenarians.

"Come, Mr. Schwartz. Let us go home. I'll help with the telephone calls. We must make sure there are ten for *Kaddish*."